Patricia Cornwell sold her first novel, *Postmortem*, while working as a computer analyst at the Office of the Chief Medical Examiner in Richmond, Virginia. It would go on to win the Edgar, Creasey, Anthony, and Macavity awards as well as the French Prix du Roman d'Aventure prize – the first book ever to claim all these distinctions in a single year. To date, Cornwell's books have sold some 100 million copies in thirty-six languages in over 120 countries, winning Cornwell the Sherlock Award for best detective created by an American [illegible]hor, the Gold Dagger Award, the RBA Thriller Award, a[illegible]edal of Chevalier of the Order of Arts and Letters f[illegible]ns to literary and artistic development.

Though Cornwell n[illegible]orn in Miami and grew up in [illegible]fter earning her degree in En[illegible] in 1979, she began working at th[illegible]moving to a job with the Office of the Ch[illegible]iner of Virginia – a post she would later bestow [illegible]ctional Kay Scarpetta.

When not writing [illegible]n her Boston home, Patricia tirelessly researches cutting-edge forensic technologies to include in her work. Her interests span outside the literary: Patricia co-founded of the Conservation Scientist Chair at the Harvard University Art Museums. She appears as a forensic consultant on CNN and serves as a member of Harvard-affiliated McLean Hospital's National Council, where she advocates for psychiatric research. She's helped fund the ICU at Cornell's Animal Hospital, the scientific study of a Confederate submarine, the archaeological excavation of Jamestown, and a variety of law enforcement charities.

Also by Patricia Cornwell

THE SCARPETTA NOVELS

Postmortem
Body of Evidence
All That Remains
Cruel and Unusual
The Body Farm
From Potter's Field
Cause of Death
Unnatural Exposure
Point of Origin
Black Notice
The Last Precinct
Blow Fly
Trace
Predator
Book of the Dead
Scarpetta
The Scarpetta Factor
Port Mortuary
Red Mist
The Bone Bed
Dust

ANDY BRAZIL SERIES

Hornet's Nest
Southern Cross
Isle of Dogs

WIN GARANO SERIES

The Front
At Risk

NONFICTION

Portrait of a Killer: Jack the Ripper – Case Closed

BIOGRAPHY

Ruth, A Portrait: The Story of Ruth Bell Graham

OTHER WORKS

Food to Die For: Secrets from Kay Scarpetta's Kitchen
Life's Little Fable
Scarpetta's Winter Table

Patricia Cornwell

Point of Origin

sphere

SPHERE

First published in the United States in 1998 by G.P. Putnam's Sons
First published in Great Britain in 1998 by Little, Brown and Company
This reissue published in 2010 by Sphere
This edition published in 2020 by Sphere

1 3 5 7 9 10 8 6 4 2

A CIP catalogue record for this book is available from the British Library.

ISBN 978-0-7515-8269-7

Printed and bound in Great Britain by Clays Ltd, Elcograf S.p.A.

Papers used by Sphere are from well-managed forests and other responsible sources.

Sphere
An imprint of
Little, Brown Book Group
Carmelite House
50 Victoria Embankment
London EC4Y 0DZ

An Hachette UK Company
www.hachette.co.uk

www.littlebrown.co.uk

With Love to Barbara Bush

(for the difference you make)

Every man's work shall be made manifest: for the day shall declare it, because it shall be revealed by fire; and the fire shall try every man's work of what sort it is.

– I Corinthians 3:13

DAY 523.6
ONE PHEASANT PLACE
KIRBY WOMEN'S WARD
WARDS ISLAND, NY

Hey DOC,

Tick Tock

Sawed bone and fire.

Still home alone with FIB the liar? Watch the clock BIG DOC!

Spurt dark light and fright TRAINSTRAINSTRAINS. GKSFWFY wants photos.

Visit with we. On floor three. YOU trade with we.

TICK TOC DOC! (Will Lucy talk?)

LUCY-BOO on TV. Fly through window. Come with we. Under covers. Come til dawn. Laugh and sing. Same ole song. LUCY LUCY LUCY and we!

Wait and see.

Carrie

1

Benton Wesley was taking off his running shoes in my kitchen when I ran to him, my heart tripping over fear and hate and remembered horror. Carrie Grethen's letter had been mixed in a stack of mail and other paperwork, all of it put off until a moment ago when I had decided to drink cinnamon tea in the privacy of my Richmond, Virginia home. It was Sunday afternoon, thirty-two minutes past five, June eighth.

"I'm assuming she sent this to your office," Benton said.

He did not seem disturbed as he bent over, peeling off white Nike socks.

"Rose doesn't read mail marked personal and confidential." I added a detail he already knew as my pulse ran hard.

"Maybe she should. You seem to have a lot of fans out there." His wry words cut like paper.

I watched him set pale bare feet on the floor, his elbows on his knees and head low. Sweat trickled over shoulders and arms well defined for a man his age, and my eyes drifted down knees and calves, to tapered ankles still imprinted with the weave of his socks. He ran his fingers through wet silver hair and leaned back in the chair.

"Christ," he muttered, wiping his face and neck with a towel. "I'm too old for this crap."

He took a deep breath and blew out slowly with mounting anger. The stainless steel Breitling Aerospace watch I had given to him for Christmas was on the table. He picked it up and snapped it on.

"Goddamn it. These people are worse than cancer. Let me see it," he said.

The letter was penned by hand in bizarre red block printing, and drawn at the top was a crude crest of a bird with long tail feathers. Scrawled under it was the enigmatic Latin word *ergo*, or *therefore*, which in this context meant nothing to me. I unfolded the simple sheet of white typing paper by its corners and set it in front of him on the antique French oak breakfast table. He did not touch a document that might be evidence as he carefully scanned Carrie Grethen's weird words and began running them through the violent database in his mind.

"The postmark's New York, and of course there's been publicity in New York about her trial," I said as I continued to rationalize and deny. "A sensational article just two weeks ago. So anyone could have gotten Carrie Grethen's name from that. Not to mention, my office address is public information. This letter's probably not from her at all. Probably some other cuckoo."

"It probably is from her." He continued reading.

"She could mail something like this from a forensic psychiatric hospital and nobody would check it?" I countered as fear coiled around my heart.

"Saint Elizabeth's, Bellevue, Mid-Hudson, Kirby." He did not glance up. "The Carrie Grethens, the John Hinckley Juniors, the Mark David Chapmans are patients, not inmates. They enjoy our same civil rights as they sit around in penitentiaries and forensic psychiatric centers and create pedophile bulletin boards on computers and sell serial killer tips through the mail. And write taunting letters to chief medical examiners."

His voice had more bite, his words more clipped. Benton's eyes burned with hate as he finally lifted them to me.

"Carrie Grethen is mocking you, *big chief*. The FBI. Me," he went on.

"*FIB*," I muttered, and on another occasion, I might have found this funny.

Wesley stood and draped the towel over a shoulder.

"Let's say it's her," I started in again.

"It is." He had no doubt.

"Okay. Then there's more to this than mockery, Benton."

"Of course. She's making sure we don't forget that she and Lucy were lovers, something the general public doesn't know *yet*," he said. "The obvious point is Carrie Grethen hasn't finished ruining people's lives."

I could not stand to hear her name, and it enraged me that she was now, this moment, inside my West End home. She might as well be sitting at my breakfast table with us, curdling the air with her foul, evil presence. I envisioned her condescending smile and blazing eyes and wondered what she looked like now after five years of steel bars and socializing with the criminally insane. Carrie was not crazy. She had never been that. She was a character disorder, a psychopath, a violent entity with no conscience.

I looked out at wind rocking Japanese maples in my yard and the incomplete stone wall that scarcely kept me from my neighbors. The telephone rang abruptly and I was reluctant to answer it.

"Dr. Scarpetta," I said into the receiver as I watched Benton's eyes sweep back down that red-penned page.

"Yo," Pete Marino's familiar voice came over the line. "It's me."

He was a captain with the Richmond Police Department, and I knew him well enough to recognize his tone. I braced myself for more bad news.

"What's up?" I said to him.

"A horse farm went up in flames last night in Warrenton. You may have heard about it on the news," he said. "Stables, close to twenty high-dollar horses, and the house. The whole nine yards. Everything burned to the ground."

So far, this wasn't making any sense. "Marino, why are you calling me about a fire? In the first place, Northern Virginia is not your turf."

"It is now," he said.

My kitchen seemed to get small and airless as I waited for the rest.

"ATF's just called out NRT," he went on.

"Meaning us," I said.

"Bingo. Your ass and mine. First thing in the morning."

The Bureau of Alcohol, Tobacco and Firearms' National Response Team, or NRT, was deployed when churches or businesses burned, and in bombings or any other disaster in which ATF had jurisdiction. Marino and I were not ATF, but it was not unusual for it and other law enforcement agencies to recruit us when the need arose. In recent years I had worked the World Trade Center and Oklahoma City bombings and the crash of TWA Flight 800. I had helped with the identifications of the Branch Davidians at Waco and reviewed the disfigurement and death caused by the Unabomber. I knew from stressful experience that ATF included me in a call-out only when people were dead, and if Marino was recruited, too, then the suspicion was murder.

"How many?" I reached for my clipboard of call sheets.

"It's not how many, Doc. It's *who*. The owner of the farm is media big shot Kenneth Sparkes, the one and only. And right now it's looking like he didn't make it."

"Oh God," I muttered as my world suddenly got too dark to see. "We're sure?"

"Well, he's missing."

"You mind explaining to me why I'm just now being told about this?"

I felt anger rising, and it was all I could do not to hurl it at him, for all unnatural deaths in Virginia were my responsibility. I shouldn't have needed Marino to inform me about this one, and I was furious with my Northern Virginia office for not calling me at home.

"Don't go getting pissed at your docs up in Fairfax," said Marino, who seemed to read my mind. "Fauquier County asked ATF to take over here, so that's the way it's going."

I still didn't like it, but it was time to get on with the business at hand.

"I'm assuming no body has been recovered yet," I said, and I was writing fast.

"Hell no. That's going to be your fun job."

I paused, resting the pen on the call sheet. "Marino, this is a single-dwelling fire. Even if arson is suspected, and it's a high-profile case, I'm not seeing why ATF is interested."

"Whiskey, machine guns, not to mention buying and selling fancy horses, so now we're talking about a business," Marino answered.

"Great," I muttered.

"Oh yeah. We're talking a goddamn nightmare. The fire marshal's gonna call you before the day's out. Better get packed because the whirlybird's picking us up before dawn.

Timing's bad, just like it always is. I guess you can kiss your vacation goodbye."

Benton and I were supposed to drive to Hilton Head tonight to spend a week at the ocean. We had not had time alone so far this year and were burned out and barely getting along. I did not want to face him when I hung up the phone.

"I'm sorry," I said to him. "I'm sure you've already figured out there's a major disaster."

I hesitated, watching him, and he would not give me his eyes as he continued to decipher Carrie's letter.

"I've got to go. First thing in the morning. Maybe I can join you in the middle of the week," I went on.

He was not listening because he did not want to hear any of it.

"Please understand," I said to him.

He did not seem to hear me, and I knew he was terribly disappointed.

"You've been working those torso cases," he said as he read. "The dismemberments from Ireland and here. 'Sawed-up bone.' And she fantasizes about Lucy, and masturbates. Reaching orgasm multiple times a night under the covers. Allegedly."

His eyes ran down the letter as he seemed to talk to himself.

"She's saying they still have a relationship, Carrie and Lucy," he continued. "The *we* stuff is her attempt to make a case for disassociation. She's not present when she commits her crimes. Some other party doing them. Multiple personalities. A predictable and pedestrian insanity plea. I would have thought she'd be a little more original."

"She is perfectly competent to stand trial," I answered with a wave of fresh anger.

"You and I know that." He drank from a plastic bottle of Evian. "Where did *Lucy Boo* come from?"

A drop of water dribbled down his chin and he wiped it with the back of his hand.

I stumbled at first. "A pet name I had for her until she was in kindergarten. Then she didn't want to be called that anymore. Sometimes I still slip." I paused again as I imagined her back then. "So I guess she told Carrie the nickname."

"Well, we know that at one time, Lucy confided in Carrie quite a lot," Wesley stated the obvious. "Lucy's first lover. And we all know you never forget your first, no matter how lousy it was."

"Most people don't choose a psychopath for their first," I said, and I still could not believe that Lucy, my niece, had.

"Psychopaths are us, Kay," he said as if I had never heard the lecture. "The attractive, intelligent person sitting next to you on a plane, standing behind you in line, meeting you backstage, hooking up with you on the Internet. Brothers, sisters, classmates, sons, daughters, lovers. Look like you and me. Lucy didn't have a chance. She was no match for Carrie Grethen."

The grass in my backyard had too much clover, but spring had been unnaturally cool and perfect for my roses. They bent and shivered in gusting air and pale petals fell to the ground. Wesley, the retired chief of the FBI's profiling unit, went on.

"Carrie wants photos of Gault. Scene photos, autopsy photos. You bring them to her, and in exchange she'll tell you investigative details, forensic jewels you've supposedly missed. Ones that might help the prosecution when the case goes to court next month. Her taunt. That you might have missed something. That it might in some way be connected with Lucy."

His reading glasses were folded by his place mat, and he thought to slip them on.

"Carrie wants you to come see her. At Kirby."

His face was tight as he peered at me.

"It's her."

He pointed at the letter.

"She's surfacing. I knew she would." He spoke from a spirit that was tired.

"What's the dark light?" I asked, getting up because I could not sit a moment longer.

"Blood." He seemed sure. "When you stabbed Gault in the thigh, severing his femoral artery, and he bled to death. Or would have had the train not finished the job. Temple Gault."

He took his glasses off again, because he was secretly agitated.

"As long as Carrie Grethen is around, so is he. The evil twins," he added.

In fact, they were not twins, but had bleached their hair and shaved it close to their skulls. They were prepubescently thin and androgenously dressed alike when I last saw them in New York. They had committed murder together until we had captured her in the Bowery and I had killed him in the subway tunnel. I had not intended to touch him or see him or exchange one word with him, for it was not my mission in this life to apprehend criminals and commit judicial homicide. But Gault had willed it so. He had made it happen because to die by my hand was to bond me to him forever. I could not get away from Temple Gault, though he had been dead five years. In my mind were gory pieces of him scattered along gleaming steel rails and rats moiling out of dense shadows to attack his blood.

In bad dreams his eyes were ice blue with irises

scattered like molecules, and I heard the thunder of trains with lights that were blinding full moons. For several years after I had killed him, I avoided autopsying the victims of train deaths. I was in charge of the Virginia medical examiner system and could assign cases to my deputy chiefs, and that was what I had done. Even now, I could not look at dissecting knives with the same clinical regard for their cold sharp steel, because he had set me up to plunge one into him, and I had. In crowds I saw dissipated men and women who were him, and at night I slept closer to my guns.

"Benton, why don't you shower and then we'll talk more about our plans for the week," I said, dismissing recollections I could not bear. "A few days alone to read and walk the beach would be just what you need. You know how much you love the bike trails. Maybe it would be good for you to have some space."

"Lucy needs to know." He got up, too. "Even if Carrie's confined at the moment, she's going to cause more trouble that involves Lucy. That's what Carrie's promising in her letter to you."

He walked out of the kitchen.

"How much more trouble can anybody cause?" I called after him as tears rose in my throat.

"Dragging your niece into the trial," he stopped to say. "Publicly. Splashed across *The New York Times*. Out on the AP, *Hard Copy*, *Entertainment Tonight*. Around the world. *FBI agent was lesbian lover of deranged serial killer* . . ."

"Lucy's left the FBI with all its prejudices and lies and preoccupations with how the mighty Bureau looks to the world." Tears flooded my eyes. "There's nothing left. Nothing further they can do to crush her soul."

"Kay, this is about far more than the FBI," he said, and he sounded spent.

"Benton, don't start . . ." I could not finish.

He leaned against the doorway leading into my great room, where a fire burned, for the temperature had not gotten above sixty degrees this day. His eyes were pained. He did not like me to talk this way, and he did not want to peer into that darker side of his soul. He did not want to conjure up the malignant acts Carrie might carry out, and of course, he worried about me, too. I would be summoned to testify in the sentencing phase of Carrie Grethen's trial. I was Lucy's aunt. I supposed my credibility as a witness would be impeached, my testimony and reputation ruined.

"Let's go out tonight," Wesley said in a kinder tone. "Where would you like to go? La Petite? Or beer and barbecue at Benny's?"

"I'll thaw some soup." I wiped my eyes as my voice faltered. "I'm not very hungry, are you?"

"Come here," he said to me sweetly.

I melted into him and he held me to his chest. He was salty when we kissed, and I was always surprised by the supple firmness of his body. I rested my head, and the stubble on his chin roughed my hair and was white like the beach I knew I would not see this week. There would be no long walks on wet sand or long talks over dinners at La Polla's and Charlie's.

"I think I should go see what she wants," I finally said into his warm, damp neck.

"Not in a million years."

"New York did Gault's autopsy. I don't have those photographs."

"Carrie knows damn well what medical examiner did Gault's autopsy."

"Then why is she asking me, if she knows?" I muttered.

My eyes were closed as I leaned against him. He paused and kissed the top of my head again and stroked my hair.

"You know why," he said. "Manipulation, jerking you around. What people like her do best. She wants you to get the photos for her. So she can see Gault mangled like chopped meat, so she can fantasize and get off on that. She's up to something and the worst thing you could do is respond to her in any way."

"And this GKSWF—something or other? Like out of a personal?"

"I don't know."

"And the One Pheasant Place?"

"No idea."

We stayed a long time in the doorway of this house I continued to think of singularly and unequivocally as my own. Benton parked his life with me when he was not consulting in big aberrant cases in this country and others. I knew it bothered him when I consistently said *I* this and *my* that, although he knew we were not married and nothing we owned separately belonged to both of us. I had passed the midline of my life and would not legally share my earnings with anyone, including my lover and my family. Maybe I sounded selfish, and maybe I was.

"What am I going to do while you're gone tomorrow?" Wesley got back to that subject.

"Drive to Hilton Head and get groceries," I replied. "Make sure there's plenty of Black Bush and Scotch. More than usual. And sunblock SPF 35 and 50, and South Carolina pecans, tomatoes, and Vidalia onions."

Tears filled my eyes again, and I cleared my throat.

"As soon as I can, I'll get on a plane and meet you, but I don't know where this case in Warrenton is going to go.

And we've already been over this. We've done it before. Half the time you can't go, the rest of the time it's me."

"I guess our lives suck," he said into my ear.

"Somehow we ask for it," I replied, and most of all I felt an uncontrollable urge to sleep.

"Maybe."

He bent down to my lips and slid his hands to favorite places.

"Before soup, we could go to bed."

"Something very bad is going to happen during this trial," I said, and I wanted my body to respond to him but didn't think it could.

"All of us in New York again. The Bureau, you, Lucy, at her trial. Yes, I'm sure for the past five years she has thought of nothing else and will cause all the trouble she can."

I pulled away as Carrie's sharp, drawn face suddenly jumped out of a dark place in my mind. I remembered her when she was strikingly pretty and smoking with Lucy on a picnic table at night near the firing ranges of the FBI Academy at Quantico. I could still hear them teasing in low playful voices and saw their erotic kisses on the mouth, deep and long, and hands tangled in hair. I remembered the strange sensation running through my blood as I silently hurried away, without them knowing what I had seen. Carrie had begun the ruination of my only niece's life, and now the grotesque coda had come.

"Benton," I said. "I've got to pack my gear."

"Your gear is fine. Trust me."

He hungrily had undone layers of my clothing, desperate for skin. He always wanted me more when I was not in sync with him.

"I can't reassure you now," I whispered. "I can't tell you everything is going to be all right, because it won't be.

Attorneys and the media will go after Lucy and me. They will dash us against the rocks, and Carrie may go free. There!"

I held his face in my hands.

"Truth and justice. The American way," I concluded.

"Stop it."

He went still and his eyes were intense on mine.

"Don't start again," he said. "You didn't used to be this cynical."

"I'm not cynical, and I'm not the one who started anything," I answered him as my anger rose higher. "I'm not the one who started with an eleven-year-old boy and cut off patches of his flesh and left him naked by a Dumpster with a bullet in his head. And then killed a sheriff and a prison guard. And Jayne—Gault's own twin sister. Remember that, Benton? Remember? Remember Central Park on Christmas Eve. Bare footprints in snow and her frozen blood dripping from the fountain!"

"Of course I remember. I was there. I know all the same details you do."

"No, you don't."

I was furious now and moved away from him and gathered together my clothes.

"You don't put your hands inside their ruined bodies and touch and measure their wounds," I said. "You don't hear them speak after they're dead. You don't see the faces of loved ones waiting inside my poor, plain lobby to hear heartless, unspeakable news. You don't see what I do. Oh no, you don't, Benton Wesley. You see clean case files and glossy photos and cold crime scenes. You spend more time with the killers than with those they ripped from life. And maybe you sleep better than I do, too. Maybe you still dream because you aren't afraid to."

He walked out of my house without a word, because I had gone too far. I had been unfair and mean, and not even truthful.

Wesley knew only tortured sleep. He thrashed and muttered and coldly drenched the sheets. He rarely dreamed, or at least he had learned not to remember. I set salt and pepper shakers on corners of Carrie Grethen's letter to keep it from folding along its creases. Her mocking, unnerving words were evidence now and should not be touched or disturbed.

Ninhydrin or a Luma Lite might reveal her fingerprints on the cheap white paper, or exemplars of her writing might be matched with what she had scrawled to me. Then we would prove she had penned this twisted message at the brink of her murder trial in Superior Court of New York City. The jury would see that she had not changed after five years of psychiatric treatment paid for with their taxes. She felt no remorse. She reveled in what she had done.

I had no doubt Benton would be somewhere in my neighborhood because I had not heard his BMW leave. I hurried along new paved streets, passing big brick and stucco homes, until I caught him beneath trees staring out at a rocky stretch of the James River. The water was frigid and the color of glass, and cirrus clouds were indistinct chalky streaks in a fading sky.

"I'll head out to South Carolina as soon as I get back to the house. I'll get the condo ready and get your Scotch," he said, not turning around. "And Black Bush."

"You don't need to leave tonight," I said, and I was afraid to move closer to him as slanted light brightened his hair and the wind stirred it. "I've got to get up early tomorrow. You can head out when I do."

He was silent, staring up at a bald eagle that had followed me since I had left my house. Benton had put on a red windbreaker, but he looked chilled in his damp running shorts, and his arms were crossed tightly at his chest. His throat moved as he swallowed, his pain radiating from a hidden place that only I was allowed to see. At moments like this I did not know why he put up with me.

"Don't expect me to be a machine, Benton," I said quietly for the millionth time since I had loved him.

Still he did not speak, and water barely had the energy to roll toward downtown, making a dull pouring sound as it unwittingly headed closer to the violence of dams.

"I take as much as I can," I explained. "I take more than most people could. Don't expect too much from me, Benton."

The eagle soared in circles over the tops of tall trees, and Benton seemed more resigned when he spoke at last.

"And I take more than most people can," he said. "In part, because you do."

"Yes, it works both ways."

I stepped closer to him from behind and slipped my arms around the slick red nylon covering his waist.

"You know damn well it does," he said.

I hugged him tight and dug my chin into his back.

"One of your neighbors is watching," he said. "I can see him through sliding glass. Did you know you have a peeper in this ritzy white-bread place?"

He placed his hands over mine, then lifted one finger at a time with nothing special in mind.

"Of course, if I lived here, I would peep at you too," he added with a smile in his tone.

"You do live here."

"Naw. I just sleep here."

"Let's talk about the morning. As usual, they'll pick me up at the Eye Institute around five," I told him. "So I guess if I get up by four . . ." I sighed, wondering if life would always be like this. "You should stay the night."

"I'm not getting up at four," he said.

2

The next morning came unkindly on a field that was flat and barely blue with first light. I had gotten up at four, and Wesley had gotten up, too, deciding he would rather leave when I did. We had kissed briefly and barely looked at each other as we had headed to our cars, for brevity at goodbyes was always easier than lingering. But as I had followed West Cary Street to the Huguenot Bridge, a heaviness seemed to spread through every inch of me and I was suddenly unnerved and sad.

I knew from weary experience that it was unlikely I would be seeing Wesley this week, and there would be no rest or reading or late mornings to sleep. Fire scenes were never easy, and if nothing else, a case involving an important personage in a wealthy bedroom community of D.C. would tie me up in politics and paperwork. The more attention a death caused, the more public pressure I was promised.

There were no lights on at the Eye Institute, which was not a place of medical research nor called such in honor of some benefactor or important personage named *Eye*. Several times a year I came here to have glasses adjusted or my vision checked, and it always seemed strange to park near fields where I was often lifted into the air, headed toward chaos. I opened my car door as the familiar distant sound moved over dark waves of trees, and I imagined burned bones and teeth scattered through black watery debris. I imagined Sparkes's sharp suits and strong face, and shock chilled me like fog.

The tadpole silhouette flew beneath an imperfect moon as I gathered water repellent duffle bags, and the scratched silver Halliburton aluminum flight case that stored my various medical examiner instruments and needs, including photography equipment. Two cars and a pickup truck began slowing on Huguenot Road, the city's twilight travelers unable to resist a helicopter low and about to land. The curious turned into the parking lot and got out to stare at blades slicing air in a slow sweep for power lines, puddles and muck, or sand and dirt that might boil up.

"Must be the governor coming in," said an old man who had arrived in a rusting heap of a Plymouth.

"Could be someone delivering an organ," said the driver of the pickup truck as he briefly turned his gaze on me.

Their words scattered like dry leaves as the black Bell LongRanger thundered in at a measured pitch and perfectly flared and gently descended. My niece Lucy, its pilot, hovered in a storm of fresh-mown grass flooded white by landing lights, and settled sweetly. I gathered my belongings and headed into beating wind. Plexiglas was tinted dark enough that I could not see through it as I pulled open the back door, but I recognized the big arm that reached down to grab my baggage. I climbed up as more traffic slowed to watch the aliens, and threads of gold bled through the tops of trees.

"I was wondering where you were." I raised my voice above rotors chopping as I latched my door.

"Airport," Pete Marino answered as I sat next to him. "It's closer."

"No, it's not," I said.

"At least they got coffee and a john there," he said, and I knew he did not mean them in that order. "I guess Benton headed out on vacation without you," he added for the effect.

Lucy was rolling the throttle to full power, and the blades were going faster.

"I can tell you right now I got one of those feelings," he let me know in his grumpy tone as the helicopter got light and began to lift. "We're headed for big trouble."

Marino's specialty was investigating death, although he was completely unnerved by possibilities of his own. He did not like being airborne, especially in something that did not have flight attendants or wings. The *Richmond Times Dispatch* was a mess in his lap, and he refused to look down at fast retreating earth and the distant city skyline slowly rising from the horizon like someone tall standing up.

The front page of the paper prominently displayed a story about the fire, including a distant AP aerial photograph of ruins smoldering in the dark. I read closely but learned nothing new, for mostly the coverage was a rehash of Kenneth Sparkes's alleged death, and his power and wealthy lifestyle in Warrenton. I had not known of his horses before or that one named Wind had sailed in last one year at the Kentucky Derby and was worth a million dollars. But I was not surprised. Sparkes had always been enterprising, his ego as enormous as his pride. I set the newspaper on the opposite seat and noted that Marino's seat belt was unbuckled and collecting dust from the floor.

"What happens if we hit severe turbulence when you're not belted in?" I talked loudly above the turbine engine.

"So I spill my coffee." He adjusted the pistol on his hip, his khaki suit a sausage skin about to split. "In case you ain't figured it out after all those bodies you've cut up, if this bird goes down, Doc, a seat belt ain't gonna save you. Not airbags either, if we had them."

In truth, he hated anything around his girth and had come to wear his pants so low I marveled that his hips could keep them up. Paper crackled as he dug two Hardee's biscuits out of a bag stained gray with grease. Cigarettes bunched in his shirt pocket, and his face had its typical hypertensive flush. When I had moved to Virginia from my native city of Miami, he was a homicide detective as obnoxious as he was gifted. I remembered our early encounters in the morgue when he had referred to me as *Mrs. Scarpetta* as he bullied my staff and helped himself to any evidence he pleased. He had taken bullets before I could label them, to infuriate me. He had smoked cigarettes with bloody gloves and made jokes about bodies that had once been living human beings.

I looked out my window at clouds skating across the sky and thought of time going by. Marino was almost fifty-five, and I could not believe it. We had defended and irritated each other almost daily for more than eleven years.

"Want one?" He held up a cold biscuit wrapped in waxy paper.

"I don't even want to look at it," I said ungraciously.

Pete Marino knew how much his rotten health habits worried me and was simply trying to get my attention. He carefully stirred more sugar in the plastic cup of coffee he was floating up and down with the turbulence, using his meaty arm for suspension.

"What about coffee?" he asked me. "I'm pouring."

"No thanks. How about an update?" I got to the point

as my tension mounted. "Do we know anything more than we did last night?"

"The fire's still smoldering in places. Mostly in the stables," he said. "A lot more horses than we thought. Must be twenty cooked out there, including thoroughbreds, quarter horses, and two foals with racehorse pedigrees. And of course you know about the one that ran the Derby. Talk about the insurance money alone. A so-called witness said you could hear them screaming like humans."

"What witness?" It was the first I'd heard of it.

"Oh, all kinds of drones have been calling in, saying they saw this and know that. Same old shit that always happens when a case gets a lot of attention. And it don't take an *eyewitness* to know the horses would have been screaming and trying to kick down their stalls." His tone turned to flint. "We're gonna get the son of a bitch who did this. Let's see how he likes it when it's his ass burning."

"We don't know that there is a son of a bitch, at least not for a fact," I reminded him. "No one has said it's arson yet, although I certainly am assuming you and I haven't been invited along for the ride."

He turned his attention out a window.

"I hate it when it's animals." He spilled coffee on his knee. "Shit." He glared at me as if I were somehow to blame. "Animals and kids. The thought makes me sick."

He did not seem to care about the famous man who may have died in the fire, but I knew Marino well enough to understand that he targeted his feelings where he could tolerate them. He did not hate human beings half as much as he led others to believe, and as I envisioned what he had just described, I saw thoroughbreds and foals with terror in their eyes.

I could not bear to imagine screams, or battering hooves splintering wood. Flames had flowed like rivers of lava over the Warrenton farm with its mansion, stables, reserve aged whiskey, and collection of guns. Fire had spared nothing but hollow walls of stone.

I looked past Marino into the cockpit, where Lucy talked into the radio, making comments to her ATF copilot as they nodded at a Chinook helicopter below horizon and a plane so distant it was a sliver of glass. The sun lit up our journey by degrees, and it was difficult to concentrate as I watched my niece and felt wounded again.

She had quit the FBI because it had made certain she would. She had left the artificial intelligence computer system she had created and robots she had programmed and the helicopters she had learned to fly for her beloved Bureau. Lucy had walked off from her heart and was no longer within my reach. I did not want to talk to her about Carrie.

I silently leaned back in my seat and began reviewing paperwork on the Warrenton case. Long ago I had learned how to focus my attention to a very sharp point, no matter what I thought and in spite of my mood. I felt Marino staring again as he touched the pack of cigarettes in his shirt pocket, making sure he was not without his vice. The chopping and flapping of blades was loud as he slid open his window and tapped his pack of cigarettes to shake one loose.

"Don't," I said, turning a page. "Don't even think about it."

"I don't see a No Smoking sign," he said, stuffing a Marlboro into his mouth.

"You never do, no matter how many of them are posted." I reviewed more of my notes, puzzling again over one particular statement the fire marshal had made to me over the phone yesterday.

"Arson for profit?" I commented, glancing up. "Implicating the owner, Kenneth Sparkes, who may have accidentally been overcome by the fire he started? Based on what?"

"Is his the name of an arsonist or what?" Marino said. "Gotta be guilty." He inhaled deeply and with lust. "And if that's the case, he got what he deserves. You know, you can take them off the street but can't take the street out of them."

"Sparkes was not raised on the street," I said. "And by the way, he was a Rhodes scholar."

"*Road* scholar and *street* sound like the same damn thing to me," Marino went on. "I remember when all the son of a bitch did was criticize the police through his newspaper chain. Everybody knew he was doing cocaine and women. But we couldn't prove it because nobody would come forward to help us out."

"That's right, no one could prove it," I said. "And you can't assume someone is an arsonist because of his name or his editorial policy."

"Well, it just so happens you're talking to the expert in weird-ass names and how they fit the squirrels who have them." Marino poured more coffee as he smoked. "*Gore* the coroner. *Slaughter* the serial killer. *Childs* the pedophile. *Mr. Bury* buried his victims in cemeteries. Then we got *Judges Gallow* and *Frye*. Plus Freddie *Gamble*. He was running numbers out of his restaurant when he got whacked. *Dr. Faggart* murdered five homosexual males. Stabbed their eyes out. You remember *Crisp?*" He looked at me. "Struck by lightning. Blew his clothes all over the church parking lot and magnetized his belt buckle."

I could not listen to all this so early in the morning and reached behind me to grab a headset so I could drown Marino out and monitor what was being said in the cockpit.

"I wouldn't want to get struck by lightning at no church and have everybody read something into it," Marino went on.

He got more coffee, as if he did not have prostate and urinary troubles.

"I've been keeping a list all these years. Never told no one. Not even you, Doc. You don't write down shit like this, you forget." He sipped. "I think there's a market for it. Maybe one of those little books you see up by the cash register."

I put the headset on and watched rural farms and dormant fields slowly turn into houses with big barns and long drives that were paved. Cows and calves were black-spotted clusters in fenced-in grass, and a combine churned up dust as it slowly drove past fields scattered with hay.

I looked down as the landscape slowly transformed into the wealth of Warrenton, where crime was low and mansions on hundreds of acres of land had guest houses, tennis courts and pools, and very fine stables. We flew lower over private airstrips and lakes with ducks and geese. Marino was gawking.

Our pilots were silent for a while as they waited to be in range of the NRT on the ground. Then I caught Lucy's voice as she changed frequencies and began transmitting.

"Echo One, helicopter niner-one-niner Delta Alpha. Teun, you read me?"

"That's affirmative, niner Delta Alpha," T. N. McGovern, the team leader, came back.

"We're ten miles south, inbound-landing with passengers," Lucy said. "ETA about eight hundred hours."

"Roger. It feels like winter up here and not getting any warmer."

Lucy switched over to the Manassas Automated Weather Observation Service, or AWOS, and I listened to a long mechanical rendition of wind, visibility, sky condition, temperature, dew point, and altimeter setting according to Sierra time, which was the most recent update of the day. I wasn't thrilled to learn that the temperature had dropped five degrees Celsius since I had left home, and I imagined Benton on his way to warm sunshine and the water.

"We got rain over there," Lucy's copilot said into his mike.

"It's at least twenty miles west and the winds are west," Lucy replied. "So much for June."

"Looks like we got another Chinook coming this way, below horizon."

"Let's remind 'em we're out here," Lucy said, switching to a different frequency again. "Chinook over Warrenton, helicopter niner-one-niner Delta Alpha, you up this push? We're at your three o'clock, two miles northbound, one thousand feet."

"We see you, Delta Alpha," answered the twin rotor Army helicopter named for an Indian tribe. "Have a good'n."

My niece double-clicked the transmit switch. Her calm, low voice seemed unfamiliar to me as it radiated through space and bounced off the antennae of strangers. I continued to eavesdrop and, as soon as I could, butted in.

"What's this about wind and cold?" I asked, staring at the back of Lucy's head.

"Twenty, gusting to twenty-five out of the west," she

sounded in my headset. "And gonna get worse. You guys doing all right back there?"

"We're fine," I said as I thought of Carrie's deranged letter again.

Lucy flew in blue ATF fatigues, a pair of Cébé sunglasses blacking out her eyes. She had grown her hair, and it gracefully curled to her shoulders and reminded me of red jarrah wood, polished and exotic, and nothing like my own short silver-blond strands. I imagined her light touch on the collective and cyclic as she worked anti-torque pedals to keep the helicopter in trim.

She had taken to flying like everything else she had ever tried. She had gotten her private and commercial ratings in the minimum required hours and next got her certificated flight instructor rating simply because it gave her joy to pass on her gifts to others.

I needed no announcement that we were reaching the end of our flight as we skimmed over woods littered with felled trees scattered haphazardly like Lincoln Logs. Dirt trails and lanes wound narrowly, and on the other side of gentle hills, gray clouds got vertical as they turned into vague columns of tired smoke left by an inferno that had killed. Kenneth Sparkes's farm was a shocking black pit, a scorched earth of smoldering carnage.

The fire had left its trail as it had slaughtered, and from the air I followed the devastation of splendid stone dwellings and stables and barn to wide charred swaths that had denuded the grounds. Fire trucks had rolled over sections of the white fence surrounding the property and had churned up acres of manicured grass. Miles in the distance were more pasture land and a narrow paved public road, then a Virginia Power substation, and farther off, more homes.

We invaded Sparkes's privileged Virginia farm at not quite eight A.M., landing far enough away from ruins that our rotor wash did not disturb them. Marino climbed out and went on without me as I waited for our pilots to brake the main rotor and turn off all switches.

"Thanks for the lift," I said to Special Agent Jim Mowery, who had helped Lucy fly this day.

"She did the driving."

He popped open the baggage door.

"I'll tie her down if you guys want to go on," he added to my niece.

"Seems like you're getting the hang of that thing," I lightly teased Lucy as we walked away.

"I limp along the best I can," she said. "Here, let me get one of those bags."

She relieved me of my aluminum case, which did not seem to weigh much in her firm hand. We walked together, dressed alike, although I did not wear gun or portable radio. Our steel-reinforced boots were so battered they were peeling and almost gray. Black mud sucked at our soles as we drew closer to the gray inflatable tent that would be our command post for the next few days. Parked next to it was the big white Pierce supertruck with Department of the Treasury seals and emergency lights, and ATF and EXPLOSIVES INVESTIGATION announced in vivid blue.

Lucy was a step ahead of me, her face shadowed by a dark blue cap. She had been transferred to Philadelphia, and would be moving from D.C. soon, and the thought made me feel old and used up. She was grown. She was as accomplished as I had been at her age, and I did not want her moving farther away. But I had not told her.

"This one's pretty bad." She initiated the conversation.

"At least the basement is ground level, but there's only one door. So most of the water's in a pool down there. We got a truck on the way with pumps."

"How deep?"

I thought of thousands of gallons of water from fire hoses and imagined a cold black soup thick with dangerous debris.

"Depends on where you're stepping. If I were you, I wouldn't have taken this call," she said in a way that made me feel unwanted.

"Yes, you would have," I said, hurt.

Lucy had made little effort to hide her feelings about working cases with me. She wasn't rude, but often acted as if she barely knew me when she was with her colleagues. I remembered earlier years when I would visit her at UVA and she did not want students to see us together. I knew she was not ashamed of me but perceived me as an overwhelming shadow that I had worked very hard not to cast over her life.

"Have you finished packing?" I asked her with an ease that was not true.

"Please don't remind me," she said.

"But you still want to go."

"Of course. It's a great opportunity."

"Yes, it is, and I am so pleased for you," I said. "How's Janet? I know this must be hard . . ."

"It's not like we'll be in different hemispheres," Lucy answered back.

I knew better, and so did she. Janet was an FBI agent. The two of them had been lovers since their early training days at Quantico. Now they worked for different federal law enforcement agencies and soon would live in separate cities.

It was quite possible their careers would never permit their relationship again.

"Do you suppose we can carve out a minute to talk today?" I spoke again as we picked our way around puddles.

"Sure. When we finish up here, we'll have a beer, if we can find an open bar out here in the sticks," she replied as the wind blew harder.

"I don't care how late it is," I added.

"Here goes," Lucy muttered with a sigh as we approached the tent. "Hey gang," she called out. "Where's the party?"

"You're looking at it."

"Doc, you making house calls these days?"

"Naw, she's babysitting Lucy."

In addition to Marino and me, NRT on this call-out were nine men, two women, including team leader McGovern. All of us were dressed alike in the familiar dark blue fatigues, which were worn and patched and supple like our boots. Agents were restless and boisterous around the back of the open tailgate of the supertruck with its shiny aluminum interior divided into shelves and jump seats, and its outside compartments packed with reels of yellow crime-scene tape, and dustpans, picks, floodlights, whisk brooms, wrecking bars, and chop saws.

Our mobile headquarters was also equipped with computers, a photocopier and fax machine, and the hydraulic spreader, ram, hammer, and cutter used to deconstruct a scene or save a human life. In fact, I could not think of much the truck did not have except, perhaps, a chef, and more importantly, a toilet.

Some agents had begun decontaminating boots, rakes, and shovels in plastic tubs filled with soapy water. It was a never-ending effort, and in brisk weather, hands and feet never dried or thawed. Even exhaust pipes were swabbed for petroleum residues, and all power tools were run by electricity or hydraulic fluid instead of gasoline, preparing for that day in court when all would be questioned and judged.

McGovern was sitting on a table inside the tent, her boots unzipped, and a clipboard on her knee.

"All right," she addressed her team. "We've been through most of this already at the fire station, where you guys missed good coffee and donuts," she added for the benefit of those of us who had just gotten here. "But listen up again. What we know so far is the fire is believed to have started day before yesterday, on the evening of the seventh at twenty hundred hours."

McGovern was about my age and based in the Philadelphia field office. I looked at her and saw Lucy's new mentor, and I felt a stiffening in my bones.

"At least that's the time the fire alarm went off in the house," McGovern went on. "When the fire department got here, the house was fully involved. Stables were burning. Trucks really couldn't get close enough to do anything but surround and drown. Or at least make an attempt at it. We're estimating about thirty thousand gallons of water in the basement. That's about six hours total to pump all of it out, assuming we're talking about four pumps going and don't have millions of clogs. And by the way, the power's off, and our local friendly fire department is going to set up lights inside."

"What was the response time?" Marino asked her.

"Seventeen minutes," she replied. "They had to grab people off duty. Everything around here is volunteer."

Someone groaned.

"Now don't be too hard on them. They used every tanker

around to get enough water in, so that wasn't the problem," McGovern chided her troops. "This thing went up like paper, and it was too windy for foam, even though I don't think it would have helped." She got up and moved to the supertruck. "The deal is, this was a *fast, hot fire*. That much we know for a fact."

She opened a red-paneled door and began handing out rakes and shovels.

"We got not a clue as to point of origin or cause," she continued, "but it's believed that the owner, Kenneth Sparkes, the newspaper tycoon, was inside the house and did not get out. Which is why we got the doc here."

McGovern looked straight at me with piercing eyes that did not miss much.

"What makes us think he was home at the time?" I asked.

"For one thing, he seems to be MIA. And a Mercedes burned up in the back. We haven't run the tags yet but assume it's probably his," a fire investigator answered. "And the farrier who shoes his horses was just here two days before the fire, on Thursday, the fifth, and Sparkes was home then and the farrier didn't say that he indicated he was headed out somewhere."

"Who took care of his horses when he was out of town?" I asked.

"We don't know," McGovern said.

"I'd like the farrier's name and number," I said.

"No problem. Kurt?" she said to one of her investigators.

"Sure. I got it." He flipped pages in a spiral notebook, his young hands big and rough from years of work.

McGovern grabbed bright blue helmets out of another compartment and began tossing them around as she reminded individuals of their assignments.

"Lucy, Robby, Frank, Jennifer, you're in the hole with me. Bill, you're general assignment, and Mick's going to help him, since this is Bill's first NRT."

"Lucky you."

"Ohhh, a virgin."

"Give me a break, man," said the agent named Bill. "It's my wife's fortieth birthday. She'll never speak to me again."

"Rusty's in charge of the truck," McGovern resumed. "Marino and the doc are here as needed."

"Had Sparkes been receiving any threats?" Marino asked, because it was his job to think murder.

"You know about as much as we do at this point," the fire investigator named Robby said.

"What's this about this alleged witness?" I asked.

"We got that through a telephone call," he explained. "A male, he wouldn't leave his name, and it was an out-of-the-area call, so we got no idea. Got no idea if it's legit."

"But he said he heard the horses as they were dying," I persisted.

"Yeah. Screaming like humans."

"Did he explain how he might have been close enough to have heard that?" I was getting upset again.

"Said he saw the fire from the distance and drove in for a closer look. Says he watched for maybe fifteen minutes and then got the hell out of Dodge when he heard the fire trucks."

"Now I didn't know that and it bothers me," Marino said ominously. "What he's saying is consistent with the response time. And we know how much these squirrels like to hang around and watch their fires burn. Got any idea about race?"

"I didn't talk to him more than thirty seconds," Robby

answered. "But he had no discernible accent. Was soft-spoken and very calm."

There was silence for a pause as everyone processed their disappointment in not knowing who this witness was, or if he had been genuine. McGovern went on with her roster of who was doing what this day.

"Johnny Kostylo, our beloved ASAC in Philly, will be working the media and local bigwigs, like the mayor of Warrenton, who's already been calling because he doesn't want his town to look bad."

She glanced up from her clipboard, scanning our faces.

"One of our auditors is on his way," she went on. "And Pepper will be showing up shortly to help us out."

Several agents whistled their appreciation of Pepper the arson dog.

"And thankfully, Pepper doesn't hit on alcohol." McGovern put her own helmet on. "Because there's about a thousand gallons of bourbon out here."

"We know anything more about that?" Marino asked. "We know if Sparkes might have been making or selling the stuff? I mean, that's a hell of a lot of hooch for one guy."

"Apparently Sparkes was a collector of the finer things in life," McGovern spoke of Sparkes as if he were certainly dead. "Bourbon, cigars, automatic firearms, expensive horses. We don't know how legal he was, which is one of the reasons why youze guys are here instead of the Feebs."

"Hate to tell you, but the Feebs are already sniffing around. Wanting to know what they can do to help."

"Aren't they sweet."

"Maybe they can show us what to do."

"Where are they?" McGovern asked.

"In a white Suburban about a mile down the road.

Three of 'em hanging out in their FBI flak jackets. They're already talking to the media."

"Shit. Wherever there are cameras."

There were groans and derisive laughter directed at the *Feebs*, which was what ATF rudely called the FBI. It was no secret that the two federal agencies were not fond of each other, and that the FBI routinely appropriated credit when it was not always due.

"Speaking of pains in the ass," another agent spoke up, "the Budget Motel doesn't take AmEx, boss. We're going through the heels of our boots, and we're supposed to use our own credit cards?"

"Plus, room service quits at seven."

"It stinks anyway."

"Any chance we can move?"

"I'll take care of it," McGovern promised.

"That's why we love you so much."

A bright red fire engine rumbled up the unpaved road, churning dust and small rocks, as help arrived to begin draining water from the scene. Two firefighters in turn-out gear and high rubber boots climbed down and briefly conferred with McGovern before uncoiling one-and-three-quarter-inch hoses attached to filters. These they draped over their shoulders and dragged inside the mansion's stone shell and dropped them into the water in four different locations. They returned to the truck and set heavy portable Prosser pumps on the ground and plugged extension cords into the generator. Soon the noise of engines got very loud, and hoses swelled as dirty water gushed through them and over grass.

I gathered heavy canvas fire gloves and a turn-out coat

and adjusted the size of my helmet. Then I began cleaning my faithful Red Wing boots, sloshing them through tubs of sudsy cold tap water that seeped through old leather tongues and soaked the laces. I had not thought to wear silk underwear beneath my BDUs because it was June. That had been a mistake. Winds were now strong and from the north, and every drop of moisture seemed to lower my body temperature another degree. I hated being cold. I hated not trusting my hands, because they were either stiff or heavily gloved. McGovern headed toward me as I blew on my fingertips and fastened my heavy turn-out coat up to my chin.

"It's going to be a long day," she said with a shiver. "What happened to summer?"

"Teun, I'm missing my vacation for you. You are destroying my personal life." I gave her a hard time.

"At least you have either." McGovern started cleaning her boots, too.

Teun was really an odd hybrid of the initials T. N., which stood for something Southern-awful such as Tina Nola, or so I had been told. For as long as I had been on the NRT, she had been Teun, and so that was what I called her. She was capable and divorced. She was firm and fit, her bone structure and gray eyes compelling. McGovern could be fierce. I had seen her anger flash over like a room in flames, but she could also be generous and kind. Her special gift was arson, and it was legend that she could intuit the cause of a fire simply by hearing a description of the scene.

I worked on two pairs of latex gloves as McGovern scanned the horizon, her eyes staying a long time on the blackened pit with its shell of standing granite. I followed her gaze to scorched stables, and in my mind heard screams and panicked hooves battering stalls. For an instant my throat constricted. I had seen the raw, clawed hands of people buried alive, and the defense injuries of victims who struggled with their killers. I knew about life fighting not to die, and I could not bear the vivid footage playing in my mind.

"Goddamn reporters." McGovern stared up at a small helicopter flying low overhead.

It was a white Schweizer with no identification or mounted cameras I could see. McGovern stepped forward and boldly pointed out every member of the media within five miles.

"That van there," she let me know. "Radio, some local-yokel FM dial with a celebrity talent named Jezebel who tells moving stories about life and her crippled son and his three-legged dog named Sport. And another radio over there. And that Ford Escort over that way is some fucking son-of-a-bitch newspaper. Probably some tabloid out of D.C. Then we got the *Post*." She pointed at a Honda. "So look out for her. She's the brunette with legs. Can you imagine wearing a skirt out here? Probably thinks the guys will talk to her. But they know better, unlike the Feebs."

She backed up and grabbed a handful of latex gloves from inside the supertruck. I dug my hands deeper into the pockets of my BDUs. I had gotten used to McGovern's diatribes about the *biased, mendacious media*, and I barely listened.

"And this is just the start," she went on. "These media maggots will be crawling all over the place because I already know about this one here. It doesn't take a Boy Scout to guess how this place burned and all those poor horses got killed."

"You seem more cheerful than usual," I said dryly.

"I'm not cheerful in the least."

She propped her foot on the shiny tailgate of the supertruck as an old station wagon pulled up. Pepper the arson dog was a handsome black Labrador retriever. He wore an ATF badge on his collar and was no doubt comfortably curled in the warm front seat, going nowhere until we were ready for him.

"What can I do to help?" I said to her. "Besides staying out of the way until you need me."

She was staring off. "If I were you, I'd hang out with Pepper or in the truck. Both are heated."

McGovern had worked with me before and knew if I was needed to dive into a river or sift through fire or bombing debris, I was not above the task. She knew I could hold a shovel and did not sit around. I resented her comments and felt she was somehow picking on me. I turned to address her again and found her standing very still, like a bird dog pointing. She had an incredulous expression on her face as she remained fixed to some spot on the horizon.

"Holy Jesus," she muttered.

I followed her stare to a lone black foal, maybe a hundred yards due east of us, just beyond the smoky ruins of the stables. The magnificent animal looked carved from ebony from where we stood, and I could make out twitching muscles and tail as he seemed to return our attention.

"The stables," McGovern said, in awe. "How the hell did he get away?"

She got on her portable radio.

"Teun to Jennifer," she said.

"Go ahead."

"Take a look maybe beyond the stables. See what I do?"

"Ten-four. Got the four-legged subject in sight."

"Make sure the locals know. We need to find out if subject is a survivor from here or a runaway from somewhere else."

"You got it."

McGovern strode off, a shovel over her shoulder. I watched her move into the stinking pit and pick a spot near what appeared to have once been the wide front door, cold water up to her knees. Far off, the aloof black horse wavered as if made of fire. I slogged ahead in soggy boots, my fingers getting increasingly uncooperative. It was only a matter of time before I would need a toilet, which typically would be a tree, a mound, an acre somewhere in what was sworn to be a blind with no men within a mile.

I did not enter the remaining stone shell at first but walked slowly around it from the outside perimeter. The caving-in of remaining structures was an obvious and extreme danger at scenes of mass destruction, and although the two-story walls looked sturdy enough, it would have suited me better had they been pulled down by a crane and trucked away. I continued my scan in the bright, cool wind, my heart sinking as I wondered where to begin. My shoulders ached from my aluminum case, and just the thought of dragging a rake through water-logged debris sent pain into my back. I was certain McGovern was watching to see how long I would last.

Through gaping wounds of windows and doors I could see the sooty pit coiling with thousands of flat steel whiskey-barrel hoops that drifted in black water. I imagined reserve bourbon exploding from burning white oak kegs and pouring through the door in a river of fire downhill to the stables that had housed Kenneth Sparkes's precious horses. While investigators began the task of determining where the fire had started and hopefully its cause, I stepped through puddles and climbed atop anything that looked sturdy enough to bear my weight.

Nails were everywhere, and with a Buckman tool that

had been a gift from Lucy, I pulled one of them out of my left boot. I stopped inside the perfect stone rectangle of a doorway in the front of the former mansion. For minutes I stood and looked. Unlike many investigators, I did not take photographs with every inch I moved closer into a crime scene. I had learned to bide my time and let my eyes go first. As I quietly scanned around me, I was struck by many things.

The front of the house, unsurprisingly, would have afforded the most spectacular view. From upper stories no longer there, one should have seen trees and gentle hills, and the various activities of the horses that the owner bought, traded, bred, and sold. It was believed that Kenneth Sparkes had been home the night of the fire, on June seventh, and I remembered that the weather had been clear and a little warmer, with a light wind and full moon.

I surveyed the empty shell of what must have been a mansion, looking at soggy couch parts, metal, glass, the melted guts of televisions and appliances. There were hundreds of partially burned books, and paintings, mattresses, and furniture. All had fallen from upper stories and settled into soupy layers in the basement. As I imagined Sparkes in the evening when the fire alarm went off, I imagined him in the living room with its view, or in the kitchen, perhaps cooking. Yet the more I explored where he might have been, the less I understood why he had not escaped, unless he were incapacitated by alcohol or drugs, or had tried to put out the fire until carbon monoxide had overcome him.

Lucy and comrades were on the other side of the pit, prying open an electrical box that heat and water had caused to rust instantly.

"Good luck," McGovern's voice carried as she waded closer to them. "That's not going to be what started this one."

She kept talking as she slung a blackened frame of an ironing board to one side. The iron and what was left of its cord followed. She kicked more barrel hoops out of the way as if she were mad at whoever had caused this mess.

"You notice the windows?" she went on to them. "The broken glass is on the inside. Makes you think someone broke in?"

"Not necessarily." It was Lucy who answered as she squatted to look. "You get thermal impact to the inside of the glass and it heats up and expands more and faster than the exterior, causing uneven stress and heat cracks, which are distinctively different from mechanical breakage."

She handed a jagged piece of broken glass to McGovern, her supervisor.

"Smoke goes out of the house," Lucy went on, "and the atmosphere comes in. Equalization of pressure. It doesn't mean someone broke in."

"You get a B-plus," McGovern said to her.

"No way. I get an A."

Several of the agents laughed.

"But I have to agree with Lucy," one of them said. "So far I'm not seeing any sign that someone broke in."

Their team leader continued turning our disaster site into a classroom for her soon-to-be Certificated Fire Investigators, or CFIs.

"Remember we talked about smoke coming through brick?" she continued, pointing up to areas of stone along the roofline that looked as if they had been scrubbed with steel brushes. "Or is that erosion from blasts of water?"

"No, the mortar's partially eaten away. That's from smoke."

"That's right. From smoke pushing through the joints." McGovern was matter-of-fact. "Fire establishes its own vent paths. And low around the walls here, here and here'—she pointed—"the stone is burned clean of all incomplete combustion or soot. We've got melted glass and melted copper pipes."

"It started low, on the first floor," Lucy said. "The main living area."

"Looks like that to me."

"And flames went up as high as ten feet to engage the second floor and roof."

"Which would take a pretty decent fuel load."

"Accelerants. But forget finding a pour pattern in this shit."

"Don't forget anything," McGovern told her team. "And we don't know if an accelerant was necessary because we don't know what kind of fuel load was on that floor."

They were splashing and working as they talked, and all around was the constant sound of dripping water and rumbling of the pumps. I got interested in box springs caught in my rake and squatted to pull out rocks and charred wood with my hands. One always had to consider that a fire victim might have died in bed, and I peered up at what once had been the upper floors. I continued excavating, producing nothing remotely human, only the sodden, sour trash of all that had been ruined in Kenneth Sparkes's fine estate. Some of his former possessions still smoldered on tops of piles that were not submerged, but most of what I raked was cold and permeated with the nauseating smell of scorched bourbon.

Our sifting went on throughout the morning, and as I moved from one square of muck to the next, I did what

I knew how to do best. I groped and probed with my hands, and when I felt a shape that worried me, I took off my heavy fire gloves and felt some more with fingers barely sheathed by latex. McGovern's troops were scattered and lost in their own hunches, and at almost noon she waded back to me.

"You holding up?" she asked.

"Still standing."

"Not bad for an armchair detective." She smiled.

"I'll take that as a compliment."

"You see how even everything is?" She pointed a sooty gloved finger. "High-temperature fire, constant from one corner of the house to the other. Flames so hot and high they burned up the upper two floors and pretty near everything in them. We're not talking some electrical arc here, not some curling iron left on or grease that caught fire. Something big and smart's behind this."

I had noticed over the years that people who battled fire spoke of it as if it were alive and possessed a will and personality of its own. McGovern began working by my side, and what she couldn't sling out of the way, she piled into a wheelbarrow. I polished what turned out to be a stone that could have passed for a finger bone, and she pointed the wooden butt of her rake up at an empty overcast sky.

"The top level's gonna be the last one to fall," she told me. "In other words, debris from the roof and second floor should be on top down here. So I'm assuming that's what we're rooting around in right now." She stabbed the rake at a twisted steel I-beam that once had supported the roof. "Yes sir," she went on, "that's why there's all this insulation and slate everywhere."

This went on and on, with no one taking breaks that were longer than fifteen minutes. The local fire station kept us supplied in coffee, sodas, and sandwiches, and had set up quartz lights so we could see as we worked in our wet hole. At each end a Prosser pump sucked water through its hose and disgorged it outside granite walls, and after thousands of gallons were gone, our conditions did not seem much better. It was hours before the level dipped perceptibly.

At half past two I could stand it no longer and went outside again. I scanned for the most inconspicuous spot, which was beneath the sweeping boughs of a large fir tree near the smoking stables. My hands and feet were numb, but beneath heavy protective clothing I was sweating as I squatted and kept a nervous watch for anyone who might wander this way. Then I steeled myself to walk past every charred stall. The stench of death pushed itself up into my nostrils and seemed to cling to spaces inside my skull.

Horses were pitifully piled on top of each other, their legs pugilistically drawn, and skin split from the swelling and shrinking of cooking flesh. Mares, stallions, and geldings were burned down to bone with smoke still drifting from carcasses charred like wood. I hoped they had succumbed to carbon monoxide poisoning before flames had touched them.

I counted nineteen bodies, including two yearlings and a foal. The miasma of burned horse hair and death was choking and enveloped me like a heavy cloak as I headed across grass back to the mansion's shell. On the horizon, the sole survivor was watching me again, standing very still, alone and mournful.

McGovern was still sloshing and shoveling and pitching trash out of her way, and I could tell she was getting tired, and I was perversely pleased by that. It was getting late in the day. The sky had gotten darker, and the wind had a sharper edge.

"The foal is still there," I said to her.

"Wish he could talk." She straightened up and massaged the small of her back.

"He's running loose for a reason," I said. "It doesn't make sense to think he got out on his own. I hope someone plans to take care of him?"

"We're working on it."

"Couldn't one of the neighbors help?" I would not stop, because the horse was really getting to me.

She gave me a long look and pointed straight up.

"Master bedroom and bath were right up there," she announced as she lifted a broken square of white marble out of the filthy water. "Brass fixtures, a marble floor, the jets from a Jacuzzi. The frame of a skylight, which, by the way, was open at the time of the fire. If you reach down six inches to your left, you'll run right into what's left of the tub."

The water level continued to lower as pumps sucked and formed small rivers over grass. Nearby, agents were pulling out antique oak flooring that was deeply charred on top with very little unburned wood left. This went on, and added to mounting evidence that the origin of the fire was the second floor in the area of the master suite, where we recovered brass pulls from cabinets and mahogany furniture, and hundreds of coat hangers. We dug through burnt cedar and remnants of men's shoes and clothing from the master closet.

By five o'clock, the water had dropped another foot, revealing a ruined landscape that looked like a burned land-fill, with scorched hulls of appliances and the carcasses of couches. McGovern and I were still excavating in the area of the master bath, fishing out prescription bottles of pills, and shampoos and body lotions, when I finally discovered the first shattered edge of death. I carefully wiped soot from a jagged slab of glass.

"I think we've got something," I said, and my voice seemed swallowed by dripping water and the sucking of pumps.

McGovern shone her flashlight on what I was doing and went still.

"Oh Jesus," she said, shocked.

Milky dead eyes gleamed at us through watery broken glass.

"A window, maybe a glass shower door fell on top of the body, preserving at least some of it from being burned to the bone," I said.

I moved more broken glass aside, and McGovern was momentarily stunned as she stared at a grotesque body that I instantly knew was not Kenneth Sparkes. The upper part of the face was pressed flat beneath thick cracked glass, and the eyes were a dull bluish-gray because their original color had been cooked out of them. They peered up at us from the burned bone of the brow. Strands of long blond hair had gotten free and eerily flowed as dirty water seeped, and there was no nose or mouth, only chalky, calcined bone and teeth that had been burned until there was nothing organic left in them.

The neck was partially intact, the torso covered with more broken glass, and melted into cooked flesh was a dark fabric that had been a blouse or shirt. I could still make out the weave. Buttocks and pelvis were also spared beneath glass. The victim had been wearing jeans. The legs were burned down to bone, but leather boots had protected the feet.

There were no lower arms or hands, and I could not find any trace of those bones.

"Who the hell is this?" McGovern said, amazed. "Did he live with someone?"

"I don't know," I said, scooping more water out of the way.

"Can you tell if it's a female?" McGovern said as she leaned closer to look, her flashlight still pointed.

"I wouldn't want to swear to it in court until I can examine her more closely. But yes, I'm thinking female," I answered.

I looked up at empty sky, imagining the bathroom the woman possibly had died in, and then got cameras out of my kit as cold water lapped around my feet. Pepper the arson dog and his handler had just filled a doorway, and Lucy and other agents were wading our way as word of our find hummed down the line. I thought of Sparkes, and nothing here made sense, except that a woman had been inside his home the night of the fire. I feared his remains might be somewhere in here, too.

Agents came nearer, and one of them brought me a body bag. I unfolded it and took more photographs. Flesh had cooked to glass and would have to be separated. This I would do in the morgue, and I instructed that any debris around the body would need to be sent in as well.

"I'm going to need some help," I said to everyone. "Let's get a backboard and some sheets in here, and someone needs to call whatever local funeral home is responsible for body removals. We're going to need a van. Be careful, the glass is sharp. As she is, *in situ*. Face up, just like she is now, so we don't put too much stress on the body and tear the skin. That's good. Now open the bag more. As wide as we can get it."

"It ain't gonna fit."

"Maybe we could break off more of the glass around the edges here," McGovern suggested. "Somebody got a hammer?"

"No, no. Let's just cover her as is." I issued more commands, for I was in charge now. "Drape this over and around the edges to protect your hands. Everybody got their gloves on?"

"Yeah."

"Those of you who aren't helping here, there may be another body. So let's keep looking."

I was tense and irritable as I waited for two agents to return with a backboard and blue plasticized sheets to cover it.

"Okay," I said. "We're going to lift. On the count of three."

Water sloshed and splashed as four of us struggled for leverage and balance. It was awful groping for sure footing as we gripped slippery wet glass that was sharp enough to cut through leather.

"Here we go," I said. "One, two, three, lift."

We centered the body on the backboard. I covered it as best I could with the sheets and fastened it snugly with straps. Our steps were small and hesitant as we felt our way through water that no longer came over our boots. The Prosser pumps and generator were a constant humming throb that we scarcely noticed as we ferried our morbid cargo closer to the empty space that once had been a door. I smelled cooked flesh and death, and the acrid rotting odor of fabric, food, furniture, and all that had burned in Kenneth Sparkes's home. I was breathless and numb with stress and cold as I emerged into the pale light of the fast-retreating day.

We lowered the body to the ground, and I kept watch over it as the rest of the team continued their excavation. I opened the sheets and took a close long look at this pitifully disfigured human being, and got a flashlight and lens out of my aluminum case. Glass had melted around the head at the bridge of the nose, and bits of pinkish material and ash were snared in her hair. I used light and magnification to study areas of flesh that had been spared, and wondered if it was my imagination when I discovered hemorrhage in charred tissue in the left temporal area, about an inch from the eye.

Lucy suddenly was by my side, and Wiser Funeral Home was pulling up in a shiny dark blue van.

"Find something?" Lucy asked.

"Don't know with certainty, but this looks like hemorrhage, versus the drying you find with skin splitting."

"Skin splitting from fire, you mean."

"Yes. Flesh cooks and expands, splitting the skin."

"Same thing that happens when you cook chicken in the oven."

"You got it," I said.

Damage to skin, muscle, and bone is easily mistaken for injuries caused by violence if one is not familiar with the artifacts of fire. Lucy squatted closer to me. She looked on.

"Anything else turning up in there?" I asked her. "No other bodies, I hope."

"Not so far," she said. "It will be dark soon, and all we can do is keep the scene secured until we can start again in the morning."

I looked up as a man in a pinstripe suit climbed out of the funeral home van and worked on latex gloves. He loudly pulled a stretcher out from the back and metal clacked as he unfolded the legs.

"You gonna get started tonight, Doc?" he asked me, and I knew I'd seen him somewhere before.

"Let's get her to Richmond and I'll start in the morning," I said.

"Last time I saw you was the Moser shooting. That young girl they was fighting over's still causing trouble round here."

"Oh yes." I vaguely remembered, for there were so many shootings and so many people who caused trouble. "Thank you for your help," I said to him.

We lifted the body by gripping the edges of the heavy vinyl pouch. We lowered the remains onto the stretcher and slid it into the back of the van. He slammed shut tailgate doors.

"I hope it's not Kenneth Sparkes in there," he said.

"No identification yet," I told him.

He sighed and slid into the driver's seat.

"Well, let me tell you something," he said, cranking the engine. "I don't care what anybody says. He was a good man."

I watched him drive away and could sense Lucy's eyes on me. She touched my arm.

"You're exhausted," she said. "Why don't you spend the night and I'll fly you back in the morning. If we find anything else, we'll let you know right away. No point in your hanging around."

I had very difficult work ahead and the sensible thing to do was to head back to Richmond now. But in truth, I did not feel like walking inside my empty home. Benton would be at Hilton Head by now, and Lucy was staying in Warrenton. It was too late to call upon any of my friends, and I was too spent for polite conversation. It was one of those times when I could think of nothing that might soothe me.

"Teun's moved us to a better place and I got an extra bed

in my room, Aunt Kay," Lucy added with a smile as she pulled a car key out of her pocket.

"So now I'm Aunt Kay again."

"As long as nobody's around."

"I've got to get something to eat," I said.

3

We bought drive-thru Whoppers and fries at a Burger King on Broadview, and it was dark out and very cool. Approaching headlights hurt my eyes, and no amount of Motrin would relieve the hot pain in my temples or the dread in my heart. Lucy had brought her own CDs and was playing one of them loudly as we glided through Warrenton in a rented black Ford LTD.

"What's this you're listening to?" I asked as a way of registering a complaint.

"Jim Brickman," she said sweetly.

"Not hardly," I said over flutes and drums. "Sounds Native American to me. And maybe we could turn it down a bit?"

Instead, she turned it up.

"David Arkenstone. *Spirit Wind*. Got to open your mind, Aunt Kay. This one right now is called 'Destiny'."

Lucy drove like the wind, and my mind began to float.

"You're getting kooky on me," I said as I imagined wolves and campfires in the night.

"His music's all about connectivity and finding your way and positive force," she went on as the music got lively and added guitars. "Don't you think that fits?"

I couldn't help but laugh at her complicated explanation. Lucy had to know how everything worked and the reason why. The music, in truth, was soothing, and I felt a brightening and calm in frightening places in my mind.

"What do you think happened, Aunt Kay?" Lucy suddenly broke the spell. "I mean, in your heart of hearts."

"Right now it's impossible to say," I answered her the way I would anybody else. "And we shouldn't assume anything, including gender or who might have been staying in the house."

"Teun is already thinking arson, and so am I," she matter-of-factly stated. "What's weird is Pepper didn't alert on anything in any areas where we thought he might."

"Like the master bathroom on the first floor," I said.

"Nothing there. Poor Pepper worked like a dog and didn't get fed."

The Labrador retriever had been food-reward trained since his youth to detect hydrocarbon petroleum distillates, such as kerosene, gasoline, lighter fluid, paint thinner, solvents, lamp oil. All were possible, if not common, choices for the arsonist who wanted to start a major fire with the drop of a match. When accelerants are poured at a scene, they pool and flow as their vapors burn. The liquid soaks into fabric or bedding or carpet. It seeps under furniture and between the cracks in flooring. It is not water-soluble or easy to wash away, so if Pepper had found nothing to excite his nose, chances were good that nothing was there.

"What we got to do is find out exactly what was in the house so we can begin to calculate the fuel load," Lucy went on as the music turned to violins, and strings and drums got sadder. "Then we can begin to get a better idea about what and how much would have been needed to get something like that going."

"There was melted aluminum and glass, and tremendous burning of the body in the upper legs and lower arms, any areas that weren't spared by the glass door," I said. "That suggests to me the victim was down, possibly in the bathtub, when the fire reached her."

"It would be bizarre to think a fire like this started in a marble bathroom," my niece said.

"What about electrical? Any possibility of that?" I asked, and our motel's red and yellow lighted sign floated above the highway, maybe a mile ahead.

"Look, the place had been electrically upgraded. When fire reached the wires and insulation was degraded by heat, the ground wires came in contact with each other. The circuit failed, the wires arced and the circuit breakers tripped," she said. "That's exactly what I would expect to happen whether the fire was set or not. It's hard to say. There's a lot left to look at, and of course the labs will do their thing. But whatever got that fire going, got it going fast. You can tell from some of the flooring. There's a sharp demarcation between really deep charring and the unburned wood, and that means hot and fast."

I remembered wood near the body looking just as she had described. It was alligatored, or blistered black on top, versus slowly burned all the way through.

"First floor again?" I asked as my private suspicions about this case grew darker.

"Probably. Plus, we know things happened fast anyway based on when the alarm went off and what the firefighters found seventeen minutes later." She was quiet for a moment, then went on, "The bathroom, the possible hemorrhage in tissue near her left eye. What? Maybe she was taking a bath or shower? She's overcome by carbon monoxide and falls and hits her head?"

"It appears she was fully dressed when she died," I reminded her. "Including boots. If the smoke alarm goes off while you're in the bath or shower, I doubt you'd take time to put on all that."

Lucy turned the volume up even louder and adjusted the bass. Bells jingled with drums and I thought oddly of incense and myrrh. I wanted to lie in the sun with Benton and sleep. I wanted the ocean to roll over my feet as I walked in the morning exploring the beach, and I remembered Kenneth Sparkes as I had seen him last. I envisioned what was left of him turning up next.

"This is called 'The Wolf Hunt,'" Lucy said as she turned into a white brick Shell Food Mart. "And maybe that's what we're on, huh? After the big bad wolf."

"No," I said as she parked. "I think we're looking for a dragon."

She threw a Nike windbreaker over her gun and BDUs.

"You didn't see me do this," she said as she opened her door. "Teun would kick my ass to the moon."

"You've been around Marino too long," I said, for he rarely minded rules and was known to carry beer home in the trunk of his unmarked police car.

Lucy went inside, and I doubted that she fooled anyone in her filthy boots and faded blue pants with so many pockets, and the tenacious smell of fire. A keyboard and cowbell began a different rhythm on the CD as I waited in the car and longed for sleep. Lucy returned with a six-pack of Heineken, and we drove on as I drifted with flute and percussion until sudden images shocked me straight up in my seat. I envisioned bared chalky teeth and dead eyes the grayish-blue of boiled eggs. Hair strayed and floated like dirty cornsilk in black water, and crazed, melted glass was an intricate sparkling web around what was left of the body.

"Are you all right?" Lucy sounded worried as she looked over at me.

"I think I fell asleep," I said. "I'm fine."

Johnson's Motel was just ahead of us on the other side of the highway. It was stone with a red and white tin awning, and a red and yellow lit-up sign out front promised it was open twenty-four hours a day and had air conditioning. The NO part of the vacancy sign was dark, which boded well for those in need of a place to stay. We got out, and a welcome mat announced HELLO outside the lobby. Lucy rang a bell. A big black cat came to the door, and then a big woman seemed to materialize from nowhere to let us in.

"We should have a reservation for a room for two," Lucy said.

"Check-out's eleven in the morning," the woman stated as she went around to her side of the counter. "I can give you fifteen down there at the end."

"We're ATF," Lucy said.

"Honey, I already figured out that one. The other lady was just in here. You're all paid up."

A sign posted above the door said no checks but encouraged MasterCard and Visa, and I thought of McGovern and her resourceful ways.

"You need two keys?" the clerk asked us as she opened a drawer.

"Yes, ma'am."

"Here's you go, honey, and there's two nice beds in there. If I'm not around when you check out, just leave the keys on the counter."

"Glad you got security," Lucy said drolly.

"Sure do. Double locks on every door."

"How late does room service stay open?" Lucy played with her again.

"Until that Coke machine out front quits," the woman said with a wink.

She was at least sixty with dyed red hair and jowls, and a squat body that pushed against every inch of her brown polyester slacks and yellow sweater. It was obvious that she was fond of black and white cows. There were carvings and ceramic ones on shelves and tables and fastened to the wall. A small fish tank was populated with an odd assortment of tadpoles and minnows, and I couldn't help asking her about them.

"Home grown?" I said.

She gave me a sheepish smile. "I catch 'em in the pond out back. One of them turned into a frog not long ago and it drowned. I didn't know frogs can't live under water."

"I'm gonna use the pay phone," Lucy said, opening the screen door. "And by the way, what happened to Marino?"

"I think some of them went out to eat somewhere," I said.

She left with our Burger King bag, and I suspected she was calling Janet and that our Whoppers would be cold by the time we got to them. As I leaned against the counter, I noticed the clerk's messy desk on the other side, and the local paper with its front page headline: MEDIA MOGUL'S FARM DESTROYED BY FIRE. I recognized a subpoena among her clutter and posted notices of reward money for information about murders, accompanied by composite sketches of rapists, thieves, and killers. All the same, Fauquier was the typical quiet county where people got lulled into feeling safe.

"I hope you aren't working here all by yourself at night," I said to the clerk, because it was my irrepressible habit to give security tips whether or not anyone wanted them.

"I've got Pickle," she affectionately referred to her fat black cat.

"That's an interesting name."

"You leave an open pickle jar around, and she'll get into it. Dips her paw right in, ever since she was a kitten."

Pickle was sitting in a doorway leading into a room that I suspected was the clerk's private quarters. The cat's eyes were gold coins fixed on me as her fluffy tail twitched. She looked bored when the bell rang and her owner unlocked the door for a man in a tank top who was holding a burned-out lightbulb.

"Looks like it done it again, Helen." He handed her the evidence.

She went into a cabinet and brought out a box of lightbulbs as I gave Lucy plenty of time to get off the pay phone so I could use it. I glanced at my watch, certain Benton should have made it to Hilton Head by now.

"Here you go, Big Jim." She exchanged a new lightbulb for bad. "That's sixty watts?" She squinted at it. "Uh huh. You here a little longer?" She sounded as if she hoped he would be.

"Hell if I know."

"Oh dear," said Helen. "So things still aren't too good."

"When have they ever been?" He shook his head as he went out into the night.

"Fighting with his wife again," Helen the clerk commented to me as she shook her head, too. "Course, he's been here before, which is partly why they fight so much. Never knew there'd be so many people cheating on each other. Half the business here is from folks just three miles down the road."

"And they can't fool you," I said.

"Oh no-sir-ree-bob. But it's none of my business as long as they don't wreck the room."

"You're not too far from the farm that burned," I then said.

She got more animated. "I was working that night. You could see the flames shooting up like a volcano going off." She gestured broadly with her arms. "Everyone staying here was out front watching and listening to the sirens. All those poor horses. I can't get over it."

"Are you acquainted with Kenneth Sparkes?" I wondered out loud.

"Can't say I've ever seen him in person."

"What about a woman who might have been staying in his house?" I asked. "You ever heard anything about that?"

"Only what people say." Helen was looking at the door as if someone might appear any second.

"For example," I prodded.

"Well, I guess Mr. Sparkes is quite the gentleman, you know," Helen said. "Not that his ways are popular around here, but he's quite a figure. Likes them young and pretty."

She thought for a moment and gave me her eyes as moths flickered outside the window.

"There are those who got upset when they'd see him around with the newest one," she said. "You know, no matter what anybody says, this is still the Old South."

"Anybody in particular who got upset?" I asked.

"Well, the Jackson boys. They're always in one sort of trouble or another," she said, and she was still watching the door. "They just don't like colored people. So for him to be sporting something pretty, young, and white, he tended to do that a lot . . . Well, there's been talk. I'll just put it like that."

I was imagining Ku Klux Klansmen with burning crosses, and white supremacists with cold eyes and guns. I had seen hate before. I had dipped my hands in its carnage for most of my life. My chest was tight as I bid Helen the clerk good night. I was trying not to leap to assumptions about prejudice and arson and an intended victim, which may have been only Sparkes and not a woman whose body was now on its way to Richmond. Of course, it may simply have been the former governor's vast property that the perpetrators had been interested in, and they did not know anyone was home.

The man in the tank top was on the pay phone when I went out. He was absently holding his new lightbulb and talking in an intense, low voice. As I walked past, his anger flared.

"Dammit, Louise! That's what I mean. You never shut up," he snarled into the phone as I decided to call Benton later.

I unlocked the red door to room fifteen, and Lucy pretended that she hadn't been waiting for me as she sat in a wing chair, bent over a spiral notebook, making notes and calculations. But she had not touched her fast-food dinner, and I knew she was starved. I took Whoppers and French fries out of the bag and set paper napkins and food on a nearby table.

"Everything's cold," I said simply.

"You get used to it." Her voice was distant and distracted.

"Would you like to shower first?" I asked politely.

"Go ahead," she replied, buried in math, a scowl furrowing her brow.

Our room was impressively clean for the price and decorated in shades of brown, with a Zenith TV almost as old as my niece. There were Chinese lamps and long-tasseled lanterns, porcelain figurines, static oil paintings and flower-printed spreads. Carpeting was a thick shag Indian design, and wallpaper was woodland scenes. Furniture was Formica or so thickly shellacked that I could not see the grain of the wood.

I inspected the bath and found it a solid pink and white tile that probably went back to the fifties, with Styrofoam cups and tiny wrapped bars of Lisa Luxury soap on the sink. But it was a single plastic red rose in a window that touched me most. Someone had done the best with the least to make strangers feel special, and I doubted that most patrons noticed or cared. Maybe forty years ago such resourcefulness and attention to detail would have mattered when people were more civilized than they seemed to be now.

I lowered the toilet lid and sat to remove my dirty wet boots. Then I fought with buttons and hooks until my clothes retreated to a wilted heap on the floor. I showered until I was warm and cleansed of the smell of fire and death. Lucy was working on her laptop when I emerged in an old Medical College of Virginia T-shirt and popped open a beer.

"What's up?" I asked as I sat on the couch.

"Just screwing around. I don't know enough to do much more than that," she replied. "But that was a big fucking fire, Aunt Kay. And it doesn't appear to have been set with gasoline."

I had nothing to say.

"And someone died in it? In the master bathroom? Maybe? How did that happen? At eight o'clock at night?"

I did not know.

"I mean, she's in there brushing her teeth and the fire horn goes off?"

Lucy stared hard at me.

"And what?" she asked. "She just stays there and dies?"

She paused to stretch sore shoulders.

"You tell me, Chief. You're the expert."

"I can offer no explanation, Lucy," I said.

"And there we have it, ladies and gentlemen. World famous expert Dr. Kay Scarpetta doesn't know." She was getting irritable. "Nineteen horses," she went on. "So who took care of them? Sparkes doesn't have a stable hand? And why did one of the horses get away? The little black stallion?"

"How do you know it's a boy?" I said as someone knocked on our door. "Who is it?" I asked through wood.

"Yo. It's me," Marino announced gruffly.

I let him in and could tell by the expression on his face that he had news.

"Kenneth Sparkes is alive and well," he announced.

"Where is he?" I was very confused again.

"Apparently, he's been out of the country and flew back when he heard the news. He's staying in Beaverdam and don't seem to have a clue about anything, including who the victim is," Marino told us.

"Why Beaverdam?" I asked, calculating how long the trip would take to that remote part of Hanover County.

"His trainer lives there."

"His?"

"Horse trainer. Not his trainer, like in weight lifting or nothing."

"I see."

"I'm heading out in the morning, around nine A.M.," he said to me. "You can go on to Richmond or go with me."

"I have a body to identify, so I need to talk to him whether he claims to know anything or not. I guess I'm going with you," I said as Lucy met my eyes. "Are you planning on our fearless pilot dropping us off, or have you managed to get a car?"

"I'm skipping the whirlybird," Marino retorted. "And do I need to remind you that the last time you had a chat with Sparkes, you pissed him off?"

"I don't remember," I said, and I really did not, for I had irritated Sparkes on more than one occasion when we disagreed about case details he thought should be released to the media.

"I can guarantee he does, Doc. You gonna share the beer or what?"

"I can't believe you don't have your own stash," Lucy said as she resumed working on her laptop, keys clicking.

He went to the refrigerator and helped himself to one.

"You want my opinion at the end of the day?" he said. "It's the same as it was."

"Which is?" Lucy asked without looking up.

"Sparkes is behind this."

He set the bottle opener on the coffee table and stopped at the door, resting his hand on the knob.

"For one thing, it's just too friggin' convenient that he was suddenly out of the country when it happened," he talked on as he yawned. "So he gets someone to do his dirty work. Money." He slid a cigarette out of the pack in his shirt pocket and shoved it between his lips. "That's all the bastard's ever cared about, anyway. Money and his dick."

"Marino, for God's sake," I complained.

I wanted to shut him up, and I wanted him to leave. But he ignored my cue.

"The worst news of all is now we probably got a homicide on our hands, on top of everything else," he said as he opened the door. "Meaning yours truly here is stuck on this case like a fly on a pest strip. And that goes for the two of you. Shit."

He got out his lighter, the cigarette moving with his lips.

"The last thing I feel like doing right now. You know how many people that asshole's probably got in his pocket?" Marino would not stop. "Judges, sheriffs, fire marshals . . ."

"Marino," I interrupted him because he was making everything worse. "You're jumping to conclusions. In fact, you're jumping to Mars."

He pointed his unlit cigarette at me. "Just wait," he said on his way out. "Everywhere you turn on this one, you're going to run into a briar patch."

"I'm used to it," I said.

"You just think you are."

He shut the door too hard.

"Hey, don't wreck the joint," Lucy called out after him.

"Are you going to work on that laptop all night?" I asked her.

"Not all night."

"It's getting late, and there's something you and I need to discuss," I said, and Carrie Grethen was back in my mind.

"What if I told you I don't feel like it?" Lucy wasn't kidding.

"It wouldn't matter," I replied. "We have to talk."

"You know, Aunt Kay, if you're going to start in on Teun and Philly . . ."

"What?" I said, baffled. "What does Teun have to do with anything?"

"I can tell you don't like her."

"That's utterly ridiculous."

"I can see through you," she went on.

"I have nothing against Teun, and she is not relevant to this conversation."

My niece got silent. She began taking off her boots.

"Lucy, I got a letter from Carrie."

I waited to see a response and was rewarded with none.

"It's a bizarre note. Threatening, harassing, from Kirby Forensic Psychiatric Center in New York."

I paused again as Lucy dropped a boot to the shag carpeting.

"She's basically making sure we know that she intends to cause a lot of trouble during her trial," I explained. "Not that this should come as any great surprise. But, well, I . . ." I stumbled as she tugged off wet socks and massaged her pale feet. "We just need to be prepared, that's all."

Lucy unbuckled her belt and unzipped her pants as if she had not heard a word I'd said. She pulled her filthy shirt over her head and threw it on the floor, stripping down to sports bra and cotton panties. She stalked toward the bathroom, her body beautiful and fluid, and I sat staring after her, stunned, until I heard water run.

It was as if I had never really noticed her full lips and breasts and her arms and legs curved and strong like a hunter's bow. Or maybe I simply had refused to see her as someone apart from me and sexual, because I chose not to understand her or the way she lived. I felt shamed and confused, when for an electric instant, I envisioned her as Carrie's supple, hungry lover. It did not seem so foreign that a woman would want to touch my niece.

Lucy took her time in the shower, and I knew this was deliberate because of the discussion we were about to have.

She was thinking. I suspected she was furious. I anticipated she would vent her rage on me. But when she emerged a little later, she was wearing a Philadelphia fire marshal T-shirt that did nothing but darken my mood. She was cool and smelled like lemons.

"Not that it's any of my business," I said, staring at the logo on her chest.

"Teun gave it to me," she answered.

"Ah."

"And you're right, Aunt Kay, it's none of your business."

"I just wonder why you don't learn . . ." I started in as my own temper flared.

"Learn?"

She feigned a clueless expression that was meant to irritate, eliminate, and make one feel vapid.

"About sleeping with people you work with."

My emotions hurled down their own treacherous track. I was being unfair, jumping to conclusions with little evidence. But I was scared for Lucy in every way imaginable.

"Someone gives me a T-shirt and suddenly I'm sleeping with this person? Hmmm. Quite a deduction, Dr. Scarpetta," Lucy said with gathering fury. "And by the way, you're one to talk about sleeping with people you work with. Look who you practically live with, hello?"

I was certain Lucy would have stormed out into the night if she had been dressed. Instead, she stood with her back to me, staring at a curtained window. She wiped outraged tears from her face as I tried to salvage what was left of a moment that I had never intended to turn out like this.

"We're both tired," I said softly. "It's been an awful day, and now Carrie has gotten just what she wanted. She has turned us on each other."

My niece did not move or utter a sound as she wiped her face again, her back solidly to me like a wall.

"I am not at all implying that you are sleeping with Teun," I went on. "I'm only warning you of the heartbreak and chaos . . . Well, I can see how it could happen."

She turned around and stared at me with a challenge in her eyes.

"What do you mean, *you can see how it could happen*?" she demanded to know. "She's gay? I don't remember her telling me that."

"Maybe things aren't so good with Janet right now," I went on. "And people are people."

She sat on the foot of my bed, and it was clear she intended to hold me to this conversation.

"Meaning?" she asked.

"Just that. I wasn't born in a cave. Teun's gender makes no difference to me. I do not know a thing about her proclivities. But if you are attracted to each other? Why wouldn't anyone be attracted to either of you? Both of you are striking and compelling and brilliant and heroic. I'm just reminding you that she's your supervisor, Lucy."

My blood pounded as my voice got more intense.

"And then what?" I asked. "Will you move from one federal agency to another until you've screwed yourself out of a career? That's my point, like it or not. And that's the last time I will ever bring it up."

My niece just stared at me as her eyes filled again. She did not wipe them this time, and tears rolled down her face and splashed the shirt Teun McGovern had given to her.

"I'm sorry, Lucy," I said gently. "I know your life isn't easy."

We were silent as she looked away and wept. She took a deep, long breath that trembled in her chest.

"Have you ever loved a woman?" she asked me.

"I love you."

"You know what I mean."

"Not in love with one," I said. "Not to my knowledge."

"That's rather evasive."

"I didn't mean it to be."

"Could you?"

"Could I what?"

"Love a woman," she persisted.

"I don't know. I'm beginning to think I don't know anything." I was as honest as I knew how to be. "Probably that part of my brain is shut."

"It has nothing to do with your brain."

I wasn't sure what to say.

"I've slept with two men," she said. "So I know the difference, for your information."

"Lucy, you don't need to plead your case to me."

"My personal life should not be a *case*."

"But it's about to become one," I went back to that subject. "What do you think will be Carrie's next move?"

Lucy opened another beer and glanced to see that I still had plenty.

"Send letters to the media?" I speculated for her. "Lie under oath? Take the stand and go into gory detail about everything the two of you ever said and did and dreamed?"

"How the hell can I know?" Lucy retorted. "She's had five years to do nothing but think and scheme while the rest of us have been rather busy."

"What else might she know that could come out?" I had to ask.

Lucy got up and began to pace.

"You trusted her once," I went on. "You confided in her,

and all the while she was an accomplice to Gault. You were their pipeline, Lucy. Right into the heart of all of us."

"I'm really too tired to talk about this," she said.

But she was going to talk about it. I was determined about that. I got up and turned off the overhead light, because I had always found it easier to talk in an atmosphere soft and full of shadows. Then I plumped pillows on her bed and mine and turned down the spreads. At first she did not take me up on my invitation, and she paced some more like a wild thing as I silently watched. Then she reluctantly sat on her bed and settled back.

"Let's talk about something besides your reputation for a moment," I began in a calm voice. "Let's talk about what this New York trial is all about."

"I know what it's all about."

I was going to give her an opening argument anyway and raised my hand to make her listen.

"Temple Gault killed at least five people in Virginia," I began, "and we know Carrie was involved in at least one of these since we have her on videotape pumping a bullet into the man's head. You remember that."

She was silent.

"You were in the room when we watched that horrific footage right there in gory color on TV," I went on.

"I know all this."

Anger was crawling into Lucy's voice again.

"We've been over it a million times," she said.

"You watched her kill," I went on. "This woman who was your lover when you were all of nineteen and naive and doing an internship at ERF, programming CAIN."

I saw her draw up more into herself as my monologue became more painful. ERF was the FBI's Engineering

Research Facility, which housed its Criminal Artificial Intelligence Network computer system known as CAIN. Lucy had conceived CAIN and been the driving force behind its creation. Now she was locked out of it and could not bear to hear its name.

"You watched your lover kill, after she had set you up in her cold-blooded premeditated way. You were no match for her," I said.

"Why are you doing this?" Lucy's voice was muffled, her face resting on her arm.

"A reality check."

"I don't need one."

"I think you do. And by the way, we won't even go into the personal details both Carrie and Gault learned about me. And this brings us to New York, where Gault murdered his own sister and at least one police officer, and now forensic evidence shows that he didn't do it alone. Carrie's fingerprints were later recovered on some of Jayne Gault's personal effects. When she was captured in the Bowery, Jayne's blood was found on Carrie's pants. For all we know, Carrie pulled that trigger, too."

"She probably did," Lucy said. "And I already know about that."

"But not about Eddie Heath. Remember the candy bar and can of soup he bought at the 7-Eleven? The bag found with his dying, mutilated body? Carrie's thumbprint has since been recovered."

"No way!" Lucy was shocked.

"There's more."

"Why haven't you told me this before? She was doing this all along, with him. And probably helped him break out of prison back then, too."

"We have no doubt. They were Bonnie and Clyde long before you met her, Lucy. She was killing when you were seventeen and had never been kissed."

"You don't know that I'd never been kissed," my niece said inanely.

No one spoke for a moment.

Then Lucy said, and her voice quavered, "So you think she spent two years plotting a way to meet me and become . . . And do the things she did to . . ."

"To seduce you," I cut in. "I don't know if she planned it that far in advance. Frankly, I don't care." My outrage mounted. "We've moved heaven and earth to extradite her to Virginia for those crimes, and we can't. New York won't let her go."

My beer bottle was limp and forgotten in my hands as I shut my eyes, and flashes of the dead played through my mind. I saw Eddie Heath propped up against a Dumpster as rain diluted the blood from his wounds, and the sheriff and prison guard killed by Gault and probably Carrie. I had touched their bodies and translated their pain into diagrams and autopsy protocols and dental charts. I could not help it. I wanted Carrie to die for what she had done to them, to my niece and me.

"She's a monster," I said as my voice shook with grief and fury. "I will do anything I can to make sure she is punished."

"Why are you preaching all this to me?" Lucy said in a louder, upset voice. "Do you somehow think I don't want the same thing?"

"I'm sure you do."

"Just let me throw the switch or stick the needle in her arm."

"Don't let your former relationship distract you from justice, Lucy."

"Jesus Christ."

"It's already an overwhelming struggle for you. And if you lose perspective, Carrie will have her way."

"Jesus Christ," Lucy said again. "I don't want to hear any more."

"You wonder what she wants?" I would not stop. "I can tell you exactly. To manipulate. The thing she does best. And then what? She'll be found not guilty by reason of insanity and the judge will send her back to Kirby. Then she'll suddenly and dramatically improve, and the Kirby doctors will decide she's not insane. Double jeopardy. She can't be tried twice for the same crime. She ends up back on the street."

"If she walks," Lucy said coldly, "I will find her and blow her brains out."

"What kind of answer is that?"

I watched her silhouette sitting straight up against pillows on her bed. She was very stiff and I could hear her breathing as hatred pounded inside her.

"The world really won't care who or what you slept or sleep with unless you do," I said to her more quietly. "In fact, I think the jury will understand how it could have happened back then. When you were so young. And she was older and brilliant and striking to look at. When she was charismatic and attentive, and your supervisor."

"Like Teun," Lucy said, and I could not tell if she was mocking me.

"Teun is not a psychopath," I said.

4

The next morning, I fell asleep in the rented LTD, and woke up to cornfields and silos, and stands of trees as old as the Civil War. Marino was driving, and we passed vast acres of vacant land strung with barbed wire and telephone lines, and front yards dotted with mailboxes painted like flower gardens and Uncle Sam. There were ponds and creeks and sod farms, and cattle fields high with weeds. Mostly I noticed small houses with leaning fences, and clotheslines sagging with scrubbed garments billowing in the breeze.

I covered a yawn with my hand and averted my face, for I had always considered it a sign of weakness to look tired or bored. Within minutes, we turned right on 715, or Beaverdam Road, and we began to see cows. Barns were bleached gray and it seemed people never thought to haul away their broken-down trucks. The owner of Hootowl Farm lived in a large white brick house surrounded by endless vistas of pasture and fence. According to the sign out front, the house had been built in 1730. Now it had a swimming pool and a satellite dish that looked serious enough to intercept signals from other galaxies.

Betty Foster was out to greet us before we had gotten out of the car. She was somewhere in her fifties with sharp regal features and skin deeply creased by the sun. Her long white hair was tucked in a bun. But she walked with the athletic spring of someone half her age, and her hand was hard and strong when she shook mine and looked at me with pained hazel eyes.

"I'm Betty," she said. "And you must be Dr. Scarpetta. And you must be Captain Marino."

She shook his hand too, her movements quick and confident. Betty Foster wore jeans and a sleeveless denim shirt, her brown boots scarred and crusted with mud around the heels. Beneath her hospitality other emotions smoldered, and she seemed slightly dazed by us, as if she did not know where to begin.

"Kenneth is in the riding ring," she told us. "He's been waiting for you, and I'll go on and tell you now that he's terribly upset. He loved those horses, everyone of them, and of course, he's devastated that someone died inside his house."

"What exactly is your relationship to him?" Marino asked as we started walking up the dusty road toward the stables.

"I've bred and trained his horses for years," she said. "Ever since he left office and moved back to Warrenton. He had the finest Morgans in the Commonwealth. And quarter horses and thoroughbreds."

"He would bring his horses to you?" I asked.

"Sometimes he did that. Sometimes it was yearlings he would buy from me and just leave them here to be trained for two years. Then he'd add them to his stable. Or he'd breed racehorses and sell them when they were old enough to be trained for the track. And I also went up there to his farm, sometimes two or three times a week. Basically, I supervised."

"And he has no stable hand?" I asked.

"The last one quit several months ago. Since then Kenny has been doing most of the work himself. It's not like he can hire just anyone. He has to be careful."

"I'd like to know more about the stable hand," Marino said, taking notes.

"A lovely old guy with a very bad heart," she said.

"It may be that one horse survived the fire," I told her.

She didn't comment at first, and we drew nearer to a big red barn and a *Beware of Dog* sign on a fence post.

"It's a foal, I guess. Black," I went on.

"A filly or a colt?" she asked.

"I don't know. I couldn't tell the gender."

"What about a star-strip-snip?" she asked, referring to the white stripe on the horse's forehead.

"I wasn't that close," I told her.

"Well, Kenny had a foal named Windsong," Foster said. "The mother, Wind, ran the Derby and came in last, but just being in it was enough. Plus the father had won a few big stake races. So Windsong was probably the most valuable horse in Kenny's stables."

"Well, Windsong may have gotten out somehow," I said again. "And was spared."

"I hope he's not still out there running around."

"If he is, I doubt he will be for long. The police know about him."

Marino was not particularly interested in the surviving horse, and as we entered the indoor ring, we were greeted by the sound of hooves and the clucking of bantam roosters and guinea hens that wandered about freely. Marino coughed and squinted because red dust was thick in the air, kicked up by the cantering of a chestnut Morgan mare. Horses in their stalls neighed and whinnied as horse and rider went by, and although I recognized Kenneth Sparkes in his English saddle, I had never seen him in dirty denim and boots. He was an excellent equestrian, and when he met my eyes as he went by, he showed no sign of recognition or relief. I knew right then he did not want us here.

"Is there someplace we can talk to him?" I asked Foster.

"There are chairs outside." She pointed. "Or you can use my office."

Sparkes picked up speed and thundered toward us, and the guinea hens lifted up their feathery skirts to hurry out of the way.

"Did you know anything about a lady maybe staying with him in Warrenton?" I asked as we headed back outside again. "Did you ever see anyone when you went to work with his horses?"

"No," Foster said.

We picked plastic chairs and sat with our backs to the arena, overlooking woods.

"But Lord knows, Kenny's had girlfriends before, and I don't always know about them," Foster said, turning around in her chair to look back inside the ring. "Unless you're right about Windsong, the horse Kenny's on now is the only one he has left. Black Opal. We call him Pal for short."

Marino and I did not respond as we turned around to see Sparkes dismount and hand the reins to one of Foster's stable hands.

"Good job, Pal," Sparkes said, patting the horse's handsome neck and head.

"Any special reason this horse wasn't with the others on his farm?" I asked Foster.

"Not quite old enough. He's a barely three-year-old gelding who still needs training. That's why he's still here, lucky for him."

For a flicker, her face was contorted by grief, and she quickly looked away. She cleared her throat and got up from her chair. She walked away as Sparkes came out of the arena adjusting his belt and the fit of his jeans. I got up and Marino and I respectfully shook his hand. He was sweating through a faded red Izod shirt, and he wiped his face with a yellow bandanna he untied from his neck.

"Please sit down," he said graciously, as if he were granting us an audience with him.

We took our chairs again, and he pulled his out and turned it around to face us, the skin tight around eyes that were resolute but bloodshot.

"Let me begin by telling you what I firmly believe right now as I sit in this chair," he said. "The fire was not an accident."

"That's what we're here to investigate, sir," Marino said, more politely than usual.

"I believe the motivation was racist in nature." Sparkes's jaw muscles began to flex and fury filled his voice. "And they—whoever *they* are—intentionally murdered my horses, destroying everything I love."

"If the motive was racism," Marino said, "then why wouldn't they have checked to make sure you were home?"

"Some things are worse than death. Perhaps they want me alive to suffer. You put two and two together."

"We're trying to," Marino said.

"Don't even consider pinning this on me."

He pointed a finger at both of us.

"I know exactly how people like you think," he went on.

"Huh. I torched my own farm and horses for money. Now you listen to me good."

He leaned closer to us.

"I'm telling you now that I didn't do it. Would never, could never do it, will never do it. I had nothing to do with what happened. I'm the victim here and probably lucky to be alive."

"Let's talk about the other victim," I spoke quietly. "A white female with long blond hair, as it looks now. Is there anyone else who might have been in your house that night?"

"No one should have been in my house!" he exclaimed.

"We are speculating that this person may have died in the master suite," I went on. "Possibly the bathroom."

"Whoever she was, she must have broken in," he said. "Or maybe she was the one who set the fire, and couldn't get out."

"There's no evidence that anyone broke in, sir," Marino responded. "And if your burglar alarm was set, it never went off that night. Only the smoke alarm."

"I don't understand." Sparkes seemed to be telling the truth. "Of course, I set the alarm before I left town."

"And you were headed where?" Marino probed.

"London. I got there and was immediately notified. I never even left Heathrow and instantly caught the next flight back," he said. "I got off in D.C. and drove straight here."

He stared blankly at the ground.

"Drove in what?" Marino asked.

"My Cherokee. I'd left it at Dulles in long-term parking."

"You've got the receipt?"

"Yes."

"What about the Mercedes at your house?" Marino went on.

Sparkes frowned. "What Mercedes? I don't own a Mercedes. I have always bought American cars."

I remembered that this had been one of his policies that he had been quite vocal about.

"There's a Mercedes behind the house. It burned up, too, so we can't tell much about it yet," Marino said. "But it doesn't look like a recent model to me. A sedan, sort of boxy like they were earlier on."

Sparkes just shook his head.

"Then we might wonder if it was the victim's car," Marino deduced. "Maybe someone who had come to see you unexpectedly? Who else had a key to your house, and your burglar alarm code?"

"Good Lord," Sparkes said as he groped for an answer. "Josh did. My stable hand, honest as the day is long. He quit for health reasons and I never bothered changing the locks."

"You need to tell us where to find him," Marino said.

"He would never . . ." Sparkes started to say, but he stopped and an incredulous expression came over his face. "My God," he muttered with an awful sigh. "Oh my God."

He looked at me.

"You said she was blond," he asked.

"Yes," I said.

"Can you tell me anything else about the way she looked?" His voice was getting panicky.

"Appears to be slender, possibly white. Wearing jeans, some sort of shirt, and boots. Lace-up boots, versus Western."

"How tall?" he had to know.

"I can't tell. Not until I've examined her."

"What about jewelry?"

"Her hands were gone."

He sighed again, and when he spoke his voice trembled. "Was her hair very long, like down to the middle of her back, and a very pale gold?"

"That's the way it appears at this time," I replied.

"There was a young woman," he began, clearing his throat several times. "My God . . . I have a place at Wrightsville Beach and met her there. She was a student at the university, or at least on and off she was. It didn't last long, maybe six months. And she did stay with me on the farm, several times. The last time I saw her was there, and I ended the relationship because it couldn't go on."

"Did she own an old Mercedes?" Marino asked.

Sparkes shook his head. He covered his face with his hands as he struggled for composure.

"A Volkswagen thing. Light blue," he managed to say. "She didn't have any money. I gave her some in the end, before she left. A thousand dollars cash. I told her to go back to school and finish. Her name is Claire Rawley, and I suppose she could have taken one of my extra keys without my knowing while she was staying on the farm. Maybe she saw the alarm code when I punched it in."

"And you've had no contact with Claire Rawley for more than a year?" I said.

"Not one word," he replied. "That seems so far in my past. It was a foolish fling, really. I saw her surfing and started talking to her on the beach, in Wrightsville. I have to say, she was the most splendid-looking woman I have ever seen. For a while, I was out of my mind, then I came to my senses. There were many, many complications and problems. Claire needed a caretaker, and I couldn't be that."

"I need to know everything about her that you can tell me," I said to him with feeling. "Anything about where she was from, her family. Anything that might help me identify the body or rule Claire Rawley out. Of course, I will contact the university, as well."

"I've got to tell you the sad truth, Dr. Scarpetta," my former boss said to me. "I never knew anything about her, really. Our relationship was mainly sexual, with me helping her out with money and her problems as best I could. I did care about her." He paused. "But it was never serious, at least not on my side. I mean, marriage was never in the offing."

He did not need to explain further. Sparkes had power. He exuded it and had always enjoyed almost any woman he wanted. But I felt no judgment now.

"I'm sorry," he said, getting up. "I can only tell you that she was rather much a failed artist. A want-to-be actor who spent most of her time surfing or wandering the beach. And after I'd been around her for a while, I began to see that something wasn't right about her. The way she seemed so lacking in motivation, and would act so erratic and glazed sometimes."

"Did she abuse alcohol?" I asked.

"Not chronically. It has too many calories."

"Drugs?"

"That's what I began to suspect, and it was something I could have no association with. I don't know."

"I need for you to spell her name for me," I said.

"Before you go walking off," Marino jumped in, and I recognized the bad-cop edge to his tone, "you sure this couldn't be some sort of a murder-suicide? Only she kills everything you own and goes up in flames along with it? You sure there's no reason she might have done that, Mr. Sparkes?"

"At this point, I can't be sure of anything," Sparkes answered him as he paused near the barn's open door.

Marino got up, too.

"Well, this ain't adding up, no disrespect intended," Marino said. "And I do need to see any receipts you have for your London trip. And for Dulles airport. And I know ATF's hot to know about your basement full of bourbon and automatic weapons."

"I collect World War II weapons, and all of them are registered and legal," he said with restraint. "I bought the bourbon from a Kentucky distillery that went out of business five years ago. They shouldn't have sold it to me and I shouldn't have bought it. But so be it."

"I think ATF's got bigger fish to fry than your barrels of bourbon," Marino said. "So if you got any of those receipts with you now, I'd appreciate your handing them over to me."

"Will you strip search me next, Captain?" Sparkes fixed hard eyes on him.

Marino stared back as guinea hens kicked past again like breakdancers.

"You can deal with my lawyer," Sparkes said. "And then I'll be happy to cooperate."

"Marino," it was my turn to speak, "if you'd give me just a minute alone with Mr. Sparkes."

Marino was taken aback and very annoyed. Without a word, he stalked off into the barn, several hens trotting after him. Sparkes and I stood, facing each other. He was a strikingly handsome man, tall and lean, with thick gray hair. His eyes were amber, his features aristocratic, with a straight Jeffersonian nose and skin dark and as smooth as a man half his age. The way he tightly gripped his riding crop seemed to fit his mood. Kenneth Sparkes was capable of violence but had never given in to it, as best I knew.

"All right. What's on your mind?" he asked me suspiciously.

"I just wanted to make sure you understand that our differences of the past . . ."

He shook his head and would not let me finish.

"The past is past," he said curtly.

"No, Kenneth, it isn't. And it's important for you to know that I don't harbor bad feelings about you," I replied. "That what's going on now is not related."

When he had been more actively involved with the publishing of his newspapers, he had basically accused me of racism when I had released statistics about black on black homicides. I had shown citizens how many deaths were drug-related or involved prostitution or were just plain hate of one black for another.

His own reporters had taken several of my quotes out of context and had distorted the rest, and by the end of the day, Sparkes had summoned me to his posh downtown office. I would never forget being shown into his mahogany space of fresh flowers and colonial furniture and lighting. He had ordered me, as if he could, to demonstrate more sensitivity to African-Americans and publicly retract my bigoted professional assessments. As I looked at him now, with sweat on his face and manure on his boots, it did not seem I was talking to the same arrogant man. His hands were trembling, his strong demeanor about to break.

"Will you let me know what you find out?" he asked as tears filled his eyes, his head held high.

"I'll tell you what I can," I promised evasively.

"I just want to know if it's her, and that she didn't suffer," he said.

"Most people in fires don't. The carbon monoxide renders

them unconscious long before the flames get close. Usually, death is quiet and painless."

"Oh, thank God."

He looked up at the sky.

"Oh, thank you, God," he muttered.

5

I got home that night in time for a dinner I did not feel like cooking. Benton had left me three messages, and I had not returned any one of them. I felt strange. I felt an odd sensation of doom, and yet I felt a lightness around my heart that spurred me into working in my garden until dark, pulling weeds and clipping roses for the kitchen. The ones I chose were pink and yellow, tightly furled like flags before glory. At dusk, I went out to walk and wished I had a dog. For a while I fantasized about that, wondering just what sort of dog I would have, were it possible and practical.

I decided on a retired greyhound rescued from the track and from certain extermination. Of course, my life was too unkind for a pet. I pondered this as one of my neighbors came out of his grand stone home to walk his small white dog.

"Good evening, Dr. Scarpetta," the neighbor said grimly. "How long are you in town for?"

"I never know," I said, still imagining my greyhound.

"Heard about the fire."

He was a retired surgeon, and he shook his head.

"Poor Kenneth."

"I suppose you know him," I said.

"Oh yes."

"It is too bad. What kind of dog do you have?"

"He's a salad bar dog. Little bit of everything," my neighbor said.

He walked on, taking out a pipe and lighting up, because his wife, no doubt, would not let him smoke in the house. I walked past the homes of my neighbors, all different but the same because they were brick or stucco and not very old. It seemed fitting that the sluggish stretch of the river in the back of the neighborhood made its way over rocks the same way it had two hundred years before. Richmond was not known for change.

When I reached the spot where I had found Wesley when he had been somewhat mad at me, I stood near that same tree, and soon it was too dark to spot an eagle or the river's rocks. For a time, I stood staring at my neighbors' lights in the night, suddenly not having the energy to move as I contemplated that Kenneth Sparkes was either a victim or a killer. Then heavy footsteps sounded on the street behind me. Startled, I whipped around, gripping the canister of red pepper spray attached to my keys.

Marino's voice was quickly followed by his formidable shape.

"Doc, you shouldn't be out here this late," he said.

I was too drained to resent his having an opinion on how I was spending my evening.

"How did you know I was here?" I asked.

"One of your neighbors."

I did not care.

"My car's right over there," he went on. "I'll drive you home."

"Marino, can I never have a moment's peace?" I said with no rancor, for I knew he meant no harm to me.

"Not tonight," he said. "I got some really bad news and think you might want to sit down."

I immediately thought of Lucy and felt the strength go out of my knees. I swayed and put my hand on his shoulder as my mind seemed to shatter into a million pieces. I had always known the day might come when someone would deliver her death notice to me, and I could not speak or think. I was miles beyond the moment, sucked down deeper and deeper into a dark and terrible vortex. Marino grabbed my arm to steady me.

"Jesus," he exclaimed. "Let me get you to the car and we'll sit down."

"No," I barely said, because I had to know. "How's Lucy?"

He paused for a moment and seemed confused.

"Well, she don't know yet, unless she's heard it on the news," he replied.

"Know what?" I asked as my blood seemed to move again.

"Carrie Grethen's escaped from Kirby," he told me. "Some time late this afternoon. They didn't figure it out until it was time to take the female inmates down for dinner."

We began walking quickly to his car as fear made him angry.

"And here you are walking around in the dark with nothing but a keychain," he went on. "Shit. Goddamn son of a bitch. Don't you do that anymore, you hear me? We got no idea where that bitch is, but one thing I know for a fact, as long as she's out, you ain't safe."

"No one in the world is safe," I muttered as I climbed into his car and thought of Benton alone at the beach.

Carrie Grethen hated him almost as much as she hated

me, or at least this was my belief. Benton had profiled her and was the quarterback in the game that had eventually resulted in her capture and Temple Gault's death. Benton had used the Bureau's every resource to lock Carrie away, and until now, it had worked.

"Is there any way she might know where Benton is?" I said as Marino drove me to my house. "He's alone on an island resort. He probably takes walks on the beach without his gun, unmindful that there might be someone looking for him . . ."

"Like someone else I know," Marino cut me off.

"Point well taken."

"I'm sure Benton already knows, but I'll call him," Marino said. "And I got no reason to think that Carrie would know about your place in Hilton Head. You didn't have it back then when Lucy was telling her all your secrets."

"That's not fair," I said as he pulled into my driveway and came to an abrupt stop. "Lucy never meant it that way. She never meant to be disloyal, to hurt me."

I lifted the handle of my door.

"At this point, it don't matter what she meant."

He blew smoke out his window.

"How did Carrie get out?" I asked. "Kirby's on an island and not easily accessible."

"No one knows. About three hours ago, she was supposed to go down to dinner with all the other lovely ladies, and that's when the guards realized she was gone. Boom, no sign of her, and about a mile away there's an old footbridge that goes over the East River into Harlem."

He tossed the cigarette butt on my driveway.

"All anyone can figure is maybe she got off the island that way. Cops are everywhere, and they got choppers out to make sure she's not still hiding somewhere on the island. But I don't think so. I think she's planned this for a while, and timed it exactly. We'll hear from her, all right. You can bet on that."

I was deeply unsettled when I went inside my house and checked every door and set the alarm. I then did something that was rare and unnerving for me. I got my Glock nine-millimeter pistol from a drawer in my office, and secured every closet in every room, on each floor. I stepped into each doorway, the pistol firm in both hands as my heart hammered. By now Carrie Grethen had become a monster with supernatural powers. I had begun to imagine that she could evade any security system, and would glide out of the shadows when I was feeling safe and unaware.

There seemed to be no presence in my two-story stone house but me, and I carried a glass of red burgundy into my bedroom and got into my robe. I called Wesley again and felt a chill when he did not pick up the phone. I tried once more at almost midnight, and still he did not answer.

"Dear God," I said, alone in my room.

Lamplight was soft and cast shadows from antique dressers and tables that had been stripped down to old gray oak, because I liked flaws and the stress marks of time. Pale rose draperies stirred as air flowed out from vents, and every movement unglued me more, no matter the explanation. With each passing moment, my brain was further overruled by fear as I tried to repress images from the past I shared with Carrie Grethen. I hoped Benton would call. I told myself he was okay and that what I needed was sleep. So I tried to read Seamus Heaney's poetry and dozed off somewhere in the middle of *The Spoonbait*. The phone rang at twenty minutes past two A.M., and my book slid to the floor.

"Scarpetta," I blurted into the receiver as my heart pounded the way it always did when I was startled awake.

"Kay, it's me," Benton said. "Sorry to call you this late, but I was afraid you were trying to reach me. Somehow the answering machine got turned off, and, well, I went out to eat and then walked the beach for more than two hours. To think. I guess you know the news."

"Yes." I was suddenly very alert.

"Are you all right?" he said, because he knew me well.

"I searched every inch of my house tonight before going to bed. I had my gun out and checked every closet and behind every shower curtain."

"I thought you probably would."

"It's like knowing a bomb is on the way in the mail."

"No, it's not like that, Kay. Because we don't know one is coming or when or in what form. I wish we did. But that's part of her game. To make us guess."

"Benton, you know how she feels about you. I don't like you there alone."

"Do you want me to come home?"

I thought about this and had no good answer.

"I'll get in my car right this minute," he added. "If that's what you want."

Then I told him about the body in the ruins of Kenneth Sparkes's mansion, and I went on and on about that, and about my meeting with the tycoon on Hootowl Farm. I talked and explained while he listened patiently.

"The point is," I concluded, "that this is turning out to be terribly complicated, if not bizarre, and there is so much to do. It makes no sense for your vacation to be ruined, too.

And Marino's right. There's no reason to suspect that Carrie knows about our place in Hilton Head. You're probably safer there than here, Benton."

"I wish she'd come here." His voice turned hard. "I'd welcome her with my Sig Sauer and we could finally put an end to this."

I knew he truly wanted to kill her, and this was, in a way, the worst damage she could have done. It was not like Benton to wish for violence, to allow a shadow of the evil he pursued to fall over his conscience and heart, and as I listened, I felt my own culpability, too.

"Do you see how destructive this is?" I said, upset. "We sit around talking about shooting her, strapping her into the electric chair or giving her a lethal injection. She has succeeded in taking possession of us, Benton. Because I admit that I want her dead about as much as I've ever wanted anything."

"I think I should come on home," he said again.

We hung up soon after, and insomnia proved the only enemy of the night. It robbed me of the few hours left before dawn and ripped my brain into fragmented dreams of anxiety and horror. I dreamed I was late for an important appointment and got stuck in the snow and was unable to dial the phone. In my twilight state I could not find answers in autopsies anymore and felt my life was over, and suddenly I drove up on a terrible car accident with bleeding bodies inside, and I could not make a move to help. I flipped this way and that, rearranging pillows and covers until the sky turned smoky blue and the stars went out. I got up and made coffee.

I drove to work with the radio on, listening to repeated news breaks about the fire in Warrenton and a body that was found. Speculation was wild and dramatic about the victim being the famed media mogul, and I could not help but wonder if this amused Sparkes just a little. I was curious why he had not issued a statement to the press, letting the world know he was quite alive, and again, doubts about him darkened my mind.

Dr. Jack Fielding's red Mustang was parked behind our new building on Jackson Street, between the restored row houses of Jackson Ward, and the Medical College of Virginia campus of Virginia Commonwealth University. My new building, which was also home to the forensic labs, was the anchor of thirty-four acres of rapidly developing data institutes known as Biotech Park.

We had just moved from our old address to this new one but two months before, and I was still adjusting to modern glass and brick, and lintels on top of windows to reflect the neighborhoods once there. Our new space was bright, with tan epoxy flooring and walls that were easily hosed down. There was much still to be unpacked and sorted and rearranged, and as thrilled as I was to finally have a modern morgue, I felt more overwhelmed than I had ever been. The low sun was in my eyes as I parked in the chief's slot inside the covered bay on Jackson Street, and I unlocked a back door to let myself in.

The corridor was spotless and smelled of industrial deodorizer, and there were still boxes of electrical wiring and switch plates and cans of paint parked against walls. Fielding had unlocked the stainless steel cooler, which was bigger than most living rooms, and he had opened the doors to the autopsy room. I tucked my keys into my pocketbook and headed to the lockers, where I slipped out of my suit jacket and hung it up. I buttoned a lab coat up to my neck, and exchanged pumps for the rather gruesome black Reeboks I called my autopsy shoes. They were spattered and stained and certainly a biological hazard. But they supported my less-than-youthful legs and feet, and never left the morgue.

The new autopsy room was much bigger than the one before as it was better designed to utilize space. No longer were large steel tables built into the floor, so they could be parked out of the way when not in use. The five new tables were transportable and could be wheeled out of the refrigerator and wall-mounted dissecting sinks accommodated both right- and left-handed doctors. Our new tables had roller trays so we no longer had to use our backs to lift or move bodies, and there were non-clogging aspirators, and eye wash stations, and a special dual exhaust duct connected to the building's ventilation system.

All in all, the Commonwealth had granted me most of what I needed to ease the Virginia Medical Examiner System into the third millennium, but in truth, there was no such thing as change, at least not for the better. Each year we explored more damage done by bullets and blades, and more people filed frivolous lawsuits against us, and the courts miscarried justice as a matter of course because lawyers lied and jurors did not seem interested in evidence or facts anymore.

Frigid air rushed as I opened the cooler's massive door, and I walked past body bags and bloody plastic shrouds and stiff protruding feet. Brown-paper-bagged hands meant a violent death, and small pouches reminded me of a sudden infant death and the toddler who had drowned in the family pool. My fire case was swathed, broken glass and all, just as I had left it. I rolled the gurney out into a blaze of fluorescent light. Then I changed shoes again and walked to the other end of the first floor, where our offices and conference room were sequestered from the dead.

It was almost eight-thirty, and residents and clerical staff were getting coffee and traveling the hall. We exchanged our usual detached good mornings as I headed toward Fielding's open door. I knocked once and walked in as he talked on the phone and hastily scribbled information on a call sheet.

"Start again?" he said in his strong blunt voice as he cradled the receiver between his shoulder and chin and absently ran his fingers through his unruly dark hair. "What's the address? What's the officer's name?"

He did not glance up at me as he wrote.

"You got a local phone number?"

He quickly read it back to make sure he'd gotten it right.

"Any idea what kind of death this is? Okay, okay. What cross street and will I see you in your cruiser? All right, you're good to go."

Fielding hung up and looked harried for so early in the morning.

"What have we got?" I asked him as the business of the day began to mount.

"Looks like a mechanical asphyxiation. A black female with a history of alcohol and drug abuse. She's hanging off the bed, head against the wall, neck bent at an angle inconsistent with life. She's nude, so I think I'd better take a look to make sure this isn't something else."

"*Someone* definitely should take a look," I agreed.

He got my meaning.

"We can send Levine if you want."

"Good idea, because I'm going to start the fire death and would like your help," I said. "At least in the early stages."

"You got it."

Fielding pushed back his chair and unfolded his powerful body. He was dressed in khakis, a white shirt with sleeves rolled up, Rockports, and an old woven leather belt around his hard, trim waist. Past forty now, he was no less diligent about his physical condition, which was no less remarkable than it had been when I had first hired him shortly after I had taken office. If only he cared about his cases quite so much. But he had always been respectful and faithful to me, and although he was slow and workmanlike, he was not given to assumptions or mistakes. For my purposes, he was manageable, reliable, and pleasant, and I would not have traded him for another deputy chief.

We entered the conference room together, and I took my seat at the head of the long glossy table. Charts and models of muscles and organs and the anatomical skeleton were the only decor, save for the same dated photographs of previous male chiefs who had watched over us in our previous quarters. This morning, the resident, a fellow, my three deputy and assistant chiefs, the toxicologist, and my administrators were present and accounted for. We had a medical student from MCV who was doing her elective here, and a forensic pathologist from London who was making the rounds in American morgues to learn more about serial murders and gunshot wounds.

"Good morning," I said. "Let's go over what we've got, and then we'll talk about our fire fatality and the implications of that."

Fielding began with the possible mechanical asphyxiation, and then Jones, the administrator for the central district, which was the physical office where we were located, quickly ran through our other cases. We had a white male who fired five bullets into his girlfriend's head before blasting away at his own misguided brain. There were the sudden infant death and the drowning, and a young man who may have been changing out of his shirt and tie when he smashed his red Miata into a tree.

"Wow," said the medical student, whose name was Sanford. "How do you figure he was doing that?"

"Tank top half on, shirt and tie crumpled on the passenger's seat," Jones explained. "Seems he was leaving work to meet some friends at a bar. We've had these cases before—someone changing clothes, shaving, putting on makeup while they're driving."

"That's when you want the little box on the death certificate that says manner of death was *stupid*," Fielding said.

"Quite possibly all of you are aware that Carrie Grethen escaped from Kirby last night," I went on. "Though this does not directly impact this office, clearly we should be more than a little concerned."

I tried to be as matter-of-fact as possible.

"Expect the media to call," I said.

"They already have," said Jones as he peered at me over his reading glasses. "The answering service has received five calls since last night."

"About Carrie Grethen." I wanted to be sure.

"Yes, ma'am," he said. "And four more calls about the Warrenton case."

"Let's get to that," I said. "There will be no information coming from this office at this point. Not about the escape from Kirby nor the Warrenton death. Fielding and I will be downstairs the better part of the day, and I want no interruptions that aren't absolutely necessary. This case is very sensitive."

I looked around the table at faces that were somber but alive with interest.

"At present I don't know if we're dealing with an accident, suicide, or homicide, and the remains have not been identified. Tim," I addressed the toxicologist, "let's get a STAT alcohol and CO. This lady may have been a drug abuser, so I'll want a drug screen for opiates, amphetamines and methamphetamine, barbiturates, cannabinoids, as fast as you can get it."

He nodded as he wrote this down. I paused long enough to scan newspaper articles that Jones had clipped for me, then I followed the hallway back to the morgue. In the ladies' locker room I removed my blouse and skirt and went to a cabinet to fetch a transmitter belt and mike that had been custom-designed for me by Lanier. The belt went around my upper waist under a long-sleeved blue surgical gown so the mike key would not come into direct contact with bloody hands. Last, I clipped the cordless mike to my collar, laced up my morgue shoes again, covered them with booties, and tied on a face shield and surgical mask.

Fielding emerged into the autopsy room the same time I did.

"Let's get her into X-ray," I said.

We rolled the steel table across the corridor into the X-ray room and lifted the body and accompanying fire debris by corners of the sheets. This we transferred onto a table beneath the C-arm of the Mobile Digital Imaging System, which was an X-ray machine and fluoroscope in one computer-controlled unit. I went through the various set-up procedures, locking in various connecting cables and turning on the work station with a key. Lighted segments and a time line lit up on the control panel, and I loaded a film cassette into the holder and pressed a floor pedal to activate the video monitor.

"Aprons," I said to Fielding.

I handed him a lead-lined one that was Carolina blue. Mine was heavy and felt full of sand as I tied it in back.

"I think we're ready," I announced as I pressed a button.

By moving the C-arm, we were able to capture the remains in real time from many different angles, only, unlike the examination of hospital patients, what we viewed did not breathe or beat or swallow. Static images of dead organs and bones were black and white on the video screen, and I saw no projectiles or anomalies. As we pivoted the C-arm some more, we discovered several radiopaque shapes that I suspected were metal objects mingled with the debris. We watched our progress on screen, digging and sifting with our gloved hands until I closed my fingers around two hard objects. One was the size and shape of a half dollar, the other smaller than that and square. I began cleaning them in the sink.

"What's left of a small silver metal belt buckle," I said as I dropped it into a plasticized carton, which I labeled with a Magic Marker.

My other find was easier, and I did not have to do much to it to determine that it was a wristwatch. The band had burned off and the sooty crystal was shattered. But I was fascinated by the face, which upon further rinsing turned out to be a very bright orange etched with a strange abstract design.

"Looks like a man's watch to me," Fielding observed.

"Women wear watches this big," I said. "I do. So I can see."

"Some kind of sports watch, maybe?"

"Maybe."

We rotated the C-arm here and there, continuing to excavate as radiation from the X-ray tube passed through the body and all the muck and charred material surrounding it. I spotted what looked like the shape of a ring located somewhere beneath the right buttock, but when I tried to grab it, nothing was there. Since the body had been on its back, much of the posterior regions had been spared, including clothing. I wedged my hands under the buttocks and worked my fingers into the back pockets of the jeans, recovering half a carrot and what appeared to be a plain wedding band that at first looked like steel. Then I realized it was platinum.

"That looks like a man's ring, too," Fielding said. "Unless she had really big fingers."

He took the ring from me to examine it more closely. The stench of burned decaying flesh rose from the table as I discovered more strange signs pointing to what this woman may have done prior to dying. There were dark, coarse animal hairs adhering to wet filthy denim, and though I couldn't be certain, I was fairly sure their origin was equine.

"Nothing engraved in it," he said, sealing the ring inside an evidence envelope.

"No," I confirmed with growing curiosity.

"Wonder why she had it in her back pocket instead of wearing it."

"Good question."

"Unless she was doing something that might have caused her to take it off," he continued to think aloud. "You know, like people taking off their jewelry when they wash their hands."

"She may have been feeding the horses."

I collected several hairs with forceps.

"Maybe the black foal that got away?" I supposed.

"Okay," he said, and he sounded very dubious. "And what? She's paying attention to the little guy, feeding him carrots, and then doesn't return him to his stall? A little later, everything burns, including the stables and the horses in them? But the foal gets away?"

He glanced at me across the table.

"Suicide?" he continued to speculate. "And she couldn't bring herself to kill the colt? What's his name, Windsong?"

But there were no answers to any of these questions right now, and we continued to make X-rays of personal effects and pathology, to give us a permanent case record. But mostly we explored, in real time on screen, recovering grommets from jeans and an intrauterine device that suggested she had been sexually active with males.

Our findings included a zipper and a blackened lump the size of a baseball that turned out to be a steel bracelet with small links and a serpent silver ring that held three copper keys. Other than sinus configurations, which are as distinct as fingerprints in every human being, and a single porcelain crown on the right maxillary central incisor, we discovered nothing else obvious that might effect an identification.

At close to noon, we rolled her back across the corridor into the autopsy room and attached her table to a dissecting sink in the farthest corner, out of the main traffic. Other sinks were busy and loud as water drummed stainless steel, and stepladders were scooted as other doctors weighed and sectioned organs and dictated their findings into tiny mikes while various detectives looked on. The chatter was typically blunt with fractured sentences, our communication as random and disjointed as the lives of our cases.

"Excuse me, need to be right about where you are."

"Darn, I need a battery."

"What kind?"

"Whatever the hell goes in this camera."

"Twenty dollars, right front pocket."

"Probably not robbery."

"Who's gonna count pills. Got a shitload."

"Dr. Scarpetta, we just got another case. Possible homicide," a resident said loudly as he hung up a phone that was designated for clean hands.

"We may have to hold it until tomorrow," I responded as our workload worsened.

"We've got the gun from the murder-suicide," one of my assistant chiefs called out.

"Unloaded?" I answered back.

"Yeah."

I walked over to make sure, for I never made assumptions when firearms came in with bodies. The dead man was big and still dressed in Faded Glory jeans, the pockets turned inside out by police. Potential gunshot residue on his hands was protected by brown paper bags, and blood trickled from his nose when a wooden block was placed beneath his head.

"Do you mind if I handle the gun?" I asked the detective, above the whine of a Stryker saw.

"Be my guest. I've already lifted prints."

I picked up the Smith & Wesson pistol and pulled back the slide to check for a cartridge, but the chamber was clear. I dabbed a towel over the bullet wound in the head, as my morgue supervisor, Chuck Ruffin, honed a knife with long sweeps over a sharpening stone.

"See the black around there and the muzzle imprint?" I said as the detective and a resident leaned close. "You can see the sight here. It's contact right-handed. The exit's here, and you can see by the dripping he was lying on his right side."

"That's how we found him," the detective said as the saw whined on and a bony dust drifted through the air.

"Be sure to note the caliber, make, and model," I said as I returned to my own sad chore. "And is the ammunition ball versus hollow point?"

"Ball. Remington nine-mill."

Fielding had parallel-parked another table nearby and covered it with a sheet that he had piled with the fire debris that we had already sifted through. I began measuring the lengths of her badly burned femurs in hopes I could make an estimate of height. The rest of her legs were gone from just above the knees to the ankles, but her feet had been spared by her boots. In addition, she had burn amputations of her forearms and hands. We collected fragments of fabric and drew diagrams and collected more animal hairs, doing all that we could before beginning the difficult task of removing the glass.

"Let's get the warm water going," I said to Fielding. "Maybe we can loosen without tearing skin."

"It's like a damn roast stuck to the pan."

"Why are you guys always making food analogies?" came a deep, sure voice I recognized.

Teun McGovern, in full morgue protective garb, was walking toward our table. Her eyes were intense behind her face shield, and for an instant we stared straight at each other. I was not the least bit surprised that ATF would have sent a fire investigator to watch the postmortem examination. But I had never expected McGovern to show up.

"How's it going in Warrenton?" I asked her.

"Working away," she replied. "We haven't found Sparkes's body, which is a good thing, since he's not dead."

"Cute," Fielding said.

McGovern positioned herself across from me, standing far enough back from the table to suggest to me that she had seen very few autopsies.

"So what exactly are you doing?" she asked as I picked up a hose.

"We're going to run warm water between the skin and the glass in hopes we can peel the two apart without further damage," I replied.

"And what if that doesn't work?"

"Then we got a big fat mess," Fielding said.

"Then we use a scalpel," I explained.

But this was not necessary. After several minutes of a constant warm bath, I began to very slowly and gently separate the thick broken glass from the dead woman's face, the skin pulling and distorting as I peeled, making her all the more horrible to look at. Fielding and I worked in silence for a while, gently laying shards and sections of heat-stressed glass into a plastic tub. This took about an hour, and when we were done, the stench was stronger. What was left of the poor woman seemed more pitiful and small, and the damage to her head was even more striking.

"My God," McGovern said as she stepped closer. "That's the weirdest thing I've ever seen."

The lower part of the face was chalky bone, a barely discernible human skull with open jaws and crumbling teeth. Most of the ears were gone, but from the eyes up, the flesh was cooked and so remarkably preserved that I could see the blond fuzz along the hairline. The forehead was intact, although slightly abraded by the removal of the glass, so that it was no longer smooth. If there had been wrinkles, I could not find them now.

"I can't figure out what the hell this is," Fielding said as he examined the bits of material mingled with hair. "It's everywhere, all the way down to her scalp."

Some of it looked like burned paper, while other small pieces were pristinely preserved and a neon pink. I scraped some of it onto my scalpel and placed it into another carton.

"We'll let the labs take a crack at it," I said to McGovern.

"Absolutely," she answered.

The hair was eighteen and three-quarters inches long, and I saved a strand of it for DNA should we ever have a premortem sample for comparison.

"If we trace her back to someone missing," I said to McGovern, "and you guys can get hold of her toothbrush, we can look for buccal cells. They line the mucosa of the mouth and can be used for DNA comparison. A hairbrush would be good, too."

She made a note of this. I moved a surgical lamp closer to the left temporal area, using a lens to painstakingly examine what appeared to be hemorrhage in tissue that had been spared.

"It seems we have some sort of injury here," I said. "Definitely not skin splitting or an artifact of fire. Possibly an incision with some sort of shiny debris imbedded inside the wound."

"Could she have been overcome by CO and fallen and hit her head?" McGovern voiced the same question others had.

"She would have had to have hit it on something very sharp," I said as I took photographs.

"Let me look," Fielding said, and I handed him the lens.

"I don't see any torn or ragged edges," he remarked as he peered.

"No, not a laceration," I agreed. "This looks more like something inflicted by a sharp instrument."

He returned the lens to me, and I used plastic forceps to delicately scrape the shiny debris from the wound. I swiped it onto a square of clean cotton twill. On a nearby desk was a dissecting microscope, and I placed the cloth on the stage and moved the light source so that it would reflect off the debris. I looked through the eyepiece lens as I manipulated the coarse and fine adjustments.

What I saw in the circle of reflected illumination were several silvery segments that had the striated, flattened surfaces of metal shavings, such as the turnings made by a lathe. I fitted a Polaroid MicroCam to the microscope and took high-resolution instant color photographs.

"Take a look," I said.

Fielding, then McGovern, bent over the microscope.

"Either of you ever seen anything like that?" I asked.

I peeled open the developed photographs to make certain they had turned out all right.

"It reminds me of Christmas tinsel when it gets old and wrinkled," Fielding said.

"Transferred from whatever cut her," was all McGovern had to say.

"I would think so," I agreed.

I removed the square of white cloth from the stage and preserved the shavings between cotton balls, which I sealed inside a metal evidence button.

"One more thing for the labs," I said to McGovern.

"How long will it take?" McGovern said. "Because if there's a problem, we can do the work at our labs in Rockville."

"There won't be a problem." I looked at Fielding and said, "I think I can handle it from here."

"Okay," he said. "I'll get started on the next one."

I opened up the neck to look for trauma to those organs and muscles, beginning with the tongue, which I removed while McGovern looked on with stoicism. It was a grim procedure that separated the weak from the strong.

"Nothing there," I said, rinsing the tongue and blotting it dry with a towel. "No bite marks that might be indicative of a seizure. No other injuries."

I looked inside the glistening smooth walls of the airway and found no soot, meaning she was no longer breathing when heat and flames had reached her. But I also found blood, and this was further ominous news.

"More premortem trauma," I said.

"Possible something fell on her after she was dead?" McGovern asked.

"It didn't happen that way."

I noted the injury on a diagram and dictated it into the transmitter.

"Blood in the airway means she inhaled it—or aspirated," I explained. "Meaning, obviously, that she was breathing when the trauma occurred."

"What sort of trauma?" she then asked.

"A penetrating injury. The throat stabbed or cut. I see no other signs of trauma to the base of the skull or lungs or to the neck, no contusions or broken bones. Her hyoid's intact, and there's fusion of the greater horn and body, possibly indicating she's older than twenty and most likely wasn't strangled manually or with a ligature."

I began to dictate again.

"The skin under the chin and superficial muscle are burned away," I said into the small mike on my gown. "Heat-coagulated blood in the distal trachea, primary, secondary, and tertiary bronchi. Hemoaspiration, and blood in the esophagus."

I made the Y incision to open up the dehydrated, ruined body, and for the most part, the rest of the autopsy proved to be rather routine. Although the organs were cooked, they were within normal limits, and the reproductive organs verified the gender as female. There was blood in her stomach, too; otherwise it was empty and tubular, suggesting she hadn't been eating very much. But I found no disease and no other injuries old or new.

Height I could not positively ascertain, but I could estimate by using Trotter and Gleser regression formula charts to correlate femur length to the victim's stature. I sat at a nearby desk and thumbed through Bass's *Human Osteology* until I found the appropriate table for American white females. Based on a 50.2 millimeter, or approximately twenty-inch, femur, the predicted height would have been five-foot-ten.

Weight was not so exact, for there was no table, chart, or scientific calculation that might tell me that. In truth, we usually got a hint of weight from the size of clothing left, and in this case, the victim had been wearing size eight jeans. So based on the data I had, I intuited that she had been between one hundred and twenty and one hundred and thirty pounds.

"In other words," I said to McGovern, "she was tall and very slim. We also know she had long blond hair, was probably sexually active, may have been comfortable around horses, and was already dead inside Sparkes's Warrenton house before the fire got to her. I also know that she received significant premortem injury to her upper neck and was cut right here on her left temple." I pointed. "How these were inflicted, I can't tell you."

I got up from my chair and gathered paperwork while McGovern looked at me, her eyes shadowed by thought. She took off her face shield and mask and untied her gown in back.

"If she had a drug problem, is there any way you might be able to tell that?" she asked me as the phone rang and rang.

"Toxicology will certainly tell us if she had drugs on board," I said. "There may also be crystals in her lungs or foreign body granulomas from cutting agents like talc, and fibers from the cotton used to strain out impurities. Unfortunately, the areas where we might be most likely to find needle tracks are missing."

"What about her brain? Would chronic drug abuse cause any damage that you might be able to see? For example, if she started having severe mental problems, was getting psychotic and so on? It sounds like Sparkes thought she had some sort of mental illness," McGovern then said. "For example, what if she were depressive or manic-depressive? Could you tell?"

By now the skull had been opened, the rubbery, fire-shrunken brain sectioned and still on the cutting board.

"In the first place," I answered, "nothing is going to be helpful postmortem because the brain is cooked. But even if that were not the case, looking for a morphological correlate to a particular psychiatric syndrome is, in most cases, still theoretical. A widening of the sulci, for example, and reduced gray matter due to atrophy might be a signpost if we knew what the weight of the brain originally was when she was healthy. Then maybe I could say, *Okay, her brain weighs a hundred grams less now than it did, so she might have been suffering from some sort of mental disease.* Unless she has a lesion or old head injury that might suggest a problem, the answer to your question is no, I can't tell."

McGovern was silent, and it was not lost on her that I was clinical and not the least bit friendly. Even though I was aware of my rather brittle demeanor around her, I could not seem to soften it. I looked around for Ruffin. He was at the first dissecting sink, suturing a Y incision in long strokes of needle and twine. I motioned to him and walked over. He was too young to worry about turning thirty anytime soon, and had gotten his training in an O.R. and a funeral home.

"Chuck, if you can finish up here and put her back in the fridge," I said to him.

"Yes, ma'am."

He returned to his station to finish his present task while I peeled off gloves and dropped them and my mask into one of many red biological hazard containers scattered around the autopsy room.

"Let's go to my office and have a cup of coffee," I suggested to McGovern in an attempt to be a little more civil. "And we can finish this discussion."

In the locker room, we washed with antibacterial soap and I got dressed. I had questions for McGovern, but in truth, I was curious about her, too.

"Getting back to the possibility of drug-induced mental illness," McGovern said as we followed the corridor. "Many of these people self-destruct, right?"

"In one way or another."

"They die in accidents, commit suicide, and that gets us back to the big question," she said. "Is that what happened here? Possible she was whacked out and committed suicide?"

"All I know is, she has injury that was inflicted before death," I pointed out again.

"But that could be self-inflicted if she were not in her right mind," McGovern said. "God knows the kinds of self-mutilation we've seen when people are psychotic."

This was true. I had worked cases in which people had cut their own throats, or stabbed themselves in the chest, or amputated their limbs, or shot themselves in their sexual organs, or walked into a river to drown. Not to mention leaps from high places and self-immolations. The list of horrendous things people did to themselves was much too long, and whenever I thought I'd seen it all, something new and awful was rolled into our bay.

The phone was ringing as I unlocked my office, and I grabbed it just in time.

"Scarpetta," I said.

"I've got some results for you," said Tim Cooper, the toxicologist. "Ethanol, methanol, isopropanol, and acetone are zero. Carbon monoxide is less than seven percent. I'll keep working on the other screens."

"Thanks. What would I do without you?" I said.

I looked at McGovern as I hung up, and I told her what Cooper had just said.

"She was dead before the fire," I explained, "her cause of death exsanguination and asphyxia due to aspiration of blood due to acute neck injury. As for manner, I'm pending that until further investigation, but I think we should work this as a homicide. In the meantime, we need to get her identified, and I'll do what I can to get started on that."

"I guess I'm supposed to imagine that this woman torched the place and maybe cut her own throat before the fire got her first?" she said as anger flickered.

I did not answer as I measured coffee for the coffeemaker on a nearby countertop.

"Don't you think that's rather far-fetched?" she went on.

I poured in bottled water and pressed a button.

"Kay, no one's going to want to hear homicide," she said. "Because of Kenneth Sparkes and what all of this may imply. I hope you realize what you're up against."

"And what ATF is up against," I said, sitting across my hopelessly piled desk from her.

"Look, I don't care who he is," she replied. "I do every job like I fully intend to make an arrest. I'm not the one who has to deal with the politics around here."

But my mind wasn't on the media or Sparkes right now. I was thinking that this case disturbed me at a deeper level and in ways I could not fathom.

"How much longer will your guys be at the scene?" I asked her.

"Another day. Two at the most," she said. "Sparkes has supplied us and the insurance company with what was inside his house, and just the antique furniture and old wood flooring and paneling alone were a massive fuel load."

"What about the master bath?" I asked. "Saying this was the point of origin."

She hesitated. "Obviously, that's the problem."

"Right. If an accelerant wasn't used, or at least not a petroleum distillate, then how?"

"The guys are beating their brains out," she said, and she was frustrated. "And so am I. If I try to predict how much energy would be needed in that room for a flashover condition, the fuel load isn't there. According to Sparkes, there was nothing but a throw rug and towels. Cabinets and fixtures were customized brushed steel. The shower had a glass door, the window had sheer curtains."

She paused as the coffeemaker gurgled.

"So what are we talking about?" she went on. "Five, six hundred kilowatts total for a ten-by-fifteen-foot room? Clearly, there are other variables. Such as how much air was flowing through the doorway . . ."

"What about the rest of the house? You just said there was a big fuel load there, right?"

"We're only concerned with one room, Kay. And that's the room of origin. Without an origin, the rest of the fuel load doesn't matter."

"I see."

"I know a flame was impinged on the ceiling in that bathroom, and I know how high that flame had to be and how many kilowatts of energy were needed for flashover. And a throw rug and maybe some towels and curtains couldn't even come close to causing something like that."

I knew her engineering equations were pristinely mathematical, and I did not doubt anything she was saying. But it did not matter. I was still left with the same problem. I had reason to believe that we were dealing with a homicide and that when the fire started, the victim's body was inside the master bath, with its noncombustible marble floors, large mirrors, and steel. Indeed, she may have been in the tub.

"What about the open skylight?" I asked McGovern. "Does that fit with your theory?"

"It could. Because once again, the flames had to be high enough to break the glass, and then heat would have vented through the opening like a chimney. Every fire has its own personality, but certain behaviors are always the same because they conform to the laws of physics."

"I understand."

"There are four stages," she went on, as if I knew nothing. "First is the fire plume, or column of hot gases, flames, and smoke rising from the fire. That would have been the case, let's say, if the throw rug in the bathroom had ignited. The higher above the flame the gases rise, the cooler and denser they become. They mix with combustion by-products, and the hot gases now begin to fall, and the cycle repeats itself creating turbulent smoke that spreads horizontally. What should have happened next was this hot smoky layer would have continued to descend until it found an opening for ventilation—in this case, we'll assume the bathroom doorway. Next, the smoky layer flows out of the opening while fresh air flows in. If there's enough oxygen, the temperature at the ceiling's going to go up to more than six hundred degrees Celsius, and boom, we have flashover, or a fully developed fire."

"A fully developed fire in the master bath," I said.

"And then on into other oxygen-enriched rooms where the fuel loads were enough to burn the place to the ground," she replied. "So it's not the spread of the fire that bothers me. It's how it got started. Like I said, a throw rug, curtains, weren't enough, unless something else was there."

"Maybe something was," I said, getting up to pour coffee. "How do you take yours?" I asked.

"Cream and sugar."

Her eyes followed me.

"None of that artificial stuff, please."

I drank mine black, and set mugs on the desk as

McGovern's gaze wandered around my new office. Certainly, it was brighter and more modern than what I had occupied in the old building on Fourteenth and Franklin, but I really had no more room to evolve. Worst of all, I had been honored with a CEO corner space with windows, and anybody who understood physicians knew that what we needed were walls for bookcases, and not bulletproof glass overlooking a parking lot and the Petersburg Turnpike. My hundreds of medical, legal, and forensic science reviews, journals and formidable volumes were crammed together and, in some cases, double-shelved. It was not uncommon for Rose, my secretary, to hear me swearing when I could not find a reference book I needed right that minute.

"Teun," I said, sipping my coffee, "I'd like to take this opportunity to thank you for taking care of Lucy."

"Lucy takes care of herself," she said.

"That has not always been true."

I smiled in an effort to be more gracious, to hide the hurt and jealousy that were a splinter in my heart.

"But you're right," I said. "I think she does a pretty admirable job of it now. I'm sure Philadelphia will be good for her."

McGovern was reading every signal I was sending, and I could tell she was aware of more than I wanted her to be.

"Kay, hers will not be an easy road," she then stated. "No matter what I do."

She swirled the coffee in her mug, as if about to taste the first sip of fine wine.

"I'm her supervisor, not her mother," McGovern said.

This irked me considerably, and it showed when I abruptly picked up the phone and instructed Rose to hold all calls. I got up and shut my door.

"I would hope she's not transferring to your field office because she needs a mother," I replied coolly as I returned to my desk, which served as a barrier between us. "Above all else, Lucy is a consummate professional."

McGovern held up her hand to stop me.

"Whoa," she protested. "Of course she is. I'm just not promising anything. She's a big girl, but she's also got a lot of big obstacles. Her FBI background will be held against her by some, who will assume right off the bat that she has an attitude and has never really worked cases."

"That stereotype shouldn't last long," I said, and I was finding it very difficult to objectively discuss my niece with her.

"Oh, about as long as it takes for them to see her land a helicopter or program a robot to remove a bomb from a scene," she quipped. "Or zip through Q-dot calculations in her head while the rest of us can't even figure them out on a calculator."

Q-dot was slang for the mathematical equations, or scientific evaluations, used to estimate the physics and chemistry of a fire as it related to what the investigator observed at the scene or was told by witnesses. I wasn't sure Lucy would make many friends by being able to work such esoteric formulas in her head.

"Teun," I said, softening my tone. "Lucy's different, and that isn't always good. In fact, in many ways it is just as much a handicap to be a genius as it is to be retarded."

"Absolutely. I am more aware of this than you might imagine."

"As long as you understand," I said as if I were reluctantly handing her the baton in the relay race of Lucy's difficult development.

"And as long as you understand that she has and will continue to be treated like everybody else. Which includes the other agents' reactions to her baggage, which includes rumors about why she left the FBI and about her alleged personal life," she stated frankly.

I looked at her long and hard, wondering just how much she really knew about Lucy. Unless McGovern had been briefed by someone at the Bureau, there was no reason I could think of why she should know about my niece's affair with Carrie Grethen and the implications of what that might mean when the case went to court, assuming Carrie was caught. Just the reminder cast a shadow over what had already been a dark day, and my uncomfortable silence invited McGovern to fill it.

"I have a son," she said quietly, staring into her coffee. "I know what it's like to have children grow up and suddenly vanish. Go their own way, too busy to visit or get on the phone."

"Lucy grew up a long time ago," I said quickly, for I did not want her to commiserate with me. "She also never lived with me, not permanently, I mean. In a way, she's always been gone."

But McGovern just smiled as she got out of her chair.

"I've got troops to check on," she said. "I guess I'd better be on my way."

6

At four o'clock that afternoon, my staff was still busy in the autopsy room, and I walked in looking for Chuck. He and two of my residents were working on the burned woman's body, defleshing her as best they could with plastic spatulas, because anything harder might scratch the bones.

Chuck was sweating beneath his surgical cap and mask as he scraped tissue from the skull, his brown eyes rather glazed behind his face shield. He was tall and wiry with short, sandy blond hair that tended to stick out in every direction no matter how much gel he used. He was attractive in an adolescent way and, after a year on the job, still terrified of me.

"Chuck?" I said again, inspecting one of the more ghoulish tasks in forensic medicine.

"Yes, ma'am."

He stopped scraping and looked up furtively at me. The stench was getting worse by the minute as unrefrigerated flesh continued to decompose, and I was not looking forward to what I needed to do next.

"Let me just check this one more time," I said to Ruffin,

who was so tall he tended to stoop, his neck jutting out like a turtle when he looked at whoever he was talking to. "Our old battered pots and pans didn't make it in the move."

"I think somehow they got tossed out," he said.

"And probably should have," I told him. "Which means you and I have an errand to run."

"Now?"

"Now."

He wasted no time heading into the men's locker room to get out of his dirty, stinking scrubs and shower just long enough to get the shampoo out of his hair. He was still perspiring, his face pink from scrubbing, when we met in the corridor and I handed him a set of keys. The dark red office Tahoe was parked inside the bay, and I climbed up into the passenger's seat, letting Ruffin drive.

"We're going to Cole's Restaurant Supply," I told him as the big engine came to life. "About two blocks west of Parham, on Broad. Just get us on 64 and take the West Broad exit. I'll show you from there."

He pushed a remote control on the visor and the bay door rolled up heavily, letting in sunlight that I had not noticed all day. Rush hour traffic had just begun and would be awful in another half hour. Ruffin drove like an old woman, dark glasses on and hunched forward as he kept his speed about five miles an hour less than the limit.

"You can go a little faster," I told him calmly. "It closes at five, so we sort of need to hurry along."

He stepped on the gas, lurching us forward, and fumbled in the ashtray for toll tokens.

"You mind if I ask you something, Dr. Scarpetta?" he said.

"Please. Go right ahead."

"It's kind of bizarre."

He glanced in the rearview mirror again.

"That's all right."

"You know, I've seen a lot of things, at the hospital and the funeral home and all," he began nervously. "And nothing got to me, you know?"

He slowed at the toll plaza and tossed a token into the basket. The red striped arm went up and we rolled on as people in a hurry darted past us. Ruffin rolled his window back up.

"It's normal for what you're seeing now to get to you," I finished his thought for him, or thought I did.

But this was not what he wanted to tell me.

"You see, most of the time I get to the morgue before you in the morning," he said instead, his eyes riveted forward as he drove. "So I'm the one who answers the phones and gets things ready for you, right? You know, because I'm there alone."

I nodded, having not a clue as to what he was about to say.

"Well, starting about two months ago, when we were still in the old building, the phone started ringing at around six-thirty in the morning, just after I got in. And when I would pick it up, nobody was there."

"How often has this happened?" I asked.

"Maybe three times a week. Sometimes every day. And it's still happening."

He was getting my attention now.

"It's happening since we moved." I wanted to make sure.

"Of course, we have the same number," he reminded me. "But yes, ma'am. In fact it happened again this morning, and I've started getting a little spooked. I'm just wondering if we should try to get the calls traced to see what's going on."

"Tell me exactly what happens when you pick up the

phone," I said as we drove exactly at the speed limit along the interstate.

"I say 'Morgue,'" he said. "And whoever it is doesn't say a word. There's silence, almost like the line is dead. So I say 'Hello?' a few times and finally hang up. I can tell there's someone there. It's just something I sense."

"Why haven't you told me this before?"

"I wanted to make sure it wasn't just me overreacting. Or maybe being too imaginative, because I got to tell you it's kind of creepy in there first thing in the morning when the sun's not up yet and no one else is around."

"And you say this started about two months ago?"

"More or less," he answered. "I didn't really count the first few, you know."

I was irritated that he had waited until now to pass this along to me, but there was no point in belaboring that.

"I'll pass this along to Captain Marino," I said. "In the meantime, Chuck, you need to tell me if this happens again, okay?"

He nodded, his knuckles white on the steering wheel.

"Just beyond the next light, we're looking for a big beige building. It will be on our left, in the nine thousand block, just past JoPa's."

Cole's was fifteen minutes from closing, and there were but two other cars in the lot when we parked. Ruffin and I got out, and air conditioning was frigid as we entered a wide open space with aisles of metal shelves all the way up to the ceiling. Crowded on them was everything from restaurant-sized ladles and spoons, to food warmers for cafeteria lines, to giant coffeemakers and mixers. But it was potware that I was interested in, and after a quick scan I found the section I needed, halfway to the back, near electric skillets and measuring cups.

I began lifting great aluminum pans and pots when a

sales clerk suddenly appeared. He was balding and big-bellied, and sporting a tattoo of a naked woman playing cards on his right forearm.

"Can I help you?" he said to Ruffin.

"I need the biggest cooking pot you've got," I answered.

"That'd be forty quarts."

He reached up to a shelf too high for me and handed the monstrous pot to Ruffin.

"I'll need a lid," I said.

"Will have to be ordered."

"What about something deep and rectangular," I then said as I envisioned long bones.

"Got a twenty-quart pan."

He reached up to another shelf, and metal clanged as he lifted out a pan that had probably been intended for vats of whipped potatoes, vegetables or cobbler.

"And I don't suppose you have a lid for that either," I said.

"Yeah."

Different-sized lids clattered as he pulled one out.

"It's got the notch right here for the ladle. I guess you'll be wanting a ladle, too."

"No, thank you," I said. "Just something long to stir with, either wooden or plastic. And heat-resistant gloves. Two pairs. What else?"

I looked at Ruffin as I thought.

"Maybe we should get a twenty-quart pot, too, for smaller jobs?" I mused.

"That'd be a good idea," he agreed. "That big pot's going to be mighty heavy when it's filled with water. And there's no point in using it if something smaller will work, but I think you're going to need the bigger pot this time, or it all won't fit. You know?"

The salesman was getting more confused as he listened to our evasive conversation.

"You tell me what you're planning to cook, and maybe I can give you some advice," he offered, again to Ruffin.

"Different things," I replied. "Mostly I'll be boiling things."

"Oh, I see," he said, even though he didn't. "Well, will there be anything else?"

"That's it," I answered him with a smile.

At the counter, he rang up one hundred and seventy-seven dollars of restaurant cookware while I got out my billfold and hunted for my MasterCard.

"Do you by chance give discounts to state government?" I asked as he took my card from me.

"No," he said, rubbing his double chin as he frowned at my card. "I think I've heard your name on the news before."

He stared suspiciously at me.

"I know."

He snapped his fingers.

"You're the lady who ran for the senate a few years back. Or maybe it was for lieutenant governor?" he said, pleased.

"Not me," I answered. "I try to stay out of politics."

"You and me both," he said loudly as Ruffin and I carried our purchases out the door. "They're all crooks, every single one of 'em!"

When we returned to the morgue, I gave Ruffin instructions to remove the remains of the burn victim from the refrigerator and wheel them and the new pots into the decomposition room. I shuffled through telephone messages, most of them from reporters, and realized I was nervously pulling at my hair when Rose appeared in the doorway that joined my office to hers.

"You look like you've had a bad day," she said.

"No worse than usual."

"How about a cup of cinnamon tea?"

"I don't think so," I said. "But thanks."

Rose placed a stack of death certificates on my desk, adding to the never-ending pile of documents for me to initial or sign. She was dressed this day in a smart navy blue pants suit and bright purple blouse, her shoes, typically, black leather lace-ups for walking.

Rose was well past retirement age, although it didn't show in her face, which was regal and subtly made up. But her hair had gotten finer and had turned completely white, while arthritis nibbled at her fingers, lower back, and hips, making it increasingly uncomfortable for her to sit at her desk and take care of me as she had from my first day at this job.

"It's almost six," she said, looking kindly at me.

I glanced up at the clock as I began to scan paperwork and sign my name.

"I have a dinner at the church," she diplomatically let me know.

"That's nice," I said, frowning as I read. "Damn it, how many times do I have to tell Dr. Carmichael that you don't sign out a death as *cardiac arrest*. Jesus, everybody dies of cardiac arrest. You die, your heart quits, right? And he's done the *respiratory arrest* number too, no matter how many times I've amended his certificates."

I sighed in annoyance.

"He's been the M.E. in Halifax County for how many years?" I continued my tirade. "Twenty-five at least?"

"Dr. Scarpetta, don't forget he's an obstetrician. And an ancient one at that," Rose reminded me. "A nice man who's not capable of learning anything new. He still types his reports on an old manual Royal, flying capitals and all. And the reason I mentioned the church dinner is, I'm supposed to be there in ten minutes."

She paused, regarding me over her reading glasses.

"But I can stay if you want me to," she added.

"I've got some things to do," I told her. "And the last thing I would think of is to interfere with a church dinner. Yours or anyone's. I'm always in enough trouble with God as is."

"Then I'll say good night," Rose said. "My dictations are in your basket. I'll see you in the morning."

After her footsteps vanished down the corridor, I was enveloped by silence broken only by the sounds of paper I was moving around on my desk. I thought of Benton several times and warded off my desire to call him, because I was not ready to relax, or maybe I simply did not want to feel human quite yet. It is, after all, hard to feel like a normal person with normal emotions when one is about to boil human remains in what is essentially a large soup pot. A few minutes after seven, I followed the corridor to the decomposition room, which was two doors down and across from the cooler.

I unlocked the door and entered what was nothing more than a small autopsy room with a freezer and special ventilation. The remains were covered by a sheet on a transportable table, a new forty-quart pot filled with water on an electric burner beneath a chemical hood. I put on a mask and gloves and turned the burner on a low heat that would not further damage the bones. I poured in two scoops of laundry detergent and a cup of bleach to hasten the loosening of fibrous membranes, cartilage, and grease.

I opened the sheets, exposing bones stripped of most of their tissue, the extremities pitifully truncated like burned sticks. I gently placed femurs and tibias into the pot, then the pelvis and parts of the skull. Vertebrae and ribs followed as water got hotter and a sharp-smelling steam began to rise. I needed to see her bare, clean bones because they might have something to tell me, and there simply was no other way to do it.

For a while I sat in that room, the hood loudly sucking up air as I drifted in my chair. I was tired. I was emotionally drained and feeling all alone. Water heated up, and what was left of a woman I believed had been murdered began to process in the pot, in what seemed one more indignity and callous slight to who she was.

"Oh God," I sighed, as if God might somehow hear me. "Bless her, wherever she is."

It was hard to imagine being reduced to bones cooking in a pot, and the more I thought about it the more depressed I got. Somewhere someone had loved this woman, and she had accomplished something in this life before her body and identity had been so cruelly stripped away. I had spent my existence trying to ward off hate, but by now it was too late. It was true that I hated sadistic evil people whose purpose in life was to torment life and take it, as if it were theirs to appropriate. It was true that executions deeply disturbed me, but only because they resurrected heartless crimes and the victims society barely remembered.

Steam rose in a hot, moist vapor, tainting the air with a nauseating stench that would lessen the longer the bones were processed. I envisioned someone thin and tall and blond, someone wearing jeans and lace-up boots, with a platinum ring tucked in her back pocket. Her hands were gone, and

I probably would never know the size of her fingers or if the ring had fit, but it wasn't likely. Fielding probably was right, and I knew I had one more thing to ask Sparkes.

I thought of her wounds and tried to reconstruct how she might have gotten them, and why her fully clothed body had been in the master bathroom. That location, if we were correct about it, was unexpected and odd. Her jeans had not been undone, for when I had recovered the zipper it had been zipped shut, and certainly her buttocks had been covered. Based on the synthetic fabric that had melted into her flesh, I also had no reason to suspect that her breasts had been exposed, not that any of these findings ruled out a sexual assault. But they certainly argued against one.

I was checking the bones through a veil of steam when the telephone rang, startling me. At first I thought it might be some funeral home with a body to deliver, but then I realized that the flashing light was one of the lines for the autopsy room. I could not help but remember what Ruffin had said about spooky early morning calls, and I halfway expected to hear no one on the other end.

"Yes," I said abruptly.

"Geez, who pissed in your cornflakes?" Marino answered back.

"Oh," I said, relieved. "Sorry, I thought it was someone playing pranks."

"What do you mean, *pranks*?"

"Later," I said. "What's going on?"

"I'm sitting in your parking lot and was hoping you might let me in."

"I'll be right there."

In fact, I was very pleased to have company. I hurried to the enclosed bay, and I pushed a button on a wall. The huge door began to crank up, and Marino ducked under it, the dark night smudged with sodium vapor lights. I realized the sky had gotten overcast with clouds that portended rain.

"Why are you here so late?" Marino asked in his usual grumpy way as he sucked on a cigarette.

"My office is smoke-free," I reminded him.

"Like anybody in this joint's gotta worry about secondary smoke."

"A few of us are still breathing," I said.

He flicked the cigarette to the concrete floor and irritably crushed it with his foot, as if we had never been through this routine, not even once in our lives. In fact, this had gotten to be a standard act with us that in its own dysfunctional way somehow reaffirmed our bond to each other. I was quite certain that Marino's feelings would be injured if I didn't nag him about something.

"You can follow me into the decomp room," I said to him as I shut the bay door. "I'm in the middle of something."

"I wish I'd known before," he complained. "I would've just dealt with you over the phone."

"Don't worry. It's not too bad. I'm just cleaning up some bones."

"Maybe that ain't bad to you," he said, "but I've never gotten used to smelling people cook."

We walked inside the decomposition room and I handed him a surgical mask. I checked the processing to see how it was going and turned the heat down fifty degrees to make sure the water did not boil over and knock bones against each other and the sides of the pot. Marino bent the mask to fit over his nose and mouth and tied sloppy bows in the back. He spotted a box of disposable gloves, snatched a pair and worked them on. It was ironical that he was obsessive in his concerns about outside agents invading his health, when in fact the gravest danger was simply the way he lived. He was sweating in khakis and a white shirt and tie and at some point during the day had been assaulted by ketchup.

"Got a couple interesting things for you, Doc," he said, leaning against a brightly polished sink. "We ran the tags on the burned-up Mercedes behind Kenneth Sparkes's house, and it comes back to an '81 Benz 240D, blue. The odometer's probably rolled over at least twice. Registration's a little scary, comes back to a Dr. Newton Joyce in Wilmington, North Carolina. He's in the book but I couldn't get him, just his answering machine."

"Wilmington is where Claire Rawley went to school, and close to where Sparkes had his beach house," I reminded him.

"Right. So far the signs are still pointing that way."

He stared blankly at the steaming pot on the burner.

"She drives someone else's car to Warrenton and somehow gets inside Sparkes's house when he's not home, and gets murdered and burns up in a fire," he said, rubbing his temples. "I tell you, this one stinks about as bad as what you're cooking there, Doc. We're missing a really big piece, because nothing's making sense."

"Are there any Rawleys in the Wilmington area?" I asked. "Any possibility she has relatives there?"

"They got two listings, and neither of them have ever heard of a Rawley named Claire," he said.

"What about the university?"

"Haven't gotten to that yet," he answered as I went over to check the pot again. "Thought you were going to do that."

"In the morning."

"So. You gonna hang out here all night cooking this shit?"

"As a matter of fact," I said, turning off the burner, "I'm going to let it sit so I can go home. What time is it anyway? Oh God, almost nine o'clock. And I've got court in the morning."

"Let's blow this joint," he said.

I locked the door to the decomposition room, and I opened the bay door again. Through it I saw mountainous dark clouds blowing across the moon like boats in full sail, and the wind was wild and making eerie rushing sounds around the corners of my building. Marino walked me to my car and seemed in no hurry as he got out his cigarettes and lit one.

"I don't want to put any hinky ideas in your head," he said, "but there's something I think you ought to know."

I unlocked my car door and slid behind the wheel.

"I'm afraid to ask," I said, and I meant it.

"I got a call about four-thirty this afternoon from Rex Willis at the paper. The editorial columnist," he said.

"I know who he is."

I fastened my seat belt.

"Apparently he got a letter today from an anonymous source, kind of in the format of a press release. It's pretty bad."

"About what?" I said as an alarm shot through my blood.

"Well, it's supposedly from Carrie Grethen, and she's saying that she escaped from Kirby because she was framed by the feds and knew they'd execute her for something she didn't do unless she got away. She claims that at the time of the murders you were having an affair with the chief profiler in the case, Benton Wesley, and all the so-called evidence against her was doctored, made up, a conspiracy between the two of you to make the Bureau look good."

"And this was mailed from where?" I asked as outrage heated me up.

"Manhattan."

"And it was addressed specifically to Rex Willis?"

"Yup."

"And of course, he's not going to do anything with it."

Marino hesitated.

"Come on, Doc," he said. "When's the last time a reporter didn't do something with something?"

"Oh for God's sake!" I blurted out as I started the engine. "Has the media gone totally mad? They get a letter from a psycho and print it in the paper?"

"I've got a copy if you want to see it."

He dug a folded sheet of paper out of his back pocket and handed it to me.

"It's a fax," he explained. "The original's already at the lab. Documents is going to see what they can do with it."

I unfolded the copy with shaking hands, and did not recognize the neat printing in black ink. It was nothing like the bizarre red printing that was on the letter I had received from Carrie, and in this epistle, the words were very articulate and clear. For a moment I read, skimming over the ridiculous claims that she had been framed, my eyes stopping cold on the last long paragraph.

As for Special Agent Lucy Farinelli, she has enjoyed a successful career only because the ever influential chief medical examiner, Dr. Scarpetta, her aunt, has covered up her niece's mistakes and transgressions for years. When Lucy and I were both at Quantico, it was she who came on to me, not the other way around as it would most certainly be alleged in court. While it is true that we were lovers for a while, this was all manipulation on her part to get me to cover for her when she screwed up CAIN time and time again. Then she went on to take credit for work she'd never done. I'm telling you this is the God's truth. I swear it. And I'm asking you to please print this letter for all to see. I don't want to stay in hiding the rest of my life, convicted by society for terrible deeds I did not do. My only hope for freedom and justice is for people to see the truth and do something about it.

Have Mercy, Carrie Grethen

Marino quietly smoked until I was finished reading, then he said, "This person knows too much. I got no doubt the bitch wrote it."

"She writes me a letter that seems the work of someone deranged and then follows it with this, something that seems completely rational?" I said, and I was so upset I felt sick. "How does that make sense, Marino?"

He shrugged as the first drops of rain began to fall.

"I'll tell you what I think," he said. "She was sending you a signal. She wants you to know she's jerking everybody around. It wouldn't be fun for her if she couldn't piss you off and ruin your day."

"Does Benton know about this?"

"Not yet."

"And you really think the paper's going to print it," I asked again, hoping his answer would be different this time.

"You know how it goes."

He dropped the cigarette butt and it glowed to the ground and scattered in sparks.

"The story will be that this notorious psychopathic killer has contacted them while half of law enforcement is out there looking for the bitch," he said. "And the other bad news is that there's nothing to say she hasn't sent the same letter other places, too."

"Poor Lucy," I muttered.

"Yeah, well, poor everybody," Marino said.

7

Rain was slanted and flying down like nails as I made my way home, scarcely able to see. I had turned the radio off because I did not want to hear any more news this day, and I was certain this would be one night when I was too keyed up to sleep. Twice I slowed to thirty miles an hour as my heavy Mercedes sedan splashed through water like a cigarette boat. On West Cary Street, dips and potholes were filled like tubs, and emergency lights streaking red and blue through the downpour reminded me to take my time.

It was almost ten o'clock when I finally pulled into my driveway and a note of fear was plucked in my heart when motion sensor lights did not come on near the garage door. The darkness was complete, with only the rumble of my car engine and drumming of rain to orient my senses as to what world I was in. For a moment, I deliberated about opening the garage door or speeding away.

"This is ridiculous," I said to myself as I pressed a button on the visor.

But the door did not respond.

"Damn!"

I shifted the car into reverse and backed up without being able to see the driveway or brick border or even the shrubbery, for that matter. The tree I swiped was small and did no harm, but I felt sure I had churned up part of the lawn as I maneuvered to the front of my house, where timers inside had at least turned lamps on and the light in the foyer. As for motion sensor lights on either side of the front steps, they were out, too. I reasonably told myself that the weather had caused a power outage earlier in the evening, causing a circuit breaker to be thrown.

Rain swept into my car as I opened the door. I grabbed my pocketbook and briefcase and bolted up the front steps. I was soaked to the skin by the time I unlocked the front door, and the silence that greeted me thrilled me with fear. Lights dancing across the keypad by the door meant the burglar alarm had gone off, or perhaps an electrical surge had screwed that up, too. But it did not matter. By now I was terrified and afraid to move. So I stood in the foyer, water dripping on the hardwood floor as my brain raced to the nearest gun.

I could not remember if I had returned the Glock to a drawer of the kitchen desk. That certainly would be closer than my office or bedroom, which were on the other side of the house. Stone walls and windows were buffeted by the wind and lashed by rain, and I strained to hear any other sounds, such as the creaking of an upstairs floor or feet on carpet. In a burst of panic, I suddenly dropped my briefcase and pocketbook from my hands and ran through the dining room and into the kitchen, my wet feet almost going out from under me. I yanked open the bottom right drawer in the desk and almost cried out in relief when I grabbed my Glock.

For a while I searched my house again, flipping on lights in every room. Satisfied that I had no unwanted guests, I checked the fuse box in the garage and flipped on the breakers that had tripped. Order was restored, the alarm reset, and I poured a tumbler of Black Bush Irish whiskey on the rocks and waited for my nerves to tuck themselves back inside their sheaths. Then I called Johnson's Motel in Warrenton, but Lucy was not there. So I tried her apartment in D.C. and Janet answered the phone.

"Hi, it's Kay," I said. "I hope I didn't wake anyone."

"Oh, hello, Dr. Scarpetta," said Janet, who could not call me by my first name no matter how many times I had told her to. "No, I'm just sitting here having a beer and waiting for Lucy."

"I see," I said, very disappointed. "She's on her way home from Warrenton?"

"Not for long. You ought to see this place. Boxes everywhere. It's a wreck."

"How are you holding up through all this, Janet?"

"I don't know yet," she said, and I detected a quiver in her voice. "It will be an adjustment. God knows, we've been through adjustments before."

"And I'm sure you'll get through this one with flying colors."

I sipped my whiskey and had no faith in what I'd just said, but at the moment I was grateful to hear a warm human voice.

"When I was married—ancient years ago—Tony and I were on two totally different planes," I said. "But we managed to find time for each other, quality time. In some ways, it was better like that."

"And you also got divorced," she politely pointed out.

"Not at first."

"Lucy won't be here for at least another hour, Dr. Scarpetta. Is there a message I can give her?"

I hesitated, not sure what to do.

"Is everything all right?" Janet then asked.

"Actually, no," I said. "I guess you haven't heard. I guess she hasn't heard either, for that matter."

I gave her a quick summary of Carrie's letter to the press, and after I had finished, Janet was as silent as a cathedral.

"I'm telling you because you'd better be prepared," I added. "You could wake up tomorrow and see this in the paper. You might hear it on the late news tonight."

"It's best you told me," Janet said so quietly I could barely hear her. "And I'll let Lucy know when she gets in."

"Tell her to call me, if she's not too tired."

"I'll tell her."

"Good night, Janet."

"No, it isn't. It isn't a good night at all," she said. "That bitch has been ruining our lives for years. One way or another. And I've fucking had enough of it! And I'm sorry to use that word."

"I've said it before."

"I was there, for God's sake!" She began to cry. "Carrie was all over her, the manipulative psycho bitch. Lucy never stood a chance. My God, she was just a kid, this genius kid who probably should have stayed in college where she belonged instead of doing an internship with the Fucking Bureau of Investigation. Look, I'm still FBI, okay? But I see the shit. And they haven't done right by her, which just makes her all the more vulnerable to what Carrie is doing."

My whiskey was half gone, and there wasn't enough of it in the world to make me feel better right now.

"She doesn't need to get upset, either," Janet went on in a gush of frankness about her lover that I had never before heard. "I don't know if she's told you. In fact, I don't think she ever intended to, but Lucy's been seeing a psychiatrist for two years, Dr. Scarpetta."

"Good. I'm glad to hear it," I said, disguising my hurt. "No, she hasn't told me, but I wouldn't necessarily expect her to," I added with the perfect voice of objectivity as the ache in my heart got more intense.

"She's been suicidal," Janet said. "More than once."

"I'm glad she's seeing someone," was all I could think to say as tears welled.

I was devastated. Why had Lucy not reached out to me?

"Most of the great achievers have their very dark passages," I said. "I'm just glad she's doing something about it. Is she taking anything?"

"Wellbutrin. Prozac weirded her out. One minute a zombie and bar-hopping the next."

"Oh." I could barely speak.

"She doesn't need any more stress or upheavals or rejections," Janet went on. "You don't know what it's like. Something knocks her off balance, and she's down for weeks, up and down, up and down, morbid and miserable one minute and Mighty Mouse the next."

She placed her hand over the receiver and blew her nose. I wanted to know the name of Lucy's psychiatrist but was afraid to ask. I wondered if my niece were bipolar and undiagnosed.

"Dr. Scarpetta, I don't want her . . ." She struggled, choking. "I don't want her to die."

"She won't," I said. "I can promise you that."

We hung up and I sat for a while on my bed, still dressed

and afraid to sleep because of the chaos inside my head. For a while I wept in fury and in pain. Lucy could hurt me more than anyone, and she knew it. She could bruise me to the bone and crush my heart, and what Janet had told me was, by far, the most devastating blow. I could not help but think of Teun McGovern's inquisitive mind when we had talked in my office, and she had seemed to know so much about Lucy's difficulties. Had Lucy told her and not me?

I waited for Lucy to call, and she didn't. Since I had not called Benton, at midnight, he finally called me.

"Kay?"

"Have you heard?" I said with feeling. "What Carrie has done?"

"I know about her letter."

"Damn it, Benton. Damn it all."

"I'm in New York," he surprised me by saying. "The Bureau's called me in."

"Well, okay. And they should have. You know her."

"Unfortunately."

"I'm glad you're there," I decided out loud. "Somehow it seems safer. Isn't that an ironical thing to say? Since when is New York safer?"

"You're very upset."

"Do you know anything more about where she is?" I swirled melting ice in my glass.

"We know she mailed her latest letter from a 10036 zip code, which is Times Square. The postdate is June tenth, yesterday, Tuesday."

"The day she escaped."

"Yes."

"And we still don't know how she did that."

"We still don't know," he said. "It's as if she beamed herself across the river."

"No, it's not like that," I said, weary and out of sorts. "Someone saw something and someone probably helped her. She's always been skilled at getting people to do what she wants."

"The profiling unit's had too many calls to count," he said. "Apparently she did a blitz mailing, all the major newspapers, including the *Post* and *The New York Times*."

"And?"

"And this is too juicy for them to drop in a basket, Kay. The hunt for her is as big as the one for the Unabomber or Cunanan, and now she's writing to the media. The story's going to run. Hell, they'll print her grocery list and broadcast her belches. To them she's gold. She's magazine covers and movies in the making."

"I don't want to hear anymore," I said.

"I miss you."

"You wouldn't if you were around me right now, Benton."

We said good night and I fluffed the pillow behind my back and contemplated another whiskey but thought better of it. I tried to imagine what Carrie would do, and the twisted path always led back to Lucy. Somehow, that would be Carrie's tour de force because she was consumed by envy. Lucy was more gifted, more honorable, more everything, and Carrie would not rest until she had appropriated that fierce beauty and sucked up every drop of Lucy's life. It was becoming clear to me that Carrie did not even need to be present to do it. All of us were moving closer to her black hole, and the power of her pull was shockingly strong.

My sleep was tortured, and I dreamed of plane crashes and sheets soaked with blood. I was in a car and then a train, and someone was chasing me. When I awakened at half past six, the sun was announcing itself in a royal blue sky, and puddles gleamed in the grass. I carried my Glock into the bathroom, locked the door and took a quick shower. When I shut the water off, I listened closely to make sure my burglar alarm wasn't going, and then I checked the keypad in my bedroom to make sure the system was still armed. All the while, I was aware of how paranoid and downright irrational my behavior was. But I could not help it. I was scared.

Suddenly Carrie was everywhere. She was the thin woman in sunglasses and baseball cap walking along my street, or the driver pulling up close behind me at the toll plaza, or the homeless woman in a shapeless coat who stared at me as I crossed Broad Street. She was anyone white with punk hair and body piercing, or anyone androgynous or oddly dressed, and all the while I kept telling myself I had not seen Carrie in more than five years. I had no idea what she looked like now and quite possibly would not recognize her until it was too late.

The bay door was open when I parked behind my office, and Bliley's Funeral Home was loading a body into the back of a shiny black hearse, as the rhythm continued of bringing and taking away.

"Pretty weather," I said to the attendant in his neat dark suit.

"Fine, how are you?" came the reply of someone who no longer listened.

Another well-dressed man climbed out to help, and stretcher legs clacked and the tailgate slammed shut. I waited for them to drive off, and I rolled down the big door after them.

My first stop was Fielding's office. It was not quite quarter after eight.

"How are we doing?" I asked as I knocked on his door.

"Come in," he said.

He was scanning books on his shelves, his lab coat straining around his powerful shoulders. Life was difficult for my deputy chief, who rarely could find clothes that fit, since he basically had no waist or hips. I remembered our first company picnic at my house, when he had lounged in the sun with nothing but cut-offs on. I had been amazed and slightly embarrassed that I could scarcely take my eyes off him, not because I had any thoughts of bed, but rather his raw physical beauty had briefly held me hostage. I could not comprehend how anyone could find time to look like that.

"I guess you've seen the paper," he said.

"The letter," I said as my mood sunk.

"Yes."

He slid out an outdated PDR and set it on the floor.

"Front page with a photo of you and an old mug shot of her. I'm sorry you have to put up with shit like this," he said, hunting for other books. "The phones up front are going crazy."

"What have we got this morning?" I changed the subject.

"Last night's car wreck from Midlothian Turnpike, passenger and driver killed. They're views, and DeMaio's already started on them. Other than that, nothing else."

"That's enough," I said. "I've got court."

"Thought you were on vacation."

"So did I."

"Seriously. Didn't get it continued. What? You were gonna have to come back from Hilton Head?"

"Judge Bowls."

"Huh," Fielding said with disgust. "He's done this to you how many times now? I think he waits to find out your void dates so he can decide on a court date that will totally screw you. Then what? You bust your butt to get back here and half the time he continues the case."

"I'm on the pager," I said.

"And you can guess what I'll be doing."

He pointed at the paperwork cascading from piles on his desk.

"I'm so behind I need a rearview mirror," he quipped.

"There's no point in nagging you," I said.

The John Marshall Courts Building was but a ten-minute walk from our new location, and I thought the exercise would do me good. The morning was bright, the air cool and clean as I followed the sidewalk along Leigh Street and turned south on Ninth, passing police headquarters, my pocketbook over my shoulder and an accordion file tucked under an arm.

This morning's case was the mundane result of one drug dealer killing another, and I was surprised to see at least a dozen reporters on the third floor, outside the courtroom door. At first I thought Rose had made a mistake on my schedule, for it never occurred to me that the media might have been there for me.

But the minute I was spotted, they hurried my way with television cameras shouldered, microphones pointed, and flashguns going off. At first I was startled, then I was angry.

"Dr. Scarpetta, what is your response to Carrie Grethen's letter?" asked a reporter from Channel 6.

"No comment," I said as I frantically cast about for the

commonwealth's attorney who had summoned me here to testify in his case.

"What about the conspiracy allegation?"

"Between you and your FBI lover?"

"That would be Benton Wesley?"

"What is your niece's reaction?"

I shoved past a cameraman, my nerves hopping like faulty wiring as my heart flew. I shut myself inside the small windowless witness room and sat in a wooden chair. I felt trapped and foolish, and wondered how I could have been so thick as not to consider that something like this might happen after what Carrie had done. I opened the accordion file and began going through various reports and diagrams, envisioning gunshot entrances and exits and which had been fatal. I stayed in my airless space for almost half an hour until the Commonwealth's attorney found me. We spoke for several minutes before I took the stand.

What ensued brought to fruition what had happened in the hallway moments before, and I found myself disassociating from the core of myself to survive what was nothing more than a ruthless attack.

"Dr. Scarpetta," said defense attorney Will Lampkin, who had been trying to get the best of me for years, "how many times have you testified in this court?"

"I object," said the C.A.

"Overruled," said Judge Bowls, my fan.

"I've never counted," I replied.

"But surely you can give us an estimate. More than a dozen? More than a hundred? A million?"

"More than a hundred," I said as I felt his lust for blood.

"And you have always told the truth to the juries and the judges?"

Lampkin paced slowly, a pious expression on his florid face, hands clamped behind his back.

"I have always told the truth," I answered.

"And you don't consider it somewhat dishonest, Dr. Scarpetta, to sleep with the FBI?"

"I object!" The C.A. was on his feet.

"Objection sustained," said the judge as he stared down at Lampkin, egging him on, really. "What is your point, Mr. Lampkin?"

"My point, Your Honor, is conflict of interest. It is widely known that Dr. Scarpetta has an intimate relationship with at least one law enforcement individual she has worked cases with, and she has also influenced law enforcement—both the FBI and ATF—when it comes to her niece's career."

"I object!"

"Overruled. Please get to the point, Mr. Lampkin," said the judge as he reached for his water and goaded some more.

"Thank you, Your Honor," Lampkin said with excruciating deference. "What I'm trying to illustrate is an old pattern here."

The four whites and eight blacks sat politely in the jury box, staring back and forth from Lampkin to me as if they were watching a tennis match. Some of them were scowling. One was picking at a fingernail while another seemed asleep.

"Dr. Scarpetta, isn't it true that you tend to manipulate situations to suit you?"

"I object! He's badgering the witness!"

"Overruled," the judge said. "Dr. Scarpetta, please answer the question."

"No, I absolutely do not tend to do that," I said with feeling as I looked at the jurors.

Lampkin plucked a sheet of paper off the table where his felonious nineteen-year-old client sat.

"According to this morning's newspaper," Lampkin hurried ahead, "you've been manipulating law enforcement for years . . ."

"Your Honor! I object! This is outrageous!"

"Overruled," the judge coolly stated.

"It says right here in black and white that you have conspired with the FBI to send an innocent woman to the electric chair!"

Lampkin approached the jurors and waved the photocopied article in their faces.

"Your Honor, for God's sake!" exclaimed the C.A., sweating through his suit jacket.

"Mr. Lampkin, please get on with your cross-examination," Judge Bowls said to the overweight, thick-necked Lampkin.

What I said about distance and trajectories, and what vital organs had been struck by ten-millimeter bullets, was a blur. I could scarcely remember a word of it after I hurried down the courthouse steps and walked swiftly without looking at anyone. Two tenacious reporters followed me for half a block, and finally turned back when they realized it was easier to talk to a stone. The unfairness of what had happened in the witness stand went beyond words. Carrie had needed to fire but one small round and already I was wounded. I knew this would not end.

When I unlocked the back door to my building, for an instant the glare of sunlight made it hard for me to see as I stepped inside the cool shaded bay. I opened the door leading inside and was relieved to see Fielding in the corridor, heading toward me. He was wearing fresh scrubs, and I supposed another case had come in.

"Everything under control?" I asked, tucking my sunglasses inside my pocketbook.

"A suicide from Powhatan. Fifteen-year-old girl shot herself in the head. It seems daddy wouldn't let her see her dirtbag boyfriend anymore. You look terrible, Kay."

"It's called a shark attack."

"Uh oh. Damn fucking lawyers. Who was it this time?" He was ready to beat somebody up.

"Lampkin."

"Oh, good ole *Lamprey the eel*!" Fielding squeezed my shoulder. "It's gonna be all right. Trust me. It really will be. You just gotta block out the bullshit and go on."

"I know." I smiled at him. "I'll be in the decomp room if you need me."

The solitary task of patiently working on bones was a welcome relief, for I did not want anyone on my staff to detect my dejection and fear. I switched on lights and shut the door behind me. I tied a gown over my clothes and pulled on two layers of latex gloves, and turned on the electric burner and took the lid off the pot. The bones had continued processing after I had left last night, and I probed them with a wooden spoon. I spread a plasticized sheet over a table. The skull had been sawn open during autopsy, and I carefully lifted the dripping calvarium, and the bones of the face with its calcined teeth, from tepid, greasy water. I set them on the sheet to drain.

I preferred wooden tongue depressors versus plastic spatulas to scrape tissue from bone. Metal instruments were out of the question because they would cause damage that might obviate our finding true marks of violence. I worked very carefully, loosening and defleshing while the rest of the skeletal remains quietly cooked in their steamy pot. For two hours I cleaned and rinsed until my wrists and fingers ached. I missed lunch, and in fact never thought of it. At almost two P.M. I found a nick in the bone beneath the temporal region where I had found hemorrhage, and I stopped and stared in disbelief.

I pulled surgical lamps closer, blasting the table with light. The cut to bone was straight and linear, no more than an inch in length and so shallow it easily could have been missed. The only time I had ever seen an injury similar to this was in the nineteenth-century skulls of people who had been scalped. In those instances, the nicks or cuts were not generally associated with temporal bone, but that meant nothing, really.

Scalping was not an exact surgical procedure and anything was possible. Although I had found no evidence that the Warrenton victim was missing areas of scalp and hair, I could not swear to it. Certainly, when we had found her, the head was not intact, and while a scalping trophy might involve most of the cranium, it might also mean the excision of a single lock of hair.

I used a towel to pick up the phone because my hands were unfit to touch anything clean. I paged Marino. For ten minutes I waited for him to call back while I continued to carefully scrape. But I found no other marks. This did not mean, of course, that additional injury had not been lost, for at least a third of the twenty-two bones of the skull were burned away. My mind raced through what I should do. I yanked off my gloves and threw them in the trash, and I was flipping through an address book I had gotten out of my purse when Marino called.

"Where the hell are you?" I asked as stress gushed toxins through my body.

"At Liberty Valance eating."

"Thank you for getting back to me so quickly," I said irritably.

"Gee, Doc. It must've been lost in space somewhere, because I just got it. What the shit's going on?"

I could hear the background noise of people drinking and enjoying food that was guaranteed to be heavy and rich but worth it.

"Are you on a pay phone?" I asked.

"Yeah, and I'm off duty, just so you know."

He took a swallow of something that I figured was beer.

"I've got to get to Washington tomorrow. Something significant has come up."

"Uh oh. I hate it when you say that."

"I found something else."

"You gonna tell me or do I have to stay up all night pacing?"

He had been drinking, and I did not want to talk to him about this now.

"Listen, can you go with me, assuming Dr. Vessey can see us?"

"The bones man at the Smithsonian?"

"I'll call him at home as soon as we get off the phone."

"I'm off tomorrow, so I guess I can squeeze you in."

I did not say anything as I stared at the simmering pot and turned the heat down just a little.

"Point is, count me in," Marino said, swallowing again.

"Meet me at my house," I said. "At nine."

"I'll be there with bells on."

Next I tried Dr. Vessey's Bethesda home and he answered on the first ring.

"Thank God," I said. "Alex? It's Kay Scarpetta."

"Oh! Well, how are you?"

He was always a bit befuddled and missing in action in the minds of the hoi polloi who did not spend their lives putting people back together again. Dr. Vessey was one of the finest forensic anthropologists in the world, and he had helped me many times before.

"I'll be much better if you tell me you're in town tomorrow," I said.

"I'll be working on the railroad as always."

"I've got a cut mark on a skull. I need your help. Are you familiar with the Warrenton fire?"

"Can't be conscious and not know about that."

"Okay. Then you understand."

"I won't be there until about ten and there's no place to park," he said. "I got in a pig's tooth the other day with aluminum foil stuck in it," he absently went on about whatever he'd been doing of late. "I guess from a pig roast, dug up in someone's backyard. The Mississippi coroner thought it was a homicide, some guy shot in the mouth."

He coughed and loudly cleared his throat. I heard him drink something.

"Still getting bear paws now and then," he went on, "more coroners thinking they're human hands."

"I know, Alex," I said. "Nothing has changed."

8

Marino pulled into my driveway early, at quarter of nine, because he wanted coffee and something to eat. He was officially not working, so he was dressed in blue jeans, a Richmond Police T-shirt, and cowboy boots that had lived a full life. He had slicked back what little hair had weathered his years, and he looked like an old beer-bellied bachelor about to take his woman to Billy Bob's.

"Are we going to a rodeo?" I asked as I let him in.

"You know, you always have a way of pissing me off."

He gave me a sour look that didn't faze me in the least. He didn't mean it.

"Well, I think you look pretty cool, as Lucy would say. I've got coffee and granola."

"How many times do I got to tell you that I don't eat friggin' birdseed," he grumbled as he followed me through my house.

"And I don't cook steak-egg biscuits."

"Well, maybe if you did, you wouldn't spend so many evenings alone."

"I hadn't thought about that."

"Did the Smithsonian tell you where we was going to park up there? Because there's no parking in D.C."

"Nowhere in the entire district? The President should do something about that."

We were inside my kitchen, and the sun was gold on windows facing it, while the southern exposure caught the river glinting through trees. I had slept better last night, although I had no idea why, unless my brain had been so overloaded it simply had died. I remembered no dreams, and was grateful.

"I got a couple of VIP parking passes from the last time Clinton was in town," Marino said, helping himself to coffee. "Issued by the mayor's office."

He poured coffee for me, too, and slid the mug my way, like a mug of beer on the bar.

"I figured with your Benz and those, maybe the cops would think we have diplomatic immunity or something," he went on.

"I'm supposing you've seen the boots they put on cars up there."

I sliced a poppyseed bagel, then opened the refrigerator door to take an inventory.

"I've got Swiss, Vermont cheddar, prosciutto."

I opened another plastic drawer.

"And Parmesan reggiano—that wouldn't be very good. No cream cheese. Sorry. But I think I've got honey, if you'd rather have that."

"What about a Vidalia onion?" he asked, looking over my shoulder.

"That I have."

"Swiss, prosciutto, and a slice of onion is just what the doctor ordered," Marino said happily. "Now that's what I call a breakfast."

"No butter," I told him. "I have to draw the line somewhere so I don't feel responsible for your sudden death."

"Deli mustard would be good," he said.

I spread spicy yellow mustard, then added prosciutto and onion with the cheese on top, and by the time the toaster oven had heated up, I was consumed by cravings. I fixed the same concoction for myself and poured my granola back into its tin. We sat at my kitchen table and drank Columbian coffee and ate while sunlight painted the flowers in my yard in vibrant hues, and the sky turned a brilliant blue. We were on I-95 North by nine-thirty, and fought little traffic until Quantico.

As I drove past the exit for the FBI Academy and Marine Corps base, I was tugged by days that no longer were, by memories of my relationship with Benton when it was new, and my anxious pride over Lucy's accomplishments in a law enforcement agency that remained as much a politically correct all-boys club as it had been during the reign of Hoover. Only now, the Bureau's prejudices and power-mongering were more covert as it marched forward like an army in the night, capturing jurisdictions and credits wherever it could as it pushed closer to becoming the official federal police force of America.

Such realizations had been devastating to me and were largely left unspoken, because I did not want to hurt the individual agent in the field who worked hard and had given his heart to what he believed was a noble calling. I could feel Marino looking at me as he tapped ash out his window.

"You know, Doc," he said. "Maybe you should resign."

He referred to my long-held position as the consulting forensic pathologist for the Bureau.

"I know they're using other medical examiners these days,"

he went on. "Bringing them in on cases instead of calling you. Let's face it, you haven't been to the Academy in over a year, and that's not an accident. They don't want to deal with you because of what they did to Lucy."

"I can't resign," I said, "because I don't work for them, Marino. I work for cops who need help with their cases and turn to the Bureau. There's no way I'll be the one who quits. And things go in cycles. Directors and attorneys general come and go, and maybe someday things will be better again. Besides, you are still a consultant for them, and they don't seem to call you, either."

"Yo. Well, I guess I feel the same way you do."

He pitched his cigarette butt and it sailed behind us on the wind of my speeding car.

"It sucks, don't it? Going up there and working with good people and drinking beer in the Boardroom. It all gets to me, if you want to know. People hating cops and cops hating 'em back. When I was getting started, old folks, kids, parents—they was happy to see me. I was proud to put on the uniform and shined my shoes every day. Now, after twenty years, I get bricks throwed at me in the projects and citizens don't even answer if I say good morning. I work my ass off for twenty-six years, and they promote me to captain and put me in charge of the training bureau."

"That's probably the place where you can do the most good," I reminded him.

"Yeah, but that's not why I got stuck there."

He stared out his side window, watching green highway signs fly by.

"They're putting me out to pasture, hoping I'll hurry up and retire or die. And I gotta tell you, Doc, I think about it a lot. Taking the boat out, fishing, taking the RV on the road and maybe going out west to see the Grand Canyon, Yosemite, Lake Tahoe, all those places I've always heard about. But then when it gets right down to it, I wouldn't know what to do with myself. So I just think I'll croak in the saddle."

"Not anytime soon," I said. "And should you retire, Marino, you can do like Benton."

"With all due respect, I ain't the consultant type," he said. "The Institute of Justice and IBM ain't gonna hire a slob like me. Doesn't matter what I know."

I didn't disagree or offer another word, because, with rare exception, what he had said was true. Benton was handsome and polished and commanded respect when he walked into a room, and that was really the only difference between him and Pete Marino. Both were honest and compassionate and experts in their fields.

"All right, we need to pick up 395 and head over to Constitution," I thought out loud as I watched signs and ignored urgent drivers riding my bumper and darting around me because going the speed limit wasn't fast enough. "What we don't want to do is go too far and end up on Maine Avenue. I've done that before."

I flicked on my right turn signal.

"On a Friday night when I was coming up to see Lucy."

"A good way to get carjacked," Marino said.

"Almost did."

"No shit?" He looked over at me. "What'd you do?"

"They started circling my car, so I floored it."

"Run anybody over?"

"Almost."

"Would you have kept on going, Doc? I mean, if you had run one of them over?"

"With at least a dozen of his buddies left, you bet your boots."

"Well, I'll tell you one thing," he said, looking down at his feet. "They ain't worth much."

Fifteen minutes later we were on Constitution, passing the Department of the Interior while the Washington Monument watched over the Mall, where tents had been set up to celebrate African-American art, and venders sold Eastern Shore crabs and T-shirts from the backs of small trucks. The grass between kiosks was depressingly layered with yesterday's trash, and every other minute another ambulance screamed past. We had driven in circles several times, the Smithsonian coiled in the distance like a dark red dragon. There was not a parking place to be found and, typically, streets were one way or abruptly stopped in the middle of a block, while others were barricaded, and harried commuters did not yield even if it meant your running into the back of a parked bus.

"I tell you what I think we should do," I said, turning on Virginia Avenue. "We'll valet park at the Watergate and take a cab."

"Who the hell would want to live in a city like this?" Marino griped.

"Unfortunately, a lot of people."

"Talk about a place that's screwed up," he went on. "Welcome to America."

The uniformed valet at the Watergate was very gracious and did not seem to think it odd when I gave him my car and asked him to hail a cab. My precious cargo was in the backseat, packed in a sturdy cardboard box filled with Styrofoam peanuts. Marino and I were let out at Twelfth and Constitution at not quite noon, and climbed the crowded steps of the National Museum of Natural History. Security had been intensified since the Oklahoma bombing, and the guard let us know that Dr. Vessey would have to come down and escort us upstairs.

While we waited, we perused an exhibit called *Jewels of the Sea*, browsing Atlantic thorny oysters and Pacific lions' paws while the skull of a duckbill dinosaur watched us from a wall. There were eels and fish and crabs in jars, and tree snails and a mosasaur marine lizard found in a Kansas chalk bed. Marino was beginning to get bored when the bright brass elevator doors opened and Dr. Alex Vessey stepped out. He had changed little since I had seen him last, still slight of build, with white hair and prepossessed eyes that, like those of so many geniuses, were perpetually focused somewhere else. His face was tan and perhaps more lined, and he still wore the same thick black-framed glasses.

"You're looking robust," I said to him as we shook hands.

"I just got back from vacation. Charleston. I trust you've been there?" he said as the three of us boarded the elevator.

"Yes," I replied. "I know the chief there very well. You remember Captain Marino?"

"Of course."

We rose three levels above the eight-ton African bush elephant in the rotunda, the voices of children floating up like wisps of smoke. The museum was, in truth, little more than a huge granite warehouse. Some thirty thousand human skeletons were stored in green wooden drawers stacked from floor to ceiling. It was a rare collection used to study people of the past, specifically Native Americans who of late had been determined to get their ancestors' bones back. Laws had been passed, and Vessey had been through hell on the Hill, his life's work halfway out the door and headed back to the not-so-wild west.

"We've got a repatriation staff that collects data to supply to this group and that," he was saying as we accompanied him along a crowded, dim corridor. "Respective tribes have to be informed as to what we've got, and it's really up to them to determine what's done. In another couple years, our American Indian material may be back in the earth again, only to be dug up again by archaeologists in the next century, my guess is."

He talked on as he walked.

"Every group is so angry these days they don't realize how much they're hurting themselves. If we don't learn from the dead, who do we learn from?"

"Alex, you're singing to the choir," I said.

"Yeah, well, if it was my great-grandfather in one of these drawers," Marino retorted, "I'm not so sure I'd feel too good about that."

"But the point is we don't know *who* is in these drawers, and neither do any of the people who are upset," said Vessey. "What we do know is that these specimens have helped us know a lot more about the diseases of the American Indian population, which is clearly a benefit to those now feeling threatened. Oh well, don't get me started."

Where Vessey worked was a series of small laboratory rooms that were a jumble of black counter space and sinks, and thousands of books and boxes of slides, and professional journals. Displayed here and there were the usual shrunken heads and shattered skulls and various animal bones mistaken as human. On a corkboard were large, painful photographs of the aftermath of Waco, where Vessey had spent weeks recovering and identifying the decomposing burned remains of Branch Davidians.

"Let's see what you've got for me," Vessey said.

I set my package on a counter and he slit the tape with a pocket knife. Styrofoam rattled as I dug out the cranium, then the very fragile lower portion of the skull that included the bones of the face. I set these on a clean blue cloth and he turned on lamps and fetched a lens.

"Right here," I directed him to the fine cut on bone. "It corresponds with hemorrhage in the temporal area. But around it, the flesh was too burned for me to tell anything about what sort of injury we were dealing with. I didn't have a clue until I found this on the bone."

"A very straight incision," he said as he slowly turned the skull to look at it from different angles. "And we're certain this wasn't perhaps accidentally done during autopsy, when, for example, the scalp was reflected back to remove the skull cap?"

"We're certain," I said. "And as you can see by putting the two together'—I fit the cranium back in place—"the cut is about an inch and a half below where the skull was opened during autopsy. And it's an angle that would make no sense if one were reflecting back the scalp. See?"

My index finger was suddenly huge as I looked through the lens and pointed.

"This incision is vertical versus horizontal," I made my case.

"You're right," he said, and his face was vibrant with interest. "As an artifact of autopsy, that would make no sense at all, unless your morgue assistant was drunk."

"Could it be maybe some kind of defense injury?" Marino suggested. "You know, if someone was coming at her with a knife. They struggle and her face gets cut?"

"Certainly that's possible," Vessey said as he continued to process every millimeter of bone. "But I find it curious that this incision is so fine and exact. And it appears to be the same depth from one end to the other, which would be unusual if one is swinging a knife at someone. Generally, the cut to bone would be deeper where the blade struck first, and then more shallow as the blade traveled down."

He demonstrated, an imaginary knife cutting straight down through air.

"We also have to remember that a lot depends on the assailant's position in relation to the victim when she was cut," I commented. "Was the victim standing or lying down? Was the assailant in front or behind or to one side of her or on top of her?"

"Very true," said Vessey.

He went to a dark oak cabinet with glass doors and lifted an old brown skull from a shelf. He carried it over to us and handed it to me, pointing to an obvious coarse cut in the left parietal and occipital area, or on the left side, high above the ear.

"You asked about scalpings," he said to me. "An eight- or nine-year-old, scalped, then burned. Can't tell the gender, but I know the poor kid had a foot infection. So he or she couldn't run. Cuts and nicks like this are fairly typical in scalpings."

I held the skull and for a moment imagined what Vessey had just said. I envisioned a cowering crippled child, and blood running to the earth as his screaming people were massacred and the camp went up in flames.

"Shit," Marino muttered angrily. "How do you do something like that to a kid?"

"How do you do something like that at all?" I said. Then to Vessey, I added, "The cut on this'—I pointed at the skull I had brought in—"would be unusual for a scalping."

Vessey took a deep breath and slowly blew out.

"You know, Kay," he said, "it's never exact. It's whatever happened at the time. There were many ways that Indians scalped the enemy. Usually, the skin was incised in a circle over the skull down to the galea and periosteum so it could be easily removed from the cranial vault. Some scalpings were simple, others involved ears, eyes, the face, the neck. In some instances multiple scalps were taken from the same victim, or maybe just the scalplock, or small area of the crown of the head, was removed. Finally, and this is what you usually see in old westerns, the victim was violently grabbed by his hair, the skin sliced away with a knife or saber."

"Trophies," Marino said.

"That and the ultimate macho symbol of skill and bravery," said Vessey. "Of course, there were cultural, religious, and even medicinal motives, as well. In your case," he added to me, "we know she wasn't successfully scalped because she still had her hair, and I can tell you the injury to bone strikes me as having been inflicted carefully with a very sharp instrument. A very sharp knife. Maybe a razor blade or box cutter, or even something like a scalpel. It was inflicted while the victim was alive and it was not the cause of death."

"No, her neck injury is what killed her," I agreed.

"I can find no other cuts, except possibly here."

He moved the lens closer to an area of the left zygomatic arch, or bone of the cheek. "Something very faint," he muttered. "Too faint to be sure. See it?"

I leaned close to him to look.

"Maybe," I said. "Almost like the thread of a spider web."

"Exactly. It's that faint. And it may be nothing, but

interestingly enough, it's positioned at very much the same angle as the other cut. Vertical versus horizonal or slanted."

"This is getting sick," Marino said ominously. "I mean, let's cut to the chase, no pun intended. What are we saying here? That some squirrel cut this lady's throat and mutilated her face? And then torched the house?"

"I guess that's one possibility," Vessey said.

"Well, mutilating a face gets personal," Marino went on. "Unless you're dealing with a loony tune, you don't find killers mutilating the faces of victims they don't have some sort of connection with."

"As a rule, this is true," I agreed. "In my experience where it hasn't been true is when the assailant is very disorganized and turns out to be psychotic."

"Whoever burned Sparkes's farm was anything but disorganized, you ask me," Marino said.

"So you're contemplating that this might be a homicide of a more domestic nature," Vessey said, now slowly scanning the cranium with the lens.

"We have to contemplate everything," I said. "But if nothing else, when I try to imagine Sparkes killing all his horses, I just can't see it."

"Maybe he had to kill them to get away with murder," Marino said. "So people would say what you just did."

"Alex," I said, "whoever did this to her made very sure we would never find a cut mark. And were it not for a glass door falling on top of her, there probably would have been virtually nothing of her left that would have given us any clue as to what happened. If we had recovered no tissue, for example, we wouldn't have known she was dead before the fire because we wouldn't be able to get a CO level. So what happens? She gets signed out as an accidental death, unless we prove arson, which so far we've been unable to do."

"There's no doubt in my mind that this is a classic case of arson-concealed homicide," Vessey said.

"Then why the hell hang around to cut on somebody?" Marino said. "Why not kill her and torch the joint and run like hell? And usually when these whackos mutilate, they get off on people seeing their handiwork. Hell, they display the bodies in a park, on a hillside next to a road, on a jogging trail, in the middle of the living room, right there for all to see."

"Maybe this person doesn't want us to see," I said. "It's very important that we not know he left a signature this time. And I think we need to run as exhaustive a computer search as we can, to see if anything even remotely similar to this has turned up anywhere else."

"You do that, and you bring in a lot of other people," Marino said. "Programmers, analysts, guys who run the computers at the FBI and big police departments like Houston, L.A., and New York. I guarantee you, someone's going to spill the beans and next thing this shit's all over the news."

"Not necessarily," I said. "It depends on who you ask."

We caught a cab on Constitution and told the driver to head toward the White House and cut over to the six hundred block of Fifteenth Street. I intended to treat Marino to the Old Ebbitt Grill, and at half past five, we did not have to wait in line but got a green velvet booth. I had always found a special pleasure in the restaurant's stained glass, mirrors, and brass gas lamps wavering with flames. Turtles, boars, and antelopes were mounted over the bar, and the bartenders never seemed to slow down no matter the time of day.

A distinguished-looking husband and wife behind us were talking about Kennedy Center tickets and their son's entering Harvard in the fall, while two young men debated whether lunch could go on the expense account. I parked my cardboard box next to me on the seat. Vessey had resealed it with yards of tape.

"I guess we should have asked for a table for three," Marino said, looking at the box. "You sure it doesn't stink? What if someone caught a whiff of it in here?"

"It doesn't stink," I said, opening my menu. "And I think it would be wise to change the subject so we can eat. The burger here is so good that even I break down now and then and order it."

"I'm looking at the fish," he said with great affectation. "You ever had them here?"

"Go to hell, Marino."

"All right, you talked me into it, Doc. Burger it is. I wish it were the end of the day so I could have a beer. It's torture to come to a joint like this and not have Jack Black or a tall one in a frosted mug. I bet they make mint juleps. I haven't had one of those since I was dating that girl from Kentucky. Sabrina. Remember her?"

"Maybe if you describe her," I said absently as I looked around and tried to relax.

"I used to bring her into the FOP. You was in there once with Benton, and I came over and introduced her. She had sort of reddish blond hair, blue eyes, and pretty skin. She used to roller skate competitively?"

I had no earthly idea whom he was talking about.

"Well'—he was still studying the menu—"it didn't last very long. I don't think she would have given me the time of day if it wasn't for my truck. When she was sitting high in that king cab you would've thought she was waving at everybody from a float in the Rose Bowl parade."

I started laughing, and the blank expression on his face only made matters worse. I was laughing so hard my eyes were streaming and the waiter paused and decided to come back later. Marino looked annoyed.

"What's wrong with you?" he said.

"I guess I'm just tired," I said, gasping. "And if you want a beer, you go right ahead. It's your day off and I'm driving."

This improved his mood dramatically, and not much later he was draining his first pint of Samuel Adams while his burger with Swiss and my chicken Caesar salad were served. For a while we ate and drifted in and out of a conversation while people around us talked loudly and nonstop.

"I said, do you want to go away for your birthday?" one businessman was telling another. "You're used to going wherever you want."

"My wife's the same way," the other businessman replied as he chewed. "Acts like I never take her anywhere. Hell, we go out to dinner almost every week."

"I saw on *Oprah* that one out of ten people owe more money than they can pay," an older woman confided to a companion whose straw hat was hanging from the hat rack by their booth. "Isn't that wild?"

"Doesn't surprise me in the least. It's like everything else these days."

"They do have valet parking here," one of the businessmen said. "But I usually walk."

"What about at night?"

"Shooo. Are you kidding? In D.C.? Not unless you got a death wish."

I excused myself and went downstairs to the ladies' room,

which was large and built of pale gray marble. No one else was there, and I helped myself to the handicap stall so I could enjoy plenty of space and wash my hands and face in private. I tried to call Lucy from my portable phone, but the signal seemed to bounce off walls and come right back. So I used a pay phone and was thrilled to find her at home.

"Are you packing?" I asked.

"Can you hear an echo yet?" she said.

"Ummm. Maybe."

"Well, I can. You ought to see this place."

"Speaking of that, are you up for visitors?"

"Where are you?" Her tone turned suspicious.

"The Old Ebbitt Grill. At a pay phone downstairs by the restrooms, to be exact. Marino and I were at the Smithsonian this morning, seeing Vessey. I'd like to stop by. Not only to see you, but I have a professional matter to discuss."

"Sure," she said. "We're not going anywhere."

"Can I bring anything?"

"Yeah. Food."

There was no point in retrieving my car, because Lucy lived in the northwest part of the city, just off Dupont Circle, where parking would be as bad as it was everywhere else. Marino whistled for a cab outside the grill, and one slammed on its brakes and we got in. The afternoon was calm and flags were wilted over roofs and lawns, and somewhere a car alarm would not stop. We had to drive through George Washington University, past the Ritz and Blackie's Steakhouse to reach Lucy and Janet's neighborhood.

The area was bohemian and mostly gay, with dark bars like The Fireplace and Mr. P's that were always crowded with well-built, body-pierced men. I knew, because I had been here many times in the past to visit my niece, and I noted that the lesbian bookstore had moved and there seemed to be a new health food store not too far from Burger King.

"You can let us out here," I said to the driver.

He slammed on the brakes again and swerved near the curb.

"Shit," Marino said as the blue cab raced away. "You think there's any Americans in this town?"

"If it wasn't for non-Americans in towns like this, you and I wouldn't be here," I reminded him.

"Being Italian's different."

"Really? Different from what?" I asked at the two thousand block of P Street, where we entered the D.C. Cafe.

"From them," he said. "For one thing, when our people got off the boat on Ellis Island, they learned to speak English. And they didn't drive taxi cabs without knowing where the hell they was going. Hey, this place looks pretty good."

The café was open twenty-four hours a day, and the air was heavy with sautéing onions and beef. On the walls were posters of gyros, green teas, and Lebanese beer, and a framed newspaper article boasted that the Rolling Stones had once eaten here. A woman was slowly sweeping as if it were her mission in life. She paid us no mind.

"You relax," I said to Marino. "This shouldn't take but a minute."

He found a table to smoke at while I went up to the counter and studied the yellow lit-up menu over the grill.

"Yes," said the cook as he pressed sizzling beef and slapped and cut and tossed browning chopped onions.

"One Greek salad," I said. "And a chicken gyro in pita and, let me see." I perused. "I guess a Kefte Kabob Sandwesh. I guess that's how you say it."

"To go?"

"Yes."

"I call you," he said as the woman swept.

I sat down with Marino. There was a TV, and he was watching *Star Trek* through a swarm of loud static.

"It's not going to be the same when she's in Philly," he said.

"It won't be."

I stared numbly at the fuzzy form of Captain Kirk as he pointed his phaser at a Klingon or something.

"I don't know," he said, resting his chin in his hand as he blew out smoke. "Somehow it just don't seem right, Doc. She had everything all figured out and had worked hard to get it that way. I don't care what she says about her transferring, I don't think she wants to go. She just doesn't believe she's got a choice."

"I'm not sure she does if she wants to stay on the track she's chosen."

"Hell, I believe you always got a choice. You see an ashtray anywhere?"

I spotted one on the counter and carried it over.

"I guess now I'm an accomplice," I said.

"You just nag me because it gives you something to do."

"Actually, I'd like you to hang around for a while, if that's all right with you," I said. "It seems I spend half my time trying to keep you alive."

"That's kind of an irony considering how you spend the rest of your time, Doc."

"Your order!" the cook called out.

"How 'bout getting me a couple of those baklava things. The one with pistachios."

"No," I said.

9

Lucy and Janet lived in a ten-story apartment building called The Westpark that was in the two thousand block of P Street, a few minutes' walk away. It was tan brick with a dry cleaner downstairs and the Embassy Mobile station next door. Bicycles were parked on small balconies, and young tenants were sitting out enjoying the balmy night, drinking and smoking, while someone practiced scales on a flute. A shirtless man reached out to shut his window. I buzzed apartment 503.

"Who goes there?" Lucy's voice came over the intercom.

"It's us," I said.

"Who's *us*?"

"The *us* with your dinner. It's getting cold," I said.

The lock clicked free to let us into the lobby, and we took the elevator up.

"She could probably have a penthouse in Richmond for what she pays to live here," Marino commented.

"About fifteen hundred a month for a two-bedroom."

"Holy shit. How's Janet going to make it alone? The Bureau can't be paying her more than forty grand."

"Her family has money," I said. "Other than that, I don't know."

"I tell you, I wouldn't want to be starting out these days." He shook his head as elevator doors parted.

"Now back in Jersey when I was just revving up my engines, fifteen hundred could've kept me in clover for a year. Crime wasn't like it is, and people were nicer, even in my bad-ass neighborhood. And here we are, you and yours truly, working on some poor lady who was all cut up and burned in a fire, and after we finish with her, it will be somebody else. It's like what's-his-name rolling that big rock up the hill, and every time he gets close, down it rolls again. I swear, I wonder why we bother, Doc."

"Because it would be worse if we didn't," I said, stopping before the familiar pale orange door and ringing the bell.

I could hear the deadbolt flip open, and then Janet was letting us in. She was sweating in FBI running shorts and a Grateful Dead T-shirt that looked left over from college.

"Come in," she said with a smile as Annie Lennox played loudly in the background. "Something smells good."

The apartment was two bedrooms and two baths forced into a very tight space that overlooked P Street. Every piece of furniture was stacked with books and layered with clothing, and dozens of boxes were on the floor. Lucy was in the kitchen, rattling around in cupboards and drawers as she gathered silverware and plates, and paper towels for napkins. She cleared a space on the coffee table and took the bags of food from me.

"You just saved our lives," she said to me. "I was getting hypoglycemic. And by the way, Pete, nice to see you, too."

"Damn, it's hot in here," he said.

"It's not so bad," Lucy said, and she was sweating, too.

She and Janet filled their plates. They sat on the floor and ate while I propped up on an armrest of the couch and Marino carried in a plastic chair from the balcony. Lucy was in Nike running shorts and a tank top, and dirty from head to heel. Both young women looked exhausted, and I could not imagine what they were feeling. Surely this was an awful time for them. Every emptying of a drawer and taping shut a box had to be another blow to the heart, a death, an end to who you were at that time in your life.

"The two of you have lived here, what? Three years?" I asked.

"Close to it," said Janet as she speared a forkful of Greek salad.

"And you'll stay in this same apartment," I said to Janet.

"For the time being. There's really no reason to move, and when Lucy pops in and out, she'll have some room."

"I hate to bring up an unpleasant subject," Marino said. "But is there any reason Carrie might know where you guys live?"

There was silence for a moment as both women ate. I reached over to the CD player to turn down the volume.

"*Reason?*" Lucy finally spoke. "Why would there be a reason for her to know anything about my life these days?"

"Hopefully there's no reason at all," Marino said. "But we got to think about it whether you two birds like it or not. This is the sort of neighborhood she would hang in and fit right in, so I'm asking myself, if I was Carrie and back out on the street, would I want to find where Lucy is?"

No one said a word.

"And I think we all know what the answer is," he went on. "Now finding where the doc lives is no big problem.

It's been in the newspapers enough, and if you find her, you find Benton. But you?"

He pointed at Lucy.

"You're the challenge, because Carrie'd been locked up for several years by the time you moved here. And now you're moving to Philly, and Janet's left here alone. And to be honest, I don't like that worth a damn, either."

"Neither of you is listed in the phone book, right?" I asked.

"No way," Janet said, and she was listlessly picking at her salad.

"What if someone called this building and asked for either of you?"

"They're not supposed to give out info like that," Janet said.

"*Not supposed to*," Marino said sardonically. "Yeah, I'm sure this joint's got state-of-the-art security. Must be all kinds of *high profile* people living here, huh?"

"We can't sit around worrying about this all of the time," Lucy said, and she was getting angry. "Can't we talk about something else?"

"Let's talk about the Warrenton fire," I said.

"Let's do."

"I'll be packing in the other room," Janet said appropriately, since she was FBI and not involved in this case.

I watched her disappear into a bedroom, and then I said, "There were some unusual and disturbing findings during the autopsy. The victim was murdered. She was dead before the fire started, which certainly points at arson. Have we made any further headway on how the fire might have been set?"

"Only through algebra," Lucy said. "The only hope here

is fire modeling, since there's no physical evidence that points at arson, only circumstantial evidence. I've spent a lot of time fooling around with Fire Simulator on my computer, and the predictions keep coming back to the same thing."

"What the hell is Fire Simulator?" Marino wanted to know.

"One of the routines in FPEtool, the software we use for fire modeling," Lucy explained patiently. "For example, we'll assume that flashover is reached at six hundred degrees Celsius—or one thousand, one hundred and twelve degrees Fahrenheit. So we plug in the data we know, such as the vent opening, area of surface, energy available from the fuel, fire virtual point of origin, room lining materials, wall materials, and so on and so on. And at the end of the day, we should get good predictions as to the suspect, or the fire in question. And guess what? No matter how many algorithms, procedures, or computer programs you try with this one, the answer's always the same. There's no logical explanation for how a fire this fast and hot could have started in the master bathroom."

"And we're absolutely sure it did," I said.

"Oh yeah," Lucy said. "As you probably know, that bathroom was a relatively modern addition built out from the master bedroom. And if you look at the marble walls, the cathedral ceiling we recovered, you can piece together this really narrow, sharply defined V pattern, with the apex pointing somewhere in the middle of the floor, most likely where the rug was, meaning the fire developed really fast and hot in that one spot."

"Let's talk about this famous rug," Marino said. "You light it, and what kind of fire do we get?"

"A lazy flame," Lucy answered. "Maybe two feet tall."

"Well, that didn't do it," I said.

"And what's also really telling," she went on, "is the destruction to the roof directly above. Now we're talking flames at least eight feet high above the fire's origin, with the temperature reaching about eighteen hundred degrees for the glass in the skylight to melt. About eighty-eight percent of all arsons are up from the floor, in other words the radiant heat flux . . ."

"What the hell's radiant heat flux?" Marino wanted to know.

"Radiant heat is in the form of an electromagnetic wave, and is emitted from a flame almost equally in all directions, three hundred and sixty degrees. Following me so far?"

"Okay," I said.

"A flame also emits heat in the form of hot gases, which weigh less than air, so up they go," Lucy, the physicist, went on. "A *convective* transfer of heat, in other words. And in the early stages of the fire, most of the heat transfer is convective. It moves up from its point of origin. In this case, the floor. But after the fire was going for a while and hot gas-smoke layers formed, the dominant form of heat transfer became *radiant*. It was at this stage that I think the shower door fatigued and fell on top of the body."

"And what about the body?" I asked. "Where would that have been during all this?"

Lucy grabbed a legal pad off the top of a box and clicked open a pen. She drew the outline of a room with a tub and shower and, in the middle of the floor, a tall narrow fire that was impinging upon the ceiling.

"If the fire was energetic enough to project flames to the ceiling, then we're talking about a high radiant flux. The body was going to be severely damaged unless there was a barrier between it and the fire. Something that absorbed radiant heat and energy—the tub and shower door—which would have protected areas of the body. I also think the body was at least some small distance from the point of origin. We could be talking feet, maybe a yard or two."

"I don't see any other way it could have happened," I agreed. "Clearly something protected much of it."

"Right."

"How the hell do you set off a torch like that without some sort of accelerant?" Marino asked.

"All we can hope is that something turns up in the labs," my niece said. "You know, since the fuel load can't account for the observed fire pattern, then something was added or modified, indicating arson."

"And you guys are working on a financial audit," Marino said to her.

"Naturally almost all of Sparkes's records burned up in the fire. But his financial people and accountant have been pretty helpful, to give the guy credit. So far there's no indication that money was a problem."

I was relieved to hear it. Everything I knew about this case so far argued against Kenneth Sparkes being anything but a victim. But this was not an opinion that was shared by most, I felt sure.

"Lucy," I said as she finished her gyro pita, "I think we're all in agreement that the MO of this crime is distinctive."

"Definitely."

"Let's just suppose," I went on, "for the sake of argument, that something similar has happened before, somewhere else. That Warrenton is simply part of a pattern of fires used to disguise homicides that are being committed by the same individual."

"It's certainly possible," Lucy said. "Anything is."

"Can we do a search?" I then asked. "Is there any database that might connect similar MOs in fires?"

She got up and threw food containers in a large trash bag in the kitchen.

"You want to, we can," she said. "With the Arson Incident System, or AXIS."

I was well acquainted with it and the new supersonic ATF wide area computer network called ESA, which was an acronym for Enterprise System Architecture, the result of ATF being mandated by Congress to create a national arson and explosive repository. Two hundred and twenty sites were hooked up to ESA, and any agent, no matter where he was, could access the central database, could pipe himself into AXIS with his laptop as long as he had a modem or a secure cellular line. This included my niece.

She led us back to her tiny bedroom, which was now depressingly bare save for cobwebs in corners and dust balls on the scuffed hardwood floor. The box springs were empty, the mattress still made with wrinkled peach sheets and upended against a wall, and rolled up in a corner was the colorful silk rug that I had given her for her last birthday. Empty dresser drawers were stacked on the floor. Her office was a Panasonic laptop on top of a cardboard box. The portable computer was in a shark-gray steel and magnesium case that met military specifications for being ruggedized, meaning it was vapor-proof and dust-proof and everything-proof and supposedly could be dropped and run over by a Humvee.

Lucy sat before it on the floor, Indian style, as if she were about to worship the great god of technology. She hit the enter key to turn the screen saver off, and ESA lit up rows of pixels at a time in electric blue, flashing a map of the United States on the next vivid screen. At a prompt, she typed in her user name and password, answered other secure prompts to work her way into the system, invisibly cruising through secret gateways on the Web, passing through one level at a time. When she had logged on to the case repository, she motioned for me to sit next to her.

"I can get you a chair if you want," she said.

"No, this is fine."

The floor was hard and unkind to my lower lumbar spine. But I was a good sport. A prompt asked her to enter a word or words or phrases that she wished the system to search for throughout the database.

"Don't worry about the format," Lucy said. "The text search engines can handle complete stream of consciousness. We can try everything from the size of the fire hose used to the materials the house was made of—all that fire safety info and stuff that's in your set forms fire departments fill out. Or you can go with your own key queries."

"Let's try *death*, *homicide*, *suspected arson*," I said.

"*Female*," Marino added. "And *wealth*."

"*Cut*, *incision*, *hemorrhage*, *fast, hot*," I continued thinking.

"What about *unidentified*," Lucy said as she typed.

"Good," I said. "And *bathroom*, I suppose."

"Hell, put *horses* in there," Marino said.

"Let's go ahead and give it a shot," Lucy proposed. "We can always try more words as we think of them."

She executed a search and then stretched her legs out and rolled her neck. I could hear Janet in the kitchen washing dishes, and in less than a minute, the computer came back with 11,873 records searched and 453 keywords found.

"That's since 1988," Lucy let us know. "And it also includes any cases from overseas in which ATF was called in to assist."

"Can we print out the four hundred and fifty-three records?" I asked.

"You know, the printer's packed, Aunt Kay." Lucy looked up apologetically at me.

"Then how about downloading the records to my computer," I said.

She looked uncertain.

"I guess that's all right," she said, "as long as you make sure . . . Oh, never mind."

"Don't worry, I'm used to confidential information. I'll make sure no one else gets hold of them."

I knew it was stupid when I said it. Lucy stared longingly into the computer screen.

"This whole thing's UNIX-based SQL." She seemed to be talking to no one. "Makes me crazy."

"Well, if they had a brain in their head, they'd have you here doing their computer shit," Marino said.

"I haven't made an issue of it," Lucy replied. "I'm trying to pay my dues. I'll ship those files to you, Aunt Kay."

She walked out of the room. We followed her into the kitchen, where Janet was rolling glasses in newspaper and carefully packing them into a Stor-All box.

"Before I head out," I said to my niece, "could we maybe go for a walk around the block or something? And just catch up?"

She gave me a look that was something less than trustful.

"What?" she said.

"I may not see you again for a while," I said.

"We can sit out on the porch."

"That would be fine."

We chose white plastic chairs in the open air above the street, and I shut the sliders behind us and watched crowds come alive at night. Taxis were not stopping, and the fireplace in the window of The Flame danced behind glass while men drank in the dark with each other.

"I just want to know how you are," I said to her. "I don't feel like you talk to me much."

"Ditto."

She stared out with a wry smile, her profile striking and strong.

"I'm all right, Lucy. As all right as I ever am, I guess. Too much work. What else has changed?"

"You always worry about me."

"I have since you were born."

"Why?"

"Because somebody should."

"Did I tell you Mother's getting a facelift?"

Just the thought of my only sibling made my heart turn hard.

"She had half her teeth crowned last year, now this," Lucy went on. "Her current boyfriend, Bo, has hung in there for almost a year and a half. *How 'bout that?* How many times can you screw before you need something else nipped and tucked?"

"Lucy."

"Oh, don't be self-righteous, Aunt Kay. You feel the same way about her that I do. How did I end up with such a piece of shit for a mother?"

"This isn't helping you in the least," I said quietly. "Don't hate her, Lucy."

"She hasn't said one fucking word about my moving to

Philadelphia. She never asks about Janet, or you, for that matter. I'm getting a beer. Do you want one?"

"Help yourself."

I waited for her in the growing dark, watching the shapes of people flow by, some loud and holding on to each other, while others moved alone with purpose. I wanted to ask Lucy about what Janet had told me, but I was afraid to bring it up. Lucy should tell me on her own, I reminded myself, as my physician's voice ordered that I should take control. Lucy popped open a bottle of Miller Lite as she returned to the balcony.

"So let's talk about Carrie just long enough for you to put your mind at ease," Lucy matter-of-factly stated, taking a swallow. "I have a Browning High-Power, and my Sig from ATF, and a shotgun—twelve gauge, seven rounds. You name it, I can get it. But you know? I think my bare hands would be enough if she dared to come around. I've had enough, you know?"

She lifted the bottle again. "Eventually you just make a decision and move on."

"What sort of decision?" I asked.

She shrugged.

"You decide you can't give someone any more power than you already have. You can't spend your days in fear of them or hating them," she explained her mindset. "So you give it up, in a sense. You go about your business, knowing that if the monster ever steps into your path, she'd better be ready for life or death."

"I think that's a pretty good attitude," I said. "Maybe the only attitude. I'm just not sure you really feel that way, but I hope so."

She stared up at an irregular moon, and I thought she was blinking back tears, but I couldn't be sure.

"The truth is, Aunt Kay, I could do all their computer stuff with one arm. You know?"

"You could probably do all the Pentagon's computer stuff with one arm," I said gently as my heart hurt more.

"I just don't want to push it."

I did not know how to answer her.

"I pissed off enough people because I can fly a helicopter and . . . Well, you know."

"I know all the things you can do, and that the list will probably only grow longer, Lucy. It's very lonely being you."

"Have you ever felt like that?" she whispered.

"Only all my life," I whispered back. "And now you know why I've always loved you the way I do. Maybe I get it."

She looked over at me. She reached out and sweetly touched my wrist.

"You'd better go," she said. "I don't want you driving when you're tired."

10

It was almost midnight when I slowed at the guard booth in my neighborhood, and the security officer on duty stepped out to stop me. This was highly unusual, and I feared he would tell me that my burglar alarm had been going half the night or yet one more oddball had tried to drive through to see if I was at home. Marino had been dozing for the past hour and a half, and he came to as I rolled down my window.

"Good evening," I said to the guard. "How are you doing, Tom?"

"I'm fine, Dr. Scarpetta," he said, leaning close to my car. "But you've had a few unusual events within the past hour or so, and I figured something wasn't right when I kept trying to reach you and you weren't home."

"What sort of events?" I asked as I began to imagine any number of threatening things.

"Two pizza delivery guys showed up at almost the same time. Then three taxis came to take you to the airport, one right after the other. And someone tried to deliver a construction Dumpster to your yard. When I couldn't get hold of you,

I turned every one of them around. They all said you had called them."

"Well, I certainly did not," I said with feeling as my bewilderment grew. "All this since when?"

"Well, I guess the truck with the Dumpster was here maybe around five this afternoon. Everything else since then."

Tom was an old man who probably wouldn't have had a clue as to how to defend the neighborhood should true danger ever come around the bend. But he was courteous and considered himself a true officer of the law and in his mind was probably armed and experienced in combat. He was especially protective of me.

"Did you get the names of any of these guys who showed up?" Marino asked loudly from the passenger seat.

"Domino's and Pizza Hut."

Tom's animated face was shadowed beneath the brim of his baseball cap.

"And the cabs were Colonial, Metro, and Yellow Cab. The construction company was Frick. Now I took the liberty to make a few calls. Every one of 'em had orders in your name, Dr. Scarpetta, including the times you called. I got it written down."

Tom could not hide how pleased he was when he slipped a square of notepaper from a back pocket and handed it to me. His role had been more than the usual this night, and he was almost intoxicated by it. I turned on the interior light and Marino and I scanned the list. The taxi and pizza orders had been placed between ten-ten and eleven, while the Dumpster order had been placed earlier in the afternoon with instructions for a late afternoon delivery.

"I know at least Domino's said it was a woman who called. I talked to the dispatcher myself. A young kid. According to him, you called and said to just bring a large thick crust pizza supreme to the gate and you'd get it from there. I got his name written down, too," Tom reported with great pride. "So none of this came from you, Dr. Scarpetta?" He wanted to make sure.

"No sir," I answered. "And if anything else shows up tonight, I want you to call me right away."

"Yo, call me, too," said Marino, and he jotted his home number on a business card. "I don't give a shit what time it is."

I handed Marino's card out my window and Tom looked at it carefully, even though Marino had passed through these gates more times than I could guess.

"You got it, Captain," Tom said with a deep nod. "Yes sir, anybody else shows up, I'm on the horn, and I can hold 'em till you get here, if you want me to."

"Don't do that," Marino said. "Some kid with a pizza's not going to know a damn thing. And if it's real trouble, I don't want you tangling with whoever it is."

I knew right then that he was thinking about Carrie.

"I'm pretty spry. But you got it, Captain."

"You did a great job, Tom," I complimented him. "I can't thank you enough."

"That's what I'm here for."

He pointed his remote control and raised the arm to let us through.

"I'm listening," I said to Marino.

"Some asshole harassing you," he said, his face grim in the intermittent bath of street lamps. "Trying to upset you, scare you, piss you off. And doing a pretty damn good job, I might add."

"You don't think Carrie . . ." I went ahead and started to say.

"I don't know," Marino cut me off. "But it wouldn't surprise me. Your neighborhood's been in the news enough times."

"I guess what would be good to know is if the orders were placed locally," I said.

"Christ," he said as I turned into my driveway and parked behind his car. "I sure as hell hope not. Unless it's someone else who's jerking you around."

"Take a number and stand in line."

I cut the engine.

"I can sleep on your couch if you want me to," Marino said as he opened his door.

"Of course not," I said. "I'll be fine. As long as no construction Dumpsters show up. That would be the last straw with my neighbors."

"I don't know why you live here, anyway."

"Yes, you do."

He got out a cigarette and clearly did not want to go anywhere.

"Right. The guard booth. Shit, talk about a placebo."

"If you don't feel okay to drive, I'd be pleased to have you stay on my couch," I said.

"Who, me?"

He fired his lighter and puffed smoke out the open car door.

"It ain't me I'm worried about, Doc."

I got out of my car and stood on the driveway, waiting for him. His shape was big and tired in the dark, and I suddenly was overwhelmed by sad affection for him. Marino was alone and probably felt like hell. He couldn't have memories worth much, between violence on the job and bad relationships the rest of the time. I supposed I was the only constant in his life, and although I was usually polite, I wasn't always warm. It simply wasn't possible.

"Come on," I said. "I'll fix you a toddy and you can crash here. You're right. Maybe I don't want to be alone and have five more pizza deliveries and cabs show up."

"That's what I'm thinking," he said with feigned cool professionalism.

I unlocked my front door and turned off the alarm, and very shortly Marino was on the wrap-around couch in my great room, with a Booker's bourbon on the rocks. I made his nest with sweet-smelling sheets and a baby-soft cotton blanket, and for a while we sat in the dark talking.

"You ever think we might lose in the end?" he muttered sleepily.

"Lose?" I asked.

"You know, *good guys always win*. How realistic is that? Not so for other people, like that lady that burned up in Sparkes's house. Good guys don't always win. Uh uh, Doc. No fucking way."

He halfway sat up like a sick man, and took a swallow of bourbon and struggled for breath.

"Carrie thinks she's gonna win, too, in case that thought's never entered your mind," he added. "She's had five fucking years at Kirby to think that."

Whenever Marino was tired or half drunk, he said *fuck* a lot. In truth, it was a grand word that expressed what one felt by the very act of saying it. But I had explained to him many times before that not everyone could deal with its vulgarity, and for that matter, some perhaps took it all too literally. I personally never thought of *fuck* as sexual intercourse, but rather of wishing to make a point.

"I can't entertain the thought that people like her will win," I said quietly as I sipped red burgundy. "I will never think that."

"Pie in the sky."

"No, Marino. Faith."

"Yo." He swallowed more bourbon. "Fucking faith. You know how many guys I've known to drop dead of heart attacks or get killed on the job? How many of them do you think had faith? Probably every goddamn one of them. Nobody thinks they're gonna die, Doc. You and me don't think it, no matter how much we know. My health sucks, okay? You think I don't know I'm taking a bite of a poison cookie every day? Can I help it? Naw. I'm just an old slob who has to have his steak biscuits and whiskey and beer. I've given up giving a shit about what the doctors say. So soon enough, I'm gonna stoop over in the saddle and be outta here, you know?"

His voice was getting husky and he was beginning to get maudlin.

"So a bunch of cops will come to my funeral, and you'll tell the next detective to come along how it wasn't all that bad to work with me," he went on.

"Marino, go to sleep," I said. "And you know that's not how I feel at all. I can't even think of something happening to you, you big idiot."

"You really mean that?" He brightened a bit.

"You know damn well I do," I said, and I was exhausted, too.

He finished his bourbon and softly rattled the ice in the glass, but I didn't respond, because he'd had enough.

"Know what, Doc?" he said thickly. "I like you a lot, even if you are a pain in the fucking ass."

"Thank you," I said. "I'll see you in the morning."

"It is morning."

He rattled ice some more.

"Go to sleep," I said.

I did not turn off my bedside lamp until two A.M., and thank God it was Fielding's turn to spend Saturday in the morgue. It was almost nine when I got motivated to put my feet on the floor, and birds were raucous in my garden, and the sun was bouncing light off the world like a manic child with a ball. My kitchen was so bright it was almost white, and stainless steel appliances were like mirrors. I made coffee and did what I could to clear my head as I thought of the files downloaded into my computer. I thought of opening sliders and windows to enjoy spring air, and then Carrie's face was before me again.

I went into the great room to check on Marino. He slept the way he lived, struggling against his physical existence as if it were the enemy, the blanket kicked practically to the middle of the floor, pillows beaten into shape, and sheets twisted around his legs.

"Good morning," I said.

"Not yet," he mumbled.

He turned over and punched the pillow to submission under his head. He wore blue boxer shorts and an undershirt that stopped six inches short of covering his swollen belly, and I always marveled that men were not shy about fat the way women were. In my own way I very much cared about staying in shape, and when my clothes starting feeling tight around the waist, both my general disposition and libido turned much less agreeable.

"You can sleep a few more minutes," I said to him.

I gathered up the blanket and spread it across him. He resumed snoring like a wounded wild boar, and I moved to the kitchen table and called Benton at his New York hotel.

"I hope I didn't wake you," I said.

"Actually, I was almost out the door. How are you?"

He was warm but distracted.

"I'd be better if you were here and she were back behind bars."

"The problem is, I know her patterns and she knows I know them. So I may as well not know them, if you see what I mean," he said in that controlled tone that meant he was angry. "Last night, several of us disguised ourselves as homeless people and went down into the tunnels in the Bowery. A lovely way to spend the evening, I might add. We revisited the spot where Gault was killed."

Benton was always very careful to say *where Gault was killed* instead of *where you killed Gault*.

"I am convinced she's gone back there and will again," he went on. "And not because she misses him, but that any reminder of the violent crimes they committed together excites her. The thought of his blood excites her. For her it's a sexual high, a power rush that she's addicted to, and you and I both know what that means, Kay. She'll need a fix soon, if she hasn't already gotten one that we just haven't found out about yet. I'm sorry to be a doomsayer, but I have a gut feeling that whatever she does is going to be far worse than what she did before."

"It's hard to imagine anything could be worse than that," I said, though I really did not mean it.

Whenever I had thought that human beings could get no worse, they did. Or perhaps it was simply that primitive evil seemed more shocking in a civilization of highly evolved humans who traveled to Mars and communicated through cyberspace.

"And so far no sign of her," I said. "Not even a hint."

"We've gotten hundreds of leads going nowhere. NYPD's set up a special task force, as you know, and there's a command center with guys taking calls twenty-four hours a day."

"How much longer will you stay up there?"

"Don't know."

"Well, I'm sure if she's still in the area, she knows damn well where you are. The New York Athletic Club, where you always stay. Just two buildings from where she and Gault had a room back then." I was upset again. "I guess that's the Bureau's idea of sticking you in a shark cage and waiting for her to come and get it."

"A good analogy," he said. "Let's hope it works."

"And what if it does?" I said as fear cut through my blood and made me angrier. "I wish you'd come home and let the FBI do its job. I can't get over it, you retire and they don't give you the time of day until they want to use you for bait . . . !"

"Kay . . ."

"How can you let them use you . . ."

"It's not like that. This is my choice, a job I have to finish. She was my case from the start, and as far as I'm concerned, she still is. I can't just relax at the beach knowing she's loose and going to kill again. How can I just look the other way when you, Lucy, Marino—when all of us are very possibly in danger?"

"Benton, don't turn into a Captain Ahab, okay? Don't let this become your obsession. Please."

He laughed.

"Take me seriously, goddamn it."

"I promise I'll stay away from white whales."

"You're already chasing the hell out of one."

"I love you, Kay."

As I followed the hallway to my office, I wondered why I bothered saying the same old words to him. I knew his behavior almost as well as I knew my own, and the idea that he wouldn't be doing exactly what he was right now was about as unthinkable as my letting another forensic pathologist take over the Warrenton case because it was my right to take it easy at this stage in my life.

I turned on the light in my spacious paneled office, and opened the blinds to let the morning in. My work space adjoined my bedroom, and not even my housekeeper knew that all of the windows in my private quarters, like those in my downtown office, were bulletproof glass. It wasn't just the Carries of the world who worried me. Unfortunately, there were the countless convicted killers who blamed me for their convictions, and most of them did not stay locked up forever. I had gotten my share of letters from violent offenders who promised to come see me when they got out. They liked the way I looked or talked or dressed. They would do something about it.

The depressing truth, though, was that one did not have to be a detective or profiler or chief medical examiner to be a potential target of predators. Most victims were vulnerable. They were in their cars or carrying groceries into their homes or walking through a parking lot, simply, as the saying goes, in the wrong place at the wrong time. I logged onto America Online and found Lucy's ATF repository research files in my mailbox. I executed a print command and returned to the kitchen for more coffee.

Marino walked in as I was contemplating something to eat. He was dressed, his shirttail hanging out, his face dirty with stubble.

"I'm outta here," he said, yawning.

"Would you like coffee?"

"Nope. Something on the road. Probably stop at Liberty Valance," he said as if we'd never had our discussion about his eating habits.

"Thanks for staying over," I said.

"No problem."

He waved at me as he walked out, and I set the alarm after him. I returned to my study, and the growing stack of paper was rather disheartening. After five hundred pages, I had to refill the paper tray, and the printer ran another thirty minutes. The information included the expected names, dates, and locations, and narratives from investigators. In addition, there were scene drawings and laboratory results, and in some instances, photographs that had been scanned in. I knew it would take me the rest of the day, at the very least, to get through the stack. I was already feeling that this had probably been a Pollyanna idea that would prove a waste of time.

I had gone through no more than a dozen cases when I was startled by my doorbell. I was not expecting anyone, and I almost never had unannounced visitors in my private, gated neighborhood. I suspected it might be one of the local children selling raffle tickets or magazine subscriptions or candy, but when I looked into the video screen of my camera system, I was stunned to see Kenneth Sparkes standing outside my door.

"Kenneth?" I said into the Aiphone, and I could not keep the surprise out of my voice.

"Dr. Scarpetta, I apologize," he said into the camera. "But I really need to speak to you."

"I'll be right there."

I hurried across the house, and opened the front door. Sparkes looked weary in wrinkled khaki slacks and a green polo shirt spotted with sweat. He wore a portable phone and a pager on his belt, and carried a zip-up alligator portfolio.

"Please come in," I said.

"I know most of your neighbors," he said. "In case you're wondering how I got past the guard booth."

"I've got coffee made."

I caught the scent of his cologne as we entered the kitchen.

"Again, I hope you'll forgive me for just showing up like this," he said, and his concern seemed genuine. "I just don't know who else to talk to, Dr. Scarpetta, and I was afraid if I asked you first, you would say no."

"I probably would have."

I got two mugs out of a cabinet.

"How do you take it?"

"The way it comes out of the pot," he said.

"Would you like some toast or anything?"

"Oh no. But thank you."

We sat at the table before the window, and I opened the door leading outside because my house suddenly seemed warm and stuffy. Misgivings raced through my mind as I was reminded that Sparkes was a suspect in a homicide, and that I was deeply involved in the case, and here I was alone with him in my house on a Saturday morning. He set the portfolio on the table and unzipped it.

"I suppose you know everything about what goes on in an investigation," he said.

"I never know everything about anything, really."

I sipped my coffee.

"I'm not naive, Kenneth," I said. "For example, if you didn't have clout, you wouldn't have gotten inside my neighborhood, and you wouldn't be sitting here now."

He withdrew a manila envelope from the portfolio and slid it across the table to me.

"Photographs," he said quietly. "Of Claire."

I hesitated.

"I spent the last few nights in my beach house," he went on to explain.

"In Wrightsville Beach?" I said.

"Yes. And I remembered these were in a filing cabinet drawer. I hadn't looked at them or even thought of them since we broke up. They were from some photo shoot. I don't recall the details, but she gave me copies when we first started seeing each other. I guess I told you she did some photographic modeling."

I slid what must have been about twenty eight-by-ten color prints from the envelope, and the one on top was startling. It was true what the governor had said to me at Hootowl Farm. Claire Rawley was physically magnificent. Her hair was to the middle of her back, perfectly straight, and seemed spun of gold as she stood on the beach in running shorts and a skimpy tank top that barely covered her breasts. On her right wrist she wore what appeared to be a large diving watch with a black plastic band and an orange face. Claire Rawley looked like a Nordic goddess, her features striking and sharp, her tan body athletic and sensual. Behind her on the sand was a yellow surfboard, and in the distance a sparkling ocean.

Other photographs had been taken in other dramatic

settings. In some she was sitting on the porch of a decaying Gothic southern mansion, or on a stone bench in an overgrown cemetery or garden, or playing the part of hard-working mate surrounded by weathered fishermen on one of Wilmington's trawlers. Some of the poses were rather slick and contrived, but it made no difference. In all, Claire Rawley was a masterpiece of human flesh, a work of art whose eyes revealed fathomless sadness.

"I didn't know if these might be of any use to you," Sparkes said after a long silence. "After all, I don't know what you saw, I mean what was . . . Well."

He tapped the table nervously with his index finger.

"In cases such as these," I told him calmly, "a visual identification simply isn't possible. But you never know when something like this might help. At the very least, there's nothing in these photos that might tell me the body *isn't* Claire Rawley."

I scanned the photographs again, to see if I noted any jewelry.

"She's wearing an interesting watch," I said, shuffling through the photographs again.

He smiled and stared. Then he sighed.

"I gave that to her. One of these trendy sports watches that's very popular with surfers. It had an off-the-wall name. *Animal?* Does that sound right?"

"My niece may have had one of those once," I recalled. "Relatively inexpensive? Eighty, ninety dollars?"

"I don't remember what I paid. But I bought it at the surf shop where she liked to hang out. Sweetwater Surf Shop on South Lumina, where Vito's, Reddog's, and Buddy's Crab are. She lived near there with several other women. An old not-so-nice condo on Stone Street."

I was writing this down.

"But it was on the water. And that's where she wanted to be."

"And what about jewelry? Do you remember her wearing anything unusual?"

He had to think.

"Maybe a bracelet?"

"I don't recall."

"Her keychain?"

He shook his head.

"What about a ring?" I then asked.

"She wore funky ones now and then. You know, silver ones that didn't cost much."

"What about a platinum band?"

He hesitated, knocked off balance.

"You said platinum?" he asked.

"Yes. And a fairly large size, too."

I stared at his hands.

"In fact, it might fit you."

He leaned back in his chair and looked up at the ceiling.

"My God," he said. "She must have taken it. I have a simple platinum band I used to wear when Claire and I were together. She used to joke that it meant I was married to myself."

"So she took it from your bedroom?"

"From a leather box. She must have."

"Are you aware of anything else missing from the house?" I then asked.

"One gun from my collection is unaccounted for. ATF recovered all the rest. Of course, they're ruined."

He was getting more depressed.

"What kind of gun?"

"A Calico."

"I hope that's not out on the street somewhere," I said with feeling.

A Calico was an especially nasty submachine gun that looked rather much like an Uzi with a large cylinder attached to the top of it. It was nine-millimeter and capable of firing as many as a hundred rounds.

"You need to report all this to the police, to ATF," I told him.

"Some of it I already have."

"Not some. All of it, Kenneth."

"I understand," he said. "And I will. But I want to know if it's her, Dr. Scarpetta. Please understand that I don't care about much else at the moment. I will confess to you that I have called her condo. Neither of her roommates have seen her for over a week. Last she spent the night in her place was the Friday night before the fire, the day before it, in other words. The young lady I talked to said Claire seemed distracted and depressed when they ran into each other in the kitchen. She made no mention of going out of town."

"I see that you are quite an investigator," I said.

"Wouldn't you be if you were me?" he asked.

"Yes."

Our eyes met and I read his pain. Tiny beads of sweat followed the line of his hair, and he talked as if his mouth were dry.

"Let's get back to the photos," I said. "Exactly why were these photos taken? Modeling for whom? Do you know?"

"Something local, as I vaguely recall it," he said, staring past me out the window. "I think she told me it might have been a Chamber of Commerce thing, something to help advertise the beach."

"And she gave you all these for what reason?"

I continued slowly going through the pictures.

"Just because she liked you? Perhaps she wanted to impress you?"

He laughed ruefully.

"I wish those were the only reasons," he replied. "She knows I have influence, that I know people in the film industry and so on. And I'd like you to hang on to these photos, please."

"So she was hoping you might help her career," I said, looking up at him.

"Of course."

"And did you?"

"Dr. Scarpetta, it's a simple fact of life that I have to be careful of who and what I promote," he stated candidly. "And it would not have looked especially appropriate if I were handing around photos of my beautiful, young white lover in hopes that I might help her career. I tend to keep my relationships as private as possible."

Indignation shone in his eyes as he fingered his coffee mug.

"It isn't me who broadcasts my personal life. Never has been. And I might add that you shouldn't believe everything you read."

"I never do," I said. "I of all people know better than that, Kenneth. To be honest, I'm not as interested in your personal life as I am in knowing why you have chosen to give these photos to me instead of to Fauquier County investigators or ATF."

He looked steadily at me, and then replied, "For identification reasons I've already stated. But I also trust you, and that's the more important element in the equation. No matter our differences, I know you would not railroad anyone or falsely accuse."

"I see."

I was feeling more uncomfortable by the moment and frankly wished he would decide to leave so I didn't have to do it for him.

"You see, it would be far more convenient to blame everything on me. And there are plenty of people out there who have been after me for years, people who would love to see me ruined or locked up or dead."

"None of the investigators I'm working with feel that way," I said.

"It's not you or Marino or ATF I'm worried about," he quickly replied. "It's factions who have political power. White supremacists, militia types who are secretly in bed with people whose names you know. Trust me."

He stared off, his jaw muscles knotting.

"The deck's stacked against me," he went on. "If someone doesn't get to the bottom of what happened here, my days are numbered. I know it. And anyone who can slaughter innocent, helpless horses can do anything."

His mouth trembled and his eyes brightened with tears.

"Burning them alive!" he exclaimed. "What kind of monster could do something like that!"

"A very terrible monster," I said. "And it seems there are many terrible monsters in the world these days. Can you tell me about the foal? The one I saw when I was at the scene? I assumed one of your horses somehow got away?"

"Windsong," he verified what I expected as he wiped his eyes on his napkin. "The beautiful little fella. He's actually a yearling, and he was born right on my farm, both parents were very valuable racehorses. They died in the fire." He got choked up again. "How Windsong got out I have no clue. It's just bizarre."

"Unless Claire—if it is Claire—perhaps had him out and never got a chance to put him back in his stall?" I suggested. "Perhaps she had met Windsong during one of her visits to your farm?"

Sparkes took a deep breath, rubbing his eyes. "No, I don't think Windsong had been born yet. In fact, I remember Wind, his mother, was pregnant during Claire's visits."

"Then Claire might have assumed that Windsong was Wind's yearling."

"She might have figured that out."

"Where is Windsong now?" I asked.

"Thankfully he was captured and is at Hootowl Farm, where he is safe and will be well taken care of."

The subject of his horses was devastating to him, and I did not believe he was performing. Despite his skills as a public figure whose talent was to change polls and people, Sparkes could not be this good an actor. His self-control was about to collapse, and he was struggling mightily and about to succumb. He pushed back his chair and got up from my table.

"One other thing I should tell you," he said as I walked him to the front door. "If Claire were alive, I believe she would have tried to contact me, somehow. If nothing else, through a letter. Providing she knew about the fire, and I don't know how she couldn't have known about it. She was very sensitive and kind, no matter her difficulties."

"When was the last time you saw her?" I opened the front door.

Sparkes looked into my eyes, and once again I found the intensity of his personality as compelling as it was disturbing.

I could not abide the thought that he still somewhat intimidated me.

"I suppose a year ago or so."

His silver Jeep Cherokee was in the drive, and I waited until he was inside it before I shut the door. I could not help but wonder what my neighbors might have thought had they recognized him in my driveway. On another occasion, I might have laughed, but I found nothing the least bit amusing about his visit. Why he had come in person instead of having the photographs delivered to me was my first important question.

But he had not been inappropriate in his curiosity about the case. He had not used his power and influence to try to manipulate me. He had not attempted to influence my opinions or even my feelings about him, at least not that I could tell.

11

I heated up my coffee and returned to my study. For a while, I sat in my ergonomically correct chair and went through Claire Rawley's photographs again and again. If her murder was premeditated, then why did it just so happen to occur while she was somewhere she was not supposed to be?

Even if Sparkes's enemies were to blame, wasn't it a bit too coincidental for them to strike when she just happened to have showed up, uninvited, at his house? Would even the coldest racist burn horses alive, just to punish their owner?

There were no answers, and I began going through the ATF cases again, scanning page after page as hours sped by and my vision went in and out of focus. There were church burnings, residential and business fires, and a series of bowling alleys with the point of origin always the same lane. Apartments and distilleries and chemical companies and refineries had blazed into annihilation, and in all instances, the causes were suspicious even if arson could not be proven.

As for homicides, they were more unusual and usually

perpetrated by the relatively unskilled robber or spouse who did not understand that when an entire family disappears and bone fragments turn up in a pit where trash is burned in the back, the police most likely will be called. Also, people already dead don't breathe CO or have bullets in them that show up on X-ray. By ten o'clock that evening, I had, however, come across two deaths that held my attention. One had happened this past March, the other six months before that. The more recent case had occurred in Baltimore, the victim a twenty-five-year-old male named Austin Hart who was a fourth-year medical student at Johns Hopkins when he died in a house fire not far off campus. He had been the only one home at the time because it was spring break.

According to the brief police narrative, the fire started on a Sunday evening and was fully involved by the time the fire department got there. Hart was so badly burned, he could be identified only by striking similarities of tooth root and trabecular alveolar bone points in antemortem and postmortem radiographs. The origin of fire was a bathroom on the first floor, and no electrical arcing, no accelerants were detected.

ATF had been involved in the case upon invitation by the Baltimore fire department. I found it interesting that Teun McGovern had been called in from Philadelphia to lend her expertise, and that after weeks of painstaking sifting through debris and interviewing witnesses and conducting examinations at ATF's Rockville labs, the evidence suggested the fire was incendiary, and the death, therefore, a homicide. But neither could be proven, and fire modeling could not begin to account for how such a fast-burning fire could have started in a tiny tiled bathroom that had nothing in it but a porcelain sink and toilet, a window shade, and a tub enclosed in a plastic curtain.

The fire before that, in October, happened in Venice Beach, California, again at night, in an ocean front house within ten blocks of the legendary Muscle Beach gym. Marlene Farber was a twenty-three-year-old actress whose career consisted mainly of small parts on soap operas and sitcoms, with most of her income generated from television commercials. The details of the fire that burned her cedar shake house to the ground were just as sketchy and inexplicable as those of Austin Hart's.

When I read that the fire was believed to have started in the master bathroom of her spacious dwelling, adrenaline kicked in. The victim was so badly burned, she was reduced to white, calcinated fragments, and a comparison of antemortem and postmortem X-rays of her remains was made to a routine chest film taken two years before. She was identified, basically, by a rib. No accelerants were detected, nor was there any explanation of what in the bathroom could have ignited a blaze that had shot up eight feet to set fire to the second floor. A toilet, tub, sink, and countertop with cosmetics, of course, were not enough. Nor, according to the National Weather Service satellite, had lightning struck within a hundred miles of her address during the past forty-eight hours.

I was mulling over this with a glass of pinot noir when Marino called me at almost one A.M.

"You awake?" he asked.

"Does it matter?"

I had to smile, for he always asked that when he called at impolite hours.

"Sparkes owned four Mac tens with silencers that he

supposedly bought for around sixteen hundred dollars apiece. He had a claymore mine he bought for eleven hundred, and an MP40 sub. And get this, ninety empty grenades."

"I'm listening," I said.

"Says he was into World War II shit and just collected it as he went along, like his kegs of bourbon, which came from a distillery in Kentucky that went kaput five years ago. The bourbon he gets nothing more than a slap on the hand, because in light of everything else, who gives a shit about that. As for the guns, all are registered and he's paid the taxes. So he's clean on those scores, but this cockeyed investigator in Warrenton has a notion that Sparkes's secret thing is selling arms to anti-Castro groups in South Florida."

"Based on what?" I wanted to know.

"Shit, you got me, but the investigators in Warrenton are running after it like a dog chasing the postman. The theory is that the girl who burned up knew something, and Sparkes had no choice but to get rid of her, even if it meant torching everything he owned, including his horses."

"If he were dealing arms," I said impatiently, "then he would have had a lot more than a couple old submachine guns and a bunch of empty grenades."

"They're going after him, Doc. Because of who he is, it may take a while."

"What about his missing Calico?"

"How the hell do you know about that?"

"A Calico is unaccounted for, am I correct?"

"That's what he says, but how do you . . ."

"He came to see me today."

There was a long pause.

"What are you talking about?" he asked, and he was very confused. "Came to see you where?"

"My house. Uninvited. He had photographs of Claire Rawley."

Marino was silent so long this time I wondered if we had been disconnected.

"No offense," he finally said. "You sure you're not getting sucked in because of who . . ."

"No," I cut him off.

"Well, could you tell anything from what you looked at?" He backed down.

"Only that his alleged former girlfriend was extraordinarily beautiful. The hair is consistent with the victim's, and the height and weight estimates. She wore a watch that sounds similar to the one I found and hasn't been seen by her roommates since the day before the fire. A start, but certainly not enough to go on."

"And the only thing Wilmington P.D."s been able to get from the university is that there is a Claire Rawley. She's been a student off and on but not since last fall."

"Which would have been close to the time Sparkes broke up with her."

"If what he said was true," Marino pointed out.

"What about her parents?"

"The university's not telling us anything else about her. Typical. We got to get a court order. And you know how that goes. I'm thinking you could try to talk to the dean or someone, soften them up a little. People would rather deal with doctors than cops."

"What about the owner of the Mercedes? I guess he still hasn't turned up?"

"Wilmington P.D."s got his house under surveillance," Marino answered. "They've looked through windows, sniffed through the mail slot to see if anyone's decomposing in there.

But so far, nothing. It's like he disappeared in thin air, and we don't have probable cause to bust in his door."

"He's how old?"

"Forty-two. Brown hair and eyes, five-foot-eleven and weighs one-sixty."

"Well, someone must know where he is or at least when he was seen last. You don't just walk away from a practice and not have anyone notice."

"So far it's looking like he has. People have been driving up to his house for appointments. They haven't been called or nothing. He's a no-show. Neighbors haven't seen him or his car in at least a week. Nobody noticed him driving off, either with somebody or alone. Now apparently some old lady who lives next door spoke to him the morning of June fifth—the Thursday before the fire. They was both picking up their newspapers at the same time, and waved and said good morning. According to her, he was in a hurry and not as friendly as usual. At the moment, that's all we got."

"I wonder if Claire Rawley might have been his patient."

"I just hope he's still alive," Marino said.

"Yes," I said with feeling. "Me, too."

A medical examiner is not an enforcement officer of the law, but an objective presenter of evidence, an intellectual detective whose witnesses are dead. But there were times when I did not care as much about statutes or definitions.

Justice was bigger than codes, especially when I believed that no one was listening to the facts. It was little more than intuition when I decided Sunday morning at breakfast to visit Hughey Dorr, the farrier who had shoed Sparkes's horses two days before the fire.

The bells of Grace Baptist and First Presbyterian churches tolled as I rinsed my coffee cup in the sink. I dug through my notes for the telephone number one of the ATF fire investigators had given to me. The farrier, which was a modern name for an old-world blacksmith, was not home when I called, but his wife was, and I introduced myself.

"He's in Crozier," she said. "Will be there all day at Red Feather Point. It's just off Lee Road, on the north side of the river. You can't miss it."

I knew I could miss it easily. She was talking about an area of Virginia that was virtually nothing but horse farms, and quite frankly, most of them looked alike to me. I asked her to give me a few landmarks.

"Well, it's right across the river from the state penitentiary. Where the inmates work on the dairy farms, and all," she added. "So you probably know where that is."

Unfortunately, I did. I had been there in the past when inmates hanged themselves in their cells or killed each other. I got a phone number and called the farm to make certain it was all right for me to come. As was the nature of privileged horse people, they did not seem the least bit interested in my business but told me I would find the farrier inside the barn, which was green. I went back to my bedroom to put on a tennis shirt, jeans, and lace-up boots, and called Marino.

"You can go with me, or I'm happy to do this on my own," I told him.

A baseball game was playing loudly on his TV, and the phone clunked as he set it down somewhere. I could hear him breathing.

"Crap," he said.

"I know," I agreed. "I'm tired, too."

"Give me half an hour."

"I'll pick you up to save you a little time," I offered.

"Yeah, that will work."

He lived south of the James in a neighborhood with wooded lots just off the strip-mall-strewn corridor called Midlothian Turnpike, where one could buy handguns or motorcycles or Bullet burgers, or indulge in a brushless carwash with or without wax. Marino's small aluminum-sided white house was on Ruthers Road, around the corner from Bon Air Cleaners and Ukrop's. He had a large American flag in his front yard and a chainlink fence around the back, and a carport for his camper.

Sunlight winked off strands of unlit Christmas lights that followed every line and angle of Marino's habitat. The multi-colored bulbs were tucked in shrubs and entwined in trees. There were thousands of them.

"I still don't think you should leave those lights up," I said one more time when he opened the door.

"Yo. Then you take them down and put 'em back again come Thanksgiving," he said as he always did. "You got any idea how long that would take, especially when I keep adding to them every year?"

His obsession had reached the point where he had a separate fuse box for his Christmas decorations, which in full blaze included a Santa pulled by eight reindeer, and happy snowmen, candy canes, toys, and Elvis in the middle of the yard crooning carols through speakers. Marino's display had become so dazzling that its radiance could be seen for miles, and his residence had made it into Richmond's official *Tacky Tour*. It still bewildered me that someone so antisocial didn't mind endless lines of cars and limousines, and drunken people making jokes.

"I'm still trying to figure out what's gotten into you," I said as he got into my car. "Two years ago you would never do something like this. Then out of the blue, you turn your private residence into a carnival. I'm worried. Not to mention the threat of an electrical fire. I know I've given you my opinion before on this, but I feel strongly . . ."

"And maybe I feel strongly, too."

He fastened his seat belt and got out a cigarette.

"How would you react if I started decorating my house like that and left lights hanging around all year round?"

"Same way I would if you bought an RV, put in an above-the-ground pool and started eating Bojangles biscuits every day. I'd think you lost your friggin' mind."

"And you would be right," I said.

"Look."

He played with the unlit cigarette.

"Maybe I've reached a point in life where it's do it or lose it," he said. "The hell with what people think. I ain't going to live more than once, and shit, who knows how much longer I'm gonna be hanging around, anyway."

"Marino, you're getting entirely too morbid."

"It's called reality."

"And the reality is, if you die, you'll come to me and end up on one of my tables. That ought to give you plenty of incentive to hang around for a long time."

He got quiet, staring out his window as I followed Route 6 through Goochland County, where woods were thick and I sometimes did not see another car for miles. The morning was clear but on its way to being humid and warm, and I passed unassuming homes with tin roofs and gracious porches, and bird baths in the yards. Green apples bent gnarled branches to the ground, and sunflowers hung their heavy heads as if praying.

"Truth is, Doc," Marino spoke again. "It's like a premonition, or something. I keep seeing my time running short. I think about my life, and I've pretty much done it all. If I didn't do nothing else, I still would have done enough, you know? So in my mind I see this wall ahead and there's nothing behind it for me. My road ends. I'm out of here. It's just a matter of how and when. So I'm sort of doing whatever the hell I want. May as well, right?"

I wasn't sure what to say, and the image of his garish house at Christmas brought tears to my eyes. I was glad I was wearing sunglasses.

"Don't make it a self-fulfilled prophecy, Marino," I said quietly. "People think about something too much and get so stressed out they make it happen."

"Like Sparkes," he said.

"I really don't see what this has to do with Sparkes."

"Maybe he thought about something too much and made it happen. Like you're a black man with a lot of people who hate your guts, and you worry so much about the assholes taking what you got, you end up burning it down yourself. Killing your horses and white girlfriend in the process. Ending up with nothing. Hell, insurance money won't replace what he lost. No way. Truth is, Sparkes is screwed any way you slice it. Either he's lost everything he loved in life, or he's gonna die in prison."

"If we were talking about arson alone, I'd be more inclined to suspect he was the torch," I said. "But we're also talking about a young woman who was murdered. And we're talking about all his horses being killed. That's where the picture gets distorted for me."

"Sounds like O.J. again, you ask me. Rich, powerful black guy. His former white girlfriend gets her throat slashed.

Don't the parallels bother you just a little bit? Listen, I gotta smoke. I'll blow it out the window."

"If Kenneth Sparkes murdered his former girlfriend, then why didn't he do it in some place where nobody might associate it with him?" I pointed out. "Why destroy everything you own in the process and cause all the signs to point back at you?"

"I don't know, Doc. Maybe things got out of control and went to shit. Maybe he never planned to whack her and torch his joint."

"There's nothing about this fire that strikes me as impetuous," I said. "I think someone knew exactly what he was doing."

"Either that or he got lucky."

The narrow road was dappled with sunlight and shade, and birds on telephone lines reminded me of music. When I drew upon the North Pole restaurant, with its polar bear sign, I was reminded of lunches after court in Goochland, of detectives and forensic scientists who since had retired. Those old homicide cases were vague because by now there were so many murders in my mind, and the thought of them and colleagues I missed made me sad for an instant. Red Feather Point was at the end of a long gravel road that led to an impressive farm overlooking the James River. Dust bloomed behind my car as I wound through white fences surrounding smooth green pastures scattered with leftover hay.

The three-story white frame house had the imperfect slanted look of a building not of this century, and silos cloaked in creeper vines were also left over from long ago. Several horses wandered a distant field, and the red dirt riding ring was empty when we parked. Marino and I walked inside a big green barn and followed the noise of steel ringing from the blows of a hammer. Fine horses stretched their splendid necks out of their stalls, and I could not resist stroking the velvet noses of fox hunters, thoroughbreds, and Arabians. I paused to say sweet things to a foal and his mother as both stared at me with huge brown eyes. Marino kept his distance, waving at flies.

"Looking at them is one thing," he commented. "But being bit by one once was enough for me."

The tack and feed rooms were quiet, and rakes and coils of hoses hung from wooden walls. Blankets were draped over the backs of doors, and I encountered no one but a woman in riding clothes and helmet who was carrying an English saddle.

"Good morning," I said as the distant hammering grew silent. "I'm looking for the farrier. I'm Dr. Scarpetta," I added. "I called earlier."

"He's that way."

She pointed, without slowing down.

"And while you're at it, Black Lace doesn't seem to be feeling so hot," she added, and I realized she thought I was a veterinarian.

Marino and I turned a corner to find Dorr on a stool, with a large white mare's right front hoof clamped firmly between his knees. He was bald, with massive shoulders and arms, and wore a leather farrier's apron that looked like baggy chaps. He was sweating profusely and covered with dirt as he yanked nails out of an aluminum shoe.

"Howdy," he said to us as the horse laid her ears back.

"Good afternoon, Mr. Dorr. I'm Dr. Scarpetta and this is Captain Pete Marino," I said. "Your wife told me I might find you here."

He glanced up at us.

"Folks just call me Hughey, 'cause that's my name. You a vet?"

"No, no, I'm a medical examiner. Captain Marino and I are involved with the Warrenton case."

His eyes darkened as he tossed the old shoe to one side. He snatched a curved knife out of a pocket in his apron and began trimming the frog until marbled white hoof showed underneath. An embedded rock kicked out a spark.

"Whoever did that ought to be shot," he said, grabbing nippers from another pocket and trimming the hoof wall all the way around.

"We're doing everything we can to find out what happened," Marino let him know.

"My part in it is to identify the woman who died in the fire," I explained, "and get a better idea of exactly what happened to her."

"For starters," Marino said, "why that lady was in his house."

"I heard about that. Strange," Dorr answered.

Now he was using a rasp as the mare irritably drew her lips back.

"Don't know why anybody should have been in his house," he said.

"As I understand it, you had just been on his farm several days earlier?" Marino went on, scribbling in a notepad.

"The fire was Saturday night," Dorr said.

He began cleaning the bottom of the hoof with a wire brush.

"I was there the better part of Thursday. Everything was just business as usual. I shoed eight of his horses and took care of one that had white line disease, where bacteria gets inside the hoof wall. Painted it with formaldehyde—something I guess you know all about," he said to me.

He lowered the right leg and picked up the left, and the mare jerked a little and swished her tail. Dorr tapped her nose.

"That's to give her something to think about," he explained to us. "She's having a bad day. They're nothing more than little children, will test you any way they can. And you think they love you, and all they want is food."

The mare rolled her eyes and showed her teeth as the farrier yanked out more nails, working with amazing speed that never slowed as he talked.

"Were you ever there when Sparkes had a young woman visiting?" I asked. "She was tall and very beautiful with long blond hair."

"Nope. Usually when I showed up, we spent our time with the horses. He'd help out any way he could, was absolutely nuts about them."

He picked up the hoof knife again.

"All these stories about how much he ran around," Dorr went on. "I never saw it. He's always seemed like a kind of lonely guy, which surprised me at first because of who he is."

"How long have you worked for him?" Marino asked, shifting his position in a way that signaled he was taking charge.

"Going on six years," Dorr said, grabbing the rasp. "A couple times a month."

"When you saw him that Thursday, did he mention anything to you about going out of the country?"

"Oh sure. That's why I came when I did. He was leaving the next day for London, and since his ranch hand had quit, Sparkes had no one else to be there when I came around."

"It appears that the victim was driving an old blue Mercedes. Did you ever see a car like that on his ranch?"

Dorr pushed himself back on his low wooden stool, scooting the shoeing box with him. He picked up a hind leg.

"I don't remember ever seeing a car like that."

He tossed aside another horseshoe.

"But nope. Can't say I remember the one you just described. Now *whoa*."

He steadied the horse by placing his hand on her rump.

"She's got bad feet," he let us know.

"What's her name?" I asked.

"Molly Brown."

"You don't sound as if you're from around here," I said.

"Born and raised in South Florida."

"So was I. Miami," I said.

"Now that's so far south it's South America."

12

A beagle had trotted in and was snuffling around the hay-strewn floor, going after hoof shavings. Molly Brown daintily perched her other hind leg on the hoof stand as if about to be treated to a manicure in a salon.

"Hughey," I said, "there are circumstances about this fire that raise many, many questions. There's a body, yet no one was supposed to have been inside Sparkes's house. The woman who died is my responsibility, and I want to do absolutely everything I can to find out why she was there and why she didn't get out when the fire started. You may have been the last person to visit the farm before the fire, and I'm asking you to search your memory and see if there's anything—absolutely anything—that might have struck you as unusual that day."

"Right," Marino said. "For example, did it appear that Sparkes might have been having a private, personal conversation on the phone? You get any idea that he might have been expecting company? You ever heard him mention the name Claire Rawley?"

Dorr got up and patted the mare on her rump again,

while my instincts kept me far out of the reach of her powerful hind legs. The beagle bayed at me as if suddenly I were a complete stranger.

"Come here, little fella."

I bent down and held out my hand.

"Dr. Scarpetta, I can tell you trust Molly Brown, and she can tell. As for you'—he nodded at Marino—"you're scared of 'em, and they can sense that. Just letting you know."

Dorr walked off, and we followed him. Marino clung to the wall as he walked behind a horse that was at least fourteen hands high. The farrier went around a corner to where his truck was parked. It was a red pickup, customized with a forge in back that burned propane gas. He turned a knob and a blue flame popped up.

"Since her feet aren't so great, I have to draw clips on shoes to make them fit. Kind of like orthotics for humans," he commented, gripping an aluminum shoe in tongs and holding it in the fire.

"I give it a count of fifty unless the forge's warmed up," he went on as I smelled heating metal. "Otherwise I go to thirty. There's no color change in aluminum, so I just warm it a bit to make it malleable."

He carried the shoe to the anvil and punched holes. He fashioned clips and hammered them flat. To take off sharp edges he used a grinder, which sounded like a loud Stryker saw. Dorr seemed to be using his trade to stall us, to buy himself time to ponder or perhaps work his way around what we wanted to know. I had no doubt that he was fiercely loyal to Kenneth Sparkes.

"At the very least," I said to him, "this lady's family has a right to know. I need to notify them about her death, and I can't do that until I am certain who she is. And they're going to ask me what happened to her. I need to know that."

But he had nothing to say, and we followed him back to Molly Brown. She had defecated and stepped in it, and he irritably swept manure away with a worn-out broom while the beagle wandered around.

"You know, the horse's biggest defense is flight," Dorr finally spoke again as he secured a front leg between his knees. "All he wants is to get away, no matter how much you think he loves you."

He drove nails through the shoe, bending points down as they went through the outside wall of the hoof.

"People aren't all that different, if you corner them," he added.

"I hope I'm not making you feel cornered," I said as I kneaded the beagle behind his ears.

Dorr bent the sharp ends of the nails over with a clincher and rasped them smooth, once again taking his time to answer me.

"Whoa," he said to Molly Brown, and the smell of metal and manure was heavy on the air. "Point is," he went on as he tapped the rounding hammer, "you two walking in here and thinking I'll trust you just like that is no different than your thinking you could shoe this horse."

"I don't blame you for feeling like that," I said.

"No way I could shoe that horse," Marino said. "No way I'd want to, either."

"They can pick you up by the teeth and throw you. They paw, cow kick, slap their tail in your eyes. It better'd be plain as day who's in charge, or you're in for a world of trouble."

Dorr straightened up, rubbing his lower back. He returned to his forge to fire another shoe.

"Look, Hughey," Marino said as we followed. "I'm asking you to help because I think you want to. You cared about those horses. You gotta care that someone's dead."

The farrier dug in a compartment on the side of his truck. He pulled out a new shoe and grabbed it with tongs.

"All I can do is give you my private theory."

He held the shoe in the forge's flame.

"I'm all ears," Marino said.

"I think it was a professional hit and that the woman was part of it but for some reason didn't get out."

"So you're saying she was an arsonist."

"Maybe one of them. But she got the short end of the stick."

"What makes you think that?" I asked.

Dorr clamped the warm shoe into a foot vice.

"You know, Mr. Sparkes's lifestyle pisses off a lot of people, especially your Nazi types," he answered.

"I'm still not clear why you think the woman had anything to do with it," Marino said.

Dorr paused to stretch his back. He rotated his head and his neck cracked.

"Maybe whoever did it didn't know he was leaving town. They needed a girl to get him to open his door—maybe even a girl he had a past with."

Marino and I let him talk.

"He's not the kind of guy to turn someone he knew away from his door. In fact, in my opinion he's always been too laid back and nice for his own damn good."

The grinding and hammering punctuated the farrier's anger, and the shoe seemed to hiss a soft warning as Dorr dipped it in a bucket of water. He said nothing to us as he returned to Molly Brown, seating himself on the stool again. He began trying on the new shoe, rasping away an edge and pulling out the hammer. The mare was fidgety, but mostly she seemed bored.

"I may as well tell you another thing that in my mind fits with my theory," he said as he worked. "While I was on his farm that Thursday, this same damn helicopter kept flying overhead. It's not like they do crop dusting around there, so Mr. Sparkes and I couldn't figure if it was lost or having a problem and looking for a place to land. It buzzed around for maybe fifteen minutes and then took off to the north."

"What color was it?" I asked as I recalled the one that had circled the fire scene when I was there.

"White. Looked like a white dragonfly."

"Like a little piston-engine chopper?" Marino asked.

"I don't know much about whirlybirds, but yup, it was small. A two-seater, my guess is, with no number painted on it. Kind of makes you wonder, now, doesn't it? Like maybe somebody doing a little surveillance from the air?"

The beagle's eyes were half shut and his head was on my shoe.

"And you've never seen that helicopter around his farm before?" Marino asked, and I could tell he remembered the white helicopter, too, but didn't want to seem especially interested.

"No sir. Warrenton's not a fan of helicopters. They spook the horses."

"There's an air park, flying circus, a bunch of private air strips in the area," Marino added.

Dorr got up again.

"I've put two and two together for you the best I can," he said.

He grabbed a bandanna out of a back pocket and mopped his face.

"I've told you all I know. Damn. I'm sore all over."

"One last thing," Marino said. "Sparkes is an important, busy man. He must've used helicopters now and then. To get to the airport, for example, since his farm was sort of out in the middle of nowhere."

"Sure, they've landed on his farm," Dorr said.

He gave Marino a lingering look that was filled with suspicion.

"Anything like the white one you saw?" Marino then asked.

"I already told you I've never seen it before."

Dorr stared at us while Molly Brown jerked against her halter and bared long stained teeth.

"And I'll tell you another thing," Dorr said. "If you're out to railroad Mr. Sparkes, don't bother poking your nose around me again."

"We're not out to railroad anyone," Marino said, and he was getting defiant, too. "Just looking for the truth. Like they say, it speaks for itself."

"That would be nice for a change," Dorr said.

I drove home deeply troubled as I tried to sort through what I knew and what had been said. Marino had few comments, and the closer we got to Richmond, the darker his mood. As we pulled into his driveway, his pager beeped.

"The helicopter ain't fitting with nothing," he said as I parked behind his truck. "And maybe it has nothing to do with nothing."

There was always that possibility.

"Now what the hell is this?"

He held up his pager and read the display.

"Shit. Looks like something's up. Maybe you better come in."

It was not often that I was inside Marino's house, and it seemed that the last time was during the holidays when I had stopped by with home-baked bread and a container of my special stew. Of course, his outlandish decorations had been up then, and even the inside of his house was strung with lights and crowded with an overburdened tree. I remembered an electric train whirring in circles along its tracks, going around and around a Christmas town dusted with snow. Marino had made eggnog with one hundred proof Virginia Lightning moonshine, and quite frankly, I should not have driven home.

Now his home seemed dim and bare, with its shag-carpeted living room centered by his favorite reclining chair. It was true the mantle over his fireplace was lined with various bowling trophies he had won over the years, and yes, the big-screen television was his nicest piece of furniture. I accompanied him to the kitchen and scanned the greasy stovetop and overflowing garbage can and sink. I turned on hot water and ran it through a sponge, then I began wiping up what I could while he dialed the phone.

"You don't need to do that," he whispered to me.

"Someone has to."

"Yo," he said into the receiver. "Marino here. What's up?"

He listened for a long, tense time, his brow furrowed and his face turning a deeper red. I started on the dishes, and there were plenty of them.

"So how closely do they check?" Marino asked. "No, I mean, do they make sure someone's in their seat? Oh, they do? And we know they did it this time? Yeah, right. No one remembers. The whole friggin' world's full of people who don't remember shit. That and they didn't see a thing, right?"

I rinsed glasses carefully and set them on a towel to drain.

"I agree the luggage thing raises a question," he went on.

I used the last of Marino's dishwashing liquid and had to resort to a dried-out bar of soap I found under the sink.

"While you're at it," he was saying, "how 'bout seeing what you can find out about a white helicopter that was flying around Sparkes's farm." He paused, then said, "Maybe before, and definitely after because I saw it with my own two eyes when we were at the scene."

Marino listened some more as I started on the silverware, and to my amazement he said, "Before I hang up, you want to say hi to your aunt?"

My hands went still as I stared at him.

"Here."

He handed me the phone.

"Aunt Kay?"

Lucy sounded as surprised as I was.

"What are you doing in Marino's house?" she asked.

"Cleaning."

"What?"

"Is everything all right?" I asked her.

"Marino will fill you in. I'll check out the white bird. It had to get fuel from somewhere. Maybe filed a flight plan with FSS in Leesburg, but somehow I doubt it. Gotta go."

I hung up and suddenly felt preempted and angry, and I wasn't completely sure why.

"I think Sparkes is in a lot of trouble, Doc," Marino said.

"What's happened?" I wanted to know.

"Turns out that the day before the fire, Friday, he showed up at Dulles for a nine-thirty P.M. flight. He checked baggage but never picked it up at the other end, in London. Meaning it's possible he could have checked his bags and given the flight attendant the ticket at the gate, then turned right around and left the airport."

"They do head counts on international flights," I argued. "His absence on the plane would have been noticed."

"Maybe. But he didn't get where he is without being clever."

"Marino . . ."

"Hold on. Let me finish giving you the rundown. What Sparkes is saying is that security was waiting for him the minute his plane landed at Heathrow at nine-forty-five the next morning—on Saturday. And we're talking England time, making it four-forty-five A.M. back here. He was told about the fire and turned right around and caught a United flight back to Washington without bothering with his bags."

"I guess if you were upset enough, you might do that," I said.

Marino paused, looking hard at me as I set the soap on top of the sink and dried my hands.

"Doc, you got to quit sticking up for him," he said.

"I'm not. I'm just trying to be more objective than I think some people are being. And certainly security at Heathrow should remember notifying him when he got off that plane?"

"Not so far. And we can't quite figure out how security knew about the fire anyway. Course Sparkes has got an explanation for everything. Says security always makes special provisions when he travels and meets him at the gate. Apparently the fire had already hit the early-morning news in London, and the businessman that Sparkes was supposed to meet with called British Air to alert them to give Sparkes the news the second he was on the ground."

"And someone's talked to this businessman?"

"Not yet. Remember, this is Sparkes's story. And I hate to tell you this, Doc, but don't think people wouldn't lie for him, either. If he's behind all this, I can guarantee that he planned it right down to the fine print. And let me also add that by the time he'd arrived at Dulles to catch the flight to London, the fire was already going and the woman was dead. Who's to say he didn't kill her and then use some kind of timer to get the fire going after he'd left the farm?"

"There's nothing to say it," I agreed. "There's also nothing to prove it. And there doesn't seem to be much chance of our knowing such a thing unless some material turns up in forensic exams that might point to some sort of explosive device used remotely as an igniter."

"These days half the stuff in your house can be used as a timer. Alarm clocks, VCRs, computers, digital watches."

"That's true. But something has to initiate low explosives, like blasting caps, sparks, a fuse, fire," I said. "Unless you have any other cleaning to do," I added dryly, "I'll be heading out."

"Don't be pissed at me," Marino said. "You know, it's not like this whole damn thing is my fault."

I stopped at his front door and looked at him. Thin gray wisps of hair clung to his sweating pate. He probably had dirty clothes flung all around his bedroom, and no one could clean and tidy up enough for him, not in a million years. I remembered Doris, his wife, and could imagine her docile servitude until the day she suddenly left and fell in love with another man.

It was as if Marino had been transfused with the wrong blood type. No matter how well his meaning or brilliant his work, he was in terrible conflict with his environment. And slowly it was killing him.

"Just do me one favor," I said with my hand on the door.

He wiped his face on his shirt sleeve and got out his cigarettes.

"Don't encourage Lucy to jump to conclusions," I said. "You know as well as I do that the problem is local law enforcement, local politics. Marino, I don't believe we've even come close to what this is all about, so let's not crucify anyone just yet."

"I'm amazed," he said. "After all that son of a bitch did to run you out of office. And now suddenly he's this saint?"

"I didn't say he was a saint. Frankly, I don't know any saints."

"Sparkes-the-ladies' man," Marino went on. "If I didn't know better, I'd wonder if you were getting sweet on him."

"I won't dignify that with a response."

I walked out onto the porch, halfway tempted to slam the door in his face.

"Yeah. Same thing everyone says when they're guilty."

He stepped out after me.

"Don't think I don't know it when you and Wesley aren't getting along . . ."

I turned to face him and pointed my finger like a gun.

"Not one more word," I warned him. "You stay out of my business, and don't you dare question my professionalism, Marino. You know better than that, goddamn it."

I went down the front steps and got inside my car. I backed out slowly and with deliberate skill. I did not look at him as I drove off.

13

Monday morning was carried in on a storm that thrashed the city with violent winds and pelting rains. I drove to work with windshield wipers going fast and air conditioning on to defog the glass. When I opened my window to toss a token into the toll bin, my suit sleeve got drenched, and then of all days for this to happen, two funeral homes had parked inside the bay, and I had to leave my car outside. The fifteen seconds it took me to dash through the parking lot and unlock the back door of my building concluded my punishment. I was soaked. Water dripped from my hair and my shoes squished as I walked through the bay.

I checked the log in the morning office to see what had come in during the night. An infant had died in his parents' bed. An elderly woman appeared to be a suicidal overdose, and, of course, there was a drug-related shooting from one of the housing projects on the fringes of what had become a more civilized and healthy downtown. In the last several years, the city had been ranked as one of the most violent in the United States, with as many as one hundred and sixty homicides in one year for a population of less than a quarter of a million people.

Police were blamed. Even I was if the statistics compiled by my office didn't suit the politicians or if convictions were slow to come in court. The irrationality of it all never ceased to appall me, for it did not seem to occur to those in power that there is such a thing as preventive medicine, and it is, after all, the only way to halt a lethal disease. It truly is better to vaccinate against polio, for example, than to deal with it after the fact. I closed the log and walked out of the office, my shoes carrying me wetly along the empty corridor.

I turned into the locker room because I was already getting chilled. I hurried out of my sticky suit and blouse and struggled into scrubs, which were always more unwilling the more I rushed. I put on my lab coat, and dried my hair with a towel, running my fingers through it to push it out of my way. The face staring back at me in the mirror looked anxious and tired. I had been neither eating nor sleeping well, and was less disciplined with coffee and alcohol. All of it showed around my eyes. A good deal of it was due to my underlying helpless anger and fear brought about by Carrie. We had no idea where she was, but in my mind she was everywhere.

I went into the break room, where Fielding, who avoided caffeine, was making herb tea. His healthy obsessions did not make me feel any better. I had not exercised in over a week.

"Good morning, Dr. Scarpetta," he said cheerfully.

"Let's hope so," I replied, reaching for the coffeepot. "Looks like our caseload is fairly light so far. I'm leaving it up to you, and you can run staff conference. I've got a lot to do."

Fielding was crisp and fresh in a yellow shirt with

French cuffs, and vivid tie and creased black slacks. He was cleanly shaven and smelled good. Even his shoes were shined, because unlike me, he never let life's circumstances interfere with how he took care of himself.

"I don't see how you do it," I said, looking him up and down. "Jack, don't you ever suffer from normal things, like depression, stress, cravings for chocolate, cigarettes, Scotch?"

"I tend to overcondition when I get whacked out," he said, sipping his tea and eyeing me through steam. "That's when I get injured."

He thought for a moment.

"I guess the worst thing I do, now that you have me thinking about it, is I shut out my wife and kids. Find excuses not to be home. I'm an insensitive bastard and they hate me for a while. So yes, I'm self-destructive, too. But I promise," he said to me, "if you would just find time to fast-walk, ride a bike, do a few push-ups, maybe crunches, I swear you'd be amazed."

He walked off, adding, "The body's natural morphines, right?"

"Thanks," I called after him, sorry I asked.

I had barely settled behind my desk when Rose appeared, her hair pinned up, fit for a CEO in her smart, navy blue suit.

"I didn't know you were here," she said, setting dictated protocols on top of a stack. "ATF just called. McGovern."

"Yes?" I asked with interest. "Do you know about what?"

"She said she was in D.C. over the weekend and needs to see you."

"When and about what?"

I began signing letters.

"She should be here soon," Rose said.

I glanced up in surprise.

"She called from her car and told me to let you know that she was almost to Kings Dominion and should be here in twenty or thirty minutes," Rose went on.

"Then it must be important," I muttered, opening a cardboard file of slides.

I swung around and removed the plastic cover from my microscope and turned on the illuminator.

"Don't feel you have to drop everything," said the ever protective Rose. "It's not as if she made an appointment or even asked if you could fit her in."

I set a slide on the stage and peered through the eyepiece lens at a tissue section of pancreas, at pink and shrunken cells that looked hyalinized, or scarred.

"His tox came back as zip," I said to Rose as I put another slide on the stage. "Except for acetone," I added. "The byproduct of inadequate metabolism of glucose. And kidneys show hyperosmolar vacuolization of the proximal convoluted tubular lining cells. Meaning, instead of cuboidal and pink, they're clear, bulging and enlarged."

"Sonny Quinn again," Rose said dismally.

"Plus we've got a clinical history of fruity-smelling breath, weight loss, thirst, frequent urination. Nothing that insulin wouldn't have cured. Not that I don't believe in prayer, contrary to what the family has told reporters."

Sonny Quinn was the eleven-year-old son of Christian Science parents. He had died eight weeks ago, and although there had never been any question as to his cause of death, at least not in my mind, I had finalized nothing until further studies and tests had been completed. In short, the boy had died because he had not received proper medical treatment. His parents had violently protested the autopsy. They had gone on television and accused me of religious persecution and of mutilating their child's body.

Rose had endured my feelings about this many times by now, and she asked, "Do you want to call them?"

"Want has nothing to do with it. So, yes."

She shuffled through Sonny Quinn's thick case file and jotted down a phone number for me.

"Good luck," she said as she passed through the adjoining doorway.

I dialed, with dread in my heart.

"Mrs. Quinn?" I said when a woman answered.

"Yes."

"This is Dr. Kay Scarpetta. I have the results from Sonny's . . ."

"Haven't you hurt us enough?"

"I thought you might like to know why your son died . . ."

"I don't need you to tell me anything about my son," she snapped.

I could hear someone taking the phone from her as my heart hammered.

"This is Mr. Quinn," said the man whose shield was religious freedom and whose son, as a result, was dead.

"Sonny's cause of death was acute pneumonia due to acute diabetic ketoacidosis due to acute onset of diabetes mellitis. I'm sorry for your pain, Mr. Quinn."

"This is all a mistake. An error."

"There's no mistake, Mr. Quinn. No error," I said, and it was all I could do to keep the anger out of my voice. "I can only suggest that if your other young children show Sonny's same symptoms that you get them medical treatment immediately. So you don't have to suffer this way again . . ."

"I don't need some medical examiner telling me how to raise my children," he said coldly. "Lady, I'll see you in court."

That you will, I thought, for I knew the Commonwealth would charge him and his wife with felony child abuse and neglect.

"Don't you call us anymore," said Mr. Quinn, and he hung up on me.

I returned the receiver to its cradle with a heavy heart and looked up to see Teun McGovern standing in the hallway, just outside my door. I could tell by the look on her face that she had heard every word.

"Teun, come in," I said.

"And I thought my job was hard." Her eyes were on mine as she took a chair and moved it directly across from me. "I know you have to do this all the time, but I guess I've never really heard it. It's not that I don't talk to families all the time, but thankfully it's not my job to tell them exactly what inhaling smoke did to their loved one's trachea or lungs."

"It's the hardest part," I said simply, and the weight inside me would not go away.

"I guess you're the messenger they want to kill."

"Not always," I said, and I knew that in the solitude of my raw inner self, I would hear the Quinns' accusing, harsh words replay for the rest of my days.

There were so many voices now, screams and prayers of rage and pain and sometimes blame, because I had dared to touch the wounds, and because I would listen. I did not want to talk about this with McGovern. I did not want her to get any closer to me.

"I've got one more phone call to make," I said. "So if you want to get coffee? Or just relax for a minute. I'm sure you'll be interested in what I find out."

I called the University of North Carolina at Wilmington, and although it was not quite nine, the registrar was in. He was excruciatingly polite but not at all helpful.

"I completely understand why you're calling and promise that we very much want to help," he was saying. "But not without a court order. We can't simply decide to release personal information about any of our students. Certainly not over the phone."

"Mr. Shedd, we're talking about a homicide," I reminded him as impatience tugged at me.

"I understand," he said again.

This went on and got me nowhere. Finally I gave up and got off the line. I was dejected when I returned my attention to McGovern.

"They're just covering their asses in case the family tries to come after them later." McGovern told me what I already knew. "They need us to give them no choice, so I guess that's what we'll do."

"Right," I said dully. "So what brings you here?" I asked.

"I understand the lab results are in, or at least some of them. I called late Friday," she said.

"News to me."

I was irked. If the trace evidence examiner had called McGovern before me, I was going to be really hot. I picked up the phone and called Mary Chan, a young examiner who was new with the labs.

"Good morning," I said. "I understand you have some reports for me?"

"I was just getting ready to bring them downstairs."

"These are the ones you've sent to ATF."

"Yes. The same ones. I can fax them or bring them in person."

I gave her the number of the fax machine in my office, and I did not let her know my irritation. But I did give her a hint.

"Mary, in the future, it's best if you let me know about my cases *before* you start sending lab results to others," I said calmly.

"I'm sorry," and I could tell she very much was. "The investigator called at five as I was halfway out the door."

The reports were in my hands two minutes later, and McGovern opened her battered briefcase to retrieve her copies. She watched me as I read. The first was an analysis of the metal-like shaving that I had recovered from the dead woman's cut to the left temporal region. According to the scanning electron microscope and energy dispersive X-ray, or SEM/EDX, the elemental composition of the material in question was magnesium.

As for the melted debris recovered from the victim's hair, those results were just as inexplicable. A FTIR, or Fourier transform infrared spectrophotometer, had caused the fibers to selectively absorb infrared light. The characteristic pattern turned out to be that of the chemical polymer polysiloxane, or silicone.

"A little strange, don't you think?" McGovern asked me.

"Let's start with magnesium," I said. "What comes to mind is sea water. There's plenty of magnesium in that. Or mining. Or the person was an industrial chemist or worked in a research lab? What about explosives?"

"If potassium chloride came up, then yes. That could be flash powder," she answered. "Or RDX, lead styphnate, lead azide of mercury fulminate if we're talking about blasting caps, for example. Or nitric acid, sulfuric acid, glycerin, ammonium nitrate, sodium nitrate. Nitro-glycerin, dynamite, and so on and so on. And I will add that Pepper would have picked up on high explosives like that."

"And magnesium?" I asked.

"Pyrotechnics, or fireworks," she said. "To produce the brilliant white light. Or flares." She shrugged. "Although aluminum powder is preferred, because it keeps better, unless the magnesium particles are coated with something like linseed oil."

"Flares," I thought out loud. "You light flares, strategically place them, and leave? That could buy you several minutes, at least."

"With the appropriate fuel load, it could."

"But that doesn't explain an unburned turning or shaving of it embedded in her wound, that would appear to have been transferred by the sharp instrument she was cut with."

"They don't use magnesium to make knives," McGovern observed.

"No, nothing like that. It's too soft. What about the aerospace industry, because it's so light?"

"Most definitely. But in those instances, there are alloys that would have come up during testing."

"Right. Let's move on to silicone, which doesn't seem to make any sense. Unless she had silicone breast implants before they were banned, which she clearly didn't."

"I can tell you that silicone rubber is used in electrical insulation, hydraulic fluids, and for water repellency. None of which makes sense, unless there was something in the bathroom, maybe in the tub. Something pink—I don't know what."

"Do we know if Sparkes had a bathmat—anything rubbery and pink in that bathroom?" I asked.

"We've only begun going through his house with him," she said. "But he claims that the decor of the master bath was mostly black and white. The marble floor and walls were black. The sink, cabinets, and tub, white. The shower door was European and wasn't tempered glass, meaning it didn't disintegrate into a billion little glass balls when the temperature exceeded four hundred degrees Fahrenheit."

"Explaining why it basically melted over the body," I said.

"Yeah, almost shrink-wrapped it."

"Not quite," I said.

"The door had brass hinges and no frame. What we recovered was consistent with that. So your friendly media tycoon's memory holds true at least on that score."

"And on others?"

"God only knows, Kay."

She unbuttoned her suit jacket as if it suddenly occurred to her to relax, while she paradoxically glanced up at the clock.

"We're dealing with a very smart man," she said. "That much all of us know."

"And the helicopter? What do you make of that, Teun? I'm assuming you've gotten word about the little white Schweizer, or Robinson, or whatever it was that the farrier saw two days before the fire? Perhaps the same one you and I saw two days later?"

"This is just a theory," she said. "A groping one at that, okay?"

Her look was penetrating.

"Maybe he sets the fire and needs to get to the airport fast," she went on. "So the day before, the helicopter does a recon over the farm because the pilot knows he'll have to land and take off after dark. Following so far?"

I nodded.

"Saturday rolls around. Sparkes murders the girl and torches his place. He runs out to the pasture and gets on the helicopter, which transports him somewhere near Dulles, where his Cherokee is stashed. He gets to the airport and does his thing with receipts and maybe baggage. Then he makes himself scarce until it's time to show up at Hootowl Farm."

"And the reason the helicopter showed up on Monday, when we were working the scene?" I then asked. "How does that fit?"

"Pyros like to watch the fun," she stated. "Hell, for all we know, Sparkes was up there himself watching us work our asses off. Paranoid, if nothing else. Figured we'd think it was a news bird, which we did."

"This is all speculation at this point," I said, and I had heard enough.

I began rearranging the infinite flow of paperwork that began where it stopped and stopped where it began. McGovern was studying me again. She got up and shut the doors.

"Okay, I think it's time we had a little talk," she said. "I don't think you like me. And maybe if you come clean about it, maybe we can do something about it, one way or another."

"I'm not sure what I think of you, if you must know."

I stared at her.

"The most important thing is that all of us do our jobs, lest we lose perspective. Since we are dealing with someone who was murdered," I added.

"Now you're pissing me off," she said.

"Not intentionally, I assure you."

"As if someone murdered makes no difference to me?

Is that what you're implying? You think I got where I am in life by not giving a shit about who set a fire and why?"

She shoved up her sleeves, as if ready for a fight.

"Teun," I said. "I don't have time for this, because I don't think it's constructive."

"This is about Lucy. You think I'm replacing you, or God knows what. That's what this is all about, isn't it, Kay?"

Now she was making me angry, too.

"You and I have worked together before, right?" she went on. "We've never had a big problem before now. So one has to ask, what's different? I think the answer's pretty obvious. The difference is that even as we speak, your niece is moving into her new apartment in Philadelphia, to be in my field office, under my supervision. Mine. Not yours. And you don't like it. And guess what else? If I were in your shoes, maybe I wouldn't like it either."

"It is neither the time nor the place for this discussion," I said firmly.

"Fine."

She got up and draped her jacket over her arm.

"Then we'll go somewhere else," she decided. "I intend to resolve this before I drive back north."

For an instant I was stymied as I reigned from the empire of my wrap-around desk, with its foremen of files, and guards demanding the hard labor of journal articles, and legions of messages and correspondence that would never set me free. I took my glasses off and massaged my face. When McGovern was blurred, it was easier for me.

"I'll take you to lunch," I said. "If you're willing to hang around three more hours. In the meantime'—I got up from my chair—"I have bones in a pot that need heating up. You can come with me, if you have a strong stomach."

"You won't scare me off with that." McGovern seemed pleased.

McGovern was not the sort to follow anyone around, and after I had turned on the burner in the decomposition room, she lingered long enough for steam to rise. Then she headed out to ATF's Richmond field office, and reappeared suddenly within an hour. She was breathless and tense when she walked in. I was carefully stirring simmering bones.

"We got another one," she said quickly.

"Another one?" I asked.

I set the long plastic spoon on a countertop.

"Another fire. Another whacko one. This time in Lehigh County, about an hour from Philadelphia," she said. "Are you coming with me?"

My mind raced through all the possibilities of what might happen if I dropped everything and left with her. For one thing, I was unnerved by the thought of the two of us alone for five hours inside a car.

"It's residential," she went on. "It started early yesterday morning, and a body has been recovered. A woman. In the master bathroom."

"Oh no," I said.

"It's clear the fire was intended to conceal that she had been murdered," she said, and then went on to explain why it was possible the case was related to the one in Warrenton.

When the body was discovered, Pennsylvania state police had immediately requested assistance from ATF. Then ATF fire investigators at the scene had entered data on their laptops, and ESA got a hit almost instantly. By last night the Lehigh case had begun to take on huge significance, and the FBI offered agents and Benton, and the state police had accepted.

"The house was built on a slab," McGovern was explaining as we got on I-95 North. "So no basement to worry about, thank God. Our guys have been there since three o'clock this morning, and what's curious is in this case, the fire didn't do the job well at all. The areas of the master suite, a guest room right above it on the second floor, and the living room downstairs are pretty badly burned, with extensive ceiling damage in the bathroom, and spalling of the concrete floor in the garage."

Spalling occurs when rapid, intense heat causes moisture trapped in concrete to boil, fragmenting the surface.

"The garage was located where?" I asked as I tried to envision what she was describing.

"On the same side of the house as the master suite. Again, a fast, hot fire. But the burning wasn't complete, a lot of alligatoring, a lot of surface charring. As for the rest of the house, we're talking mostly smoke and water damage. Which isn't consistent with the work of the individual who torched the Sparkes farm. Except for one important thing. So far, it doesn't appear that any type of accelerant was used, and there wasn't a sufficient fuel load in the bathroom to account for the height of the flames."

"Was the body in the tub?" I asked.

"Yes. Makes my hair stand on end."

"It should. What kind of shape is she in?" I asked the most important question as McGovern held our speed ten miles over the limit in her government Ford Explorer.

"Not so burned that the medical examiner couldn't tell her throat was cut."

"Then she's already been autopsied," I assumed.

"To be honest, I really don't know how much has been done. But she's not going anywhere. That's your turf. Mine's to see what the hell else we can find at the fire scene."

"So you're not going to use me to shovel out debris?" I asked.

McGovern laughed and turned on the CD player. I was not expecting *Amadeus*.

"You can dig all you want," she said with a smile that relieved a lot of tension. "You're not bad at it, by the way, for someone who probably doesn't run unless she's being chased. Or work out anything except intellectual problems."

"You do enough autopsies and move enough bodies, and you don't need to lift weights," I distorted the truth, badly.

"Hold out your hands."

I did, and she glanced over at them, changing lanes at the same time.

"Damn. I guess it didn't occur to me what saws and scalpels and hedge pruners will do for muscle tone," she commented.

"*Hedge pruners?*"

"You know, what you use to open the chest."

"Rib shears, please."

"Well, I've seen hedge pruners in some morgues, and knitting needles used to track bullet wounds."

"Not in my morgue. At least not in the one I have now. Although I will admit that in the early days one learned to improvise," I felt compelled to say as Mozart played.

"One of those little trade secrets you don't want to ever come out in court," McGovern confessed. "Sort of like stashing the best jar of confiscated moonshine in a secret desk drawer.

Or cops keeping souvenirs from scenes, like marijuana pipes and whacko weapons. Or medical examiners hanging on to artificial hips and parts of fractured skulls that in truth should be buried with the bodies."

"I won't deny that some of my colleagues aren't always appropriate," I said. "But keeping body parts without permission is not in the same category as pinching a jar of moonshine, if you ask me."

"You're awfully straight and narrow, aren't you, Kay?" McGovern stated. "Unlike the rest of us, you never seem to use poor judgment or do anything wrong. You probably never overeat or get drunk. And to be honest, it makes the rest of us schleps afraid to be around you, afraid you'll look at us and disapprove."

"Good Lord, what an awful image," I exclaimed. "I hope that's not how I'm perceived."

She said nothing.

"Certainly I don't see myself that way," I said. "Quite to the contrary, Teun. Maybe I'm just more reserved because I have to be. Maybe I'm more self-contained because I always have been, and no, it's not my tendency to publicly confess my sins. But I don't look around and judge. And I can promise I'm much harder on myself than I'd ever be on you."

"That's not been my impression. I think you size me up and down and inside out to make sure I'm suitable to train Lucy and won't be a pernicious influence."

I could not answer that charge, because it was true.

"I don't even know where she is," I suddenly realized.

"Well, I can tell you. She's in Philly. Bouncing back and forth between the field office and her new apartment."

For a while, music was our only conversation, and as the beltway carried us around Baltimore, I could not help but think of a medical student who also had died in a suspicious fire.

"Teun," I said. "How many children do you have?"

"One. A son."

I could tell this was not a happy subject.

"How old is he?" I asked.

"Joe is twenty-six."

"He lives nearby?"

I stared out the window at reflective signs flowing by, announcing exits to Baltimore streets I used to know very well when I studied medicine at Johns Hopkins.

"I don't know where he lives, to tell you the truth," she said. "We were never close. I'm not sure anyone has ever been close to Joe. I'm not sure anyone would want to be."

I did not pry, but she wanted to talk.

"I knew something was wrong with him when he started sneaking into the liquor cabinet at the tender age of ten, drinking gin, vodka, and putting water in the bottles, thinking he would fool us. By sixteen, he was a raging alcoholic, in and out of treatment, DUIs, drunk and disorderlies, stealing, one thing after another. He left home at nineteen, skipping around here and there and eventually cut off all contact. To be honest, he's probably a street person somewhere."

"You've had a hard life," I said.

14

The Atlanta Braves were staying at the Sheraton Hotel on Society Hill when McGovern dropped me off at almost seven P.M. Groupies, old and young, were dressed in baseball jackets and caps, prowling hallways and bars with huge photographs in hand to be signed by their heroes. Security had been called, and a desperate man stopped me as I was coming through the revolving door.

"Have you seen them?" he asked me, his eyes wildly darting around.

"Seen who?" I said.

"The Braves!"

"What do they look like?" I asked.

I waited in line to check in, not interested in anything but a long soak in the tub. We had been held up two hours in traffic just south of Philadelphia, where five cars and a van had smashed into each other, sending broken glass and twisted metal across six lanes. It was too late to drive another hour to the Lehigh County morgue. That would have to wait until morning, and I took the elevator to the fourth floor and slid in my plastic card to open the electronic lock. I opened curtains and looked out at the Delaware River, and masts of the *Moshulu* moored at Penn's Landing. Suddenly, I was in Philadelphia with a turn-out bag, my aluminum case, and my purse.

My message light was blinking, and I listened to Benton's recorded voice saying that he was staying at my same hotel, and should be arriving as soon as he could break free of New York and its traffic. I was to expect him around nine. Lucy had left me her new phone number and didn't know if she'd see me or not. Marino had an update that he would relay when I called, and Fielding said the Quinns had gone on the television news earlier this evening to say they were suing the medical examiner's office and me for violating the separation of church and state and causing irreparable emotional damage.

I sat on the edge of the bed and took off my shoes. My pantyhose had a run, and I wadded them and hurled them into the trash. My clothes had bitten into me because I had worn them too long, and I imagined the stench of cooking human bones lingering in my hair.

"Shit!" I exclaimed under my breath. "What kind of goddamn life is this?"

I snatched off my suit, blouse, and slip and flung them inside out on the bed. I made sure the deadbolt was secure and began filling the tub with water as hot as I could stand it. The sound of it pouring on top of itself began to soothe me, and I dribbled in foaming bath gel that smelled like sun-ripened raspberries. I was confused about seeing Benton. How had it all come to this? Lovers, colleagues, friends, whatever we were supposed to be had blended into a mixture, like paintings in sand. Our relationship was a design of delicate colors, intricate and dry and easily disturbed. He called as I was drying off.

"I'm sorry it's so late," he said.

"How are you?" I asked.

"Are you up for the bar?"

"Not if the Braves are there. I don't need a riot."

"The Braves?" he asked.

"Why don't you come to my room? I have a mini-bar."

"In two minutes."

He showed up in his typical uniform of dark suit and white shirt. Both showed the harshness of his day, and he needed to shave. He gathered me in his arms and we held each other without speaking for a very long time.

"You smell like fruit," he said into my hair.

"We're supposed to be in Hilton Head," I muttered. "How did we suddenly end up in Philadelphia?"

"It's a bloody mess," he said.

Benton gently pulled away from me and took off his jacket. He draped it over my bed and unlocked the mini-bar.

"The usual?" he asked.

"Just some Evian."

"Well, I need something stronger."

He unscrewed the top of a Johnnie Walker.

"In fact, I'll make that a double, and the hell with ice," he let me know.

He handed me the Evian, and I watched him as he pulled out the desk chair and sat. I propped up pillows on the bed and made myself comfortable as we viewed each other from a distance.

"What's wrong?" I asked. "Besides everything."

"The usual problem when ATF and the Bureau are suddenly thrown together on a case," he said, sipping his drink. "It makes me glad I'm retired."

"You don't seem very retired," I said wryly.

"That's the damn truth. As if Carrie isn't enough for me to worry about. Then I'm called in on this homicide, and to be honest, Kay, ATF has its own profilers and I don't think the Bureau should be poking its nose into this at all."

"Tell me something I don't know, Benton. And I don't see how they're justifying their involvement, for that matter, unless they're saying this lady's death is an act of terrorism."

"The potential link to the Warrenton homicide," he told me. "As you know. And it wasn't hard for the unit chief to call state police investigators to let them know the Bureau would do anything to help. So then the Bureau's invited in, and here I am. There were two agents at the fire scene earlier today, and already everybody's pissed off."

"You know, Benton, supposedly we're all on the same side," I said, and this same old subject made me angry again.

"Apparently this one FBI guy who's with the Philly field office hid a nine-millimeter cartridge at the scene to see if Pepper would hit on it."

Benton slowly swirled Scotch in his glass.

"Of course Pepper didn't because he hadn't even been told to go to work yet," he went on. "And the agent thought this was funny, saying something about the dog's nose needing to go back to the shop."

"What kind of fool would do something like that?" I asked, incensed. "He's lucky the handler didn't beat the hell out of him."

"So here we are," he went on with a sigh. "Same old shit. In the good ole days, FBI agents had better sense than that. They weren't always flashing their shields in front of the camera and taking over investigations they aren't qualified to handle. I'm embarrassed. I'm more than embarrassed, I'm enraged that these new idiots out there are ruining my reputation along with their own, after I worked twenty-five years . . . Well. I just don't know what I'm going to do, Kay."

He met my eyes as he drank.

"Just do your good job, Benton," I said to him quietly. "Trite as that may sound, it's all any of us can do. We're not doing it for the Bureau, not for ATF or the Pennsylvania state police. It's for the victims and potential victims. Always for them."

He drained his glass and set it on the desk. The lights of Penn's Landing were festive outside my window, and Camden, New Jersey, glittered on the other side of the river.

"I don't think Carrie's in New York anymore," he then said as he stared out into the night.

"A comforting thought."

"And I have no evidence for that beyond there being no sightings or any other indicators that she is in the city. Where is she getting money, for example? Often that's how the trail begins. Robbery, stolen credit cards. Nothing so far to make us think she's out there doing things like that. Of course, that doesn't mean she isn't. But she has a plan, and I feel quite confident that she's following it."

His profile was sharp in shadows as he continued staring out at the river. Benton was depressed. He sounded worn out and defeated, and I got up and went to him.

"We should go to bed," I said, massaging his shoulders. "We're both tired, and everything seems worse when we're tired, right?"

He smiled a little and closed his eyes as I worked on his temples and kissed the back of his neck.

"How much do you charge per hour?" he muttered.

"You can't afford me," I said.

We did not sleep together because the rooms were small and both of us needed rest. I liked my shower in the morning and he liked his, and that was the difference between being new with each other versus comfortable. There had been a time when we stayed up all night consuming each other, because we worked together and he was married and we could not help our hunger. I missed feeling that alive. Often when we were with each other now, my heart was dull or felt sweet pain, and I saw myself getting old.

The skies were gray and the streets were wet from washing when Benton and I drove through downtown on Walnut Street a little past seven the following morning. Steam rose from grates and manholes, the morning damp and cool. The homeless slept on sidewalks or beneath filthy blankets in parks, and one man looked dead beneath a *No Loitering* sign across from the police department. I drove while Benton went through his briefcase. He took notes on a yellow legal pad and thought about matters beyond my ken. I turned onto Interstate 76 West, where taillights were strung like red glass beads as far ahead as I could see, and the sun behind us was bright.

"Why would someone pick a bathroom as a point of origin?" I asked. "Why not some other area of the house?"

"Obviously, it means something to him, if we're talking about serial crimes," he said, flipping a page. "Symbolic, perhaps. Maybe convenient for some other reason. My guess is that if we're dealing with the same offender, and the bathroom is the point of origin that all of the fires have in common, then it is symbolic. Represents something to him, perhaps his own point of origin for his crimes. If something happened to him in a bathroom when he was a young child, for example. Sexual abuse, child abuse, witnessing something terribly traumatic."

"Too bad we can't search prison records for that."

"Problem is, you'd come up with half the prison population. Most of these people come from abuse. Then they do unto others."

"They do worse unto others," I said. "They weren't murdered."

"They were, in a sense. When you are beaten and raped as a child, your life is murdered even if your body isn't. Not that any of this really explains psychopathy. Nothing I know of does, unless you believe in evil and that people make choices."

"That's exactly what I believe."

He looked over at me and said, "I know."

"What about Carrie's childhood? How much do we know about why she's made the choices she has?" I asked.

"She would never let us interview her," he reminded me. "There isn't much in her psychiatric evaluations, except whatever her manipulation of the moment was. Crazy today, not tomorrow. Disassociating. Depressed and noncompliant. Or a model patient. These squirrels have more civil rights than we do, Kay. And prisons and forensic psychiatric centers are often so protective of their wards that you would think we're the bad guys."

The morning was getting lighter and the sky was streaked violet and white in perfect horizontal bands. We drove through farmland and intermittent cliffs of pink granite corrugated with drill holes from the dynamite that had blasted in the roads. Mist rising from ponds reminded me of pots of simmering water, and when we passed tall smokestacks with steamy plumes, I thought of fire. In the distance, mountains were a shadow, and water towers dotted the horizon like bright balloons.

It took an hour to reach Lehigh Valley Hospital, a sprawling concrete complex still under construction, with a helicopter hangar and level one trauma center. I parked in a visitor's lot, and Dr. Abraham Gerde met us inside the bright, new lobby.

"Kay," he said warmly, shaking my hand. "Who would have ever thought you'd be visiting me here some day? And you must be Benton? We have a very good cafeteria here if you'd like coffee or something to eat first?"

Benton and I politely declined. Gerde was a young forensic pathologist with dark hair and startling blue eyes. He had rotated through my office three years earlier, and was still new enough at his profession to rarely have his status as an expert witness stipulated in court. But he was humble and meticulous, and those attributes were far more valuable to me than experience, especially in this instance. Unless Gerde had changed dramatically, it was unlikely he had touched the body after learning I was coming.

"Tell me where we are in this," I said as we walked down a wide, polished gray hallway.

"I had her weighed, measured and was doing the external exam when the coroner called. As soon as he said ATF was involved and you were on the way, I stopped the presses."

Lehigh County had an elected coroner who decided which cases would be autopsied and then determined the manner of death. Fortunately for Gerde, the coroner was a former police officer who did not interfere with the forensic pathologists and usually deferred to the decisions they made. But this was not true in other states or other counties in Pennsylvania, where autopsies were sometimes performed on embalming tables in funeral homes, and some coroners were consummate politicians who did not know an entrance from an exit wound, or care.

Our footsteps echoed in the stairwell, and at the bottom, Gerde pushed through double doors and we found ourselves in a warehouse stacked with collapsed cardboard boxes and busy with people in hard hats. We passed through to a different part of the building and followed another hallway to the morgue. It was small, with a pink tile floor and two stationary stainless steel tables. Gerde opened a cabinet and handed us sterile single-use surgical gowns, plastic aprons, and full coverage disposable boots. We pulled these over our clothes and shoes and then donned latex gloves and masks.

The dead woman had been identified as Kellie Shephard, a thirty-two-year-old black female who had worked as a nurse at the very hospital where she was now being stored with the dead. She was inside a black pouch on top of a gurney inside a small walk-in refrigerator that held no other guests this day except bright orange packages of surgical specimens and stillborn infants awaiting cremation. We rolled the dead woman into the autopsy room and unzipped the pouch.

"Have you X-rayed her?" I asked Gerde.

"Yes, and we've gotten her fingerprints. The dentist charted her teeth yesterday, as well, and matched them with premortem records."

Gerde and I unzipped the pouch and opened it, and we unwrapped bloody sheets, exposing the mutilated body to the harsh glare of surgical lamps. She was rigid and cold, her blind eyes half open in a gory face. Gerde had not washed her yet, and her skin was crusty with blackish-red blood, her hair stiff with it like a Brillo pad. Her wounds were so numerous and violent that they radiated an aura of rage. I could feel the killer's fury and hate, and I began to envision her fierce struggle with him.

The fingers and palms of both hands had been cut to the bone when she had tried to protect herself by grabbing the knife blade. She had deep cuts to the backs of her forearms and wrists, again from trying to shield herself, and slashes to her legs that most likely were from her being down on the floor and trying to kick the swings of the knife away. Stab wounds were clustered in a savage constellation over her breasts, abdomen, and shoulders, and also on her buttocks and back.

Many of the wounds were large and irregular, and caused by the knife twisting as the victim moved or from the blade being withdrawn. The pattern of the individual wound configurations suggested a single-edged knife with a guard that had left squared-off abrasions. A somewhat superficial cut ran from her right jaw up to her cheek, and her throat had been laid open in a direction that began below the right ear and went downward, and then across the midline of the neck.

"Consistent with her throat being cut from behind," I said as Benton looked on silently and took notes. "Head pulled back, throat exposed."

"I'm assuming cutting her throat was his grand finale," Gerde said.

"If she had received an injury like this in the beginning, she would have bled out too quickly to put up any kind of fight. So yes, it's very possible he cut her throat last, perhaps when she was face down on the floor. What about clothing?"

"I'll get it," Gerde said. "You know, I get the strangest cases here. All these awful car crashes that turn out to be from some guy having a heart attack while he's driving.

So he ends up airborne and takes out three or four other people. We had an Internet murder not so long ago. And husbands don't just shoot their wives around here, either. They strangle and bludgeon and decapitate them."

He kept talking as he headed to a distant corner where clothing dried from hangers over a shallow basin. The garments were separated by sheets of plastic, to insure that trace evidence and body fluids from one weren't inadvertently transferred to another. I was covering the second autopsy table with a sterile sheet when Teun McGovern was shown in by a morgue assistant.

"Thought I'd check by before heading out to the scene," she said.

She was dressed in BDUs and boots, and carrying a manila envelope. McGovern did not bother with gown or gloves as she slowly surveyed the carnage.

"Good Lord," she said.

I helped Gerde spread out a pair of pajamas on top of the table I had just covered. Tops and bottoms reeked of dirty smoke and were so sooty and saturated with blood that I could not tell their color. The cotton fabric was cut and punctured front and back.

"She came in clothed in these?" I wanted to make sure.

"Yes," Gerde replied. "Everything buttoned and snapped. And I have to wonder if possibly some of the blood is his. In a fight like this, I wouldn't be surprised if he cut himself."

I smiled at him. "Someone taught you well," I said.

"Some lady in Richmond," he answered.

"At a glance this would seem domestic." It was Benton who spoke. "She's home in her pajamas, perhaps late at night. A classic case of overkill, such as you often find in homicides where the two people had a relationship. But what's a little unusual'—he stepped closer to the table—"is her face. Other than this one cut here," he pointed, "there doesn't appear to be any injury. Typically, when the assailant has a relationship with the victim, he directs much of his violence at the face, because the face is the person."

"The cut to her face is shallower than the others," I noted, gently spreading open the wound with my gloved fingers. "Deepest at her jaw, and then tapering off as it travels up her cheek."

I stepped back and looked at the pajamas again.

"It's interesting that none of the buttons or snaps are missing," I said. "And no tears, such as you might expect after a struggle like this when the assailant grabs the victim and tries to control her."

"I think *control* is the important word here," Benton said.

"Or lack of it," said McGovern.

"Exactly," Benton agreed. "This is a blitz attack. Something set this guy off and he went berserk. I seriously doubt he intended for this to go down anything like it did, which is also evidenced by the fire. It appears he lost control of that, too."

"In my mind, the guy didn't hang around very long after he killed her," McGovern said. "He torched the place on his way out, thinking it would cover up his dirty work. But you're absolutely right. He didn't do a good job. And added to that, when the lady's fire alarm went off at one-fifty-eight A.M., trucks got there in less than five minutes. So the damage was minimal."

Kellie Shephard had second-degree burns to her back and feet, and that was all.

"What about a burglar alarm?" I asked.

"Wasn't armed," McGovern replied.

She opened the manila envelope and began spreading scene photographs over a desk. Benton, Gerde, and I took our time studying them. The victim in her bloody pajamas was facedown in the bathroom doorway, one arm under her body, the other straight out in front of her as if she had been reaching for something. Her legs were straight and close together, her feet almost reaching the toilet. Sooty water on the floor made it impossible to find bloody drag marks, had they existed, but close-ups of the door frame and surrounding wall showed obvious cuts to the wood that appeared fresh.

"The fire's point of origin," McGovern said, "is right here."

She pointed to a photograph of the interior of the scorched bathroom.

"This corner near the tub where there's an open window with a curtain," she said. "And in that area, as you can see, are burned remnants of wooden furniture and pillows from a couch."

She tapped the photograph.

"So we've got an open door and an open window, or a flue and a chimney, so to speak. Just like a fireplace," she went on. "The fire starts here on the tile floor, and involves the curtains. But the flames didn't quite have the energy this time to fully engage the ceiling."

"Why do you suppose that is?" I asked.

"Can only be one good reason," she replied. "The damn thing wasn't built right. I mean, it's clear as day the killer piled furniture, couch cushions, and whatever into the bathroom to build his fire. But it just never got going the way it needed to. The initial fire was unable to involve the piled fuel load because of the open window and the flame bending toward it. He also didn't stand around and watch, either, or he would have realized he screwed up. This time his fire didn't do much more than lick over the body like a dragon's tongue."

Benton was so silent and still he looked like a statue as his eyes traveled over photographs. I could tell he had much on his mind, but typically, he was guarded in his words. He had never worked with McGovern before, and he did not know Dr. Abraham Gerde.

"We're going to be a long time," I said to him.

"I'm heading out to the scene," he replied.

His face was stony, the way it got when he felt evil like a cold draft. I gave him my eyes, and his met mine.

"You can follow me," McGovern offered him.

"Thanks."

"One other thing," McGovern said. "The back door was unlocked, and there was an empty cat pan in the grass by the steps."

"So you think she went outside to empty the cat pan?" Gerde asked both of them. "And this guy was waiting for her?"

"It's just a theory," said McGovern.

"I don't know," Wesley said.

"Then the killer knew she had a cat?" I said dubiously. "And that she eventually was going to let it out that night or clean out the cat pan?"

"We don't know that she didn't empty the litter box earlier that evening and leave it in the yard to air out," Wesley pointed out as he ripped off his gown. "She may have turned off her alarm and opened the door late that night or in the early morning hours for some other reason."

"And the cat?" I asked. "Has it shown up?"

"Not yet," McGovern said, and she and Benton left.

"I'm going to start swabbing," I said to Gerde.

He reached for a camera and started shooting as I adjusted a light. I studied the cut to her face, and collected several fibers from it, and a wavy brown hair, four and a half inches long, that I suspected was her own. But there were other hairs, red and short, and I could tell they had been recently dyed because one-sixteenth of an inch at the root was dark. Of course, cat fur was everywhere, most likely transferred to bloody surfaces of the body when the victim was on the floor.

"A Persian, maybe?" Gerde asked. "Long, very fine fur?"

"Sounds good to me," I said.

15

The task of collecting trace evidence was overwhelming and had to be done before anything else. People generally have no idea what a microscopic pigpen they carry with them until someone like me starts scouring clothing and bodies for barely visible debris. I found splinters of wood, likely from the floor and walls, and cat litter, dirt, bits and pieces of insects and plants, and the expected ash and trash from the fire. But the most telling discovery came from the tremendous injury to her neck. Through a lens, I found two shiny, metallic specks. I collected them with the tip of my little finger, and delicately transferred them to a square of clean white cotton cloth.

There was a dissecting microscope on top of an old metal desk, and I set the magnification to twenty and adjusted the illuminator. I could scarcely believe it when I saw the tiny flattened and twisted silvery shavings in the bright circle of light.

"This is very important," I started talking fast. "I'm going to pack them in cotton inside an evidence container, and we need to make double sure there's no other debris like this in any of the other wounds. To the naked eye, it flashes like a piece of silver glitter."

"Transferred from the weapon?"

Gerde was excited, too, and he came over to take a look.

"They were embedded deep inside the wound to her neck. So yes, I'd say that was a transfer, similar to what I found in the Warrenton case," I answered him.

"And we know what about that?"

"A magnesium turning," I answered. "And we don't mention anything about this to anyone. We don't want this leaking to the press. I'll let Benton and McGovern know."

"You got it," he said with feeling.

There were twenty-seven wounds, and after a painful scrutinizing of all of them, we found no other bits of the shiny metal, and this struck me as a little puzzling since I had assumed the throat had been cut last. If that were the case, why wasn't the turning transferred to an earlier wound? I believed it would have been, especially in those instances when the knife had penetrated up to the guard and was swiped clean by muscular and elastic tissue as the blade was withdrawn.

"Not impossible but inconsistent," I said to Gerde as I began measuring the cut to the throat. "Six and three-quarters inches long," I said, jotting it down on a body diagram. "Shallow up around the right ear, then deep, through the strap muscles and trachea, then shallow again higher on the opposite side of the neck. Consistent with the knife drawn across the neck from behind, by a left-handed assailant."

It was almost two P.M. when we finally began washing the body, and for minutes, water draining through the steel tabletop was bright red. I scrubbed stubborn blood with a big soft sponge, and her wounds seemed even more gaping and mutilating when her taut brown skin was clean. Kellie Shephard had been a beautiful woman, with high cheekbones and a flawless complexion as smooth as polished wood. She was five-foot-eight, with a lean, athletic figure. Her fingernails were unpainted, and she had been wearing no jewelry when she was found.

When we opened her up, her pierced chest cavity was filled with almost a liter of blood that had hemorrhaged from the great vessels leading to and from her heart and from her lungs. After receiving these injuries, she would have bled to death in, at the most, minutes, and I placed the timing of those attacks later in the struggle, when she was weakening and slowing down. The angles of those wounds were slight enough for me to suspect she had been moving very little on the floor when they had been inflicted from above. Then she had managed to roll over, perhaps in her last dying effort to protect herself, and I conjectured that this was when her throat was slashed.

"Someone should have had an awful lot of blood on him," I commented as I began measuring the cuts to the hands.

"No kidding."

"He had to clean up somewhere. You don't walk into a motel lobby looking like that."

"Unless he lives around here."

"Or got into his vehicle and hoped he didn't get pulled for something."

"She's got a little brownish fluid in her stomach."

"So she hadn't eaten recently, probably not since dinner, at any rate," I said. "I guess we need to find out if her bed was unmade."

I was getting an image of a woman asleep when something happened either late Saturday night or in the early hours of Sunday morning. For some reason, she got up and turned off the alarm and unlocked the back door. Gerde and I used surgical staples to close the Y incision at shortly past four. I cleaned up in the morgue's small dressing room, where a mannikin used for staging violent deaths in court was in a state of disarray and undress on the shower floor.

Other than teenagers burning down old farmhouses, arsons in Lehigh were rare. Violence in the tidy middle-class subdivision called Wescosville where Shephard had lived was unheard of, as well. Crime there had never been more serious than smash and grabs, when a thief spied a pocketbook or wallet in plain view inside a house, and broke in and grabbed. Since there was no police department in Lehigh, by the time state troopers responded to the clanging fire alarm, the thief was long gone.

I got my BDUs and steel-reinforced boots from my turn-out bag and shared the same changing room with the mannikin. Gerde was kind enough to give me a ride to the fire scene, and I was impressed by lush fir trees and road-side flower gardens, and every now and then, a well-kept, unassuming church. We turned on Hanover Drive, where homes were modern brick and wood, two-story and spacious, with basketball hoops, bicycles, and other signs of children.

"Do you have any idea of the price range?" I said, watching more houses flow past.

"Two-to-three-hundred-K range," he said. "Got a lot of engineers, nurses, stock brokers, and executives back here. Plus, I-78 is the main artery through Lehigh Valley, and you can shoot straight out on that and be in New York in an hour and a half. So some people commute back and forth to the city."

"What else is around here?" I asked.

"A lot of industrial parks are just ten or fifteen minutes away. Coca-Cola, Air Products, Nestlé warehouses, Perrier. You pretty much name it. And farmland."

"But she worked at the hospital."

"Right. And that's at most a ten-minute drive, as you can tell."

"Are you aware of ever having seen her before?"

Gerde thought for a minute as thin smoke drifted up from behind trees at the end of the street.

"I'm fairly certain I've seen her in the cafeteria before," he answered. "It's hard not to notice someone who looked like that. She may have been at a table with other nurses, I don't really recall. But I don't think we ever spoke."

Shephard's house was yellow clapboard with white trim, and although the fire may not have been difficult to contain, the damage from water, and from axes chopping great holes to vent the fire out of the roof, was devastating. What was left was a sad, sooty face with a caved-in head, and shattered windows that were depressed, lifeless eyes. Borders of wild-flowers were trampled, the neatly mown grass turned to mud, and a late-model Camry parked in the drive was covered with cinders. Fire department and ATF investigators were working inside, while two FBI agents in flak jackets were prowling the perimeter.

I found McGovern in the backyard talking to an intense young woman dressed in cut-off jeans, sandals, and a T-shirt.

"And that was what? Close to six?" McGovern was saying to her.

"That's right. I was getting dinner ready and saw her pull into her driveway, parking exactly where her car is now," the woman recounted excitedly. "She went inside, then came out maybe thirty minutes later and began pulling weeds.

She liked to work in the yard, cut her own grass and everything."

McGovern watched me as I walked up.

"This is Mrs. Harvey," she said to me. "The next-door neighbor."

"Hello," I said to Mrs. Harvey, whose eyes were bright with excitement that bordered on fear.

"Dr. Scarpetta is a medical examiner," McGovern explained.

"Oh," said Mrs. Harvey.

"Did you see Kellie again that night?" McGovern then asked.

The woman shook her head.

"She went in," she said, "I guess, and that was it. I know she worked real hard and usually didn't stay up late."

"What about a relationship? Was there anybody she saw?"

"Oh, she's been through them," Mrs. Harvey said. "A doctor here and there, different folks from the hospital. I remember last year she started seeing this man who had been her patient. Nothing lasted very long, it seems to me. She's so beautiful, that's the problem. The men wanted one thing, and she had something different in mind. I know because she used to make remarks about it."

"But nobody recently?" McGovern asked.

Mrs. Harvey had to think.

"Just her girlfriends," she replied. "She has a couple people she works with, and sometimes they dropped by or went off somewhere together. But I don't remember any activity that night. I mean, that's not saying I would know. Someone could have come over, and I wouldn't necessarily have heard a thing."

"Have we found her cat?" I asked.

McGovern did not answer.

"That darn cat," Mrs. Harvey said. "Pumpkin. Spoiled, spoiled, spoiled."

She smiled and her eyes filled with tears.

"That was her child," Harvey said.

"An indoor cat?" I then asked.

"Oh, absolutely. Kellie never let that cat out of the house, treated him like a hothouse tomato."

"His litter box was found in the backyard," McGovern told her. "Did Kellie sometimes empty it and leave it out all night? Or for that matter, did she have a habit of emptying it at night? Going out after dark, the door unlocked and the alarm off."

Harvey looked confused, and I suspected she had no idea that her neighbor had been murdered.

"Well," she said, "I do know that I've seen her empty the litter before, but always in a trash bag that went into the super can. So it wouldn't make sense for her to do that at night. My guess is she might have emptied it and left it outside to air, you know? Or maybe she just didn't have time to hose it off and was going to do it the next morning. But whatever the case, that cat knew how to use the toilet. So it wouldn't be any big deal for him to be without his litter box for a night."

She stared off at a state police car cruising by.

"No one's said how the fire started," Harvey went on. "Do we know?"

"We're working on it," McGovern said.

"She didn't die . . . well, it was quick, wasn't it?"

She squinted in the setting sun, and she bit her lower lip.

"I just don't want to think she suffered," she said.

"Most people who die in fires don't suffer," I answered, evading her question with gentle words. "Usually carbon monoxide overcomes them and they aren't conscious."

"Oh, thank God," she said.

"I'll be inside," McGovern said to me.

"Mrs. Harvey," I said, "did you know Kellie very well?"

"We've been neighbors for almost five years. Not that we did a whole lot together, but I certainly knew her."

"I'm wondering if you might have any recent photographs of her, or know someone who might?"

"I might have something."

"I have to make sure of the identification," I then said, although my motive was other than that.

I wanted to see for myself what Shephard had looked like in life.

"And if there's anything else you can tell me about her, I would appreciate it," I went on. "For example, does she have family here?"

"Oh no," Harvey said, staring at her neighbor's ruined house. "She was from all over. Her father was military, you know, and I think he and her mom live somewhere in North Carolina. Kellie was very worldly from having moved around so much. I used to tell her I wished I could be as strong and smart as her. She didn't take crap off anyone, let me tell you. One time there was a snake on my deck, and I called her, all hysterical. She came on and chased it in the yard and killed it with a shovel. I guess she had to get that way because the men just wouldn't leave her alone. I always told her she could be a movie star, and she would say, *But Sandra, I can't act*. And I would say, *But neither can most of them!*"

"She was pretty streetwise, then," I said.

"You bet. That's why she had that burglar alarm put in. Feisty and streetwise, that's Kellie. If you want to come in with me, I'll see what I can do about pictures."

"If you don't mind," I said. "That's very nice of you."

We cut through a hedge and I followed her up steps into her big, bright kitchen. It was apparent that Harvey liked to cook, based on a well-stocked pantry and every conceivable appliance. Cookware hung from hooks in the ceiling, and whatever was simmering on the stove smelled rich with beef and onions, perhaps a stroganoff or stew.

"If you want to sit right over there by the window, I'll go get what I've got from the den," she said.

I took a seat at the breakfast table and looked out the window at Kellie Shephard's house. I could see people passing behind broken windows, and someone had set up lights because the sun was low and smoldering. I wondered how often her neighbor had watched her come and go.

Certainly, Harvey was curious about the life of a woman exotic enough to be a movie star, and I wondered if someone could have stalked Shephard without her neighbor noticing a strange car or person in the area. But I had to be careful what I asked, because it was not publicly known that Shephard had died a violent death.

"Well, I can't believe it," Harvey called out to me as she returned to the kitchen. "I got something better. You know, some television crew was at the hospital last week filming a feature about the trauma center. It showed on the evening news, and Kellie was in it, so I taped it. I can't believe it took me this long to think of it, but my brain's not working all that well, if you know what I mean."

She was holding a videotape. I accompanied her into the living room, where she inserted the tape into the VCR. I sat in a blue wing chair in a sea of blue carpet while she rewound and then hit the *play* button. The first few frames were of Lehigh Valley hospital from the perspective of a helicopter swooping in with an emergency case. It was then I realized that Kellie was really a medflight paramedic, and not merely a nurse on a ward.

Footage showed Kellie in a jumpsuit dashing down a corridor with other members of the flight crew who had just been paged.

"Excuse me, excuse me," she said on tape as they darted around people in the way.

She was a spectacular example of the human genome working just right, her teeth dazzling, and the camera in love with every angle of her fine features and bones. It was not hard to imagine patients getting major crushes on her, and then the film showed her in the cafeteria after another impossible mission had been accomplished.

"It's always a race against time," Shephard was telling the reporter. "You know even a minute's delay could cost a life. Talk about an adrenaline rush."

As she continued her rather banal interview, the angle of the camera shifted.

"I can't believe I taped that, but it's not often someone I know is on TV," Harvey was saying.

It didn't penetrate at first.

"Stop the tape!" I said. "Rewind. Yes, right there. Freeze it."

The frame was of someone in the background eating lunch.

"No," I said under my breath. "No way."

Carrie Grethen was wearing jeans and a tie-dye shirt, and

eating a sandwich at a table with other busy hospital personnel. I had not recognized her at first because her hair was below her ears and henna red, and last I had seen her, it was short and bleached white. But it was her eyes that finally pulled at me like a black hole. She was staring straight into the camera as she chewed, her eyes as coldly bright and evil as I remembered.

I came out of the chair and went straight to the VCR and popped out the tape.

"I need to take this," I said, my voice on the verge of panic. "I promise you'll get it back."

"Okay. As long as you don't forget. It's my only copy." Sandra Harvey got up, too. "Are you all right? You look like you've seen a ghost."

"I've got to go. Thank you again," I said.

I ran next door and trotted up steps into the back of the house, where cold water was an inch deep on the floor and dripping slowly from the roof. Agents were moving about, taking photographs and talking amongst themselves.

"Teun!" I called out.

I carefully moved further inside, stepping over missing areas of flooring and doing my best not to trip. I was vaguely aware of an agent dropping the burned carcass of a cat into a plastic bag.

"Teun!" I called out again.

I heard sure feet splashing and stepping over fallen roofing and collapsed walls. Then she was mere inches from me and steadying my arm with her hand.

"Whoa. Careful," she started to say.

"We've got to find Lucy," I said.

"What's going on?"

She began to carefully escort me out.

"Where is she?" I demanded.

"There's a two-alarm fire downtown. A grocery store, probably an arson. Kay, what the hell . . . ?"

We were out on the lawn and I was clutching the videotape as if it were my only hope in life.

"Teun, please." I held her gaze. "Take me to Philadelphia."

"Come on," she said.

16

McGovern made the trip back to Philadelphia in forty-five minutes, because she was speeding. She had radioed her field office and talked on a secure tac channel. Although she was still very careful what she relayed, she had made it clear that she wanted every available agent out on the street looking for Carrie. While this was going on, I reached Marino on my cellular phone and told him to get on a plane now.

"She's here," I said.

"Oh shit. Do Benton and Lucy know?"

"As soon as I find them."

"I'm out the door," he said.

I did not believe, nor did McGovern, that Carrie was still in Lehigh County. She wanted to be where she could do the most damage, and I was convinced she somehow knew that Lucy had moved to Philadelphia. Carrie could have been stalking Lucy, for that matter. One thing I believed but could not make sense of was that the murders in Warrenton and now here were intended to lure those of us who had defeated Carrie in the past.

"But Warrenton happened before she escaped from Kirby,"

McGovern reminded me as she turned onto Chestnut Street.

"I know," I said as fear turned my pulse to static. "I don't understand any of it except that somehow she's involved. It's not coincidence that she was on that news clip, Teun. She knew that after Kellie Shephard's murder we would review everything we could find. Carrie knew damn well we would see that tape."

The fire was located on a seedy strip on the western fringes of the University of Pennsylvania. Darkness had fallen, and flashing emergency lights were visible miles away. Police cars had closed off two blocks of the street. There were at least eight fire engines and four ladder trucks, and more than seventy feet in the air, firefighters in buckets blasted the smoking roof with deluge guns. The night rumbled with diesel engines, and the blasting of high pressure water drummed over wood and shattered more glass. Tumescent hoses snaked across the street, and water was up to the hubcaps of parked cars that would be going nowhere anytime soon.

Photographers and news crews prowled sidewalks and were suddenly on alert when McGovern and I got out of her car.

"Is ATF involved in this case?" asked a TV reporter.

"We're just here taking a look," McGovern answered as we walked without pause.

"Then it's a suspected arson, like the other grocery stores?" The microphone followed as our boots splashed.

"It's under investigation," McGovern said. "And you need to stay back, ma'am."

The reporter was left at the hood of a fire engine while McGovern and I drew closer to the store. Flames had jumped to the barbershop next door, where firefighters with axes and pike poles chopped square holes in the roof. Agents in ATF flak jackets were interviewing potential witnesses, and investigators in turn-outs and helmets moved in and out of a basement. I overheard something about toggle switches and the meter and stealing service. Black smoke billowed, and there seemed to be only one area in the plenum that stubbornly smoldered and spurted flame.

"She might be inside," McGovern said in my ear.

I followed her in closer. The plate-glass storefront was wide open, and part of the inventory flowed out on a cold river of water. Cans of tuna fish, blackened bananas, sanitary napkins, bags of potato chips, and bottles of salad dressing flowed by, and a firefighter rescued a can of coffee and shrugged as he tossed it inside his truck. The strong beams of flashlights probed the smoky, black interior of the devastated store, illuminating girders twisted like taffy and exposed wires hanging in tangles from I-beams.

"Is Lucy Farinelli in there?" McGovern called inside.

"Last I saw her she was out back talking to the owner," a male voice called back.

"Be careful in there," McGovern said loudly.

"Yeah, well, we're having a real problem getting the power to shut down. Must be an underground feed. Maybe if you could look into that?"

"Will do."

"So this is what my niece does," I said as McGovern and I waded back out to the street and more ruined produce and canned goods floated past.

"On her good days. I think her unit number's 718. Let me see if I can raise her."

McGovern held the portable radio to her lips and searched for Lucy on the air.

"What'cha got?" my niece's voice came back.

"You in the middle of something?"

"Finishing up."

"Can you meet us in front?"

"On my way."

My relief was apparent, and McGovern smiled at me as lights strobed and water arched. Firefighters were black with soot and sweating. I watched them moving slowly in their boots, dragging hoses over their shoulders and drinking cups of a green thirst quencher that they mixed in plastic jugs. Bright lights had been set up in a truck, and the glare was harsh and confusing as the scene became surreal. Fire buffs, or *whackers*, as ATF agents called them, had crawled out of the dark and were taking photographs with disposable cameras, while entrepreneurial venders hawked incense and counterfeit watches.

By the time Lucy got to us, the smoke had thinned and was white, indicating a lot of steam. Water was getting to the source.

"Good," McGovern commented, observing the same thing. "I think we're almost there."

"Rats chewing wires," Lucy said first thing. "That's the owner's theory."

She looked at me oddly.

"What brings you out?" she asked.

"It's looking like Carrie is involved in the Lehigh arson-homicide," McGovern answered for me. "And it's possible she's still in the area, maybe even here in Philadelphia."

"What?" Lucy looked stunned. "How? What about Warrenton?"

"I know," I replied. "It seems inexplicable. But there are definite parallels."

"So maybe this one's a copycat," my niece then said. "She read about it and is jerking us around."

I thought of the metal shaving again, and of the point of origin. There had been nothing in the news about details like that. Nor had it ever been released that Claire Rawley had been killed with a sharp cutting instrument, such as a knife, and I could not get away from one other similarity. Both Rawley and Shephard were beautiful.

"We've got a lot of agents on the street," McGovern said to Lucy. "The point is for you to be aware and alert, all right? And Kay." She looked at me. "This may not be the best place for you to be."

I did not answer her, but instead said to Lucy, "Have you heard from Benton?"

"No."

"I just don't understand," I muttered. "I wonder where he could be."

"When did you have contact with him last?" Lucy asked.

"At the morgue. He left saying he was going to the scene. And he what? Stayed there maybe an hour?" I said to McGovern.

"If that. You don't think he would have gone back to New York, or maybe Richmond?" she asked me.

"I'm sure he would have told me. I'll keep paging him. Maybe when Marino gets here, he'll know something," I added as fire hoses blasted and a fine mist settled over us.

It was almost midnight when Marino came to my hotel room, and he knew nothing.

"I don't think you should be here by yourself," he said right off, and he was keyed up and disheveled.

"You want to tell me where I might be safer? I don't know what's happening. Benton's left no messages. He isn't answering his pager."

"You two didn't get in a fight or something, did you?"

"For God's sake," I said in exasperation.

"Look, you asked me, and I'm just trying to help."

"I know."

I took a deep breath and tried to settle down.

"What about Lucy?"

He sat on the edge of my bed.

"There was a pretty big fire near the university. She's probably still there," I answered.

"Arson?"

"I'm not sure they know yet."

We were quiet for a moment, and my tension grew.

"Look," I said. "We can stay here and wait for God knows what. Or we can go out. I can't sleep."

I began to pace.

"I'm not sitting here all night worrying that Carrie might be lying in wait, damn it."

Tears filled my eyes.

"Benton's out there somewhere. Maybe at the fire scene with Lucy. I don't know."

I turned my back to him and stared out at the harbor. My breath trembled in my breast, and my hands were so cold the fingernails had turned blue.

Marino got up, and I knew he was watching me.

"Come on," he said. "Let's check it out."

When we reached the fire scene on Walnut Street, the activity had diminished considerably. Most of the fire trucks had left, and those few firefighters still on the job were exhausted and coiling hoses. Steamy smoke drifted up from the plenum area of the store, but I could see no flames, and from within voices and footsteps sounded as the strong beam of flashlights cut the darkness and were caught in shards of broken glass. I sloshed through water as more groceries and debris floated past, and when I reached the entrance, I heard McGovern's voice. She was saying something about a medical examiner.

"Get him here now," she barked. "And watch it over there, okay? No telling where it's all scattered, and I don't want us stepping on anything."

"Someone got a camera?"

"Okay, I got a watch, stainless steel, men's. Crystal's shattered. And we got one pair of handcuffs?"

"What did you say?"

"You heard me. Handcuffs, Smith & Wesson, the genuine article. Closed and locked like someone had them on. In fact, they're *double* locked."

"You're shittin' me."

I made my way inside as large drops of cold water smacked my helmet and dripped down my neck. I recognized Lucy's voice, but I could not make out what she was saying. She sounded almost hysterical, and there was suddenly a lot of splashing and commotion.

"Hold on, hold on!" McGovern commanded. "Lucy! Someone get her out of here!"

"No!" Lucy screamed.

"Come on, come on," McGovern was saying. "I've got your arm. Take it easy, okay?"

"No!" Lucy screamed. "NO! NO! NO!"

Then there was a loud splash and a surprised outcry.

"My God. Are you all right?" McGovern said.

I was halfway inside when I saw McGovern helping Lucy to her feet. My niece was hysterical, and her hand was bleeding, but she didn't seem to care. I waded to them as my heart constricted and my blood seemed to turn as cold as the water I waded through.

"Let me see," I said as I gently took Lucy's hand and shone my light on it.

She was shaking all over.

"When's the last time you had a tetanus shot?" I asked.

"Aunt Kay," she moaned. "Aunt Kay."

Lucy locked her arms around my neck, and both of us almost fell. She was crying so hard she could not speak, and her embrace was a vise against my ribs.

"What's happened?" I demanded of McGovern.

"Let's get both of you out of here now," she said.

"Tell me what's happened!"

I wasn't going anywhere until she told me. She hesitated again.

"We've found some remains. A burn victim. Kay, please."

She took my arm and I yanked it away.

"We need to go out," she said.

I pulled away from her as I looked toward the back corner, where investigators were talking amongst themselves and splashing and wading as fingers of light probed.

"More bones over here," someone was saying. "Nope, scratch that. Burned wood."

"Well, this isn't."

"Shit. Where the fuck's the medical examiner?"

"I'll take care of this," I said to McGovern as if this were my scene. "Get Lucy out and wrap a clean towel around her hand. I'll tend to her shortly. Lucy," I then said to my niece. "You're going to be fine."

I unlocked her arms from my neck, and I was beginning to tremble. Somehow I knew.

"Kay, don't go over there," McGovern raised her voice. "Don't!"

But by now I knew I must, and I abruptly left them for that corner, splashing and almost tripping as I got weak in the knees. The investigators grew quiet with my approach, and at first I did not know what I was looking at as I followed the beams of their flashlights to something charred that was mingled with soggy paper and insulation, something on top of fallen plaster and chunks of blackened wood.

Then I saw the shape of a belt and its buckle, and the protruding femur that looked like a thick, burned stick. My heart was beating out of my chest as the shape became the burned ruins of a body attached to a blackened head that had no features, only patches of sooty silver hair.

"Let me see the watch," I said, staring wildly at the investigators.

One of them held it out and I took it from his hand. It was a men's stainless steel Breitling, an Aerospace.

"No," I muttered as I knelt in the water. "Please, no."

I covered my face with my hands. My mind shorted out. My vision failed as I swayed. Then a hand was steadying me. Bile crept up my throat.

"Come on, Doc," a male voice said gently as hands lifted me to my feet.

"It can't be him," I cried out. "Oh, God, please don't let it be. Please, please, please."

I couldn't seem to keep my balance, and it took two agents to get me out as I did what I could to gather the fragments that were left of me. I spoke to no one when I was returned to the street, and I walked weirdly, woodenly, to McGovern's Explorer, where she was with Lucy in the back, holding a blood-soaked towel around Lucy's left hand.

"I need a first aid kit," I heard myself say to McGovern.

"It might be better to get her to the hospital," her voice came back as she stared hard at me, fear and pity shining in her eyes.

"Get it," I said.

McGovern reached in back, over the seat to grab something. She set an orange Pelican case on the seat and unfastened the latches. Lucy was almost in shock, shaking violently, her face white.

"She needs a blanket," I said.

I removed the towel and washed her hand with bottled water. A thick flap of skin on her thumb was almost avulsed, and I swabbed it profusely with betadine, the iodine odor piercing my sinuses as all that I had just seen became a bad dream. It was not true.

"She needs stitches," McGovern said.

It had not happened. A dream.

"We should go to the hospital so she can get stitches."

But I already had out the steri-strips and benzoin glue, because I knew that stitches would not work with a wound like this. Tears were streaming down my face as I topped off my work with a thick layer of gauze. When I looked up and out the window, I realized Marino was standing by my door. His face was distorted by pain and rage. He looked like he might vomit. I got out of the Explorer.

"Lucy, you need to come on with me," I said, taking her arm. I had always been able to function better when I was taking care of someone else. "Come on."

Emergency lights flashed in our faces, the night and the people in it disconnected and strange. Marino drove away with us as the medical examiner's van pulled up. There would be X-rays, dental charts, maybe even DNA used to confirm the identification. The process most likely would take a while, but it did not matter. I already knew. Benton was dead.

17

As best anyone could reconstruct events at this time, Benton had been lured to his dreadful death. We had no clue as to what had drawn him to the small grocery store on Walnut Street, or if, perhaps, he simply had been abducted somewhere else and then forced up a ladder into the plenum of that small building in its bad part of town. We believed he had been handcuffed at some point, and the continuing search had also turned up wire twisted into a figure eight that most likely had restrained the ankles that had burned away.

His car keys and wallet were recovered, but not his Sig Sauer nine-millimeter pistol or gold signet ring. He had left several changes of clothing in his hotel room, and his briefcase, which had been searched and turned over to me. I stayed the night in Teun McGovern's house. She had posted agents on the property, because Carrie was still out there somewhere, and it was only a matter of time.

She would finish what she had started, and the important question, really, was who would be next and if she would succeed. Marino had moved into Lucy's tiny apartment and was keeping watch from her couch. The three of us had nothing to say to each other because there was nothing to say, really. What was done was done.

McGovern had tried to get through to me. Several times the previous night she had brought tea or food into my room with its blue-curtained window overlooking the old brick and brass lanterns of the row houses in Society Hill. She was wise enough not to force anything, and I was too ruined to do anything but sleep. I continued to wake up feeling sick and then remember why.

I did not remember my dreams. I wept until my eyes were almost swollen shut. Late Thursday morning, I took a long shower and walked into McGovern's kitchen. She was wearing a Prussian blue suit, drinking coffee and reading the paper.

"Good morning," she said, surprised and pleased that I had ventured out from behind my closed door. "How are you doing?"

"Tell me what's happening," I said.

I sat across from her. She set her coffee cup on the table and pushed back her chair.

"Let me get you coffee," she said.

"Tell me what is going on," I repeated. "I want to know, Teun. Have they found out anything yet? At the morgue, I mean?"

She was at a loss for a moment, staring out the window at an old magnolia tree heavy with blossoms that were limp and brown.

"They're still working on him," she finally spoke. "But based on indications so far, it appears his throat may have been cut. There were cuts to the bones of his face. Here and here."

She pointed to her left jaw and space between his eyes.

"There was no soot or burns in his trachea, and no CO. So he was already dead when the fire was set," she said to me. "I'm sorry, Kay. I . . . Well, I don't know what to say."

"How can it be that no one saw him enter the building?" I asked as if I had not comprehended the horror of what she had just said. "Someone forces him inside at gunpoint, maybe, and no one saw a thing?"

"The store closed at five P.M.," she answered. "There's no sign of forcible entry and for some reason the burglar alarm hadn't been set, so it didn't go off. We've had trouble with these places being torched for insurance money. Same Pakistani family always involved one way or another."

She sipped her coffee.

"Same MO," she went on. "Small inventory, the fire starts shortly after business hours, and no one in the neighborhood saw a thing."

"This has nothing to do with insurance money!" I said with sudden rage.

"Of course, it doesn't," she answered quietly. "Or at least not directly. But if you want to hear my theory, I'll tell you."

"Tell me."

"Maybe Carrie was the torch . . ."

"Of course!"

"I'm saying she might have conspired with the owner to torch the place for him. He may have even paid her to do it, not having any idea what her real agenda was. Granted, this would have taken some planning."

"She's had nothing to do for years but plan."

My chest tightened again and tears formed a lump in my throat and filled my eyes.

"I'm going home," I told her. "I've got to do something. I can't stay here."

"I think you are better off . . ." she started to protest.

"I've got to figure out what she will do next," I said, as if this were possible. "I've got to figure out how she's doing what she's doing. There's some master plan, some routine, something more to all this. Did they find any metal shavings?"

"There wasn't much left. He was in the plenum, the point of origin. There was some kind of big fuel load up there, but we don't know what, except there were a lot of Styrofoam peanuts floating around. And those things will really burn. No accelerants detected, so far."

"Teun, the metal shavings from the Shephard case. Let us take them to Richmond so we can compare them with what we've got. Your investigators can receipt them to Marino."

She looked at me with eyes that were skeptical, tired, and sad.

"You need to deal with this, Kay," she said. "Let us do the rest of it."

"I am dealing with it, Teun."

I got up from my chair and looked down at her.

"The only way I can," I said. "Please."

"You really should not be on this case anymore. And I'm placing Lucy on administrative leave for at least a week."

"You won't pull me off this case," I told her. "Not in this life."

"You're not in a position to be objective."

"And what would you do if you were me?" I demanded. "Would you go home and do nothing?"

"But I'm not you."

"Answer me," I said.

"No one could stop me from working the case. I would be obsessed. I would do just what you're doing," she said, getting up, too. "I'll do what I can to help."

"Thank you," I said. "Thank God for you, Teun."

She studied me for a while, leaning against the counter, her hands in the pockets of her slacks.

"Kay, don't blame yourself for this," she said.

"I blame Carrie," I replied with a sudden flow of bitter tears. "That's exactly who I blame."

18

Several hours later, Marino was driving Lucy and me back to Richmond. It was the worst car trip I could remember, with the three of us staring out and saying nothing, an oppressive depression heavy on the air. It did not seem true, and whenever truth struck again, it was with the blow of a heavy fist into my chest. Images of Benton were vivid. I did not know if it were grace or a bigger tragedy that we had not spent our last night together in the same bed.

In a way, I wasn't sure I could bear the fresh memories of his touch, his breath, the way he felt in my arms. Then I wanted to hold him and make love again. My mind tumbled down different hills into dark spaces where thoughts got caught on the realities of dealing with his possessions at my house, including his clothing.

His remains would have to be shipped to Richmond, and despite all I knew about death, the two of us had never devoted much attention to our own or the funeral service we might want and where we should be buried. We had not wanted to think about our own, and so we hadn't.

I-95 South was a blur of highway running forever through

stopped time. When tears filled my eyes, I turned to my window and hid my face. Lucy was silent in the back seat, her anger, grief, and fear as palpable as a concrete wall.

"I'm going to quit," she finally said when we passed through Fredericksburg. "This is it for me. I'll find something somewhere. Maybe in computers."

"Bullshit," Marino answered, his eyes on her in the rearview mirror. "That's just what the bitch wants you to do. Quit law enforcement. Be a loser and a big fuck-up."

"I am a loser and a fuck-up."

"Bull fucking shit," he said.

"She killed him because of me," she went on in the same heartless monotone.

"She killed him because she wanted to. And we can sit here and have a pity party, or we can figure out what we're gonna do before she whacks the next one of us."

But my niece was not to be consoled. Indirectly, she had exposed all of us to Carrie a long time ago.

"Carrie wants you to blame yourself for this," I said to her.

Lucy did not respond, and I turned around to look at her. She was dressed in dirty BDUs and boots, her hair a mess. She still smelled of fire, because she had not bathed. She had not eaten or slept, as best I knew. Her eyes were flat and hard. They glinted coldly of the decision she had made, and I had seen the look before, when hopelessness and hostility made her self-destructive. A part of her wanted to die, or maybe a part of her already had.

We reached my house at half past five, and the slanted rays of the sun were hot and bright, the sky hazy blue but cloudless. I carried in newspapers from the front steps and was sickened again by this morning's front-page headline about Benton's death. Although identification was tentative, it was believed he had died in a fire under very suspicious circumstances while assisting the FBI in the nationwide hunt for the escaped killer Carrie Grethen. Investigators would not say why Benton had been inside the small grocery store that had burned, or if he might have been lured there.

"What do you want to do with this?" Marino asked.

He had opened the car trunk, where three large brown paper bags contained the personal effects collected from Benton's hotel room. I could not decide.

"Want me to just put them in your office?" he asked. "Or I can go through them if you want, Doc."

"No, no, just leave them," I said.

Stiff paper crackled as he carried the bags into the house and down the hall. His footsteps were burdened and slow, and when he returned to the front of the house, I was still standing by the open door.

"I'll talk to you later," he said. "And don't go leaving this door open, you hear me? The alarm stays on and you and Lucy shouldn't go out anywhere."

"I don't think you have a worry."

Lucy had dropped her luggage in her bedroom near the kitchen and was staring out the window at Marino driving away. I came behind her and gently put my hands on her shoulders.

"Don't quit," I said, and I leaned my forehead against the back of her neck.

She did not turn around, and I felt grief shudder through her.

"We're in this together, Lucy," I went on quietly. "We're all that's left, really. Just you and me. Benton would want us united in this. He wouldn't want you giving up. Then what will I do, huh? If you give up, you'll be giving up on me, too."

She began to sob.

"I need you." I could barely talk. "More than ever."

She turned around and clung to me the way she used to when she was a frightened child starved for someone who cared. Her tears wet my neck, and for a while we stood in the middle of a room still packed with computer equipment and school books, and plastered with posters of her adolescent heroes.

"It's my fault, Aunt Kay. It's all my fault. I killed him!" she cried out.

"No," I said, holding her tight as my own tears flowed.

"How can you ever forgive me? I took him away from you!"

"That's not the way it is. You did nothing, Lucy."

"I can't live with this."

"You can and you will. We need to help each other live with this."

"I loved him, too. Everything he did for me. Getting me started with the Bureau, giving me a chance. Being supportive. About everything."

"It's going to be all right," I said.

She pulled away from me and collapsed on the edge of the bed, wiping her face with the tail of her sooty blue shirt. She rested her elbows on her knees and hung her head, staring at her own tears falling like rain on the hardwood floor.

"I'm telling you, and you've got to listen," she said in a low, hard voice. "I'm not sure I can go on, Aunt Kay. Everybody has a point. Where it begins and ends." Her breath shook. "Where they can't go on. I wish she had killed me instead. Maybe she would have done me a favor."

I watched her with gathering resolve as she willed herself to die before my eyes.

"If I don't go on, Aunt Kay, you've got to understand and not blame yourself or anything," she muttered, wiping her face with her sleeve.

I went over to her and lifted her chin. She was hot and smoky, her breath and body odor bad.

"You listen to me," I said with an intensity that would have frightened her in the past. "You get this goddamn notion out of your head right now. You are glad you didn't die, and you aren't committing suicide, if that's what you're implying, and I believe it is. You know what suicide is all about, Lucy? It's about anger, about payback. It's the final *fuck-you*. You will do that to Benton? You will do that to Marino? You will do that to me?"

I held her face in my hands until she looked at me.

"You're going to let that no-good piece of trash Carrie do that to you?" I demanded. "Where's that fierce spirit I know?"

"I don't know," she whispered with a sigh.

"Yes you do," I said. "Don't you dare ruin my life, Lucy. It's been damaged enough. Don't you dare make me spend the rest of my days with the echo of a gunshot sounding on and on in my mind. I didn't think you were a coward."

"I'm not."

Her eyes focused on mine.

"Tomorrow we fight back," I said.

She nodded, swallowing hard.

"Go take a shower," I said.

I waited until I heard the water in her bathroom running, and then went into the kitchen. We needed to eat, although I doubted either of us felt like it. I thawed chicken breasts and cooked them in stock with whatever fresh vegetables

I could find. I was liberal with rosemary, bay leaves, and sherry, but nothing stronger, not even pepper, for we needed to be soothed. Marino called twice while we were eating, to make certain we were all right.

"You can come over," I said to him. "I've made soup, although it might be kind of thin by your standards."

"I'm okay," he said, and I knew he did not mean it.

"I've got plenty of room, if you'd like to stay the night. I should have thought to ask you earlier."

"No, Doc. I got things to do."

"I'm going to the office first thing in the morning," I said.

"I don't know how you can," he replied in a judgmental way, as if my thinking about work meant I wasn't showing what I should be showing right now.

"I have a plan. And come hell or high water, I'm going to carry it out," I said.

"I hate it when you start planning things."

I hung up and collected empty soup bowls from the kitchen table, and the more I thought about what I was going to do, the more manic I got.

"How hard would it be for you to get a helicopter?" I said to my niece.

"What?" She looked amazed.

"You heard me."

"Do you mind if I ask what for? You know, I can't just order one like a cab."

"Call Teun," I said. "Tell her I'm taking care of business and need all of the cooperation I can get. Tell her if all goes as I'm hoping, I'm going to need her and a team to meet us in Wilmington, North Carolina. I don't know when yet. Maybe right away. But I need free rein. They're going to have to trust me."

Lucy got up and went to the sink to fill her glass with more water.

"This is nuts," she said.

"Can you get a helicopter or not?"

"If I get permission, then yes. Border Patrol has them. That's usually what we use. I can probably get one in from D.C."

"Good," I said. "Get it as fast as you can. In the morning I'm hitting the labs to confirm what I think I already know. Then we may be going to New York."

"Why?"

She looked interested but skeptical.

"We're going to land at Kirby and I intend to get to the bottom of things," I answered her.

Marino called again at close to ten, and I reassured him one more time that Lucy and I were as fine as could be expected, and that we felt safe inside my house, with its sophisticated alarm system, lighting, and guns. He sounded bleary and thick, and I could tell he had been drinking, his TV turned up loud.

"I need you to meet me at the lab at eight," I said.

"I know, I know."

"It's very important, Marino."

"It's not like you need to tell me that, Doc."

"Get some sleep," I said.

"Ditto."

But I couldn't. I sat at my desk in my study, going through the suspicious fire deaths from ESA. I studied the Venice Beach death, and then the one from Baltimore, struggling to see what, if anything, the cases and victims had in common besides the point of origin and the fact that although arson was suspected, investigators could find no evidence of it. I called the Baltimore police department first, and found someone in the detective division who seemed amenable to talking.

"Johnny Montgomery worked that one," the detective said, and I could hear him smoking.

"Do you know anything about it?" I asked.

"Best you talk to him. And he probably will need some way of knowing you're who you say you are."

"He can call me at my office in the morning for verification." I gave him the number. "I should be no later than eight. What about e-mail? Does Investigator Montgomery have an address I could send a note to?"

"Now that I can give you."

I heard him open a drawer, and then he gave me what I needed.

"Seems I've heard of you before," the detective said thoughtfully. "If you're the ME I'm thinking of. I know it's a lady. A good-looking one, too, based on what I've seen on TV. Hmmm. You ever get up to Baltimore?"

"I went to medical school in your fair city."

"Well, now I know you're smart."

"Austin Hart, the young man who died in the fire, was also a student at Johns Hopkins." I prodded him.

"He was also a homo. I personally think it was a hate crime."

"What I need is a photograph of him and anything about his life, his habits, his hobbies." I took advantage of the detective's momentary lapse.

"Oh yeah." He smoked. "One of these pretty boys. I heard he did modeling to pay his way through med school. Calvin Klein underwear ads, that sort of thing. Probably some jealous lover. You come to Baltimore next, Doc, and you got to try Camden Yards. You know about the new stadium, right?"

"Absolutely," I replied as I excitedly processed what he had just said.

"I can get you tickets if you want."

"That would be very nice. I'll get in touch with Investigator Montgomery, and I thank you so much for your help."

I got off the phone before he could ask me about my favorite baseball team, and I immediately sent Montgomery an e-mail that outlined my needs, although I felt I already had enough. Next I tried the Pacific Division of the Los Angeles Police Department, which covered Venice Beach, and I got lucky. The investigator who had worked Marlene Farber's case was on evening shift and had just come in. His name was Stuckey, and he did not seem to require much verification from me that I was who I claimed to be.

"Wish somebody would solve this one for me," he said right off. "Six months and still nothing. Not one tip that's turned out to be worth anything."

"What can you tell me about Marlene Farber?" I asked.

"Was on *General Hospital* now and then. And *Northern Exposure*. I guess you've seen that?"

"I don't watch much TV. PBS, that's about it."

"What else, what else? Oh right. *Ellen*. No big parts, but who knows how far she might have gone. Prettiest thing you ever saw. Was dating some producer, and we're pretty sure he had nothing to do with what happened. Only thing that guy really cared about was coke and screwing all the young stars he got parts for. You know, after I got the case, I went through a bunch of tapes of shows she was on. She wasn't bad. It's a shame."

"Anything unusual about the scene?" I asked.

"Everything was unusual about that scene. Don't have a clue how a fire like that could have started in the master bathroom on the first floor, and ATF couldn't figure it out, either. There wasn't anything to burn in there except toilet paper and towels. No sign of forcible entry, either, and the burglar alarm never went off."

"Investigator Stuckey, were her remains by chance found in the bathtub?"

"That's another freaky thing, unless she was a suicide. Maybe set the fire and cut her wrists or something. A lot of people cut their wrists in the tub."

"Any trace evidence to speak of?"

"Ma'am, she was chalk. Looked like she'd been in the crematorium. There was enough left of the torso area for them to ID her through X-rays, but beyond that, we're talking a few teeth, pieces and parts of bones, and some hair."

"Did she by chance do any modeling?" I then asked.

"That, TV commercials, magazine ads. She made a pretty good living. Drove a black Viper and lived in a damn nice house right on the ocean."

"I'm wondering if you could e-mail photos and any reports to me."

"Give me your address, and I'll see what I can do."

"I need them fast, Investigator Stuckey," I said.

I hung up and my mind was whirling. Each victim was physically beautiful and involved in photography or television. It was a common denominator that could not be ignored, and I believed that Marlene Farber, Austin Hart, Claire Rawley, and Kellie Shephard had been selected for a reason that was important to the killer. This was where everything unraveled. The pattern fit that of a serial killer, like Bundy, who selected women with long straight hair who resembled his estranged girlfriend. What didn't fit was Carrie Grethen. In the first place, she had been locked up in Kirby when the first three deaths had occurred, and her MO had never been anything like this.

I was baffled. Carrie was not there and yet she was. I dozed for a while in my chair, and at six A.M., I came to with a start. My neck burned from being bent in the wrong position, and my back was achy and stiff. I got up slowly and stretched, and knew what I had to do but wasn't certain I could. Just the thought filled me with terror, and my heart kicked in with violent force. I could feel my pulse pounding like a fist against a door, and I stared at the brown paper bags Marino had placed in front of a bookcase packed with law reviews. They were taped shut and labeled, and I picked them up. I followed the hallway to Benton's room.

Although we typically had shared my bed, the opposite wing of the house had been his. Here he had worked and stored his day-to-day belongings, for as both of us had gotten older, we had learned that space was our most reliable friend. Our retreats made our battles less bloody, and absences during the day made nights more inviting. His door was open wide, as he had left it. The lights were out, the curtains drawn. Shadows got sharper as I stood, frozen for an instant, staring in. It required all of the courage I had ever demonstrated in my life to turn on the overhead light.

His bed with its bold blue duvet and sheets was neatly made, because Benton was always meticulous, no matter his hurry. He had never waited for me to change his linens or attend to his laundry, and part of this was due to an independence and strong sense of self that never really relented, not even with me. He had to do it his way. In that regard, we were so much alike, I marveled we had ever gotten together. I collected his hairbrush from the dresser, because I knew it might be useful for a DNA comparison, should there be no other avenue for identification. I went to the small cherry bedside table to look at the books and thick file folders stacked there.

He had been reading *Cold Mountain*, and had used the torn flap of an envelope to mark his place not quite halfway through. Of course, there were the pages of the latest revision of a crime classification manual he was editing, and the sight of his scratchy penmanship crashed me to earth. I tenderly turned manuscript pages and trailed my fingers over the barely legible words he had penned as tears ambushed me again. Then I set the bags on the bed and ripped them open.

Police had hastily riffled through his closet and drawers, and nothing they had packed inside the bags was neatly folded, but rather bunched and rolled. One by one I smoothed open white cotton shirts and bold ties and two pairs of suspenders. He had packed two lightweight suits, and both of them were crinkled like crêpe paper. There were dress shoes, and running clothes and socks and jockey shorts, but it was his shaving kit that stopped me.

Methodical hands had rummaged through it, and the screw cap to a bottle of Givenchy III was loose and cologne had leaked. The familiar sharp, masculine scent seized me with emotion. I could feel his smooth shaven cheeks. Suddenly, I saw him behind his desk in his former office at the FBI Academy. I remembered his striking features, his crisp dress and the smell of him, back then when I was already falling in love and did not know it. I neatly folded his clothing in a stack and fumbled, ripping and tearing open another bag. I placed the black leather briefcase on the bed and sprung open the locks.

Noticeably missing inside was the Colt Mustang .380 pistol that he sometimes had strapped to his ankle, and I found it significant that he had taken the pistol with him the night of his death. He always carried his nine-millimeter in its shoulder holster, but the Colt was his backup if he felt a situation to be threatening. This singular act indicated to me that Benton had been on a mission at some point after he had left the Lehigh fire scene. I suspected he had gone to meet someone, and I didn't understand why he hadn't let anybody know, unless he had become careless, and this I doubted.

I picked out his brown leather date book and flipped through it in search of any recent appointment that caught my eye. There were a hair cut, dentist's appointment, and trips coming up, but nothing penciled in for the day of his death except the birthday of his daughter, Michelle, the middle of next week. I imagined she and her sisters were with their mother, Connie, who was Benton's former wife. I dreaded the idea that eventually I would need to share their sorrow, no matter how they might feel about me.

He had scribbled comments and questions about the profile of Carrie, the monster who soon after had caused his death. The irony of that was inconceivable, as I envisioned him trying to dissect Carrie's behavior in hopes of anticipating what she might do. I didn't suppose he had ever entertained the notion that even as he had concentrated on her, she quite likely had been thinking about him, too. She had been planning Lehigh County and the videotape, and by now, most likely, was parading as a member of a production crew.

My eyes stumbled over penned phrases such as *offender-victim relationship/fixation*, and *fusion of identity/erotomania* and *victim perceived as someone of higher status*. On the back of the page, he had jotted *patterned life after. How fits Carrie's victimology? Kirby. What access to Claire Rawley? Seemingly none. Inconsistent. Suggestive of a different offender? Accomplice? Gault. Bonnie and Clyde. Her original MO. May be on to something here. Carrie not alone. W/M 28–45? White helicopter?*

Chills lifted my flesh as I realized what Benton had been thinking when he had been standing in the morgue taking notes and watching Gerde and me work. Benton had been contemplating what suddenly seemed so obvious. Carrie was not alone in this. She had somehow allied herself with an evil partner, perhaps while she was incarcerated at Kirby. In fact, I was certain that this allegiance predated her escape, and I wondered if during the five years she was there, she might have met another psychopathic patient who later was released. Perhaps she had corresponded with him as freely and audaciously as she had with the media and me.

It was also significant that Benton's briefcase had been found inside his hotel room, when I knew it had accompanied him earlier at the morgue. Clearly, he had returned to his room some time after leaving the Lehigh fire scene. Where he had gone after that and why remained an enigma. I read more notes about Kellie Shephard's murder. Benton had emphasized *overkill*, *frenzied* and *disorganized*. He had jotted, *lost control* and *victim response not according to plan. Ruination of ritual.* ***Wasn't supposed to happen like this.*** *Rage.* ***Will kill again soon.***

I snapped shut the briefcase and left it on the bed as my heart ached. I walked out of the bedroom, turned off the light, and shut the door, knowing that the next time I entered it would be to clean out Benton's closet and drawers, and somehow decide to live with his resounding absence. I quietly checked on Lucy, finding her asleep, her pistol on the table by her bed. My restless wanderings took me to the foyer, where I turned off the alarm long enough to snatch the paper off the porch. I went into the kitchen to make coffee. By seven-thirty I was ready to leave for the office, and Lucy had not stirred. I quietly entered her room again, and the sun glowed faintly around the windowshade, touching her face with soft light.

"Lucy?" I softly touched her shoulder.

She jerked awake, sitting half up.

"I'm leaving," I said.

"I need to get up, too."

She threw back the covers.

"Want to have a cup of coffee with me?" I asked.

"Sure."

She lowered her feet to the floor.

"You should eat something," I said.

She had slept in running shorts and a T-shirt, and she followed me with the silence of a cat.

"How about some cereal?" I said as I got a coffee mug out of a cupboard.

She said nothing but simply watched me as I opened the tin of homemade granola that Benton had eaten most mornings with fresh banana or berries. Just the toasty aroma of it was enough to crush me again, and my throat seemed to close and my stomach furled. I stood helplessly for a long moment, unable to lift out the scoop or reach for a bowl or do the smallest thing.

"Don't, Aunt Kay," said Lucy, who knew exactly what was happening. "I'm not hungry anyway."

My hands trembled as I clamped the top back on the tin.

"I don't know how you're going to stay here," she said. She poured her own coffee.

"This is where I live, Lucy."

I opened the refrigerator and handed her the carton of milk.

"Where's his car?" she asked, whitening her coffee.

"The airport at Hilton Head, I guess. He flew straight to New York from there."

"What are you going to do about that?"

"I don't know."

I got increasingly upset.

"Right now, his car is low on my list. I've got all his things in the house," I told her.

I took a deep breath.

"I can't make decisions about everything at once," I said.

"You should clear every bit of it out today."

Lucy leaned against the counter, drinking coffee and watching me with that same flat look in her eyes.

"I mean it," she went on in a tone that carried no emotion.

"Well, I'm not touching anything of his until his body has come home."

"I can help you, if you want."

She sipped her coffee again. I was getting angry with her.

"I will do this my way, Lucy," I said as pain seemed to radiate to every cell in me. "For once I'm not going to slam the door on something and run. I've done it most of my life, beginning when my father died. Then Tony left and Mark got killed, and I got better and better at vacating each relationship as if it were an old house. Walking off as if I had never lived there. And guess what? It doesn't work."

She was staring down at her bare feet.

"Have you talked to Janet?" I asked.

"She knows. Now she's all bent out of shape because I don't want to see her. I don't want to see anybody."

"The harder you run, the more you stay in one place," I said. "If you've learned nothing else from me, Lucy, at least learn that. Don't wait until half your life has passed."

"I've learned a lot of things from you," my niece said as windows caught the morning and brightened my kitchen. "More than you think."

For a long moment she stared at the empty doorway leading into the great room.

"I keep thinking he's going to walk in," she muttered.

"I know," I said. "I keep thinking it, too."

"I'll call Teun. As soon as I know something, I'll page you," she said.

The sun was strong to the east and other people heading to work squinted in the glare of what promised to be a clear, hot day. I was carried in the flow of traffic on Ninth Street past the wrought-iron-enclosed Capitol Square, with its Jeffersonian pristine white buildings and monuments to Stonewall Jackson and George Washington. I thought of Kenneth Sparkes, of his political influence. I remembered my fear and fascination when he would call with demands and complaints. I felt terribly sorry for him now.

All that had happened of late had not cleared his name of suspicion for the simple reason that even those of us who knew we might be dealing with serial murders were not at liberty to release such information to the news. I was certain that Sparkes did not know. I desperately wanted to talk to him, to somehow ease his mind, as if perhaps in doing so I might ease my own. Depression crushed my chest with cold, iron hands, and when I turned off Jackson Street into the bay of my building, the sight of a hearse unloading a black pouched body jolted me in a way it had not before.

I tried not to imagine Benton's remains enveloped so, or the darkness of his cold, steel space at the shutting of the cooler door. It was awful to know all that I did. Death was not an abstraction, and I could envision every procedure, every sound and smell in a place where there was no loving touch, only a clinical objective and a crime to be solved. I was climbing out of my car when Marino rolled up.

"Mind if I stick my car in here?" he asked, even though he knew the bay parking was not for cops.

Marino was forever breaking rules.

"Go ahead," I replied. "One of the vans is in the shop. Or at least I think it is. You're not going to be here long."

"How the hell do you know?"

He locked his car door and flicked an ash. Marino was his rude self again, and I found this incredibly reassuring.

"You going to your office first?" he asked, as we followed a ramp to doors that led inside the morgue.

"No. Straight upstairs."

"Then I'll tell you what's probably already on your desk," he said. "We got a positive I.D. for Claire Rawley. From hair in her brush."

I wasn't surprised, but the confirmation weighed me down with sadness again.

"Thanks," I told him. "At least we know."

19

The trace evidence laboratories were on the third floor, and my first stop was the scanning electron microscope, or SEM, which exposed a specimen, such as the metal shaving from the Shephard case, to a beam of electrons. The elemental composition making up the specimen emitted electrons, and images were displayed on a video screen.

In short, the SEM recognized almost all of the one hundred and three elements, whether it was carbon, copper, or zinc, and because of the microscope's depth of focus, high resolution, and high magnification, trace evidence such as gunshot residue or the hairs on a marijuana leaf could be viewed in amazing, if not eerie, detail.

The location of the Zeiss SEM was enthroned within a windowless room of teal and beige wall cupboards and shelves, counter space, and sinks. Because the extremely expensive instrument was very sensitive to mechanical vibration, magnetic fields, and electrical and thermal disturbances, the environment was precisely controlled.

The ventilation and air conditioning system were independent of the rest of the building, and photographically safe lighting was supplied by filament lamps that did not cause electrical interference and were directed up at the ceiling to dimly illuminate the room by reflection. Floors and walls were thick steel-beamed reinforced concrete impervious to human bustling or the traffic of the expressway.

Mary Chan was petite and fair-skinned, a first-rate microscopist, this minute on the phone and surrounded by her complex apparatus. With its instrument panels, power units, electron gun and optical column, X-ray analyzer, and vacuum chamber attached to a cylinder of nitrogen, the SEM looked like a console for the space shuttle. Chan's lab coat was buttoned to her chin, and her friendly gesture told me she would be but a minute.

"Take her temperature again and try the tapioca. If she doesn't keep that down, call me back, okay?" Chan was saying to someone. "I've got to go now."

"My daughter," she said to me as an apology. "A stomach upset, most likely from too much ice cream last night. She got into the Chunky Monkey when I wasn't looking."

Her smile was brave but tired, and I suspected she had been up most of the night.

"Man, I love that stuff," Marino said as he handed her our packaged evidence.

"Another metal shaving," I explained to her. "I hate to spring this on you, Mary, but if you could look at it now. It's urgent."

"Another case or the same one?"

"The fire in Lehigh County, Pennsylvania," I replied.

"No kidding?" She looked surprised as she slit taped brown paper with a scalpel. "Lord," she said, "that one sounds pretty awful, based on what I heard on the news, anyway. Then the FBI guy, too. Weird, weird, weird."

She had no reason to know about my relationship with Benton.

"Between those cases and the one in Warrenton, you have to wonder if there isn't some whacko pyro on the loose," she went on.

"That's what we're trying to find out," I said.

Chan took the cap off the small metal evidence button and with tweezers removed a layer of snowy cotton, revealing the two tiny bright turnings. She pushed back her roller chair to a counter behind her and proceeded to place a double-sided adhesive square of black carbon tape on a tiny aluminum stub. On this she mounted the shaving that seemed to have the most surface area. It was maybe half the size of a normal eyelash. She turned on a stereo-optical microscope, positioned the sample on the stage, and adjusted the light wand to take a look at a lower magnification before she resorted to the SEM.

"I'm seeing two different surfaces," she said as she adjusted the focus. "One real shiny, the other sort of dull gray."

"That's different from the Warrenton sample," I said. "Both surfaces were shiny, right?"

"Correct. My guess would be that one of the surfaces here was exposed to atmospheric oxidation. For whatever reason that might be."

"Do you mind?" I asked.

She scooted out of the way and I peered through the lenses. At a magnification of four, the metal turning looked like a ribbon of crumpled foil, and I could just barely make out the fine striations left by whatever had been used to shave the metal. Mary took several Polaroid photographs and then rolled her chair back to the SEM console. She pushed a button to vent the chamber, or release the vacuum.

"This will take a few minutes," she said to us. "You can wait or go and come back."

"I'm getting coffee," said Marino, who had never been a fan of sophisticated technology and most likely wanted to smoke.

Chan opened a valve to fill the chamber with nitrogen to keep contamination, such as moisture, out. Next she pushed a button on the console and placed our sample on an electron optics table.

"Now we got to get it to ten to the minus six millimeters of mercury. That's the vacuum level needed to turn on the beam. Usually takes two or three minutes. But I like to pump it down a little more than that to get a really good vacuum," she explained, reaching for her coffee. "I think the news accounts are very confusing," she then said. "A lot of innuendo."

"So what else is new?" I commented wryly.

"Tell me about it. Whenever I read accounts of my court testimony, I always wonder if someone else had been on the stand instead of me. My point is, first they drag Sparkes into it, and to be honest, I was about to think that maybe he had burned his own place and some girl. Probably for money, and to get rid of her because she knew something. Then, lo and behold, there are these two other fires in Pennsylvania, and two more people killed, and there's the suggestion all of it's related? And where's Sparkes been during all this?"

She reached for her coffee.

"Excuse me, Dr. Scarpetta. I didn't even ask. Can I get you some?"

"No thank you," I said.

I watched the green light move across the gauge as the mercury level slowly climbed.

"I also find it odd that this psycho woman escapes from the loony bin in New York—what's her name? Carrie something? And the FBI profiler guy in charge of that investigation suddenly ends up dead. I think we're ready to go," she said.

She turned on the electron beam and the video display. The magnification was set for five hundred, and she turned it down and we began to get a picture of the filament's current on the screen. At first it looked like a wave, then it began to flatten. She hit more keys, backing off the magnification again, this time to twenty, and we began to get a picture of the signals coming off the sample.

"I'll change the spot size of the beam to get a little more energy."

She adjusted buttons and dials as she worked.

"Looks like our shaving of metal, almost like a curled ribbon," she announced.

The topography was simply an enlarged version of what we had seen under the optical microscope moments earlier, and since the picture wasn't terribly bright, this suggested an element with a lower atomic number. She adjusted the scanning speed of the live picture and took away some of the noise, which looked like a snowstorm on the screen.

"Here you can clearly see the shiny versus the gray," she said.

"And you think that's due to oxidation," I said, pulling up a chair.

"Well, you've got two surfaces of the same material. I would venture that the shiny side was recently shaved while the other wasn't."

"Makes sense to me."

The crinkled metal looked like shrapnel suspended in space.

"We had a case last year," Chan spoke again as she pressed the frame store button to make photographs for me. "A guy bludgeoned with a pipe from a machine shop. And tissue from his scalp had a metal filing from a lathe. It was transferred right into the wound. Okay, let's change the back scatter image and see what kind of X-ray we get off that."

The video screen went gray and digital seconds began to count. Mary worked other buttons on her control panel, and a bright orange spectrum suddenly appeared on the screen against a background of vivid blue. She moved the cursor and expanded what looked like a psychedelic stalagmite.

"Let's see if there are other metals."

She made more adjustments.

"Nope," she said. "It's very clean. Think we got our same suspect again. We'll call up magnesium and see if there's an overlapping of lines."

She superimposed the spectrum for magnesium over the one for our sample, and they were the same. She called up a table of elements on the video screen, and the square for magnesium was lit up red. We had confirmed our element, and although I had expected the answer we got, I was still stunned by it.

"Do you have any explanation as to why pure magnesium might be transferred to a wound?" I asked Chan as Marino returned.

"Well, I told you my pipe story," she replied.

"What pipe?" Marino said.

"Only thing I can think of is a metal shop," Chan went on. "But I would think that machining magnesium would be unusual. I mean, I can't imagine what for."

"Thanks, Mary. We've got one more stop to go, but

I'm going to need you to let me have the shaving from the Warrenton case so I can take it over to firearms."

She glanced at her watch as the phone rang again, and I could only imagine the caseload awaiting her.

"Right away," she said to me generously.

The firearms and toolmarks labs were on the same floor and were really the same section of science, since the lands and grooves and firing pin impressions left on cartridge cases and bullets were, in fact, the toolmarks made by guns. The space in the new building was a stadium compared to the old, and this spoke sadly to the continuing deterioration of the society beyond our doors.

It was not unusual for schoolchildren to hide handguns in their lockers, or show them off in the bathrooms, and carry them on the school bus, it seemed, and it was nothing for violent offenders to be eleven and twelve years old. Guns were still the top choice for killing oneself or one's spouse, or even the neighbor with the constantly barking dog. More frightening were the disgruntled and insane who entered public places and started blasting away, explaining why my office and the lobby were protected by bulletproof glass.

Rich Sinclair's work area was carpeted and well lighted, and overlooked the coliseum, which had always reminded me of a metal mushroom about to take flight. He was using weights to test the trigger pull of a Taurus pistol, and Marino and I walked in to the sound of the hammer clicking against the firing pin. I was not in a chatty mood and did my best not to seem rude as I told Sinclair outright what I needed, and that I needed it now.

"This is the metal turning from Warrenton," I said, opening

that evidence button. "And this is the one recovered from the body in the Lehigh fire."

I opened that evidence button next.

"Both have striations that are clearly visible on SEM," I explained.

The point was to see if the striations, or toolmarks, matched, indicating that the same instrument had been used to produce the magnesium shavings that had been recovered this far. The ribbons of metal were very fragile and thin, and Sinclair used a narrow plastic spatula to pick them up. They weren't very cooperative and tended to jump around as if they were trying to escape as he coaxed them from their sea of cotton. He used squares of black cardboard to center the shaving from Warrenton on one, and the shavings from Lehigh on the other. These he placed on stages of the comparison microscope.

"Oh yeah," Sinclair said without pause. "We've got some good stuff."

He manipulated the shavings with the spatula, flattening them some as he bumped the magnification up to forty.

"Maybe a blade of some type," he said. "The striations are probably from the finishing process and end up being a defect because no finishing process is going to be perfectly smooth. I mean, the manufacturer's going to be happy, but he's not at our end seeing this. There, here's an even better area, I think."

He moved aside so we could take a look. Marino bent over the eyepieces first.

"Looks like ski tracks in snow," was his comment. "And that's from the blade, right? Or whatever?"

"Yes, imperfections, or toolmarks, made by whatever shaved this metal. Do you see the match, when one shaving is lined up with the other?"

Marino didn't.

"Here, Doc, you look." Sinclair got out of my way.

What I saw through the microscope was good enough for court, the striations of the Warrenton shaving in one field of light matching the striations of the shaving in the other. Clearly, the same tool had shaved something made of magnesium in both homicide cases. The question was what this tool might be, and because the shavings were so thin, one had to consider a sharp blade of some type. Sinclair made several Polaroid photographs for me and slid them into glyassine envelopes.

"Okay, now what?" Marino asked as he followed me through the center of the firearms lab, past scientists busy processing bloody clothing under biohazard hoods, and others examining a Phillips screwdriver and machete at a big U-shaped counter.

"Now I go shopping," I said.

I did not slow down as I talked but, in fact, was getting more frantic because I knew I was getting closer to reconstructing what Carrie or her accomplice or someone had done.

"What do you mean, *shopping*?"

Through the wall I could hear the muffled bangs of test fires in the range.

"Why don't you check on Lucy?" I said. "And I'll get back to both of you later."

"I don't like it when you do this *later* shit," Marino said as elevator doors parted. "That means you're running around on your own and poking your nose in things that maybe you shouldn't. And this ain't the time for you to be out on the street with nobody around. We got not a clue where Carrie is."

"That's right, we don't," I said. "But I'm hoping that's going to change."

We got out on the first floor, and I headed with purpose to the door leading to the bay, where I unlocked my car. Marino looked so frustrated, I thought he might launch into a tantrum.

"You want to tell me where the hell you're going?" he demanded at the top of his voice.

"A sports store," I said, cranking the engine. "The biggest one I can find."

That turned out to be Jumbo Sports south of the James, very close to the neighborhood where Marino lived, which was the only reason I was aware of the store, since prowling for basketballs, frisbees, free weights, and golf clubs rarely entered my mind.

I took the Powhite Parkway, and two toll booths later was exiting on Midlothian Turnpike, heading toward downtown. The sports store was big and built of red brick, with stick figures of red-painted athletes framed in white on the outside walls. The parking lot was unexpectedly full for this time of day, and I wondered how many well-toned people spent their lunch hours here.

I had no idea where anything was and had to take a few moments to study the signs above miles of rows. Boxing gloves were on sale, and there were exercise machines capable of tortures I did not know. Racks of clothes for every sport were endless and in blazing colors, and I wondered what had happened to civilized white, which was still what I wore on the much-appreciated occasion I found time to play tennis. I deduced that knives would be with camping and hunting gear, a generous area against the back wall. There were bows and arrows, targets, tents, canoes, mess kits, and camouflage, and at this hour, I was the only woman who seemed interested. At first, no one was inclined to wait on me as I hovered patiently over a showcase of knives.

A sunburnt man was looking for a BB gun for his son's tenth birthday, while an older man in a white suit was inquiring about snakebite kits and mosquito repellent. When my patience was no more, I interrupted.

"Excuse me," I said.

The clerk, who was college age, didn't seem to hear me at first.

"Thing is, you should check with your doctor before using a snakebite kit," the clerk was saying to the elderly man in white.

"How the hell am I supposed to do that when I'm out in the middle of the woods somewhere and some copperhead's just bit me?"

"I meant check with him before you go out in the woods, sir."

As I listened to their backward logic I could stand it no longer.

"Snakebite kits are not only useless, but they're harmful," I said. "Tourniquets and local incision, sucking out the venom and all that just make matters worse. If you get bitten," I said to the man in white, "what you need to do is immobilize that part of your body, and avoid damaging first aid, and get to a hospital."

The two men were startled.

"So there's no point in taking anything along?" the man in white asked me. "No point in buying anything, you're saying?"

"Nothing but a good pair of boots and a walking stick you can poke around with," I replied. "Stay out of tall grass and don't stick your hands into hollows or holes. Since venom is transported through the body by the lymphatic system, broad compression bandages—like an Ace bandage—are good, and a splint to keep the limb absolutely immobilized."

"You some kind of doctor?" the clerk asked.

"I've dealt with snake bites before."

I didn't add that in those instances, the victims had not lived.

"I'm just wondering if you have knife sharpeners here," I said to the clerk.

"Kitchen sharpeners or ones for camping?"

"Let's start with camping," I said.

He pointed to a wall where a vast variety of whetstones and other types of sharpeners hung from pegs. Some were metal, others ceramic. All of the brands were proprietary enough not to reveal the composition on the packages. I scanned some more, my eyes stopping on a small package on the bottom row. Beneath clear plastic was a simple rectangular block of grayish-silver metal. It was called a *fire starter* and was made of magnesium. Excitement mounted as I read the instructions. To start a fire, one simply needed to scrape a knife on the surface of the magnesium and build a pile of shavings as small as the size of a quarter. Matches weren't necessary, for the fire starter included a sparking insert for ignition.

I hurried back through the store with half a dozen of the magnesium starters in hand, and in my haste got tangled up in one section, then another. I wound through bowling balls and shoes, and baseball gloves, and ended up in swimming, where I was instantly captivated by a display of neon-colored swimming caps. One of them was hot pink. I thought of the residue found in Claire Rawley's hair. I had believed from the start that she had been wearing something on her head when she was murdered, or at least when the fire reached her.

A shower cap had been considered but briefly, for its thin, plastic material wouldn't have lasted five seconds in the heat. What had never entered my mind was a swimming cap, and as I quickly riffled through racks of them, I discovered that all were made of Lycra or latex or silicone.

The pink one was silicone, which I knew would hold up in extreme temperatures far better than the others. I purchased several of them. I drove back to my office and was lucky I didn't get a ticket because I was passing people, no matter the lane. Images seized my mind, and they were too painful and horrific to entertain. This was one time I hoped my theory was wrong. I was speeding back to the labs because I had to know.

"Oh Benton," I muttered as if he were near me. "Please don't let this be so."

20

It was one-thirty when I parked inside the bay again and got out of my car. I walked quickly to the elevator and keyed myself back up to the third floor. I was looking for Jerri Garmon, who had examined the pink residue in the beginning and reported to me that it was silicone.

Ducking into doorways, I located her inside a room housing the latest instrumentation used in analyzing organic substances, ranging from heroin to paint binders. She was using a syringe to inject a sample into a heated chamber of the gas chromatograph and did not notice me until I spoke.

"Jerri," I said, and I was out of breath. "I hate to disturb you but I've got something I think you'll want to look at."

I held up the pink swimming cap. Her reaction was completely blank.

"Silicone," I said.

Her eyes lit up.

"Wow! A swimming cap? Boy howdy. Who would have thought that?" she said. "Just goes to show you, there's too much to keep up with these days."

"Can we burn it?" I asked.

"This has got to run for a while anyway. Come on. Now you've got me curious, too."

The actual trace evidence labs, where evidence was processed before it was routed through complicated instruments such as the SEM and mass spectrometer, was spacious but already running out of room. Scores of airtight aluminum paint cans used in the collection of fire debris and flammable residues were in pyramids on shelves, and there were big jars of granular blue Drierite, and petri dishes, beakers, charcoal tubes, and the usual brown paper bags of evidence. The test I had in mind was easy and quick.

The muffle furnace was in a corner and looked rather much like a small beige ceramic crematorium, the size of a hotel mini-bar, to be exact, that could heat up to as much as twenty-five-hundred degrees Fahrenheit. She turned it on, and a gauge very soon began registering its warming up. Jerri placed the cap inside a white porcelain dish not so different from a cereal bowl, and opened a drawer to get out a thick asbestos glove that would protect her up to her elbow. She stood poised with tongs while the temperature crept to a hundred degrees. At two hundred and fifty, she checked on our cap. It wasn't the least bit affected.

"I can tell you right now that at this temperature latex and Lycra would be smoking up a storm and beginning to melt," Jerri let me know. "But this stuff's not even getting tacky yet and the color hasn't changed."

The silicone cap did not begin to smoke until five hundred degrees. At seven hundred and fifty, it was turning gray at the edges. It was getting tacky and beginning to melt. At not quite one thousand degrees, it was flaming and Jerri had to find a thicker glove.

"This is amazing," Jerri said.

"Guess we can see why silicone's used for insulation," I marveled, too.

"Better stand back."

"Don't worry."

I moved far out of harm's way as she pulled the bowl forward with tongs and carried our flaming experiment in her asbestos-covered hand. The exposure to fresh air fueled the fire more, and by the time she had placed it under a chemical hood and turned on the exhaust, the outer surface of the cap was blazing out of control, forcing Jerri to cover it with a lid.

Eventually, flames were suffocated, and she took off the lid to see what was left. My heart thudded as I noted papery white ash and areas of spared silicone that were still visibly pink. The swimming cap had not turned gooey or become a liquid at all. It simply had disintegrated until either cooling temperatures or an absence of oxygen or perhaps even a dousing with water had thwarted the process. The end result of our experiment was completely consistent with what I had recovered from Claire Rawley's long blond hair.

The image of her body in the bathtub, a pink swimming cap on her head, was ghastly, and its implication was almost more than I could comprehend. When the bathroom had gone to flashover, the shower door had caved in. Sections of glass and the sides of the tub had protected the body as flames shot up from the point of origin, engaging the ceiling. The temperature in the tub had never climbed above one thousand degrees, and a small telltale part of the silicone swimming cap had been preserved for the simple freakish reason that the shower door was old and made of a single thick sheet of solid glass.

As I drove home, rush hour traffic hemmed me in and seemed more aggressive the greater my hurry. Several times I almost reached for the phone, desperate to call Benton and tell him what I had discovered. Then I saw water and debris in the back corner of a burned-out grocery store in Philadelphia. I saw what was left of a stainless steel watch I had given to him for Christmas. I saw what was left of him. I imagined the wire that had confined his ankles, and handcuffs that had been locked with a key. I now knew what had happened and why. Benton had been killed like the others, but this time it was for spite, for revenge, to satisfy Carrie's diabolical lust to make him her trophy.

Tears blinded me as I pulled into my driveway. I ran, primitive sounds welling up in me as I slammed the front door behind me. Lucy emerged from the kitchen. She was dressed in khaki range pants and a black T-shirt, and holding a bottle of salad dressing.

"Aunt Kay!" she exclaimed, hurrying to me. "What is it, Aunt Kay? Where's Marino? My God, is he all right?"

"It's not Marino," I said chokily.

She slipped an arm around me and helped me to the couch in my great room.

"Benton," I said. "Like the others," I moaned. "Like Claire Rawley. A swimcap to keep her hair out of the way. The bathtub. Like surgery."

"What?" Lucy was dazed.

"They wanted her face!"

I sprang up from the couch.

"Don't you understand?" I yelled at her. "The nicks to bone at the temple, at the jaw. Like a scalping, only worse! He doesn't build fires to disguise homicide! He burns everything because he doesn't want us to know what he's done to them! He steals their beauty, everything beautiful about them, by removing their faces."

Lucy's lips were parted in shock.

Then she stuttered, "But Carrie? Now she's doing that?"

"Oh no," I said. "Not entirely."

I was pacing and wringing my hands.

"It's like Gault," I said. "She likes to watch. Maybe she helps. Maybe she fucked things up with Kellie Shephard, or maybe Kellie simply resisted her because Carrie was a woman. Then there was a fight, the slashing and stabbing until Carrie's partner intervened and finally cut Kellie's throat, which is where the magnesium shavings were found. From his knife, not Carrie's. He's the torch, the fire builder, not Carrie. And he didn't take Kellie's face because it had been cut, ruined, during the struggle."

"You don't think they did that to, to . . . ?" Lucy started to say, her fists clenched in her lap.

"To Benton?" I raised my voice more. "Do I think they took his face, too?"

I kicked the paneled wall and leaned against it. Inside I went still and my mind felt dark and dead.

"Carrie knew he could imagine everything she might do to him," I said in a slow, low voice. "She would have enjoyed every minute of it as he sat there, shackled. As she taunted him with the knife. Yes. I think they did that to him, too. In fact, I know it."

The last thought was almost impossible to complete.

"I just hope he was already dead," I said.

"He would have been, Aunt Kay."

Lucy was crying, too, as she came to me and wrapped her arms around my neck.

"They wouldn't have taken the chance that someone might hear him scream," she said.

Within the hour, I passed on news of the latest developments to Teun McGovern, and she agreed that it was critical for us to find out who Carrie's partner was, if possible, and how she might have met him. McGovern was more angered than she would show when I explained what I suspected and knew. Kirby might be our only hope, and she concurred that in my professional position, I had a better chance of making that visit successfully than did she. She was law enforcement. I was a physician.

Border Patrol had ferried a Bell JetRanger to HeloAir, near Richmond International Airport, and Lucy wanted to take off this minute and fly through the night. I had told her this was out of the question, if for no other reason than once we got to New York, we had no place to stay, and certainly we couldn't sleep on Ward's Island. I needed a chance first thing in the morning to alert Kirby that we were coming. It would not be a request, but a statement of fact. Marino thought he should accompany us, but I would not hear of it.

"No cops," I told him when he dropped by my house at almost ten in the evening.

"You're out of your friggin' mind," he said.

"Would you blame me if I were?"

He stared down at worn-out running shoes that had never been given a chance to perform their primary function in this world.

"Lucy's law enforcement," he said.

"As far as they're concerned, she's my pilot."

"Huh."

"I have to do this my way, Marino."

"Gee, Doc, I don't know what to say. I don't know how you can deal with any of this."

His face was deeply flushed, and when he looked up at me, his eyes were bloodshot and filled with pain.

"I want to go because I want to find those motherfuckers," he said. "They set him up. You know that, don't you? The Bureau's got a record that some guy called Tuesday afternoon at three-fourteen. Said he had a tip about the Shephard case that he'd only give to Benton Wesley. They gave the usual song and dance, that *sure, everybody says the same thing*. They're special. Got to talk to the man direct. But this informant had the goods. He said, and I quote, *Tell him it's about some weirdo woman I saw at Lehigh County Hospital. She was sitting one table away from Kellie Shephard*."

"Damn!" I exclaimed as rage thundered in my temples.

"So as best we know, Benton calls the number this asshole left. Turns out to be a pay phone near the grocery that got burned," he went on. "My guess is, Benton met up with the guy—Carrie's psycho partner. Has no idea who he's talking to until BOOM!"

I jumped.

"Benton's got a gun, maybe a knife to his throat. They cuff him, double-locking with the key. And why do that? Because he's law enforcement and knows that your average Joe don't know about double-locking. Usually, all cops do is click shut the jaws of the cuff when they're hauling somebody in. The prisoner squirms, the cuffs tighten. And if he manages to get a hairpin or something similar up there to override the ratchets, then he might even spring himself free. But with double-locking, no way. Can't get out without a key or something exactly like a key. It's something Benton would've known about when it was happening to him. A big bad signal that he was dealing with someone who knew what the shit he was doing."

"I've heard enough," I said to Marino. "Go home. Please."

I had the beginning of a migraine. I could always tell when my entire neck and head began to hurt and my stomach felt queasy. I walked Marino to the door. I knew I had wounded him. He was loaded with pain and had no place to shoot, because he did not know how to show what he felt. I wasn't even sure he knew what he felt.

"He ain't gone, you know," he said as I opened the door. "I don't believe it. I didn't see it, and I don't believe it."

"They will be sending him home soon," I said as cicadas sawed in the dark, and moths swarmed in the glow of the lamp over my porch. "Benton is dead," I said with surprising strength. "Don't take away from him by not accepting his death."

"He's gonna show up one of these days." Marino's voice was at a higher pitch. "You wait. I know that son of a bitch. He don't go down this easy."

But Benton had gone down this easy. It was so often like that, Versace walking home from buying coffee and magazines or Lady Diana not wearing her seat belt. I shut the door after Marino drove away. I set the alarm, which by now was a reflex that sometimes got me into trouble when I forgot I had armed my house and opened a slider. Lucy was stretched out on the couch, watching the Arts and Entertainment network in the great room, the lights out. I sat next to her and put my hand on her shoulder.

We did not speak as a documentary about gangsters in the early days of Las Vegas played on. I stroked her hair and her skin felt feverish. I wondered what was going on inside that mind of hers. I worried greatly about it, too. Lucy's thoughts were different. They were distinctly her own and not to be interpreted by any Rosetta stone of psychotherapy or intuition. But this much I had learned about her from the beginning of her life. What she didn't say mattered most, and Lucy wasn't talking about Janet anymore.

"Let's go to bed so we can get an early start, Madame Pilot," I said.

"I think I'll just sleep in here."

She pointed the remote control and turned down the volume.

"In your clothes?"

She shrugged.

"If we can get to HeloAir around nine, I'll call Kirby from there."

"What if they say don't come?" my niece asked.

"I'll tell them I'm on my way. New York City is Republican at the moment. If need be, I'll get my friend Senator Lord involved, and he'll get the health commissioner and mayor on the warpath, and I don't think Kirby will want that. Easier to let us land, don't you think?"

"They don't have any ground-to-air missiles there, do they?"

"Yes, they're called patients," I said, and it was the first time we had laughed in days.

Why I slept as well as I did, I could not explain, but when my alarm clock went off at six A.M., I turned over in bed. I realized I had not gotten up once since shortly before midnight, and this hinted of a cure, of a renewing that I desperately needed. Depression was a veil I could almost see through, and I was beginning to feel hope. I was doing what

Benton would expect me to do, not to avenge his murder, really, for he would not have wanted that.

His wish would have been to prevent harm to Marino, Lucy, or me. He would have wanted me to protect other lives I did not know, other unwitting individuals who worked in hospitals or as models and had been sentenced to a terrible death in the split second it took for a monster to notice them with evil eyes burning with envy.

Lucy went running as the sun was coming up, and although it unnerved me for her to be out alone, I knew she had a pistol in her butt pack, and neither of us could let our lives stop because of Carrie. It seemed she had such an advantage. If we went on as usual, we might die. If we aborted our lives because of fear, we still died, only in a way that was worse, really.

"I'm assuming everything was quiet out there?" I said when Lucy returned to the house and found me in the kitchen.

I set coffee on the kitchen table, where Lucy was seated. Sweat was rolling down her shoulders and face, and I tossed her a dishtowel. She took off her shoes and socks, and I was slammed with an image of Benton sitting there, doing the same thing. He always hung around the kitchen for a while after running. He liked to cool down, to visit with me before he took a shower and buttoned himself up in his neat clothes and deep thoughts.

"A couple people out walking their dogs in Windsor Farms," she said. "Not a sign of anybody in your neighborhood. I asked the guy at the guard gate if anything was going on, like any more taxi cabs or pizza deliveries showing up for you. Any weird phone calls or unexpected visitors trying to get in. He said no."

"Glad to hear it."

"That's chicken shit. I don't think she's the one who did that."

"Then who?" I was surprised.

"Hate to tell you, but there are other people out there who are none too fond of you."

"A large segment of the prison population."

"And people who aren't in prison, at least not yet. Like the Christian Scientists whose kid you did. You think it might occur to them to harass you? Like sending taxis, a construction Dumpster, or calling the morgue early in the morning and hanging up on poor Chuck? That's all you need, is a morgue assistant who's too spooked to be alone in your building anymore. Or worse, the guy quits. Chicken shit," she said again. "Petty, spiteful, chicken shit generated by an ignorant, little mind."

None of this had ever occurred to me before.

"Is he still getting the hang-ups?" she asked.

She eyed me as she sipped her coffee, and through the window over the sink, the sun was a tangerine on a dusky blue horizon.

"I'll find out," I said.

I picked up the phone and dialed the number for the morgue. Chuck answered immediately.

"Morgue," he said nervously.

It was not quite seven, and I suspected he was alone.

"It's Dr. Scarpetta," I said.

"Oh!" He was relieved. "Good morning."

"Chuck? What about the hang-ups? You still getting them?"

"Yes, ma'am."

"Nothing said? Not even the sound of somebody breathing?"

"Sometimes I think I hear traffic in the background, like maybe the person's at a pay phone somewhere."

"I've got an idea."

"Okay."

"Next time it happens, I want you to say, *Good morning, Mr. and Mrs. Quinn.*"

"What?" Chuck was baffled.

"Just do it," I said. "And I have a hunch the calls will stop."

Lucy was laughing when I hung up.

"Touché," she said.

21

After breakfast, I wandered about in my bedroom and study, deliberating over what to bring on our trip. My aluminum briefcase would go, because it was habit to take it almost everywhere these days. I also packed an extra pair of slacks and a shirt, and toiletries for overnight, and my Colt .38 went into my pocketbook. Although I was accustomed to carrying a gun, I had never even thought about taking one to New York, where doing so could land one in jail with no questions asked. When Lucy and I were in the car, I told her what I had done.

"It's called situational ethics," she said. "I'd rather be arrested than dead."

"That's the way I look at it," said I, who once had been a law-abiding citizen.

HeloAir was a helicopter charter service on the western edge of the Richmond airport, where some of the area's Fortune 500 companies had their own terminals for corporate King Airs and Lear Jets and Sikorskys. The Bell JetRanger was in the hangar, and while Lucy went on to take care of that, I found a pilot inside who was kind enough to let me use the phone in his office. I dug around in my wallet for my AT&T calling card and dialed the number for Kirby Forensic Psychiatric Center's administrative offices.

The director was a woman psychiatrist named Lydia Ensor who was very leery when I got her on the line. I tried to explain to her in more detail who I was, but she interrupted.

"I know exactly who you are," she said with a Midwestern tongue. "I'm completely aware of the current situation and will be as cooperative as I can. I'm not clear, however, on what your interest is, Dr. Scarpetta. You're the chief medical examiner of Virginia? Correct?"

"Correct. And a consulting forensic pathologist for ATF and the FBI."

"And of course, they've contacted me, too." She sounded genuinely perplexed. "So are you looking for information that might pertain to one of your cases? To someone dead?"

"Dr. Ensor, I'm trying to link a number of cases right now," I replied. "I have reason to suspect that Carrie Grethen may be either indirectly or directly involved in all of them and may have been involved even while she was at Kirby."

"Impossible."

"Clearly, you don't know this woman," I said firmly. "I, on the other hand, have worked violent deaths caused by her for half of my career, beginning when she and Temple Gault were on a spree in Virginia and finally in New York, where Gault was killed. And now this. Possibly five more murders, maybe more."

"I know Miss Grethen's history all too well," Dr. Ensor said, and she wasn't hostile, but defensiveness had crept into her tone. "I can assure you that Kirby handled her as we do all maximum security patients . . ."

"There's almost nothing useful in her psychiatric evaluations," I cut her off.

"How could you possibly know about her medical records . . . ?"

"Because I am part of the ATF national response team that is investigating these fire-related homicides," I measured my words. "And I work with the FBI, as I've already said. All of the cases we're talking about are my jurisdiction because I'm a consultant for law enforcement at a federal level. But my duty is not to arrest anyone or smear an institution such as yours. My job is to bring justice to the dead and give as much peace as possible to those they left behind. To do that, I must answer questions. And most important, I am driven to do anything I can to prevent one more person from dying. Carrie will kill again. She may already have."

The director was silent for a moment. I looked out the window and could see the dark blue helicopter on its pad being towed out onto the tarmac.

"Dr. Scarpetta, what would you like us to do?" Dr. Ensor finally spoke, her voice tense and upset.

"Did Carrie have a social worker? Someone in legal aid? Anyone she really talked to?" I asked.

"Obviously, she spent a fair amount of time with a forensic psychologist, but he isn't on our staff. Mainly he's there to evaluate and make recommendations to the court."

"Then she probably manipulated him," I said as I watched Lucy climb up on the helicopter's skids and begin her preflight inspection. "Who else? Anyone she may have gotten close to?"

"Her lawyer, then. Yes, legal aid. If you would like to speak to her, that can be arranged."

"I'm leaving the airport now," I said. "We should be landing in approximately three hours. Do you have a helipad?"

"I don't remember anyone ever landing here. There are several parks nearby. I'll be happy to pick you up."

"I don't think that will be necessary. My guess is we'll land close by."

"I'll watch for you, then, and take you to legal aid, or wherever it is you need to go."

"I would like to see Carrie Grethen's ward and where she spent her time."

"Whatever you need."

"You are very kind," I said.

Lucy was opening access panels to check fluid levels, wiring, and anything else that might be amiss before we took to the air. She was agile and sure of what she was doing, and when she climbed on top of the fuselage to inspect the main rotor, I wondered how many helicopter accidents happened on the ground. It wasn't until I had climbed up into the copilot's seat that I noticed the AR-15 assault rifle in a rack behind her head, and at the same time, I realized the controls on my side had not been taken out. Passengers were not entitled to have access to the collective and cyclic, and the antitorque pedals were supposed to be cranked back far enough that the uninitiated did not accidentally push them with their feet.

"What's this?" I said to Lucy as I buckled my four-point harness.

"We've got a long flight."

She cracked the throttle several times to make certain there was no binding and it was closed.

"I realize that," I said.

"Cross country's a good time to try your hand at it."

She lifted the collective and made big X's with the cyclic.

"Whose hand at what?" I said as my alarm grew.

"Your hand at flying when all you got to do is hold your altitude and speed and keep her level."

"No way."

She pressed the starter and the engine began to whirr.

"Yes, *way*."

The blades began to turn as the windy roar got louder.

"If you're going to fly with me," my niece, the pilot and certificated flight instructor, said above the noise, "then I'd like to know you could help out if there was a problem, okay?"

I said nothing more as she rolled the throttle and raised the rpms. She flipped switches and tested caution lights, then turned on the radio and we put our headsets on. Lucy lifted us off the platform as if gravity had quit. She turned us into the wind and moved forward with gathering speed until the helicopter seemed to soar on its own. We climbed above trees, the sun high in the east. When we were clear of the tower and the city, Lucy began lesson one.

I already knew what most of the controls were and what they were for, but I had an extremely limited understanding of how they worked together. I did not know, for example, that when you raise the collective and increase power, the helicopter will yaw to the right, meaning you have to depress your left antitorque pedal to counter the torque of the main rotor and keep the aircraft in trim, and as your altitude climbs, due to the pulling up on the collective, your speed decreases, meaning you have to push the cyclic forward. And so on. It was like playing the drums, as best I knew, only in this instance I had to watch for dim-witted birds, towers, antennae, and other aircraft.

Lucy was very patient, and the time moved fast as we forged ahead at one hundred and ten knots. By the time we were north of Washington, I actually could keep the helicopter relatively steady while adjusting the directional gyro at the same time to keep it consistent with the compass. Our heading was 050 degrees, and although I could juggle not one more thing, such as the Global Positioning System, or GPS, Lucy said I was doing a fine job keeping us on course.

"We got a small plane at three o'clock," she said through her mike. "See it?"

"Yes."

"Then you say, *tally-ho*. And it's above horizon. You can tell that, right?"

"Tally-ho."

Lucy laughed. "No. Tally-ho does not mean ten-four. And if something's above horizon, that means it's also above us. That's important, because if both aircraft are at horizon and the one we're looking at also doesn't seem to be moving, then that means it's at our altitude and either heading away from us or straight for us. Kind of smart to pay attention and figure out which one, right?"

Her instruction went on until the New York skyline was in view, then I was to have nothing more to do with the controls. Lucy flew us low past the Statue of Liberty and Ellis Island, where my Italian ancestors had gathered long ago to begin with nothing in a new world of opportunity. The city gathered around us and the buildings in the financial district were huge as we flew at five hundred feet, the shadow of our helicopter moving below us along the water. It was a hot, clear day, and tour helicopters were making their rounds while others carried executives who had everything but time.

Lucy was busy with the radio, and approach control did not seem to want to acknowledge us because air traffic was so congested, and controllers were not very interested in aircraft flying at seven hundred feet. At this altitude in this city, the rules were see and avoid, and that was about it. We followed the East River over the Brooklyn, Manhattan, and Williamsburg bridges, moving at ninety knots over crawling garbage barges, fuel tankers, and circling white tour boats. As we passed by the crumbled buildings and old hospitals of Roosevelt Island, Lucy let La Guardia know what we were doing. By now Ward's Island was straight ahead. It was appropriate that the part of the river at the southwestern tip was called Hell Gate.

What I knew about Ward's Island came from my enduring interest in medical history, and as was true of many of New York's islands in earlier times, it was a place of exile for prisoners, the diseased, and mentally ill. Ward's Island's past was particularly unhappy, as I recalled, for in the mid-eighteen hundreds, it had been a place of no heat or running water, where people with typhus were quarantined and Russian Jewish refugees were warehoused. At the turn of the century, the city's lunatic asylum had been moved to the island. Certainly conditions were better here now, although the population was far more maniacal. Patients had air conditioning, lawyers, and hobbies. They had access to dental and medical care, psychotherapy, support groups, and organized sports.

We entered the Class B airspace above Ward's Island in a deceptively civilized way, flying low over green parks shaded with trees as the ugly tan brick high-rises of the Manhattan Psychiatric and Children's Psychiatric Centers and Kirby loomed straight ahead. The Triborough Bridge

Parkway ran through the middle of the island, where incongruous to all was a small circus going on, with bright striped tents, ponies, and performers on unicycles. The crowd was small, and I could see kids eating cotton candy, and I wondered why they weren't in school. A little farther north was a sewage disposal plant and the New York City fire department training academy, where a long ladder truck was practicing turns in a parking lot.

The forensic psychiatric center was twelve stories of steel mesh covered windows, opaque glass, and air conditioning units. Sloppy coils of razor wire bent in over walkways and recreation areas, to prevent an escape that Carrie apparently had found so easy. The river here was about a mile wide, rough and foreboding, the current swift, and I did not think it likely that anyone could swim across it. But there was a footbridge, as I had been told. It was painted the teal of oxidized copper and was maybe a mile south of Kirby. I told Lucy to fly over it, and from the air I saw people crossing it from both directions, moving in and out of the East River Housing of Harlem.

"I don't see how she could have gotten across that in broad daylight," I transmitted to Lucy. "Not without being seen by someone. But even if she could and did, what next? The police were going to be all over the place, especially on the other side of the bridge. And how did she get to Lehigh County?"

Lucy was doing slow circles at five hundred feet, the blades flapping loudly. There were remnants of a ferry that at one time must have allowed passage from East River Drive at 106th Street, and the ruins of a pier, which was now a pile of rotting, creosote-treated wood jutting out into unfriendly waters from a small open field on Kirby's western side. The field looked suitable for landing, providing we stayed closer to the river than to the screened-in walkways and benches of the hospital.

As Lucy began a high reconnaissance, I looked down at people on the ground. All were dressed in civilian clothes, some stretching or lying in the grass, others on benches or moving along walkways between rusting barrels of trash. Even from five hundred feet, I recognized the slovenly, ill-fitting dress and odd gaits of those broken beyond repair. They stared up, transfixed, as we scoured the area for problems, such as power lines, guy wires, and soft, uneven ground. A low reconnaissance confirmed our landing was safe, and by now, more people had emerged from buildings or were looking out windows and standing in doorways to see what was going on.

"Maybe we should have tried one of the parks," I said. "I hope we don't start a riot."

Lucy lowered into a five-foot hover, weeds and tall grass thrashing violently. A pheasant and her brood were appropriately startled and darted along the bank and out of view amid rushes, and it was hard to imagine anything innocent and vulnerable living so close to disturbed humanity. I suddenly thought of Carrie's letter to me, of her odd listing of Kirby's address as *One Pheasant Place*. What was she telling me? That she had seen the pheasants, too? If so, why did it matter?

The helicopter settled softly and Lucy rolled the throttle to flight idle. It was a very long two-minute wait to cut the engine. Blades turned as digital seconds did, and patients and hospital personnel stared. Some stood perfectly still, pinning us with glazed eyes, while others were oblivious, tugging on fences or walking with jerky motions and staring at the ground. An old man rolling a cigarette waved, a woman in curlers was muttering, and a young man wearing headphones started into a loose knee rhythm on the sidewalk, for our benefit, it seemed.

Lucy rolled the throttle to idle cut-off and braked the main rotor, shutting us down. When the blades had fully stopped and we were climbing out, a woman emerged from the gathering crowd of the mentally deranged and those who took care of them. She was dressed in a smart herringbone suit, her jacket on despite the heat. Her dark hair was short and smartly styled. I knew before being told that she was Dr. Lydia Ensor, and she seemed to pick me out as well, for she shook my hand first, then Lucy's, as she introduced herself.

"I must say, you've created a lot of excitement," she said with a slight smile.

"And I apologize for that," I said.

"Not to worry."

"I'm staying with the helicopter," Lucy said.

"You sure?" I asked.

"I'm sure," she replied, looking around at the unnerving crowd.

"Most of these are outpatients at the psychiatric center right over there." Dr. Ensor pointed at another high rise. "And Odyssey House."

She nodded at a much smaller brick building beyond Kirby, where there appeared to be a garden, and an eroded asphalt tennis court with a billowing torn net.

"Drugs, drugs, and more drugs," she added. "They go in for counseling, and we've caught them rolling a joint on their way out."

"I'll be right here," Lucy said. "Or I can head out to get fuel, and then come back," she added to me.

"I'd rather you wait," I said.

Dr. Ensor and I began the brief walk to Kirby while eyes glared and poured out black unspeakable pain and hate. A man with a matted beard shouted out to us that he wanted a ride, making gestures towards the heavens, flapping arms like a bird, jumping on one foot. Ravaged faces were in some other realms or vacant or filled with a bitter contempt that could only come from being on the inside looking out at people like us who were not enslaved to drugs or dementia. We were the privileged. We were the living. We were God to those who were helpless to do anything except destroy themselves and others, and at the end of the day, we went home.

The entrance to Kirby Forensic Psychiatric Center was that of a typical state institution, with walls painted the same teal as the footbridge over the river. Dr. Ensor led me around a corner to a button on a wall, which she pressed.

"Come to the intercom," an abrupt voice sounded like the Wizard of Oz.

She moved on, needing no direction, and spoke through the intercom.

"Dr. Ensor," she said.

"Yes, ma'am." The voice became human. "Step on up."

The entrance into the heart of Kirby was typical for a penitentiary, with its airlocked doors that never allowed two of them to be opened at the same time, and its posted warnings of prohibited items, such as firearms, explosives, ammunition, alcohol, or objects made of glass. No matter how adamant politicians, health workers, and the ACLU might be, this was not a hospital. Patients were inmates. They were violent offenders housed in a maximum security facility because they had raped and beaten. They had shot their families, burned up their mothers, disemboweled their neighbors, and dismembered their lovers. They were monsters who had become celebrities, like Robert Chambers of the Yuppie murder fame, or Rakowitz, who had murdered and cooked his girlfriend and allegedly fed parts of her to street people, or Carrie Grethen, who was worse than any of them.

The teal-painted barred door unlocked with an electronic click, and peace officers in blue uniforms were most courteous to Dr. Ensor, and also to me, since I clearly was her guest. Nonetheless, we were made to pass through a metal detector, and our pocketbooks were carefully gone through. I was embarrassed when reminded that one could enter with only enough medication for one dose, while I had enough Motrin, Immodium, Tums, and aspirin to take care of an entire ward.

"Ma'am, you must not be feeling good," one of the guards said good-naturedly.

"It accumulates," I said, grateful that I had locked my handgun in my briefcase, which was safely stored in the helicopter's baggage compartment.

"Well, I'm gonna have to hold on to it until you come out. It will be waiting right here for you, okay? So make sure you ask."

"Thank you," I said, as if he had just granted me a favor.

We were allowed to pass through another door that was posted with the warning, *Keep Hands Off Bars*. Then we were in stark, colorless hallways, turning corners, passing closed doors where hearings were in session.

"You need to understand that legal aid attorneys are employed by the Legal Aid Society, which is a nonprofit, private organization under contract with New York City. Clearly, the personnel they have here are part of their criminal division. They are not on the Kirby staff."

She wanted to make sure I understood that.

"Although, after a number of years here, they certainly may get chummy with my staff," she kept talking as we walked, our heels clicking over tile. "The lawyer in question, who worked with Miss Grethen from the beginning, will most likely arch her back at any questions you might ask."

She glanced over at me.

"I have no control over it," she said.

"I understand completely," I replied. "And if a public defender or legal aid attorney didn't arch his back when I appeared, I would think the planet had changed."

Mental Hygiene Legal Aid was lost somewhere in the midst of Kirby, and I could only swear that it was on the first floor. The director opened a wooden door for me, and then was showing me into a small office that was so overflowing with paper that hundreds of case files were stacked on the floor. The lawyer behind the desk was a disaster of frumpy clothing and wild frizzy black hair. She was heavy, with ponderous breasts that could have benefited from a bra.

"Susan, this is Dr. Kay Scarpetta, chief medical examiner of Virginia," Dr. Ensor said. "Here about Carrie Grethen, as you know. And Dr. Scarpetta, this is Susan Blaustein."

"Right," said Ms. Blaustein, who was neither inclined to get up nor shake my hand as she sifted through a thick legal brief.

"I'll leave the two of you, then. Susan, I trust you will show Dr. Scarpetta around, otherwise I will get someone on staff to do it," Dr. Ensor said, and I could tell by the way she looked at me that she knew I was in for the tour from hell.

"No problem."

The guardian angel of felons had a Brooklyn accent as coarse and tightly packed as a garbage barge.

"Have a seat," she said to me as the director disappeared.

"When was Carrie remanded here?" I asked.

"Five years ago."

She would not look up from her paperwork.

"You're aware of her history, of the homicide cases that have yet to go to trial in Virginia?"

"You name it, I'm aware of it."

"Carrie escaped from here ten days ago, on June tenth," I went on. "Has anyone figured out how that might have happened?"

Blaustein flipped a page and picked up a coffee cup.

"She didn't show up for dinner. That's it," she replied. "I was as shocked as anyone when she disappeared."

"I bet you were," I said.

She turned another page and had yet to give me her eyes. I'd had enough.

"Ms. Blaustein," I said in a hard voice as I leaned against her desk. "With all due respect to your clients, would you like to hear about mine? Would you like to hear all about men, women, and children who were butchered by Carrie Grethen? A little boy abducted from a 7-Eleven where he'd been sent to buy his mother a can of mushroom soup? He's shot in the head and areas of his flesh are removed to obliterate bitemarks, his pitiful body clad only in undershorts propped against a Dumpster in a freezing rain?"

"I told you, I know about the cases." She continued to work.

"I suggest you put down that brief and pay attention to me," I warned. "I may be a forensic pathologist, but I'm also a lawyer, and your shenanigans get nowhere with me. You just so happen to represent a psychopath who as we speak is on the outside murdering people. Don't let me find out at the end of the day that you had information that might have spared even one life."

She gave me her eyes, cold and arrogant, because her only power in life was to defend losers and jerk around people like me.

"Let me just refresh your memory," I went on. "Since your client has escaped from Kirby, it is believed she has either murdered or served as an accomplice to murder in two cases, happening within a matter of days of each other. Vicious homicides in which an attempt was made to disguise them by fire. These were predated by other fire-homicides which we now believe are linked, yet in these earlier ones, your client was still incarcerated here."

Susan Blaustein was silent as she stared at me.

"Can you help me with this?"

"All of my conversations with Carrie are privileged. I'm sure you must know that," she remarked, yet I could tell she was curious about what I was saying.

"Possible she was connecting with someone on the outside?" I went on. "And if so, how and who?"

"You tell me."

"Did she ever talk to you about Temple Gault?"

"Privileged."

"Then she did," I said. "Of course, she did. How could she not? Did you know she wrote to me, Ms. Blaustein, asking me to come see her and bring her Gault's autopsy photos?"

She said nothing, but her eyes were coming alive.

"He was hit by a train in the Bowery. Scattered along the tracks."

"Did you do his autopsy?" she asked.

"No."

"Then why would Carrie ask you for the photos, Dr. Scarpetta?"

"Because she knew I could get them. Carrie wanted to see them, blood and gore and all. This was less than a week before she escaped. I'm just wondering if you knew she was sending out letters like that? A clear indication, as far as I'm concerned, that she had premeditated all she was about to do next."

"No."

Blaustein pointed her finger at me.

"What she was thinking was how she was being framed to take the heat because the FBI couldn't find its damn way out of a paper bag and needed to hang all this on someone," she accused.

"I see you read the papers."

Her face turned angry.

"I talked to Carrie for five years," she said. "She wasn't the one sleeping with the Bureau, right?"

"In a way she was." I thought honestly of Lucy. "And quite frankly, Ms. Blaustein, I'm not here to change your opinion of your client. My purpose is to investigate a number of deaths and do what I can to prevent others."

Carrie's legal aid attorney began shoving around paperwork again.

"It seems to me that the reason Carrie had been here so long is that every time an evaluation of her mental status came up, you made sure it was clear that she had not regained competency," I went on. "Meaning she is also incompetent to stand trial, right? Meaning she is so mentally ill that she's not even aware of the charges against her? And yet she must have been somewhat aware of her situation, or how else could she have trumped up this whole business about the FBI framing her? Or was it you who trumped that up?"

"This meeting has just ended," Blaustein announced, and had she been a judge, she would have slammed down the gavel.

"Carrie's nothing but a malingerer," I said. "She played it up, manipulated. Let me guess. She was very depressed, couldn't remember anything when it was important. Was probably on Ativan, which probably didn't put a dent in her. She clearly had the energy to write letters. And what other privileges might she have enjoyed? Telephone, photocopying?"

"The patients have civil rights," Blaustein said evenly. "She was very quiet. Played a lot of chess and spades. She liked to read. There were mitigating and aggravating circumstances at the time of the offenses, and she was not responsible for her actions. She was very remorseful."

"Carrie always was a great salesperson," I said. "Always a master at getting what she wanted, and she wanted to be here long enough to make her next move. And now she's made it."

I opened my pocketbook and got out a copy of the letter Carrie had written to me. I dropped it in front of Blaustein.

"Pay special attention to the return address at the top of it. *One Pheasant Place, Kirby Women's Ward*," I said. "Do you have any idea what she meant by that, or would you like me to hazard a guess?"

"I don't have a clue." She was reading the letter, a perplexed expression on her face.

"Possibly the *one-place* part is a play off *One Hogan Place*, or the address of the District Attorney that eventually would have prosecuted her."

"I don't have a clue as to what was going through her mind."

"Let's talk about *pheasants*," I then said. "You have pheasants along the riverbank right outside your door."

"I haven't noticed."

"I noticed because we landed in the field there. And that's right, you wouldn't have noticed unless you waded through half an acre of overgrown grass and weeds and went to the water's edge, near the old pier."

She said nothing, but I could tell she was getting unsettled.

"So my question is, how might Carrie or any of the inmates have known about the pheasants?"

Still, she was silent.

"You know very well why, don't you?" I forced her.

She stared at me.

"A maximum security patient should never have been in that field or even close to it, Ms. Blaustein. If you don't wish to talk to me about it, then I'll just let the police take it up with you, since Carrie's escape is rather much a priority for law enforcement these days. Indeed, I'm sure your fine mayor isn't happy about the continuing bad publicity Carrie brings to a city that has become famous for defeating crime."

"I don't know how Carrie knew," Ms. Blaustein finally said. "This is the first I've ever heard of fucking pheasants. Maybe someone on the staff said something to her. Maybe one of the delivery people from the store, someone from the outside, such as yourself, in other words."

"What store?"

"The patient privilege programs allow them to earn credits or money for the store. Snacks, mostly. They get one delivery a week, and they have to use their own money."

"Where did Carrie get money?"

Blaustein would not say.

"What day did her deliveries come?"

"Depends. Usually early in the week, Monday, Tuesday, late in the afternoon, usually."

"She escaped late in the afternoon, on a Tuesday," I said.

"That's correct." Her eyes got harder.

"And what about the deliveryperson?" I then asked. "Has anybody bothered to see if he or she might have had anything to do with this?"

"The deliveryperson was a he," Blaustein said with no emotion. "No one has been able to locate him. He was a substitute for the usual person, who apparently was out sick."

"A *substitute*? Right. Carrie was interested in more than potato chips!" My voice rose. "Let me guess. The delivery people wear uniforms and drive a van. Carrie puts on a uniform and walks right out with her deliveryman. Gets in the van and is out of here."

"Speculation. We don't know how she got out."

"Oh, I think you do, Ms. Blaustein. And I'm wondering if you didn't help Carrie with money, too, since she was so special to you."

She got to her feet and pointed her finger at me again.

"If you're accusing me of helping her escape . . ."

"You helped her in one way or another," I cut her off.

I fought back tears as I thought of Carrie free on the streets, as I thought about Benton.

"You monster," I said, and my eyes were hot on hers. "I'd like you to spend just one day with the victims. Just one goddamn day, putting your hands in their blood and touching their wounds. The innocent people the Carries of the world butcher for sport. I think there would be some people who would not be too happy to know about Carrie, her privileges, and unaccounted source of income," I said. "Others besides me."

We were interrupted by a knock on her door, and Dr. Ensor walked in.

"I thought I might take you on your tour," she said to me. "Susan seems busy. Are you finished up here?" she asked the legal aid attorney.

"Quite."

"Very good," she said with a chilly smile.

I knew then that the director was perfectly clear on how much Susan Blaustein had abused power, trust, and common decency. In the end, Blaustein had manipulated the hospital as much as Carrie had.

"Thank you," I said to the director.

I left, turning my back on Carrie's defender.

May you rot in hell, I thought.

I followed Dr. Ensor again, this time to a large stainless steel elevator that opened onto barren beige hallways closed off with heavy red doors that required codes for entry. Everything was monitored by closed circuit TV. Apparently Carrie had enjoyed working in the pet program, which entailed daily visits to the eleventh floor, where animals were kept in cages inside a small room with a view of razor wire.

The menagerie was dimly lit and moist with the musky smells of animals and wood chips, and the skittering of claws. There were parakeets, guinea pigs, and a Russian dwarf hamster. On a table was a box of rich soil thick with tender shoots.

"We grow our own birdseed here," Dr. Ensor explained. "The patients are encouraged to raise and sell it. Of course, we're not talking mass production here. There's barely enough for our own birds, and as you can see by what's in some of the cages and on the floor, the patients tend to be fond of feeding their pets cheese puffs and potato chips."

"Carrie was up here every day?" I asked.

"So I've been told, now that I've been looking into everything she did while she was here." She paused, looking around the cages as small animals with pink noses twitched and scratched.

"Obviously I didn't know everything at the time. For example, coincidentally, during the six months Carrie supervised the pet program, we had an unusual number of fatalities and inexplicable escapes. A parakeet here, a hamster there. Patients would come in and find their wards dead in their cages, or a cage door open and a bird nowhere to be found."

She walked back out into the hallway, her lips firmly pressed.

"It's too bad you weren't here on those occasions," she said wryly. "Perhaps you could have told me what they were dying from. Or who."

There was another door down the hall, and this one opened onto a small, dimly lit room where there was one relatively modern computer and printer on a plain wooden table. I also noted a phone jack in the wall. A sense of foreshadowing darkened my thoughts even before Dr. Ensor spoke.

"This was perhaps where Carrie spent most of her free time," she said. "As you no doubt know, she has an extensive background in computers. She was extremely good about encouraging other patients to learn, and the PC was her idea. She suggested we find donors of used equipment, and we now have one computer and printer on each floor."

I walked over to the terminal and sat down in front of it. Hitting a key, I turned off the screen saver and looked at icons that told me what programs were available.

"When patients worked in here," I said, "were they supervised?"

"No. They were shown in and the door was shut and locked. An hour later, they were shown back to their ward." She grew thoughtful. "I'd be the first to admit that I was impressed with how many of the patients have started learning word processing, and in some instances, spread sheets."

I went into America Online and was prompted for a username and password. The director watched what I was doing.

"They absolutely had no access to the Internet," she said.

"How do we know that?"

"The computers aren't hooked up to it."

"But they do have modems," I said. "Or at least this one does. It's simply not connecting because there's no telephone line plugged into the telephone jack."

I pointed to the tiny receptacle in the wall, then turned around to face her.

"Any chance a telephone line might have disappeared from somewhere?" I asked. "Perhaps from one of the offices? Susan Blaustein's office, for example?"

The director glanced away, her face angry and distressed as she began to see what I was getting at.

"God," she muttered.

"Of course, she may have gotten that from the outside. Perhaps from whoever delivered her snacks from the store?"

"I don't know."

"The point is, there's a lot we don't know, Dr. Ensor. We don't know, for example, what the hell Carrie was really doing when she was in here. She could have been in and out of chat rooms, putting feelers out in personals, finding pen pals. I'm sure you've kept up with the news enough to know how many crimes are committed on the Internet? Pedophilia, rape, homicide, child pornography."

"That's why this was closely supervised," she said. "Or supposed to have been."

"Carrie could have planned her escape this way. And you say she started working with the computer how long ago?"

"About a year. After a long run of ideal behavior."

"*Ideal behavior*," I repeated.

I thought of the cases in Baltimore, Venice Beach, and more recently in Warrenton. I wondered if it were possible that Carrie might have met up with her accomplice through e-mail, through a Web site or a chat room. Could it be that she committed computer crimes during her incarceration? Might she have been working behind the scenes, advising and encouraging a psychopath who stole human faces? Then she escaped, and from that point on her crimes were in person.

"Is there anyone who's been discharged from Kirby in the past year who was an arsonist, especially someone with a history of homicide? Anyone Carrie might have come to know? Perhaps someone in one of her classes?" I asked, just to be sure.

Dr. Ensor turned off the overhead light and we returned to the hall.

"No one comes to mind," she said. "Not of the sort you're talking about. I will add that a peace officer was always present."

"And male and female patients did not mix during recreational times."

"No. Never. Men and women are completely segregated."

Although I did not know for a fact that Carrie had a male accomplice, I suspected it, and I recalled what Benton had written in his notes at the end, about a white male between the ages of twenty-eight and forty-five. Peace officers, who were simply guards not wearing guns, might have insured that order was maintained in the classrooms, but I doubted seriously they would have had any idea that Carrie was making contact on the Internet. We boarded the elevator again, this time getting off on the third floor.

"The women's ward," Dr. Ensor explained. "We have twenty-six female patients at the moment, out of one hundred and seventy patients overall. That's the visitors' room."

She pointed through glass at a spacious open area with comfortable chairs and televisions. No one was in there now.

"Did she ever have visitors?" I asked as we kept walking.

"Not from the outside, not once. Inspiring more sympathy for her, I suppose." She smiled bitterly. "The women actually stay in there."

She pointed out another area, this one arranged with single beds.

"She slept over there by the window," Dr. Ensor said.

I retrieved Carrie's letter from my pocketbook and read it again, stopping at the fifth paragraph:

LUCY-BOO on TV. Fly through window. Come with we. Under covers. Come til dawn. Laugh and sing. Same ole song. LUCY LUCY LUCY and we!

Suddenly I thought about the videotape of Kellie Shephard, and of the actress in Venice Beach who played bit parts on television shows. I thought of photo shoots and production crews, becoming more convinced that there was a connection. But what did Lucy have to do with any of this? Why would Carrie see Lucy on TV? Or was it simply that she somehow knew that Lucy could fly, could fly helicopters?

There was a commotion around a corner, and female peace officers were herding the women patients in from recreation. They were sweating and loud, with tormented faces, and one was being escorted in a preventive aggressive device, or a PAD, which was a politically correct term for a restraint that chained wrists and ankles to a thick leather strap about the waist. She was young and white, with eyes that scattered when they fixed on me, her mouth bowed in a simpering smile. With her bleached hair and pale androgynous body, she could have been Carrie, and for a moment, in my imagination, she was. My flesh crawled as those irises seemed to swirl, sucking me in, while patients jostled past us, several making it a point to bump into me.

"You a lawyer?" an obese black woman almost spat as her eyes smoldered on me.

"Yes," I said, unflinching as I stared back, for I had learned long ago not to be intimidated by people who hate.

"Come on." The director pulled me along. "I'd forgotten they were due up at this time. I apologize."

But I was glad it had happened. In a sense, I had looked Carrie in the eye and had not turned away.

"Tell me exactly what happened the night she disappeared, please," I said.

Dr. Ensor entered a code into another keypad and pushed through another set of bright red doors.

"As best anyone can reconstruct it," she replied, "Carrie went out with the other patients for this same recreation hour. Her snacks were delivered, and at dinner she was gone."

We rode the elevator down. She glanced at her watch.

"Immediately, a search began and the police were contacted. Not one sign of her, and that's what continued to eat at me," she went on. "How did she get off the island in broad daylight with no one seeing her? We had cops, we had dogs, we had helicopters . . ."

I stopped her there, in the middle of the first floor hall.

"Helicopters?" I said. "More than one?"

"Oh yes."

"You saw them?"

"Hard not to," she replied. "They were circling and hovering for hours, the entire hospital was in an uproar."

"Describe the helicopters," I said as my heart began to hammer. "Please."

"Oh gosh," she answered. "Three police at first, then the media flew in like a swarm of hornets."

"By chance, was one of the helicopters small and white? Like a dragonfly?"

She looked surprised.

"I do remember seeing one like that," she said. "I thought it was just some pilot curious about all of the commotion."

22

Lucy and I lifted off from Ward's Island in a hot wind and low barometric pressure that made the Bell JetRanger sluggish. We followed the East River and continued to fly through the Class B airspace of La Guardia, where we landed long enough to refuel and buy cheese crackers and sodas from vending machines, and for me to call the University of North Carolina at Wilmington. This time I was connected to the director of student counseling. I took that as a good sign.

"I understand your need to protect yourself," I said to her from behind the shut door of a pay phone booth inside Signatures terminal. "But please reconsider. Two more people have been murdered since Claire Rawley was."

There was a long silence.

Then Dr. Chris Booth said, "Can you come in person?"

"I was planning to," I told her.

"All right then."

I called Teun McGovern next to tell her what was going on.

"I think Carrie escaped from Kirby in the same white Schweizer we saw flying over Kenneth Sparkes's farm when we were working the scene," I said.

"Does she fly?" McGovern's confused voice came back.

"No, no. I can't imagine that."

"Oh."

"Whoever she's with," I said. "That's the pilot. Whoever helped her escape and is doing all this. The first two cases were warm-ups. Baltimore and Venice Beach. We might never have known about them, Teun. I believe Carrie waited to drag us in. She waited until Warrenton."

"Then you're thinking Sparkes was the intended target," she stated thoughtfully.

"To get our attention. To make sure we came. Yes," I said.

"Then Claire Rawley figures in how?"

"That's what I'm going to Wilmington to find out, Teun. I believe she's somehow the key to all of this. She's the connection to him. Whoever he is. And I also believe that Carrie knows I will think this, and that she's expecting me."

"You think she's there."

"Oh yes. I'm betting on it. She expected Benton to come to Philadelphia, and he did. She expects Lucy and me to come to Wilmington. She knows how we think, how we work, at least as much about us as we know about her."

"You're saying that you're her next hits."

The thought was cold water in my stomach.

"Intended ones."

"Not a chance we can take, Kay. We'll be there when you land. The university must have a playing field. We'll get that arranged very discreetly. Whenever you land to refuel or whatever, page me and we'll keep up with each other."

"You can't let her know you're there," I said. "That will ruin it."

"Trust me. She won't," McGovern said.

We flew out of La Guardia with seventy-five gallons of

fuel and an unbearably long flight to look forward to. Three hours in a helicopter was always more than enough for me. The weight of the headsets and the noise and vibration gave me a hot spot on the top of my head and seemed to rattle me loose at the joints. To endure this beyond four hours generally resulted in a serious headache. We were lucky with a generous tail wind, and although our airspeed showed one hundred and ten knots, the GPS showed our ground speed was actually one hundred and twenty.

Lucy made me take the controls again, and I was smoother as I learned not to overcontrol and fight. When thermals and winds shook us like an angry mother, I gave myself up to them. Trying to outmaneuver gusts and updrafts only made matters worse, and this was hard for me. I liked to make things better. I learned to watch for birds, and now and then I spotted a plane at the same time Lucy did.

Hours became monotonous and blurred as we snuggled up to the coastline, over the Delaware River and on to the Eastern Shore. We refueled near Salisbury, Maryland, where I used the bathroom and drank a Coke, then continued into North Carolina, where hog farms slaughtered the topography with long aluminum sheds and waste treatment lagoons the color of blood. We entered the airspace of Wilmington at almost two o'clock. My nerves began to scream as I imagined what might await us.

"Let's go down to six hundred feet," Lucy said. "And lower the speed."

"You want me to do it." I wanted to make sure.

"Your ship."

It wasn't pretty, but I managed.

"My guess is, the university's not going to be on the water, and is probably a bunch of brick buildings."

"Thank you, Sherlock."

Everywhere I looked I saw water, condominium complexes, and water treatment and other plants. The ocean was to the east, sparkling and ruffled, oblivious to dark, bruised clouds gathering on the horizon. A storm was on its way and did not seem to be in a hurry but threatened to be bad.

"Lord, I don't want to get grounded here," I said over my mike as, sure enough, a cluster of Georgian brick buildings came into view.

"I don't know about this." Lucy was looking around. "If she's here. Where, Aunt Kay?"

"Wherever she thinks we are." I sounded so sure.

Lucy took over.

"I've got the controls," she said. "I don't know if I hope you're right or not."

"You hope it," I answered her. "In fact, you hope it so much it scares me, Lucy."

"I'm not the one who brought us here."

Carrie had tried to ruin Lucy. Carrie had murdered Benton.

"I know who brought us here," I said. "It was her."

The university was close below us, and we found the athletic field where McGovern was waiting. Men and women were playing soccer, but there was a clearing near the tennis courts, and this was where Lucy was to land. She circled the area twice, once high, once low, and neither of us spotted any obstructions, except for an odd tree here and there. Several cars were on the sidelines, and as we settled to the grass, I noted that one of them was a dark blue Explorer with a driver inside. Then I realized that the intramural soccer game was coached by Teun McGovern in P.E. gym shorts and shirt. She had a whistle around her neck, and her teams were co-ed and very fit.

I looked around as if Carrie were observing all this, but skies were empty, and nothing offered even the scent of her. The instant we were on the ground and in flight idle, the Explorer drove across the grass and stopped a safe distance from our blades. It was driven by an unfamiliar woman, and I was stunned to see Marino in the passenger's seat.

"I don't believe it," I said to Lucy.

"How the hell did he get here?" She was amazed, too.

Marino stared at us through the windshield as we waited out our two minutes and shut down. He didn't smile and wasn't the least bit friendly when I climbed into the back of the car while Lucy tied down the main rotor blades. McGovern and her soccer players went on with their staged game, paying no attention to us at all. But I noticed the gym bags beneath benches on the sidelines, and I had no doubt what was inside them. It was as if we were expecting an approaching army, an ambush by enemy troops, and I could not help but wonder if Carrie had made a mockery of us once again.

"I wasn't expecting to see you," I commented to Marino.

"You think it's possible US Airways could fly somewhere without dumping your ass out in Charlotte first?" he complained. "Took me as long to get here as it probably did you."

"I'm Ginny Correll." Our driver turned around and shook my hand.

She was at least forty, a very attractive blond dressed primly in a pale green suit, and had I not known the truth, I might have assumed she was on the university's faculty. But there was a scanner and a two-way radio inside the car, and I caught a flicker of the pistol in the shoulder holster beneath her jacket. She waited until Lucy was inside the

Explorer, and then began turning around in the grass as the soccer game went on.

"Here's what's going on," Correll began to explain. "We didn't know whether the suspect or suspects might be waiting for you, following you, whatever, so we prepared for that."

"I can see that you did," I said.

"They'll be heading off the field in about two minutes, and the important point is we got guys all over the place. Some dressed as students, others hanging out in town, checking out the hotels and bars, things like that. Where we're heading now is the student counseling center, where the assistant director's going to meet us. She was Claire Rawley's counselor and has all her records."

"Right," I said.

"Just so you know, Doc," Marino said, "we got a campus police officer who thinks he may have spotted Carrie yesterday in the student union."

"The Hawk's Nest, to be specific," Correll said. "That's the cafeteria."

"Short dyed red hair, weird eyes. She was buying a sandwich, and he noticed her because she stared holes in him when she walked past his table, and then when we started passing her photo around, he said it might have been her. Can't swear to it, though."

"It would be like her to stare at a cop," Lucy said. "Jerking people around is her favorite sport."

"I'll also add that it's not unusual for college kids to look like the homeless," I said.

"We're checking pawn shops around here to see if anybody fitting Carrie's description might have bought a gun, and we're also checking for stolen cars in the area," Marino said.

"Assuming if she and her sidekick stole cars in New York or Philadelphia, they aren't going to show up here with those plates."

The campus was an immaculate collection of modified Georgian buildings tucked amid palms, magnolias, crêpe myrtles, and lobolly and long-leaf pines. Gardenias were in bloom and when we got out of the car, their perfume clung to the humid, hot air and went to my head.

I loved the scents of the South, and for a moment, it did not seem possible that anything bad could happen here. It was summer session, and the campus was not heavily populated. Parking lots were half full, with many of the bike racks empty. Some of the cars driving on College Road had surfboards strapped to their roofs.

The counseling center was on the second floor of Westside Hall, and the waiting area for students with health problems was mauve and blue and full of light. Thousand-piece puzzles of rural scenes were in various stages of completion on coffee tables, offering a welcome distraction for those who had appointments. A receptionist was expecting us and showed us down a corridor, past observation and group rooms, and spaces for GRE testing. Dr. Chris Booth was energetic with kind, wise eyes, a woman approaching sixty, I guessed, and one who loved the sun. She was weathered in a way that gave her character, her skin deeply tanned and lined, her short hair white, and her body slight but vital.

She was a psychologist with a corner office that overlooked the fine arts building and lush live oak trees. I had always been fascinated by the personality behind offices. Where she worked was soothing and unprovocative but shrewd in its arrangement of chairs that suited very different personalities. There was a papasan chair for the patient who wanted to curl up on deep cushions and be open for help, and a cane-back rocker and a stiff love seat. The color scheme was gentle green, with paintings of sailboats on the walls, and elephant ear in terracotta pots.

"Good afternoon," Dr. Booth said to us with a smile as she invited us in. "I'm very glad to see you."

"And I'm very glad to see you," I replied.

I helped myself to the rocking chair, while Ginny perched on the love seat. Marino looked around with self-conscious eyes and eased his way into the papasan, doing what he could not to be swallowed by it. Dr. Booth sat in her office chair, her back to her perfectly clean desk that had nothing on it but a can of Diet Pepsi. Lucy stood by the door.

"I've been hoping that someone would come see me," Dr. Booth began, as if she had called this meeting. "But I honestly didn't know who to contact or even if I should."

She gave each of us her bright gray eyes.

"Claire was very special—and I know that's what everyone says about the dead," she said.

"Not everyone," Marino cynically retorted.

Dr. Booth smiled sadly. "I'm just saying that I have counseled many students here over the years, and Claire deeply touched my heart and I had high hopes for her. I was devastated by news of her death."

She paused, staring out of the window.

"I saw her last about two weeks prior to her death, and I've tried to think of anything I could that might hold an answer as to what might have happened."

"When you say you saw her," I said, "do you mean in here? For a session?"

She nodded. "We met for an hour."

Lucy was getting increasingly restless.

"Before you get into that," I said, "could you give us as much of her background as possible?"

"Absolutely. And by the way, I have dates and times for her appointments, if you need all that. I'd been seeing her on and off for three years."

"Off and on?" Marino asked as he sat forward in the deep seat and started sliding back into its deep cushions again.

"Claire was paying her own way through school. She worked as a waitress at the Blockade Runner at Wrightsville Beach. She'd do nothing but work and save, then pay for a term, then drop out again to earn more money. I didn't see her when she wasn't in school, and this is where a lot of her difficulties began, it's my belief."

"I'm going to let you guys handle this," Lucy said abruptly. "I want to make sure someone's staying with the helicopter."

Lucy went out and shut the door behind her, and I felt a wave of fear. I didn't know that Lucy wouldn't hit the streets alone to look for Carrie. Marino briefly met my eyes, and I could tell he was thinking the same thing. Our agent escort, Ginny, was stiff on the love seat, appropriately unobtrusive, offering nothing but her attention.

"About a year ago," Dr. Booth went on, "Claire met Kenneth Sparkes, and I know I'm not telling you something you're not already aware of. She was a competitive surfer and he had a beach house in Wrightsville. The long and short of it is they got involved in a brief, extremely intense affair, which he cut off."

"This was while she was enrolled in school," I said.

"Yes. Second term. They broke up in the summer, and she didn't return to the university until the following winter.

She didn't come in to see me until that February when her English professor noticed that she was constantly falling asleep in class and smelled of alcohol. Concerned, he went to the dean, and she was put on probation, with the stipulation that she had to come back to see me. This was all related to Sparkes, I'm afraid. Claire was adopted, the situation a very unhappy one. She left home when she was sixteen, came to Wrightsville, and did any kind of work she could to survive."

"Where are her parents now?" Marino asked.

"Her birth parents? We don't know who they are."

"No. The ones who adopted her."

"Chicago. They have had no contact with her since she left home. But they do know she's dead. I have spoken to them."

"Dr. Booth," I said, "do you have any idea why Claire would have gone to Sparkes's house in Warrenton?"

"She was completely incapable of dealing with rejection. I can only speculate she went there to see him, in hopes she might resolve something. I do know she stopped calling him last spring, because he finally changed to another unlisted phone number. Her only possible contact was to just show up, my guess is."

"In an old Mercedes that belonged to a psychotherapist named Newton Joyce?" Marino asked, adjusting his position again.

Dr. Booth was startled. "Now I didn't know that," she said. "She was driving Newton's car?"

"You know him?"

"Not personally, but certainly I know his reputation. Claire started going to him because she felt she needed a male perspective. This was within the past two months. He certainly wouldn't have been my choice."

"Why?" Marino asked.

Dr. Booth gathered her thoughts, her face tight with anger.

"This is all very messy," she said finally. "Which might begin to explain my reluctance to talk about Claire when you first began to call. Newton is a spoiled rich boy who has never had to work but decided to go into psychotherapy. A power trip for him, I suppose."

"He seems to have vanished in thin air," Marino said.

"Nothing out of the ordinary about that," she replied shortly. "He's in and out as he pleases, sometimes for months or even years at a time. I've been here at the university for thirty-some years now, and I remember him as a boy. Could charm the birds out of the trees and talk people into anything, but he's all about himself. And I was most concerned when Claire began to see him. Let's just say that no one would ever accuse Newton of being ethical. He makes his own rules. But he's never been caught."

"At what?" I asked. "Caught at what?"

"Controlling patients in a way that is most inappropriate."

"Having sexual relations with them?" I asked.

"I've never heard proof of that. It was more of a mind thing, a dominance thing, and it was very apparent that he completely dominated Claire. She was utterly dependent on him just like that." She snapped her fingers. "After their very first session. She would come in here and spend the entire time talking about him, obsessing. That's what's so odd about her going to see Sparkes. I truly thought she was over him and besotted with Newton. I honestly think she would have done anything Newton told her to do."

"Possible he might have suggested she go see Sparkes? For therapeutic reasons, such as closure?" I said.

Dr. Booth smiled ironically.

"He may have suggested she go see him, but I doubt it was to help her," she replied. "I'm sorry to say that if going there was Newton's idea, then it most likely was manipulative."

"I sure would like to know how the two of them got hooked up," Marino said, scooting forward in the papasan chair. "I'm guessing that someone referred her to him."

"Oh no," she replied. "They met on a photo shoot."

"What do you mean?" I said as my blood stopped in my veins.

"He's quite enamored with all things Hollywood and has finagled his way into working with production crews for movies and photo shoots. You know Screen Gems studio is right here in town, and Claire's minor was film studies. It was her dream to be an actress. Heaven knows, she was beautiful enough. Based on what she told me, she was doing a modeling job at the beach, for some surfing magazine, I think. And he was part of the production crew, the photographer, in this instance. Apparently he is accomplished in that."

"You said he was in and out a lot," Marino said. "Maybe he had other residences?"

"I don't know anything more about him, really," she replied.

Within an hour, the Wilmington Police Department had a warrant to search Newton Joyce's property in the historic district, several blocks from the water. His white frame house was one story with a broken-pitch gable roof that covered the porch in front at the end of a quiet street of other tired nineteenth-century homes with porches and piazzas.

Huge magnolias darkly shadowed his yard with only patches of wan sunlight seeping through, and the air was fitful with insects. By now, McGovern had caught up with us, and we waited on the slumping back porch as a detective used a tactical baton to break out a pane of glass from the door. Then he reached his hand inside and freed the lock.

Marino, McGovern, and a Detective Scroggins went first with pistols close to their bodies and pointed to shoot. I was close behind, unarmed and unnerved by the creepiness of this place Joyce called home. We entered a small sitting area that had been modified to accommodate patients. There was a rather ghastly old red velvet Victorian couch, a marble-topped end table centered by a milkglass lamp, and a coffee table scattered with magazines that were many months old. Through a doorway was his office, and it was even stranger.

Yellowed knotty pine walls were almost completely covered with framed photographs of what I assumed were models and actors in various publicity poses. Quite literally, there were hundreds of them, and I assumed Joyce had taken them himself. I could not imagine a patient pouring out his problems in the midst of so many beautiful bodies and faces. On Joyce's desk were a Rolodex, date book, paperwork, and a telephone. While Scroggins began playing messages from the answering machine, I looked around some more.

On bookcases were worn-out cloth and leather volumes of classics that were too dusty to have been opened in many years. There was a cracked brown leather couch, presumably for his patients, and next to it a small table bearing a single water glass. It was almost empty and smeared around the rim with pale peach lipstick. Directly across from the couch was an intricately carved, high-back mahogany armchair that brought to mind a throne. I heard Marino and McGovern checking other rooms while voices drifted out of Joyce's answering machine. All of the messages had been left after the evening of June fifth, or the day before Claire's death. Patients had called about their appointments. A travel agent had left word about two tickets to Paris.

"What'd you say that fire starter thing looks like?" Detective Scroggins asked as he opened another desk drawer.

"A thin bar of silvery metal," I answered him. "You'll know it when you see it."

"Nothing like that in here. But the guy sure is into rubber bands. Must be thousands of them. Looks like he was making these weird little balls."

He held up a perfectly shaped sphere made completely of rubber bands.

"Now how the hell do you think he did that?" Scroggins was amazed. "You think he started with just one and then kept winding others all around like golf ball innards?"

I didn't know.

"What kind of mind is that, huh?" Scroggins went on. "You think he was sitting here doing that while he was talking with his patients?"

"At this point," I replied, "not much would surprise me."

"What a whacko. So far I've found thirteen, fourteen . . . uh, nineteen balls."

He was pulling them out and setting them on top of the desk, and then Marino called me from the back of the house.

"Doc, think you'd better come here."

I followed the sounds of him and McGovern through a small kitchen with old appliances that were layered in the civilizations of former meals. Dishes were piled in cold scummy water in the sink, and the garbage can was overflowing, the stench awful. Newton Joyce was more slovenly than Marino, and I would not have thought that possible, nor did it square with the orderliness of Joyce's rubber band balls or what I believed were his crimes. But despite criminalist texts and Hollywood renditions, people were not a science and they were not consistent. A prime example was what Marino and McGovern had discovered in the garage.

It was connected to the kitchen by a door that had been made inaccessible by a padlock that Marino had handily removed with bolt cutters that McGovern had fetched from her Explorer. On the other side was a work area with no door leading outside, for it had been closed in with cinder block. Walls were painted white, and against one were fifty-gallon drums of aviation gasoline. There was a stainless steel Sub-Zero freezer and its door, ominously, was padlocked. The concrete floor was very clean, and in a corner were five aluminum camera cases and Styrofoam ice chests of varying sizes. Central was a large plyboard table covered with felt and here were arranged the instruments of Joyce's crimes.

Half a dozen knives were lined in a perfect row, with precisely the same spacing between each. All were in their leather cases, and in a small redwood wooden box were sharpening stones.

"I'll be damned," Marino said, pointing out the knives to me. "Let me tell you what these are, Doc. The bone-handled ones are R.W. Loveless skinner knives, made by Beretta. For collectors, numbered, and costing around six hundred bucks a pop."

He stared at them with lust but did not touch.

"The blued steel babies are Chris Reeves, at least four hundred a pop, and the butts of the handles unscrew if you want to store matches in them," he went on.

I heard a distant door shut, and then Scroggins appeared

with Lucy. The detective was as awed by the knives as Marino was, and then the two of them and McGovern resumed opening drawers of tool chests, and prying open two cabinets that held other chilling signs that we had found our killer. In a plastic Speedo bag were eight silicone swim caps, all of them hot pink. Each was zipped inside a plastic pouch with price stickers that said Joyce had paid sixteen dollars apiece for them. As for fire starters, there were four of them in a Wal-Mart bag.

Joyce also had a modular desk in his concrete cave, and we left it to Lucy to access whatever she could. She sat in a folding chair and began working the keyboard while Marino took the bolt cutters to the freezer, which, eerily, was precisely the same model I had at home.

"This is too easy," Lucy said. "He's downloaded his e-mail onto a disk. No password or anything. Stuff he sent and received. About eighteen months' worth. We got a username of FMKIRBY. *From Kirby*, I presume. Now I wonder who that pen pal might be," she added sarcastically.

I moved closer and looked over her shoulder as she scrolled through notes that Carrie had sent to Newton Joyce, whose username horrifically was *skinner*, and those he had sent to her. On May tenth he wrote:

Found her. A connection to die for. How does a major media tycoon sound? Am I good?

And the next day, Carrie had written back:

Yes, GOOD. I want them. Then fly me out of here, bird man. You can show me later. I want to look in their empty eyes and see.

"My God," I muttered. "She wanted him to kill in Virginia, and do so in a way that would insure my participation."

Lucy scrolled some more, and her tapping of the down arrow was impatient and angry.

"So he happens upon Claire Rawley at a photo shoot, and she turns out to be the bait. The perfect lure because of her past relationship to Sparkes," I went on. "Joyce and Claire go to his farm, but he's out of town. Sparkes is spared. Joyce murders and mutilates her, and burns the place." I paused, reading more old mail. "And now here we are."

"Here we are because she wants us here," Lucy said. "We were supposed to find all this."

She tapped the key hard.

"Don't you get it?" she asked.

She turned around and looked at me.

"She reeled us in, here, so we would see all this," she said.

Bolt cutters suddenly snapped loudly through steel, and the freezer door sucked open.

"Jesus fucking Christ," Marino shouted. "Fuck!" he cried.

23

On the top wire shelf were two bald mannikin heads, one male, one female, with blank faces smeared black with frozen blood. They had been used as forms for the faces Joyce had stolen, each one laid over the mannikin's face, then frozen hard to give his trophies shape. Joyce had shrouded his mask-like horrors in triple layers of plastic freezer bags that were labeled like evidence, with case numbers, locations, and dates.

The most recent was the one on top, and I robotically picked it up as my heart began to pound so hard that for an instant, the world went black. I began to shake and was aware of nothing else until I came to in McGovern's arms. She was helping me into the chair where Lucy had been seated at the desk.

"Someone bring her some water," McGovern was saying. "It's all right, Kay. It's all right."

I focused on the freezer with its wide-open door and stacks of plastic bags hinting of flesh and blood. Marino was pacing the garage, running his fingers through his thinning strands of hair. His face was the hue of a stroke about to happen, and Lucy was gone.

"Where's Lucy?" I asked with a dry mouth.

"She's gone to get a first aid kit," McGovern answered in a gentle voice. "Just be quiet, try to relax, and we're going to get you out of here. You don't need to be seeing all this."

But I already had. I had seen the empty face, the misshapen mouth and nose that had no bridge. I had seen the orange-tinted flesh sparkling with ice. The date on the freezer bag was June 17, the location Philadelphia, and that had penetrated at the same time I was looking, and then it was too late, or maybe I would have looked anyway, because I had to know.

"They've been here," I said.

I struggled to get up and got light-headed again.

"They came here long enough to leave that. So we'd find it," I said.

"Goddamn son of a bitch!" Marino screamed. "GODDAMN-MOTHER-FUCKING-SON-OF-A-BITCH!"

He roughly wiped his eyes on his fist as he continued to pace like a madman. Lucy was coming down the steps. She was pale, her eyes glassy. My niece seemed dazed.

"McGovern to Correll," she said into her portable radio.

"Correll," the voice came back.

"You guys get on over here."

"Ten-four."

"I'm calling our forensic guys," said Detective Scroggins.

He was stunned, too, but not the same way we were. For him, this wasn't personal. He had never heard of Benton Wesley. Scroggins was carefully going through the bags in the freezer, his lips moving as he counted.

"Holy God," he said in amazement. "There's twenty-seven of these things."

"Dates and locations," I said, mustering my reserved strength to walk over to him.

We looked together.

"London, 1981. Liverpool, 1983. Dublin, 1984, and one-two-three-four-five-six-seven-eight-nine-ten-eleven. Eleven, total, from Ireland, through 1987. It looks like he really started getting into it," Scroggins said, and he was getting excited, the way people do when they are on the verge of hysteria.

I was looking on with him, and the location of Joyce's kills began in Northern Ireland in Belfast, then continued into the Republic in Galway, followed by nine murders in Dublin in neighborhoods such as Malahide, Santry and Howth. Then Joyce had begun his predation in the United States, mainly out west, in remote areas of Utah, Nevada, Montana, and Washington, and once in Natches, Mississippi, and this explained a lot to me, especially when I remembered what Carrie had said in her letter to me. She had made an odd reference to *sawed bone.*

"The torsos," I said as the truth ran through me like lightning. "The unsolved dismemberments in Ireland. And then he was quiet for eight years because he killed out west and the bodies were never found, or else never centrally reported. So we didn't know about them. He never stopped, and then he came to Virginia, where his presence definitely got my attention and drove me to despair."

It was 1995 when two torsos had turned up, the first near Virginia Beach, the next in Norfolk. The following year there were two more, this time in the western part of the state, one in Lynchburg, the other in Blacksburg, very close to the campus of the Virginia Tech. In 1997, Joyce seemed to have gotten silent, and this was when I suspected Carrie had allied herself with him.

The publicity about the dismemberments had become

overwhelming, with only two of the limbless, headless bodies identified by X-rays matching the premortem films of missing people, both of them male college students. They had been my cases, and I had made a tremendous amount of noise about them, and the FBI had been brought in.

I now realized that Joyce's primary purpose was not only to foil identification, but more importantly, to hide his mutilation of the bodies. He did not want us to know he was stealing his victims' beauty, in effect, stealing who they were by taking his knife to their faces and adding them to his frigid collection. Perhaps he feared that additional dismemberments might make the hunt for him too big, so he had switched his modus operandi to fire, and perhaps it was Carrie who had suggested this. I could only assume that somehow the two of them had connected on the Internet.

"I don't get it," Marino was saying.

He had calmed a little and had brought himself to sift through Joyce's packages.

"How did he get all of these here?" he asked. "All the way from England and Ireland? From Venice Beach and Salt Lake City?"

"Dry ice," I said simply, looking at the metal camera cases and Styrofoam ice chests. "He could have packed them well and put them through baggage without anyone ever knowing."

Further searching of Joyce's house produced other incriminating evidence, all within plain view, for the warrant had listed magnesium fire starters, knives, and body parts, and that gave police license to rummage through drawers and even tear out walls, if they so chose. While a local medical examiner removed the contents of the freezer to transport it to the morgue, cabinets were gone through and a safe drilled open. Inside were foreign money and thousands of photographs of hundreds of people who had been granted the good fortune not to have turned up dead.

There also were photographs of Joyce, we presumed, sitting in the pilot's seat of his white Schweizer or leaning against it with his arms crossed at his chest. I stared at his image and tried to take it in. He was a short, slight man with brown hair, and might have been handsome had he not been terribly scarred by acne.

His skin was pitted down his neck and into the open shirt he wore, and I could only imagine his shame as an adolescent, and the mockery and derisive laughter of his peers. I had known young men like him as I was growing up, those disfigured by birth or disease and unable to enjoy the entitlement of youthfulness or being the object of love.

So he had robbed others of what he did not have. He had destroyed as he had been destroyed, the point of origin his own miserable lot in life, his own wretched self. I did not feel sorry for him. Nor did I think that he and Carrie were still here in this city, or even anywhere around. She had gotten what she'd wanted, at least for now. The trap I had set had caught only me. She had wanted me to find Benton, and I had.

The final word, I felt sure, would be what she eventually did to me, and at the moment, I was too beaten up to care. I felt dead. I found silence in sitting on an old, worn marble bench in the riotous tangle of Joyce's overgrown backyard. Hostas, begonias, and fig bushes fought with pampas grass for the sun, and I found Lucy at the edge of intermittent shadows cast by live oak trees, where red and yellow hibiscus were loud and wild.

"Lucy, let's go home."

I sat next to my niece on cold, hard stone I associated with cemeteries.

"I hope he was dead before they did that to him," she said one more time.

I did not want to think about it.

"I just hope he didn't suffer."

"She wants us to worry about things like that," I said as anger peeked through my haze of disbelief. "She's taken enough from us, don't you think? Let's not give her any more, Lucy."

She had no answer for me.

"ATF and the police will handle it from here," I went on, holding her hand. "Let's go home, and we'll move on from there."

"How?"

"I'm not sure I know." I was as truthful as I could be.

We got up together and went around to the front of the house, where McGovern was talking to an agent out by her car. She looked at both of us, and compassion softened her eyes.

"If you'll take us back to the helicopter," Lucy said with a steadiness she did not feel, "I'll take it on in to Richmond and Border Patrol can pick it up. If that's all right, I mean."

"I'm not sure you should be flying right now." McGovern suddenly was Lucy's supervisor again.

"Trust me, I'm fine," Lucy replied, and her voice got harder. "Besides, who else is going to fly it? And you can't leave it here on a soccer field."

McGovern hesitated, her eyes on Lucy. She unlocked the Explorer.

"Okay," she said. "Climb in."

"I'll file a flight plan," Lucy said as she sat in front. "So you can check on where we are, if that will make you feel better."

"It will," McGovern said, starting the engine.

McGovern got on the radio and called one of the agents inside the house.

"Put Marino on," she said.

After a brief wait, Marino's voice came over the air.

"Go ahead," he said.

"Party's taking off. You going along?"

"I'll stick to the ground," his answer came back. "Gonna help out here first."

"Got it. We appreciate it."

"Tell them to rly safe," Marino said.

A campus police officer on bicycle patrol was standing sentry at the helicopter when we got there, and tennis was going strong on the courts next door, balls clopping, while several young men practiced soccer near a goal. The sky was bright blue, trees barely stirring, as if nothing bad had happened here. Lucy went through a thorough preflight check while McGovern and I waited in the car.

"What are you going to do?" I asked her.

"Bombard the news with pictures of them and any other info that might cause someone out there to recognize them," she answered. "They've got to eat. They've got to sleep. And he's got to have Avgas. He can't fly forever without it."

"It doesn't make sense that it hasn't been spotted before, refueling, landing, flying, what all."

"Looks like he had plenty of his own Avgas right there

in his garage. Not to mention there are so many small airfields where he could land and gas up," she said. "All over. And he doesn't have to contact the tower in uncontrolled airspace, and Schweizers aren't exactly rare. Not to mention'—she looked at me—"it *has* been spotted. We saw it ourselves, and so did the farrier and the director of Kirby. We just didn't know what we were looking at."

"I suppose."

My mood was getting heavier by the moment. I did not want to go home. I did not want to go anywhere. It was as if the weather had turned gray, and I was cold and alone and could escape none of it. My mind churned with questions and answers, and deductions and screams. Whenever it went still, I saw him. I saw him in smoldering debris. I saw his face beneath heavy plastic.

". . . Kay?"

I realized McGovern was talking to me.

"I want to know how you're doing. Really." Her eyes were fastened to me.

I took a deep, shaky breath, and my voice sounded cracked when I said, "I'm going to make it, Teun. Beyond that, I don't know how I'm doing. I'm not even sure what I'm doing. But I know what I've done. I've ruined everything. Carrie played me like a hand of cards, and Benton's dead. She and Newton Joyce are still out there, ready to do something bad again. Or maybe they already have. Nothing I've done has made a goddamn difference, Teun."

Tears filled my eyes as I watched a blurry Lucy checking to make sure the fuel cap was tight. Then she began untying the main rotor blades. McGovern handed me a Kleenex. She gently squeezed my arm.

"You were brilliant, Kay. For one thing, had you not found

out what you did, we wouldn't have had a thing to list on the warrant. We couldn't have even gotten one, and then where would we be? Yes, we haven't caught them yet, but at least we know *who*. And we will find them."

"We found what they wanted us to," I told her.

Lucy had finished her inspection and looked my way.

"I guess I'd better go," I said to McGovern. "Thank you."

I took her hand and squeezed it.

"Take care of Lucy," I said.

"I think she does a pretty good job of taking care of herself."

I got out and turned around once to wave goodbye. I opened the copilot's door and climbed up in the seat, then fastened my harness. Lucy slipped her checklist out of a pocket on the door, and went down it, zeroing in on switches and circuit breakers, and making sure the collective was down, the throttle off. My heart would not beat normally, and my breathing was shallow.

We took off and nosed around into the wind. McGovern watched us climb, a hand shielding her eyes. Lucy handed me a sectional chart and said I was to help navigate. She lifted into a hover and contacted Air Traffic Control.

"Wilmington tower, this is helicopter two-one-niner Sierra Bravo."

"Go ahead, helicopter two-one-niner, Wilmington tower."

"Requesting clearance from university athletic field, direct to your location for ISO Aero. Over."

"Contact tower when entering pattern. Cleared from present position, on course, stay with me and report down and secure at ISO."

"Two Sierra Bravo, wilco."

Then Lucy transmitted to me, "We'll be following a

three-three-zero heading. So your job after we gas up will be keeping the gyro consistent with the compass and helping out with the map."

She climbed to five hundred feet and the tower contacted us again.

"Helicopter two Sierra Bravo," the voice came over the air. "Traffic is unidentified and at your six o'clock, three hundred feet, closing."

"Two Sierra Bravo is looking, no joy."

"Unidentified aircraft two miles southeast of airport, identify yourself," the tower transmitted to all who could hear.

We were answered by nothing.

"Unidentified aircraft in Wilmington airspace, identify yourself," the tower repeated.

Silence followed.

Lucy saw the aircraft first, directly behind us and below horizon, meaning its altitude was lower than ours.

"Wilmington tower," she said over the air. "Helicopter two Sierra Bravo. Have low-flying aircraft in sight. Will maintain separation.

"Something's not right," Lucy commented to me, turning around in her seat to look behind us again.

24

It was a dark speck at first, flying after us, directly in our path and gaining on us. As it got closer it became white. Then it turned into a Schweizer with sunlight glinting off the bubble. My heart jumped as I was seized by fear.

"Lucy!" I exclaimed.

"I've got it in sight," she said, instantly angry. "Fuck. I don't believe this."

She pulled up on the collective and we began a steep climb. The Schweizer maintained the same altitude, moving faster than we were for as we gained altitude, our speed dropped to seventy knots. Lucy pushed the cyclic forward as the Schweizer gained on us, swerving in closer on our starboard side, where Lucy was sitting. Lucy keyed the mike.

"Tower. Unidentified aircraft making aggressive moves," she said. "Will be making evasive maneuvers. Contact local police authorities, suspect in unidentified aircraft known armed and dangerous fugitive. Will avoid built-up areas, will take evasive actions towards water."

"Roger helicopter. Am contacting local authorities."

Then the tower switched to over-the-guard frequency.

"Attention any aircraft, this is Wilmington tower on-guard, aircraft traffic area is now closed to incoming traffic. Any ground traffic, halt movement. Repeat, aircraft traffic area is now closed to incoming traffic. Any ground traffic, halt movement. All aircraft this frequency, immediately switch to Wilmington approach control on Victor 135.75 or Uniform 343.9. I say again, all aircraft this frequency immediately switch to Wilmington approach control on Victor 135.75 or Uniform 343.9. Helicopter two Sierra Bravo, remain this frequency."

"Roger, two Sierra Bravo," Lucy returned.

I knew why she was heading toward the ocean. If we went down, she didn't want it to be in a populated area where others might get hurt or killed. I also was certain that Carrie had predicted Lucy would do exactly this, because Lucy was good. She would always put others first. She turned to the east, the Schweizer following our every move but maintaining the same distance behind us of maybe a hundred yards, as if confident that it didn't need to be in a hurry. That's when I realized that Carrie had probably been watching us all along.

"It can't go over ninety knots," Lucy said to me, and our tension was rising like heat.

"She saw us come in straight to the field earlier today," I said. "She knows we haven't refueled."

We flew at an angle over the beach and followed it briefly over bright splashes of color that were swimmers and sunbathers. They stopped what they were doing and stared straight up at two helicopters speeding over them and out to sea. Half a mile over the ocean, Lucy began to slow down.

"We can't keep this up," she told me, and it seemed a pronouncement of doom. "We lose our engine, we'll never make it back, and we're low on fuel."

The gauge read less than twenty gallons. Lucy pushed us into a sharp one-hundred-and-eighty-degree turn. The Schweizer was maybe fifty feet below us and head on. The sun made it impossible to see who was inside, but I knew. I had not a single doubt, and when it was no more than five hundred feet from us and coming up on Lucy's side, I felt several rapid-fire jolts, like quick slaps, and we suddenly swerved. Lucy grabbed her pistol from her shoulder holster.

"They're shooting at us!" she exclaimed to me.

I thought of the submachine gun, the Calico missing from Sparkes's collection.

Lucy fought to open her door. She jettisoned it and it tumbled through the air, sailing down and away. She slowed our speed.

"They're firing!" Lucy got back on the air. "Returning fire! Keep all traffic away from Wrightsville Beach area!"

"Roger! Do you request further assistance?"

"Dispatch land emergency crews, Wrightsville Beach! Expect casualty situation!"

As the Schweizer flew directly under us, I saw muzzle flashes and the tip of a barrel barely protruding from the copilot's window. I felt more quick jolts.

"I think they hit the skids," Lucy almost screamed, and she was trying to position her pistol out her open door and fly at the same time, her shooting hand bandaged.

I instantly dug inside my pocketbook, dismayed to realize my .38 was still inside my briefcase, which remained safe inside the baggage compartment. Then Lucy handed me her pistol and reached behind her head for the AR-15 assault rifle. The Schweizer swooped around, to pursue us inland, knowing we were cornered because we would not risk the safety of people on the ground.

"We've got to go back over the water!" Lucy said. "Can't shoot at them here. Kick your door open. Get it off the hinges and dump it!"

I somehow managed, the door ripping away as rushing air blasted me and the ground suddenly seemed closer. Lucy made another turn, and the Schweizer turned, too, as the needle on the fuel gauge slipped lower. This went on for what seemed forever, the Schweizer chasing us out to sea, and our trying to return to land so we could get down. It could not shoot up without hitting the rotor blades.

Then at an altitude of eleven hundred feet, when we were over water at a hundred knots, the fuselage got hit. Both of us felt the kicks right behind us, as close as the left rear passenger door.

"I'm turning right now," Lucy said to me. "Can you keep us straight at this altitude?"

I was terrified. We were going to die.

"I'll try," I said, taking the controls.

We were heading straight toward the Schweizer. It couldn't have been more than fifty feet from us, and maybe a hundred feet below when Lucy pulled back the bolt, chambering a round.

"Shove the cyclic down! Now!" she yelled at me as she pushed the barrel of the rifle out her open door.

We were going down a thousand feet per minute, and I was certain we would fly right into the Schweizer. I tried to veer out of its path, but Lucy would have none of it.

"Straight at it!" she yelled.

I could not hear the gunfire as we flew directly over the Schweizer, so close I thought we would be devoured by its blades. She fired more, and I saw flashes, and then Lucy had the cyclic and was ramming it into a hard left, cutting it away from the Schweizer as it exploded into a ball of flames that rolled us almost over on our side. Lucy had the controls as I went into a crash position.

Then as suddenly as the violent shock waves had hit, they were gone, and I caught a glimpse of flaming debris showering into the Atlantic Ocean. We were steady and making a wide turn. I stared at my niece in stunned disbelief.

"Fuck you," she said coldly as fire and broken fuselage rained into sparkling water.

She got on the air, as calm as I had ever seen her.

"Tower," she said. "Fugitive aircraft has exploded. Debris two miles off Wrightsville Beach. Negative survivors seen. Circling for signs of life."

"Roger. Do you need assistance?" came the rattled response.

"A little late. But negative. Am returning to your location for immediate refuel."

"Uh. Roger." The omnipotent tower was stuttering. "Proceed direct. Local authorities will meet you at ISO."

But Lucy circled twice more, down to fifty feet as fire engines and police cars sped toward the beach with emergency lights flashing. Panicked swimmers were running out of the water, kicking and falling and fighting waves, arms flying, as if a great white shark were in pursuit. Floating debris rocked with the surge. Bright orange life jackets bobbed, but no one was in them.

ONE WEEK LATER
HILTON HEAD ISLAND

The morning was overcast, the sky the same gray as the sea, when the few of us who had loved Benton Wesley assembled on an empty, undeveloped point on the plantation of Sea Pines.

We parked near condominiums and followed a path that led to a dune. From there we made our way through sand spurs and sea oats. The beach was more narrow here, the sand less firm, and driftwood marked the memory of many storms.

Marino was in a pinstripe suit he was sweating through, and a white shirt and dark tie, and I thought it might have been the first time I had ever seen him so properly dressed. Lucy was in black, but I knew I would not see her until later, for she had something very important to do.

McGovern had come and so had Kenneth Sparkes, not because they had known him, but because their presence was their gift to me. Connie, Benton's former wife, and their three grown daughters were a knot near the water, and it was odd looking at them now and feeling nothing but sorrow. We had no resentment, no animosity or fear left in us. Death had spent it all as completely as life had brought it about.

There were others from Benton's precious past, retired agents and the former director of the FBI Academy who long years before had believed in Benton's prison visits and research in profiling. Benton's expertise was an old, tired word now, ruined by TV and the movies, but once it had been novel. Once Benton had been the pioneer, the creator of a better way of understanding humans who were truly psychotic, or remorseless and evil.

There was no leader of a church, for Benton had not gone since I had known him, only a Presbyterian chaplain who had counseled agents in distress. His name was Judson Lloyd, and he was frail with only a faint new moon of white hair. Reverend Lloyd wore a clerical collar and carried a small black leather Bible. There were fewer than twenty of us gathered on the shore.

We had no music or flowers, no eulogies or notes in our heads, for Benton had made it clear in his will what he wanted done. He had left me in charge of his mortal remains, because, as he had drafted himself, *It is what you are so good at, Kay. I know you will guard my wishes well.*

He had desired no ceremony. He had not wanted the military burial he was entitled to, no police cars leading the way, no gun salutes or flag-draped casket. His simple request was to be cremated and scattered over the place he loved best, the civilized Never-Never-Land of Hilton Head, where we had sequestered ourselves together whenever we could, and had forgotten for the brevity of a dream what we battled.

I would always be sorry that he had spent his last days here without me, and I would never recover from the heartless irony that I had been detained by the butchery Carrie had wrought. It had been the beginning of the end that would be Benton's end.

It was easy for me to wish I had never gotten involved in the case. But had I not, someone else would be attending a funeral somewhere in the world, as others had in the past, and the violence would not have stopped. Rain began to fall lightly. It touched my face like cool, sad hands.

"Benton brought us together here this day not to say goodbye," began Reverend Lloyd. "He wanted us to gather strength from each other and go on doing what he had done. Upholding good and condemning bad, fighting for the fallen and holding it all inside, suffering the horrors alone because he would not bruise the gentle souls of others. He left the world better than he found it. He left us better than he found us. My friends, go do as he had done."

He opened his Bible to the New Testament.

"And let us not be weary in well doing: for in due season we shall reap, if we faint not," he read.

I felt hot and arid inside and could not stop the tears. I dabbed my eyes with tissues and stared down at the sand dusting the toes of my black suede shoes. Reverend Lloyd touched a fingertip to his lips and voiced more verses from Galatians, or was it Timothy?

I was vague about what he said. His words became a continuous stream, like water flowing in a brook, and I could not make out the meaning as I fought and blocked images that without fail won. Mostly I remembered Benton in his red windbreaker, standing out and staring at the river when he was hurt by me. I would have given the world to take back every harsh word. Yet he had understood. I knew he had.

I remembered his clean profile and the imperviousness of

his face when he was with people other than me. Perhaps they found him cold, when in fact his was a shell around a kind and tender life. I wondered if we had married if I would feel any different now. I wondered if my independence had been born of a seminal insecurity. I wondered if I had been wrong.

"Knowing this, that the law is not made for a righteous man, but for the lawless and disobedient, for the ungodly and for sinners, for unholy and profane, for murderers of fathers and murderers of mothers, for manslayers," the reverend was preaching.

I felt the air stir behind me as I stared at a sluggish, depressed sea. Then Sparkes was next to me, our arms barely touching. His gaze was straight ahead, his jaw strong and resolute as he stood so straight in his dark suit. He turned to me and offered eyes of great sympathy. I nodded slightly.

"Our friend wanted peace and goodness." Reverend Lloyd had turned to another book. "He wanted the harmony the victims he championed never had. He wanted to be free of outrage and sorrow, unfettered by anger and his dreamless nights of dread."

I heard the blades in the distance, the thudding that would forever be the noise of my niece. I looked up, and the sun barely shone behind clouds that danced the dance of veils, sliding endlessly, never fully exposing what we longed to see. Blue shown through, fragmented and brilliant like stained glass over the horizon to the west of us, and the dune at our backs was lit up as the troops of bad weather began to mutiny. The sound of the helicopter got louder, and I looked back over palms and pines, spotting it with nose slightly down as it flew lower.

"I will therefore ask that people pray everywhere, lifting

up holy hands, without wrath and doubting," the reverend went on.

Benton's ashes were in the small brass urn I held in my hands.

"Let us pray."

Lucy began her glide slope over trees, the chop-chop hard air against the ear. Sparkes leaned close to speak to me, and I could not hear, but the closeness of his face was kind.

Reverend Lloyd continued to pray, but all of us were no longer capable of or interested in a petition to the Almighty. Lucy held the JetRanger in a low hover beyond the shore, and spray flew up from her wind on the water.

I could see her eyes fixed on me through the chin bubble, and I gathered my splintered spirit into a core. I walked forward into her storm of turbulent air as the reverend held on to his barely present hair. I waded out into the water.

"God bless you, Benton. Rest your soul. I miss you, Benton," I said words no one else could hear.

I opened the urn and looked up at my niece who was there to create the energy he had wanted when it was his time to move on. I nodded at Lucy and she gave me a thumbs-up that rent my heart and let loose more tears. Ashes were like silk, and I felt his bits of chalky bone as I dug in and held him in my hand. I flung him into the wind. I gave him back to the higher order he would have made, had it been possible.